CAN'T BUY ME BLOOD

A HIPPOSYNC ARCHIVES NOVEL

DC FARMER

WYRMWOOD
BOOKS

COPYRIGHT

First published 2018 as Grume by Wyrmwood Books
This edition published by Wyrmwood Books 2024

A CIP catalogue record for this book is available from the British Library

eBook ISBN -978-1-915185-32-7
Print ISBN - 978-1-915185-33-4

Published by Wyrmwood Books.
An imprint of Wyrmwood Media.

EXCLUSIVE OFFER

WOULD YOU LIKE A FREE NOVELLA

Please look out for the link near the end of the book for your chance to sign up to the no-spam-guaranteed Readers Club and receive a FREE DC Farmer novella as well as news of upcoming releases. HERE ARE THE BOOKS!

FIENDS IN HIGH PLACES*
THE GHOUL ON THE HILL
BLAME IT ON THE BOGEY (MAN)
CAN'T BUY ME BLOOD
COMING SOON
TROLL LOTTA LOVE
SOMEWHERE OGRE THE RAINBOW

PROLOGUE

DEATH HAS NO BOUNDARIES. If it had a neck, dangling around it would be a laminated pass with the words *Access All Areas* embossed in gold. Indiscriminate and irrevocable, death turns up everywhere that sentient beings exist. Even places where homo sapiens remain a bit of a novelty.

The city state of New Thameswick is a prime example. Most 'people' have never heard of it and that is only right and proper, since most 'people' prefer to sleep nightmare-free. But there are those who *have* heard of it, whose job it is to listen and watch so that the boundary between our world and the other is maintained. Because if it were not, who knows what might happen.

CHAPTER ONE

NEW THAMESWICK, THE FAE WORLD (FW)

THE BODY, WHAT WAS LEFT OF IT, was no more than eight hours dead. The smell oozing out from every crevice and crack, every corner and cranny of the foetid room in which it lay, was ancient and appalling and full of decay. It was a stink with which Asher Lodge from the Bureau of Demonology was depressingly familiar.

Many of the constables carefully sifting through the debris in the shabby space had neckerchiefs soaked in lavender water tied around their lower faces. They were multipurpose masks, cutting out the smell and at the same time absorbing the reek-induced tears leaking from their eyes. It made them look like a gang of emotionally labile, uniformed bandits. But there was nothing to steal here. Someone had already stolen the only thing this victim had of any worth.

Its life.

A few yards from where Asher stood, Hawkshaw Crouch of the New Thameswick constabulary hovered over the body, dabbing at his eyes with one hand, wielding a pencil with the other to manoeuvre the tattered remnants of dark clothing that clung to the corpse.

'This has all the hallmarks,' he said.

'There is no doubt?' Asher asked, head bowed to study the corpse.

'It's him, all right.'

Asher nodded, straightened and brushed a few stray strands of long black hair from his pale forehead. They'd been trying to catch 'him' for several months now. And they might as well have been trying to bottle moonlight. This one was an arrogant bastard; he'd even painted his initials on the wall in thick, textured grume—as required for maximum dramatic effect—above his first and second victims.

S.R.—vermen extermenaator

Whether S.R. had realised that his spelling left a lot to be desired and was the source of ridicule, or whether he'd got it out of his system by the time it came to murder number three, no one knew. Regardless, the graffiti stopped to be replaced, as here, by a gruesome tag and a hallmark modus operandi in the form of a sharpened yew stake driven, with terminal effectiveness, through the victim's heart. No, there was nothing remotely doubtful as to the identity of the killer.

Sinewy was the description best suited to Sicca Rus since he was whippet thin and could bend into all sorts of shapes, especially those commensurate with wriggling out of arresting hands. And if grasping fingers did ever manage to close over a fleeing limb, they met with ropy, iron-hard muscles that coiled and uncoiled with eel-like ease. Under a mop of dark hair was a bullet-shaped head, inside which was a brain programmed solely for enjoyment. The trouble was that the programmer had left out one or two vital bits, like giving a toss and empathy. The result was a living machine built for speed, particularly with a knife, and blessed with the conscience of a rattlesnake.

The army sometimes found jobs for people like Rus,

usually of the type with the added benefit of being able to wear camouflage makeup on trips to foreign climes, headed by that old favourite, 'behind enemy lines'. But in civvy street, and especially in a place like New Thameswick, even in the shady spots where every other eye was blind and turned, the opportunities for a man like Rus to indulge himself were few.

Yet he managed.

A skilled robber and burglar, he could sneak in and out of buildings with alacrity and without the occupants ever knowing. But his trouble was that he could not bear the thought that someone might be pretending to be asleep while he rifled through his or her drawers. And so, he'd make sure of his anonymity by giving all the occupants an extra opening through which to breathe, which they did for about ten seconds with a bubbling rattle until they had no need to breathe ever again.

When examined from the point of view of likely capture, every murder that Rus committed was unnecessary. Yet, Rus' internal, circular argument was that you couldn't extract the pearl without first shucking the oyster. And what pearls he walked away with from his nocturnal escapades! Sometimes as many as twenty scruples from the properties in the least affluent parts of town. The parts he particularly favoured because of their non-existent security and reluctance to involve the constabulary thereafter.

Hardly worth all that effort, you might think.

But Rus' flawed logic would point out that five scruples would get you a hot pie supper at Mrs Thago's pie shop. And everyone, or at least everyone with a penchant for pastry and who was certifiably psychopathic, knew that Mrs T's mouthwatering gravy made all the bloodshed worthwhile. Indeed, if a passer-by happened to look in through the window of Pie Thago R Us and saw the bloke at the corner table guzzling happily after a hard evening's graft, they'd think nothing of it. Unless the eater looked up and caught the observer's eye.

Then they'd feel something loosen inside them in the same way it might if an old newspaper on a street corner suddenly ruffled in the wind to reveal the rat's nest squirming beneath.

Asher's presence in that squalid room centred around Sicca Rus' tag. The symbol; a semicircle above a straight line with a long cylinder extending out of said semicircle beneath two straight dashes, held a passing resemblance to an ancient hieroglyph found on a stone tablet dating from the eighth century. Any such symbols automatically triggered a call to the Bureau of Demonology and required investigating. The eighth century demon in question, one Smegrot the Smiter, worshipped in the hot deserts of Rainever, had been responsible for plagues and famine lasting two centuries. Though Sicca Rus had certain traits in common with Smegrot (such as the congenital absence of a moral compass), Asher felt that the scrawl was more likely to be Rus' sick and taunting attempt at a cartoon rendition of himself peeking over a wall, with just a nose and eyes on show, knowing that no one could recognise him. But both Asher and his boss, Duana Llewyn, felt that telling the constabulary that might be counterproductive when it came to finding the killer. Consequently, they let the doubt over Smegrot the Smiter linger, since it guaranteed Asher an invite to every new crime scene of this serial spree.

As a necreddo, Asher bore the gift of speaking to the dead. Though some might argue that being able to speak to the newly departed trod a thin line between curse and gift. Most of the time Asher considered it an advantage, especially now that he'd learned to close his mind to the clamouring hordes. And it came in very handy when trying to catch murderers, even if the victims were seldom calm and collected. Generally speaking, they tended to be a bit miffed when the hooded bloke with the scythe and the big white horse trundled up unannounced, and the last thing they wanted to do was have a conversation with Asher. But he'd learned to handle all of that. He'd always been a listener, not a talker. That worked very well when the perpetrator was known to the victim. Less so when some maniac crept up behind you in a dark alley with a hammer, and all you saw as you fell to the ground was a glimpse of a holey sock. Still, a holey sock had sent more than one homicidal maniac on a one-way trip to visit Mrs Mercredi, New Thameswick's high executioner.

But it was an unenviable task, being a necreddo. Listening to the confused, aggrieved, rambling dead could take its toll and certainly had done with Asher when he'd been with the constabulary's experimental necrosquads, high on psychophiltres; his channels wide open to all sorts of mental assault. He'd gone the way of many of his colleagues and succumbed to the pressure. The result had been a spell in the sanatorium and a little delicate psychosurgery. The surprising thing was that he'd come out of it much stronger. Now, though he'd lost some of his ability, what he'd been left with had somehow become much more controllable. The BOD provided the ideal job. One where he was called in to consult whenever the spectre of a demon raised its ugly, usually horned, sometimes more than one, head. Strangely enough, Crouch seemed to find a demonic link in most of the cases he was called to investigate and, more often than not, it was Asher who answered the call, keen to help, no longer coerced by the plodding bureaucracy and unremitting pressure of his previous position at the Fae Human Intelligence and Felonious Activities Agency.

Asher's skill set was also not limited to humans. He was especially good at elves, who tended towards interminable post-mortem tribal death songs given half a chance. But they were very good at remembering faces. The reason being that if you were stupid enough to try murdering an elf, they generally took a part of your face with them under their very sharp nails when they went.

Dwarves, on the other hand, usually shrugged off their

mortal coil seething with indignation and screaming for vengeance on the killer, the killer's family, property, lands and chattels, far-flung relatives, and future progeny. Their trouble was that when it came to artists' impressions of their attacker, it was difficult to do much with a drawing of a knee or a groin, since that was exactly what dwarves remembered seeing if their attacker was not of similar dwarfish persuasion. And, to cap it all, Asher was the only necreddo who would even attempt to communicate with a deceased troll. Mainly because it was like searching for a flickering candle in a cavernous labyrinth of darkness. When found, however, it could be remarkably succinct, if a little indirect. Famously, Asher had once found a killer on the basis of a dead troll's 'bald knuckle' description. The confession from a shaven-headed sailor with hands like coalscuttles had given Asher much satisfaction.

But the leech murders were proving more difficult. Not helped by the fact that recently dead leeches, or, to give them their proper name, recidivist vampires, did not behave like the rest of humanity. So much so that even mentioning them in the same sentence as the living and breathing was stretching things a bit.

Crouch had not moved for a while and Asher began to wonder if he'd morphed into a statue. Given that the moustached constabulary man was a shapeshifter with exactly that capability, it was not beyond possibility. Indeed, Asher had noted of late that Crouch had developed the morphing habit when he needed some thinking time. Turning to granite was a great trick if you could pull it off, especially when someone was stabbing or shooting you, or even bothering you in general. Stony-faced had a whole different connotation when it came to Crouch. So hearing him ask tentatively, 'What do you reckon as regards the deceased?' snapped Asher rather smartly out of his reverie.

'I'll try,' Asher said, failing to keep the cynicism out of his voice.

Asher moved forward, Crouch stood to give him room.

There was no real need to touch the body and this was not something that Asher relished, but this was a leech and it might help, given the circumstances. Asher reached out a finger to the exposed chest, mindful of all the red bits. Taking a breath, he shut his eyes and stepped into the elevator shaft. At least that was what the giddy swoop within his innards felt like, followed swiftly by his mind tumbling down through the veils until he stopped abruptly with a mental lurch.

Something loomed out of the darkness. And though he was expecting it, still Asher flinched and threw up both arms to ward off the attack. A face, wild-eyed, lips drawn back, flew at Asher's throat and passed right through him as unsubstantial as mist. Undaunted, it turned and repeated the feral attack, and lunged at his head.

Asher cursed. It was always like this with bloody leeches. Cannibal vampires that they were, seeing their souls bared after death like this was always something that sent a shudder through him. He tried to open a conversation.

'Hold on. Just wait one minute.'

The thing swooped past him, fangs extended and thrusting towards his throat.

'Tell me who did this. Did you see a face? Anyone you recognise?'

A snarl segued into a low growl, followed by a hiss.

'Farmyard impressions? *Really*?'

The hiss got louder.

'Look, I'm here to help,' Asher said, holding out both hands. But it was no good. The leech flew at him, through him, pivoting as its jaws snapped into empty air.

'A name. Just give me a name.'

Fuelled by anger and bloodlust, the vampire's formless

spirit screamed and hurled itself towards Asher once again. The time, the necreddo shook his head, shut his eyes, and felt his own projected spirit snap home into his slim, angular body.

'Any joy?' Crouch asked.

Asher gave a hollow laugh. 'Joy and dead leeches go together about as well as black pudding and treacle.'

Crouch thought about that for a moment longer than gastronomic good taste allowed before saying, 'Not that well, then.'

Asher shook his head. 'We'll get nothing from him. Just like we got nothing from the others.' He sighed. 'They're addicts. And their souls bear witness to that fact. How it is they stop themselves from attacking anything with warm blood in its veins whilst still alive is a mystery to me. Dead, their lust is red raw and unfettered.'

'Yeah, well they're still citizens of New Thameswick. So we have to try and put a stop to this. Funny thing is,' Crouch added with a nod towards the corpse, 'this one was going to join the rehab program.'

'Too little, too late, I'm afraid,' Asher muttered almost wistfully.

'Always too late.' The voice, rasping and deep, came from a passageway off to their left.

Crouch swivelled. He brandished a silver-topped night-stick in his hand. 'Who's there?'

No reply.

Crouch yelled over his shoulder, 'Tock, get in here!'

Heavy footsteps approached from an adjacent room. Tock had to bend at the waist to get through the doorway. Asher estimated he was a good six foot five with legs that could pass as tree trunks and arms as thick boughs. The arboreal analogy didn't stop there either, since Tock's default expression was as wooden as an oak door. He stood holding a lantern, eyes as wide and innocent as a baby's, exuding an air of gentleness that belies great natural strength. His demeanour had fooled many a criminal into thinking he was slow and clumsy whereas he was in fact, neither. A fact many a wrongdoer had spent much time mulling over while they waited for limbs to mend.

Crouch picked up his own lantern and stepped towards the left passage, nightstick extended. Asher saw movement. A stooping figure flinched and a face turned rapidly away from the light.

'Name,' demanded Crouch.

'Lapotaire,' said a voice tinged with challenge as the vampire turned its pale face back and Asher looked into a pair of yellow eyes that were alive and dead at the same time. Whatever it was that flickered behind them was strange and inhuman and guaranteed to make your skin crawl. Those same eyes in the head of the berserk spirit Asher had encountered a few minutes before had beamed out unmitigated hate. Lapotaire's oozed mistrust. Asher took in the standard issue tattered rags and thin limbs. It was difficult to tell vampires apart at the best of times. Something to do with all that dried blood they never managed to wipe away from their chins. That and the lank hair and the way they seemed to curl in on themselves so as not to expose their bodies to the harsh daylight. But Asher suspected that such generalisations also had a lot to do with his own prejudices; he didn't really want to get to know any of this lot well enough to recognise them, but this one looked female, judging from the vague bulges under the rags.

'Know anything about this?' Crouch asked, waving the nightstick in the direction of the corpse.

Lapotaire tilted her head back. 'I found him,' she said. 'He is mine.'

'Who was he?' Crouch asked.

'Giovaise.'

'Then I'm sorry for your loss.'

Lapotaire's thick eyebrows came together in what might pass for vampire quizzical. 'Not loss. Food.'

'I'm going to pretend I didn't hear that,' Crouch said thickly.

'We of the Kindred recycle,' Lapotaire explained, a total lack of emotion on her unnerving features.

Crouch sent Asher a look and shook his head. 'This isn't a soddin' pick'n'mix. And I've got news for you, Miss, or whatever it is you are. Recycling is when you use the same paper bag you got last week from Root the grocer to carry your turnips. What you're talking about is cannibalism.'

'Tradition.' Lapotaire's yellow eyes held Crouch's gaze and didn't waver.

'Tradition,' Crouch repeated. 'So what's to say you didn't fancy a bit of traditional supper and sneaked up on your takeaway with a traditional carving knife while he was having a traditional kip?'

Lapotaire did not flinch. Instead, her face took on a pained look. Or as much of a pained look someone with a face imagined by Hieronymus Bosch on acid could manage. 'We are not murderers.'

Crouch let out a muffled laugh. From behind, Tock coughed gently.

'No, silly me. Of course not. You're only bloodsucking cannibals.'

'But we are not murderers,' repeated Lapotaire. 'Not of our own.'

'Lucky for you this looks like Rus's handiwork. But a word of advice. Less of the skulking and sneaking up on investigative constables next time, okay? Some of my colleagues might have attacked first and asked questions later.' Crouch wrinkled his nose. 'Do any of you even think about ever having a bath?'

'Water is for throwing bones into.'

Crouch shook his head. 'I give up.' He turned back to the

hulking constable behind him. 'Get some images of all this and then, when you're done, turn the body over to this little lot for proper 'disposal'. I'm sure they'll supply their own carrots and Lyonnaise potatoes.'

Asher didn't smile, though he caught Tock stifling another cough that might have masked either a snigger or disgust.

———

OUTSIDE, grey rain drizzled from a heavy, late August sky. Asher, slight and pale and the taller of the two investigators, pulled his coat about him. Crouch looked up, searching for pigeons before placing his bowler on his head. Coming from a long line of gabbroic igneomagi who could shapeshift into statuary, pigeons were very much off the Crouch Christmas list—for obvious reasons.

'It comes to something when you look forward to a nostril full of New Thameswick air. Especially this close to the city midden,' Crouch observed.

Asher let his eyes drift over to where seagulls wheeled and bugled a quarter of a mile away above a mildly steaming hillock of refuse and waste. 'So, where do we go from here?' he asked. Rain had begun to build up on his long eyelashes and he wiped the moisture away.

'Like I said, we don't have much. I reckon we should try the rehab place, see if they know anything. That's after we grab some grub. I'm starving.'

Asher shook his head. 'Crouch, how could you possibly think of food after…that.'

'My old dad used to say that the best cure for anything was to do the opposite. So, if I'm feeling a bit nauseous, I generally snaffle a pasty. Usually does the trick. Or at least it gives my oesophagus something to work on while it whistles carrots.' Crouch stuck out his barely protruding belly and patted it with a dusky grey hand. 'Come on. I'll treat you.

There's a place on Giblet Avenue. They do a mean EBNAT.'

'I know I'm going to regret asking,' Asher said.

'Everything but nose and tail,' Crouch grinned. 'Besides, eating helps me think. And we need to think if we're going to catch that bastard, Rus. Knows what he's doing all right. Knows it and enjoys it. Maybe a bellyful of EBNAT pasty will give me some inspiration.'

'It'll give you something,' Asher observed. 'But where can Rus be? Why has no one seen him for months?'

Crouch looked up into the drizzle, letting the water bathe his face. 'Hiding in plain sight, I reckon. Laying low in some den isn't his style. But he must know his time is up. We've had orders from up top to make him number one on our list. He's got to be found. And he'll slip up, they always do.'

'But isn't it a bit worrying that he's so profligate?' Asher asked.

'What do you mean?'

'Knowing you're all after him should make him at least a tad more cautious.'

'You're talking about Sicca Rus here. He's about as cautious as a crocodile.' Crouch shook his head.

'But he's been able to stay free because of guile. This spate of killings is almost as if he's thrown caution to the wind. As if he isn't worried that you're being drawn ever closer.'

'Oh, yeah.' Crouch gave an exaggerated nod. 'Don't tell me, maybe he wants to be caught. Give it all up and follow the great God Givashit.'

'Or he knows something that we don't.'

'What do you mean?'

'Perhaps he has a plan.'

Crouch stared at his friend. 'A plan? Anyone ever tell you that comedy wasn't your strong point?''

A police cab drawn by a sleek black horse pulled up at the kerb.

'I'll make a deal with you. Let's do the rehab place first, then I'll buy you lunch,' Asher offered.

Crouch's eyes lit up. 'We'll add a couple of hundred-year-old eggs to that pasty order if you're buying.'

Asher returned a weak smile.

Crouch addressed the horse. 'Scrap Street, Terry.'

Terry snorted and gave an equine nod. Crouch and Asher clambered aboard.

'Ahh,' said Crouch, sucking in air. 'Nothing like the smell of old leather and horses.'

'You're right,' Asher said, wrinkling his nose in response to the assault it was receiving from the stink of sweat and old vomit inside the cab. 'This smells nothing like old leather and horses.'

Crouch took out a chequered handkerchief and began polishing the silvered end of his nightstick with vigour. It had a metallic fox's head, the nose of which looked pointy and sharp.

'I know we are sworn to protect. I know our duty is to truth and justice. But them leeches…' He shook his head. 'That's species correctness gone insane, that is. Five years ago, in Lowreen, we'd have rounded up the whole lot and sent them back to Oneg.'

Asher gave him a wry smile. 'Here in New Thameswick we've embraced freedom and diversity.'

'Yeah. But all it really encourages is arseholes like Rus.'

'It has resulted in a richer society,' Asher pointed out.

'Well, you would say that since you're walking out with a witch.'

'She's not a witch. Not yet.'

'As good as,' Crouch argued, giving the fox's head another vigorous polish.

Asher watched him for a few moments and then asked, 'Why do you do that every time we meet a leech?'

Crouch held up the nightstick. 'Got this on special order from Hollandia and Sons. Based on my own design. It does for leeches, werewolves, rabid venks and most other scum. Nose is on a spring. Sharp contact and it extends right out at skull-cracking speed. It's important I keep it clean. So, I'm buffing the vampire slayer.'

Asher blinked. 'Buffing the vampire slayer?'

'Yeah, that's right.' Crouch's look was sharp and narrow eyed. 'And don't say it like that. Your Ms Miracle was the same when I told her. Fell off her chair laughing, she did. What's the big joke, eh?'

Other than the vague idea that it might have passed as innuendo or a euphemism for something onanistic, for the life of him Asher didn't know why Bobby Miracle might have found the statement even slightly amusing. However, he wasn't about to tell Crouch that, preferring instead to give the hawkshaw an imperious look. Irritated, Crouch redoubled his polishing, a fleeting flash of iridescence dancing over his dusky grey skin as a sign of his annoyance.

It brought a brief grin to Asher's face on a day when, so far, there had been little to smile at.

CHAPTER TWO

Number 17 Scrap Street had housed many and varied individuals and groups over the last couple of centuries. It was a large building, full of rooms that resisted any and all attempts at heating with ceilings high enough for birds to nest in without anyone noticing. As such it lent itself to organisations such as the Thameswick Association for Befriending Young Servants, which was mercifully closed down after a couple of politicians were found wilfully over-befriending, and the Anti-Fume League in the days of open fires burning Troll dung when smog could render a hand in front of your face a thing of remembered usage. Now, as Terry the horse pulled up and Asher and Crouch got out, a painted sign next to the imposing studded door sported the initials ICHOR, with the full title in parentheses beneath.

(The International Centre for Haemophilic Obelian Rehabilitation)

'Ever been here?' Crouch asked.

Asher shook his head.

'Interesting place. Twice as creepy as the outhouse we found Giovaise in, if you want my opinion.'

'What's Obelian?'

'Obelia the Enigmatic, to give him his full title, is some hermit bloke who lived in a cave in Oneg for twenty years and never got bitten. That makes him some kind of miracle worker. The fact that he barricaded himself in and had a small arsenal of crossbows and a garlic forest seems never to be mentioned. Anyway, he came back and started telling everyone that the leeches weren't all that bad. Minted, he is. Very big with the Ladies' Institute. Does lectures and stuff. Usually wearing little but a loincloth.'

'What's wrong with that?'

'Nothing, except he wears it on his head. Says it helps his chakra. Very big on chakras, he is. And I reckon it's his big chakra that makes him very popular with the ladies. Anyway, he set up ICHORs all over the place. This one is run by one Simla DiFrance and yes, he, too is as weird as the name suggests. Obelia set the first one up in the south of Nonions, near Nancee, and so the rehabs call themselves Les Reasonables, according to Nonions lingo. Don't speak any Froag, do you?'

Asher shook his head as Crouch lifted a brass knocker shaped like a large bat to announce their presence.

The door opened to reveal a very pretty girl with dark hair wearing a white tunic. Her face was heavily powdered and as pale as the tunic, with dark painted eyelashes and a rosebud mouth.

She bowed twice and said in a high voice, 'Please come in.'

Asher found himself in a large white anteroom with dark chandeliers high above. He followed the girl, who tottered around on four-inch wooden heels. Two other clones sat behind a desk, smiling demurely.

'Please, follow me,' said the girl.

'What's with the Tealanders?' Asher whispered.

'Less intimidating aesthetic for the rehab leeches.'

'How?'

'You'll see.'

They followed her along a white painted hallway, passing an open door through which Asher glimpsed tables and chairs.

'Dining area,' chimed the girl.

At the end of the hallway was another door leading into a large subbasement and yet another door and a huge room with an even higher ceiling. Asher guessed that it might once have been a ballroom. But the dance floor was now covered with trestle tables laden with little piles of cardboard, cards, and wrapping paper. Around each table in complete silence sat groups of people. At least, they might pass for people if you didn't dwell too long on their features. Every one of them had dark hair tied back and faces completely covered in white makeup. Everyone looked up as Asher and Crouch entered the room. For a moment, Asher got the scalp-tingling impression he was a daydreaming springbok that had wandered into a patch of savannah where a pride of lions waited. It was the eyes that did it. Despite the fact that every one of Les Reasonables was dressed in clean oyster-coloured trousers and a slightly lighter tunic, their eyes were the same dirty yellow that had stared up at him from Giovaise's dead face.

The startled deer moment lasted all of two seconds, but a cold sweat sprouted under Asher's collar. The frozen silence was broken by an echoing voice hailing them from the top end of the room.

'Inspector Crouch? We've been expecting you.'

A man approached them. He stood out from the pale-faced Reasonables by dint of an almost bald head bearing a thin red fringe beneath a shining pate, and a face dominated by a nose with a downturned tip above protruding teeth. His tunic was pale blue with his name embroidered elaborately over the left breast. On the other breast, in capitals, was written *ICHOR*.

'Mr DiFrance,' said Crouch as the man approached. 'May I introduce my colleague, Asher Lodge, seconded to the constabulary from the Bureau of Demonology. He is helping us with our enquiries.'

Asher shook DiFrance's hand. It was as cold and moist as he'd expected it to be. Over DiFrance's shoulder, Les Reasonables all watched the tableau with unblinking gazes.

DiFrance's expression, which Asher had assumed because of its toothsome nature was a smile, changed. Asher took the slight downturn at the angles of the mouth as a frown but it wasn't easy. There was simply too much enamel there for the lips to close together in any form of compression.

'Such a sad state of affairs. Such a tragedy.' DiFrance's statement was followed by a prolonged hiss as sucked-in air negotiated the large dental array.

Crouch asked, 'We understand that Giovaise had been in contact with ICHOR. Can you confirm that?'

DiFrance nodded. 'Indeed, indeed. We were hoping to enrol him next week. Such an awful waste.'

'So what is it that rehabilitation entails, exactly?' Asher asked.

DiFrance beamed. 'As you can see, we insist on creativity to occupy the Kindred minds, and activity to occupy the body.' He turned back to the room and, on cue, like a class of obedient children, Les Reasonables resumed their work.

'What sort of creativity are we talking about?' Asher peered at the tables with renewed interest.

DiFrance moistened his front teeth with a surprisingly small but pointed pink tongue. 'We try and be as inventive as we can. I have tried to bring my own expertise to bear, where possible.'

'And what is that expertise, Mr DiFrance?' Crouch asked.

Asher noted a fractional movement outwards of DiFrance's chest. 'I studied for five years at the Splosh Institute. I was lucky enough to be there when Geegenhumor was in his prime. With influences as wide ranging as Conkadonk and Rickenbacker, he was able to use social tensions to craft iconic imagery. Ever since then, I've been fascinated by the unrelenting divergence of conflict, in particular the internecine nature of the Kindred's struggle. What starts out as triumph soon becomes corroded into a carnival of mistrust, leaving only a sense of unreality and the prospect of a new beginning. With Geegenhumor, subtle phenomena become distorted through diligent and critical practice and we, the observers, are left with an insight into the outposts of our future.'

There followed a prolonged silence ended by Crouch with customary candidness. 'He paints dogs doesn't he?'

DiFrance blinked, bemused momentarily at Crouch's wondrous ability to sum up the totality of Geegenhumor's canon with such flippancy. Clearing his throat, he said, 'His canine series is amongst the best known of his works.'

Crouch chuckled. 'I like the one with the dog trying to pull a stick out of that tax collector's—'

'He became a touch reactive during his absinthe period. However, my work there means that I am able to exert a little influence.' DiFrance quickly added the qualifying statement with a few extra decibels of volume to ensure it drowned out Crouch's lurid observations and walked across to a table where some of Les Reasonables were working. 'Greeting cards, calendars, bookmarks. All very high quality, all hand finished.'

Asher picked up a card. The image on the front was a simplistic rendition of a dog wearing a party hat. Underneath this was the caption, *Happy Woofday*.

Crouch grinned, 'These are great. This is your kids' range, I take it?'

DiFrance's face tripped over itself and fell. 'Not at all. We prefer a naive style to try and inject some freshness and simplicity into our cards. We want the public to appreciate a sense of fun and frivolity.'

Crouch expelled air in a way that began as a guffaw and barely disguised itself as a cough. None of the rehab leeches looked up. Suddenly they all seemed happy to keep their heads bent to their tasks.

Fun and frivolity in the workplace were not the adjectives that sprang immediately to Asher's mind. 'Do they sell?' he asked.

'Why, yes. We have markets everywhere.'

'But Giovaise never actually got to work here, is that correct?'

DiFrance shook his head. 'All our new recruits go through an initial adjustment period. The training needed for the physical aspects of lifestyle conversion needs to be matched by a mental modification.'

Asher looked back around at the silent leeches and their painted faces. He thought he saw a lip twitch in what might just have been a suggestion of a smirk. 'And after that?'

'We want to take the message out to the public. To the whole of New Thameswick and the rest of the known world. Oneg included.'

'And how is that working out for you?' Crouch asked.

'It is not easy. But then changing attitudes is never easy. So far, thirty deaths, including five stonings and six drownings. There was also one unfortunate massacre where a group of converts reverted and ended up killing a whole village. But I think we are making progress.'

Asher and Crouch exchanged a glance.

'Was Giovaise in contact with anyone in particular here?' Crouch asked.

'Apart from me, you mean?'

Crouch nodded and picked up another childish but oddly compelling card.

'No. We do not encourage individual relationships here,'

explained DiFrance. 'We believe that our strength is in the collective and by suppressing the ego, we can suppress the base desires that have caused us to be shunned and reviled.'

'You say us and we,' Asher asked. 'But you are not a vampire.'

'No. My mother had the teeth for it but I never developed fully. I am a vimp. Half human, half vampire. I carry the Kindred's blood and its potency to transmit, but it does not manifest in me.' The words were heavy with regret.

Asher stepped closer to the table for a better look at the fruits of Les Reasonables' labours. Another card and another image of a dog, this one with excessively large canines. The log line read: *Fangs very much for the present.*

Asher winced, partly at the poor pun but also because this close, Les Reasonables' odour was inescapable. Further away, the large room diluted much of the stench with a mixture of vinegar, garlic, and cloves. But underneath all of that was the butcher shop reek that had been so overpowering at the murder scene. Here, and up close, it lingered like an odiferous old shoe.

Asher stepped back and saw that Crouch had already turned away and lost interest. They thanked DiFrance and Crouch murmured he'd be back in touch. It was with some considerable relief that Asher felt a New Thameswick breeze caress his face as they stood on the pavement a few moments later.

'Enjoy that?' Crouch asked.

Asher shook his head. 'Did you smell it?'

Crouch nodded. 'That's the grume. A putrid mixture of old blood and carcasses. Les Reasonables might well have given all that up for beetroot juice but it's in their pores. Always will be.'

Asher shivered. 'I feel like I need a good scrub with carbolic soap.'

'I know a young lady at Madame Sprig's in Splatt who specialises in that sort of thing,' Crouch said with a grin.

'No thanks.'

'Oh yeah, I forgot. You've already had a ride on the witch's broom, haven't you?'

'Can't you desist from the incessant witch references for two minutes?' Asher said, bristling.

Crouch's grin broadened. 'Not to mention tasting the witch's brew.'

'Right, that's it. You can forget the EBNAT pasty. We are going vegetarian for lunch. Turnip and leek curry.'

Panic flared in Crouch's face. 'Please not Mehta Hari's curry. They use that stuff to repair cracks in walls. Okay, okay. I'll be good, I promise.'

'One more witch reference and—'

Crouch held his hands up. 'I need some proper grub. And it's you that's paying, remember?'

Asher nodded and climbed back into Terry's cab knowing he would not be partaking of anything other than a slice of dry toast and wondering, vaguely, if his appetite would ever return properly.

CHAPTER THREE

BOBBY MIRACLE SAT IN the lecture theatre at the Bureau of Demonology listening to Professor Duana Llewyn defining mythological archetypes and death deities. Next to her, Richenda, younger by a good four years, doe-eyed and with the concentration span of a goldfish, doodled on a notepad. She'd already designed three gowns for the end of year ball and had taken no lecture notes at all, whereas Bobby had two pages of neat bullet points. Richenda looked across and frowned.

'I can't *believe* you're so interested in this stuff,' she said in her usual scathing tone. 'It's just academic BS.'

Bobby said nothing, knowing full well that it was neither 'academic' nor 'BS'. Not when you worked for Hipposync Enterprises, a very venerable Oxford establishment, as she did when she wasn't attending lectures on the accelerated Wicca course at Le Fey Academy. Her official title at Hipposync was Marketing Director. The unofficial bit, what Hipposync actually did as the clandestine garrison for the Department of Fimmigration, was a very different pot of eels.

She could have explained to Richenda that her very real interest in the lecture stemmed from the case she'd been embroiled in just a few months before. In addition to being her introduction to the real Hipposync, the DOF, and New Thameswick, it encompassed a group of sectarian psychopomps who'd almost managed to bring Gazorch the Pantocrator back to existence by hitchhiking on the souls of people they'd recently murdered. And since 'Pantocrator' literally meant 'omnipotent lord of the universe', had she and her colleagues failed to usurp the plan it would have meant an end to all joy in a world full of chaos. A bit like three-thirty in the morning after a hen party on a wet weekend in Blackpool.

But one glance at Richenda with her pierced tongue protruding from the corner of her mouth as she coloured in a skirt on her pad told Bobby that explaining all of that would probably garner only a 'Wow', followed almost immediately by 'Think this shade of green is too bright?'

A rolled-up sheet of paper dropped gently onto the desk next to them, cloud-charmed to land softly. Richenda made eyes to the ceiling and unfurled the note.

'It's from that letch, Brigger. He's asking if I want to meet him for a drink afterwards and can I bring my foxy friend.'

'Oh, what friend is that?' Bobby asked.

'He means you, witch.'

'Me?'

'Don't look so surprised.' Richenda's heavily made-up eyes danced up and down Bobby's seated form. 'They all fancy you with your sexy human accent and the stylish clothes.'

Bobby did a quick mental assessment of the very practical skirt and blouse she'd put on that day and said, 'I'm—'

'Spoken for? Yes, so you keep telling me. I know and so does Brigger.' Richenda feigned a yawn, turned and pointedly played with the silver necklace at her throat so that the back row could see her. 'There, that should shut him up.'

'What should?'

'Playing with your necklace is a very subtle way of telling them to go away. It threatens a curse.'

Bobby looked horrified.

'Look at your face," Richenda said, grinning.

'That green's a bit too bright,' Bobby said, pointing to the dress in the full knowledge that this ploy was a guaranteed distraction. Richenda and Brigger was an ongoing saga.

'Do you think so? Yes, you're right.' Frowning, Richenda returned to her designing, leaving Bobby to concentrate on the lecture. When it finished, she followed Richenda out to the refectory where they joined the queue for coffee.

Duana emerged from the lecturer's entrance, searched for and found Bobby. She waved and walked across. Next to Bobby, a wide-eyed Richenda turned with sudden intense interest towards the food counter.

'Bobby, lovely to see you,' Duana said.

They hugged and Bobby stepped out of the queue, seeking privacy. 'Great lecture,' she said.

'I knew you'd like it. But then you are the only one in the room with real world experience.'

Bobby glanced up as more BOD people entered the refectory.

'If you're looking for him, he's not here," said Duana. 'Asher's helping Crouch out on a leech serial killer case in the 'scarlet swamp'.'

'Scarlet swamp?'

'Their ghetto.'

'Oh well,' said Bobby, managing, she hoped, to hide the worst of her disappointment.

'You look lovely as usual. I think that blue streak in your hair really suits you. And is that blouse midnight blue? You should wear short skirts more often. Asher doesn't know what he's missing.'

'Thank you,' Bobby replied. Was Duana flirting?

'So, how are you coping with the course?' the professor beamed.

'I'm coping. Loving it, actually. Not sure about the rest of them. They seem to have had lots of exposure to witchcraft and all the rest, so they find some of it a bit trite. But I find it all completely fascinating.'

'Well, your grandmother would be very proud. Give her my regards if you get in touch.'

'I will.'

'And I will be sure to let Asher know you were looking for him.' Duana Llewyn's glacier grey eyes twinkled. 'You two were made for each other.'

Bobby watched the professor hurry away, unable to stop herself from wondering how someone from her old life might have interpreted that conversation. Probably with a 999 call for an ambulance and a straightjacket. Especially the part about saying hello to her gran, who had been dead for a good fifteen years.

But this wasn't her old life. This was her new, weird, and very wonderful life. Still, shame about not seeing Asher. That might have made an interesting day even better. She felt an elbow in her ribs and turned to see Richenda's slitty-eyed glare.

'My, you are well connected, aren't you?'

'I know Prof Llewyn if that's what you mean, yes.'

'Gives me the creeps, she does. Those eyes—they could cut glass.'

'She's amazing and I won't have a bad word said against her,' Bobby said with an icy calmness that stopped whatever carping comment was about to leave Richenda's lips in mid bitch.

'Still, she obviously doesn't like leeches, does she?'

'Who does?'

'Exactly,' Richenda nodded. 'Hardly an ask-them-home-for-tea sort of a bunch. Why they have to dress in rags and stink so much I have no idea. And they're always skulking in the shadows and begging for money to buy that disgusting flesh and blood gloop they eat. What's it called again?'

'Grume,' Bobby said.

'There you go,' said Richenda. 'No wonder someone wants to kill them.'

'So in Richenda's world there'd be no grume at the inn for them. Lots of grume for improvement even?'

If she heard the puns, Richenda didn't let on. 'I hear they're trying to get organised. Arranging protests and the like. Demanding rights. I ask you. Venking cheek if you ask me.'

Bobby lifted her eyebrows a centimetre or two.

Richenda was not for swaying. 'Sorry, but I am never going to feel any sympathy for a vampire, end of. Brigger, meanwhile, could bite my neck whenever he likes.'

'I though you said he was a letch?'

'Yes, letch, not leech. And he does scrub up very nicely when he tries.'

'Oh, so you're prepared to letch bygones be bygones?'

Richenda frowned. 'Is that a human attempt at a joke?'

'Wouldn't dream of it,' Bobby said. 'Come on. I could murder a cappuccino.'

CHAPTER FOUR

EDINBURGH, SCOTLAND, THE HUMAN WORLD (HW)

In a different world, one where leeches were also reviled but only because of their propensity for crawling into orifices of all persuasions (the aquatic type), or for poking their sharp mouth parts through the weave of your socks (the land type), the rain had gone. This left the late evening sun to taunt city dwellers into believing that summer was not yet passed, but soon would be so they'd better get a move on and make the most of it. And this far north they did so passionately and with good cheer, as one did in Scotland, because for every funny-ha-ha the sun is out moment, there was always the possibility of an unfunny Scotch sea mist haar moment.

But the weather was not what preoccupied Captain Kylah Porter as she followed her partner through the door onto the balcony that ran around the New Amphion café in Edinburgh's Teviot building. Ahead, her partner, Matt, hesitated as several pairs of eyes flicked up in his direction. He should not have been surprised; his sudden appearance through a door that swung open on the opposite side from its hinges and was normally firmly locked to boot, should have drawn stares. And though she'd told him to expect it and not to react, it never failed to catch him off guard. It would come with practice, no doubt. To prove the point, Kylah stepped confidently through after him and felt a dozen more pairs of eyes zero in on her. She disregarded them all and walked forward.

The truth was Matt's unconventional entry had little to do with the extra attention the couple was now attracting. Though she would never knowingly acknowledge it, the reason for that attention had a lot more to do with the street-ready black jeans and loose leather jacket Kylah wore. Clothes that failed miserably to hide the athletic, shapely form beneath. Kylah drew glances wherever she went. Consequently, no one in the room saw Matt reach around to the other side of the door and detach the Aperio—a tool of their trade that let them enter or exit through any door into any place they wanted to so long as they could visualise their destination and also had a door. Aperios were standard issue for Department of Fimmigration agents and a damned site subtler than a battering ram.

Kylah moved quickly along the balcony, skirting the loose arrangement of chairs and tables and their occupants. Within seconds no one paid them any notice, it being a Friday in August and well past beer o'clock. They were just another couple out for some fun in a city peddling it by the ton. She paused at the head of the stairs, listening to the buzz of conversation rumbling up from the open area below at a volume that almost drowned out the bar's background music, and felt Matt at her elbow.

'It's loud in here,' she shouted.

Matt nodded and shrugged. 'What do you expect? It's the Fringe. Follow me.' He led the way out into the late August evening. The line of thick cloud marring the late summer afternoon drifted away to reveal a cheerful sun hanging low in the Western sky, knowing as it did that the weather had one final trick up its sleeve. Crowds of people, some ambling, others hurrying, a few simply gathered in groups, thronged the streets. This was Edinburgh's Fringe festival. Three-and-a-bit weeks that attracted thousands of people from all over the world to be entertained by drama, comedy, circus acts, and magicians.

'How far is it?' Kylah asked.

'Ten-minute walk.'

'Couldn't you have got us closer?'

'It's been a while,' Matt answered. 'The student's union was the one place I was sure of.'

'And why are there so many people in T-shirts? It can't be more than twelve degrees.'

Matt grinned. 'Its summer. Besides, we're in Edinburgh. This is positively balmy.'

They headed along Potter Row, passing the myriad posters of acts including some big names, along pavements littered with discarded flyers handed out by the countless hawkers cajoling punters to visit their shows. After Nicholson Street, Matt found a quieter passage towards Pleasance and one of the busiest venues in the biggest festival of its type in the world. You couldn't move for jokes. And because he knew they were coming, Matt had spent most of the morning trying to come up with some. He let fly with one as they walked.

'Cinderella, the social climber, was desperate to go dancing, so she asked her lisping evil stepmother, 'Shall I go to the United Nations ball?' Her stepmother replied, 'No, U Thant'.'

'Right,' said a po-faced Kylah after an uncomfortable pause.

'Right? Is that all I get after an hour of mental struggle? I mean you didn't even raise the corner of your lip.'

'There's an old saying about not wanting to encourage hopelessness.'

'But it's genius.'

'No, it's complicated if not convoluted, and requires that the listener knows U Thant actually was the secretary general of the United Nations in order for the pun to truly work. Since he died in 1975, that precludes anyone under forty.'

'Okay, Miss Clever Clogs. You come up with something.'

Kylah stayed silent.

'Come on, money where your mouth is.' Matt stopped and took Kylah's arm. They stood close together on the edge of the pavement, his eyes narrowed in challenge.

Sighing, Kylah said, 'Okay, ummm…my singing duck was in the final of *Britain's Got Talent* and needed a style makeover so she had two gold teeth fitted by her dentist. Bit flashy but they certainly fit the bill.'

Matt blinked, started to say something, but then just shook his head. 'You've been preparing stuff on the sly, haven't you?'

Kylah smiled.

'That's not fair.' Matt turned away and began walking.

'You're smiling,' Kylah said as she caught him up.

'No, there's something in my eye, that's all.'

She held up two fingers and wordlessly said, 'Two nil.'

'I could use U Thant in a different context you know.'

She sent him a warning glance and hit him playfully on his upper arm.

The 'Oww,' that followed was full of mock pain.

Kylah's fingers strayed towards her head. 'Why is my hair getting damp and the castle suddenly in badly overdone soft focus?' she asked, glancing up.

'It's the haar.'

'I know it's my hair. That's what I said.'

'Not hair, haar. A sea fog that plagues the East coast. Some say it's like being caressed by wet, ghostly fingers.'

'But the weather was clear a minute ago.'

'Exactly. Hence the saying haar today, gone tomorrow.'

They walked through an archway guarded by someone wearing a lanyard into a close surrounded by stone walls with narrow rooms accessed through dark doorways and steep steps. Black and yellow signs posted everywhere pointed towards the various venues, but once through the narrow archway, the courtyard opened up with an outdoor bar and lines of people queuing for their ticketed performances. Groups of festivalgoers stood around or sat and almost everyone held some form of alcohol in plastic glasses. The smell of frying onions and meat hung cloyingly in the air.

'Fancy a burger?' Matt asked.

'Not at the moment,' Kylah answered, peering at the signs, many of which were quickly fading as the haar descended.

'Drink?'

'No thanks. We're on the clock here, remember?'

'Yes, but it's the Fringe.'

Kylah shook her head, lips pursed. 'Where are we meant to be?'

Matt led her through another archway into a second courtyard and pointed to the black and yellow sign. 'Pleasance Up and Under. We're here. Sure you don't want a half?'

Kylah didn't answer and kept her expression neutral.

'That's your irritated look.'

'I just think we should keep a clear head. We'll grab a drink afterwards.'

'But everyone drinks at the Fringe.'

'Not me. Not when I'm working.'

The queue began moving and they joined its tail, handing over tickets to a girl with magenta hair whose voice was deep and hoarse from saying, 'Enjoy the show' at least a thousand times over the twenty days the fringe had been running. They clambered up stone steps and were ushered into a small room lined with blackout curtains. Music played: *The Sorcerer's Apprentice*.

Kylah sent Matt a dry smile under raised eyebrows. He replied with a shrug. They found some seats at the far end of a row and Kylah did a quick headcount. The room held no more than sixty people and filled up quickly. A few minutes later, the music faded, the lights dimmed and someone announced:

'Good evening, ladies and gentlemen. Prepare to be amazed. Please be aware that recording devices and flash photography are not allowed. Anyone found using these devices will be instantly turned into a slow-worm and fed to the seagulls. Now, join me in welcoming to the stage…The Alternator!'

The unassuming man who bounced onto the stage was short, squat, and podgy with a scruffy red beard. In fact, the only outstanding thing about him was his dark jacket upon which had been sewn lightning bolts and stars in orange and yellow. Despite the lack of a tie, the jacket leant him a curiously schoolboyish air, and Kylah was relieved he'd at least eschewed a cloak and a wand.

Kitsch was one thing, plagiarism something different altogether.

Still, she found herself frowning. Appearances could be very deceptive indeed, as anyone who'd ever dealt with shapeshifters would know—and she'd once dated one. Even so, she couldn't help but acknowledge the smidgen of disappointment nagging at her. The reports they'd received suggested some serious dark and disturbing wonderworking; in other words, real magic. But the man who now stood before them on this Edinburgh stage looked about as capable of real magic as a penguin was of flight.

Kylah sat back, deciding to give The Alternator a chance. The simple sleight of hand tricks he performed were delivered with well-practised slickness, but his shtick was plodding and mundane and as charismatic as a decaying frog on a June blacktop. For forty-five minutes, The Alternator did his thing, pulling signed playing cards from out of his shoe, guessing the name of one audience member's dog, sending an engagement ring into a beer bottle. Impressive, but standard fare, and by fifty minutes Kylah could sense the audience getting restless. They'd all read the four and five-star reviews, but as yet there'd been little or no evidence for this. Where was the wonderworking gold?

To his credit, the performer sensed the shift in mood and changed gear.

'Ladies and gentlemen, I'm delighted you've all made the effort to come and see me.'

His voice had a grating, nasal quality that somehow made her want to blow her own nose.

'You may have heard that during this part of the show, I have been experimenting. Something new every day. We've got to that point now.'

No one breathed.

'I've always wanted to be a magician. A real magician. Using real magic. Old magic.' He paused, looking from one face to the next. 'Some of you may not think such a thing exists. I'm here to tell you that it does. There are things in this world beyond any rational explanation and I am certain that after the next fifteen minutes, you will all agree with me. Tonight, we will be playing with fire.' He paused and smiled a smile full of confident mischief. 'I think you are all going to like what you see.'

Kylah and Matt exchanged glances. The Alternator had the audience in the palm of his hand. But if there had been a thought bubble above Matt's head, from the sceptical look on his face, it would have read: *Now where have I heard that before?*

CHAPTER FIVE

NEW THAMESWICK, FW

Simla DiFrance stood in front of the mirror in his room, tilting his head this way and that in an attempt to see if the angles improved his profile. None did. It was no use. It would take more than a good light and optimism to improve his lot. It would take something miraculous. Behind him, the room contained little other than his few possessions: newly laundered tunic on the bed, a shelf containing folded clothes, a few books on art, and a locked chest containing more books that were extremely valuable, of interest to very few people and never on public display. The walls were unadorned. No paintings, no hangings and certainly no clocks.

Because what was the use of a clock when it stopped as soon as you looked at it?

For the thousandth time, he cursed his mother. She too had been blessed with buck teeth and small eyes whilst his father donated the red hair and ruddy cheeks. By rights, he should have borne the pale skin and dark hair all Kindred possessed. But a genetic quirk had thrown up some bygone contributor to the DiFrance gene pool and quashed the worst of the vampire traits to leave Simla a diluted hybrid. Neither man nor vampire. A vimp. Someone who carried the curse and could infect others, but who had none of the…'benefits'.

The real irony was that, apart from the receptionists, all of whom were specialist greeters from Tealand, he was the only entity in the building possessed of a reflection. How much better off would he have been without one, like all the other Les Reasonables. That was why there were no mirrors in the building other than the one in his room and the very big one they'd installed in the basement. But the latter was not there for anyone to examine themselves in. It was there for another purpose altogether.

Simla sighed and ran his fingers over his facial bones. He'd tried all sorts of charms and spells and they did work for a while, but they inevitably wore off and he was always left with the teeth, the balding head, and the farmer's complexion, though he spent as little time outside as possible since the sun brought him out in blotches. There'd been nothing he could do to change his appearance.

Something rippled up his spine.

Been nothing.

A frisson of anticipation at the thought that he might have found a way made him look again into the pale brown eyes of his reflection.

What he would give to make it happen.

Turning away, he opened the door on an empty corridor. Simla realised he'd overindulged in self-loathing and wild imaginings for far too long and was now late for the gathering. He took the stairs two at a time. The door to the old ballroom stood ajar, the tables cleared, chairs stacked, Les Reasonables all gone. But he knew where they all were.

He went to the front door, locked and bolted it. The receptionists had long gone, too. Satisfied, he retraced his steps and opened the door leading down into the basement. Thirty pairs of yellow eyes locked on to him as he descended into the dim, candlelit room.

'I see we are all here,' he said, beaming. An unfortunate expression in the DiFrance range that exposed even more of his protruding incisors. 'The usual refreshments of celery sticks and semi–dried beetroot slices will be available at the intermission, as always.'

A hundred yards away in Congregation Square a clock began striking the hour.

It was time.

Simla walked between two rows of seats to a large draped oblong. He drew back the material to reveal a grand mirror with a gilded frame. From a small muslin bag slung across his shoulder he took a pinch of powder, stood back and, reciting a familiar incantation, threw the powder at the mirrored surface. Instantly, the reflected image of the hall and its rows of 'empty' seats began to change. Clouds of colour began to appear in the glass, swirling and coalescing in a rainbow kalei-doscope until finally an image was revealed to the watching audience.

The mirror showed a small room with a bookcase, a desk, and chairs. On the desk sat a sleek black rectangle of polished glass. Yet even as they watched, the background of shelving and books faded, as the oblong grew bigger until its screen filled the whole of the mirrored surface. Became the mirrored surface as new images moved across it. This was a window into another place and it never failed to take his breath away. Behind DiFrance, the leech converts so optimistically labelled Les Reasonables by the New Thameswick press were also riveted.

Simla, without taking his eyes off the screen, found a seat.

A lion roared, and then the strangeness began as the audi-ence embroiled themselves in this different world. One they could never access under normal circumstances. The human world. But a human world made all the sweeter by being one in which their own type dwelt. Living and breathing and walking under the same sun. A sun that did not cause their skin to fry until their blood boiled.

The story never changed. A human female in the bloom of early womanhood. An only child, troubled by emotional stress, befriended by a magnificent vampire who would save her from herself and from the unwanted attention of predatory males. But it was not the girl's adventures that captivated Simla and the rehabilitated leeches. What engaged their rapt attention was how the vampires looked. Simla did not need to turn around to know that he would see in the eyes of the captivated audience the very same awe, worshipfulness, longing, and need he felt himself.

This was a world where vampires remained a minority, but were the dominant species living within the weaker human society. Powerful, feared, sleek, and handsome, these vampires controlled their desires, but enjoyed all the power that came with superiority.

It had been like this once in Oneg, the Kindred's beloved fatherland. The most successful leech colonies harvested their food source. Lived with them, milking them of blood like cattle, picking off only the weak upon which to feed so as to preserve their vital resource. Yet they had not bargained for the greed and wanton bloodlust of the few within their ranks who saw farming as nowhere near as much fun as the terrifying, ripping, fangs akimbo chase. Nor the determination and inventiveness of suppressed humans when it came to being stroppy and awkward and not accepting their lot. And being bred and kept for nothing more than a ready supply of 'cellular claret' had curiously enough not seemed like a great deal when it came to 'lot' considerations.

Wars were fought and blood spilled. All that *wasted* blood spilled. Heroes emerged, treaties were signed, and laws passed. Laws that made the superior inferior. Laws that demanded integration and tolerance. Laws that gave the cattle all the power over their herders. But this new order rankled and grated. A return to the old ways could never happen. Too many battles fought and scars left unhealed to allow such a state. And yet the Kindred yearned for a new way to be found where the balance of power shifted back to the natural order of things. It was what, with the whole of their black hearts, all leeches secretly coveted. And what Simla DiFrance coveted, too. Though in his version it came with a new face, hair, and teeth you couldn't open bottles with.

And even if it remained unclear to him which exact path needed to be taken, he knew this miraculous vision they were watching had to be the first step on a journey they all would take. And this inspiration, this validation of his work and his calling, was all he could ever have hoped for. A place where power was restored, but benevolent power.

Granted, history was not the best harbinger when it came to considering the likelihood of success. Yet what they were witnessing through the enchanted mirror was the embodiment, the actuality of DiFrance's aspirations. He could not take his eyes from it.

A tear ran down his blotchy face as, on-screen, a devastatingly handsome vampire was being merciful toward the girl who wanted nothing more than to be bitten. His restraint was a thing of wonder to behold.

Halfway down the rows of seats, a pair of eyes drifted unseen from the screen towards the profile of DiFrance's face. Those eyes, unlike those of his companions glinting in wonderment, glowed with rapacious hunger and Machiavellian glee. Because he, too, knew this to be a revelation. Much like a lizard spotting a landed insect on the branch of a tree, he would move slowly, inexorably, to within striking distance before unleashing a darting, powerful, muscular tongue towards his prey.

Where DiFrance saw promise and emancipation, what burned behind these eyes was opportunity.

The eyes drifted back to the screen. They were hungry but patient enough to watch and wait.

CHAPTER SIX

EDINBURGH, SCOTLAND, HW

JORDAN, THE VOLUNTEER PLUCKED BY the audience, was a squat man wearing faded jeans that hung a tad too low over his generous belly so as to reveal a rather hairy two inches of unattractive flesh beneath a well-worn, grubby T-shirt. Written on the shirt were the words *Official Real Beer 2022 Hophead Tour*, indicating how its wearer's lifestyle choices concisely reflected the displayed excess of flesh and the rest of the scruffy package. Jordan grinned through his full beard, at his mates in the audience, who provided a barrage of good-natured heckling.

'Don't worry, Jordie, I've got your pint safe!'

'If he asks ye, take the money, mate, don't open the box…'

'Turn him into a toad, will ye? He'll have more luck with the lassies that way.'

That one got a laugh. Jordan took it all with good grace as the happily inebriated so often did.

On stage next to him, The Alternator grabbed the fire extinguisher and placed it with silent theatricality four feet from Jordan's side. He then went back to the small trestle desk where he proceeded to open the packaging of a fresh loaf of bread and remove two slices. Attaching one to a long stainless steel toasting fork, he gave it to a nervous woman in the front row.

The woman took it, giggling anxiously.

The Alternator paused, staying deadpan. 'You'll have to do without jam or marmalade, I'm afraid.'

He returned to the beaming Jordan and positioned him such that he was facing the audience. Retrieving a large galvanised metal trug, The Alternator poured in a 2kg bag of sand and asked Jordan to stand in it.

'Just in case,' The Alternator explained with a maniacal grin. It was pure cheese and the audience loved it.

Preparations complete, he turned to face the crowd. Hands held widely apart, he brought them together with a loud clap. When he separated them again by a matter of ten inches, a ball of golden flame flickered between them.

The audience applauded. A glassy-eyed Jordan smiled in anticipation.

'I don't know what you're laughing about,' said The Alternator and hurled the flaming ball at the standing man. With a great whump, Jordan burst into flames. Still standing, he became a rigid pillar with fire flickering thickly all around him, licking his body, crackling up a good foot above his head.

The audience gasped and then went strangely quiet. Horror mingled with nervous excitement in their expressions as their minds tried to make sense of what they were seeing. And feeling, because the flames *looked* real and the heat *was* real. Ordering Jordan to keep still, The Alternator fetched another piece of bread, stuck it on the end of another long steel handled fork and began toasting it, nodding at the woman in the front row to do the same.

At the very rear of the small room, Matt and Kylah looked at one another with identical frowns. They too could feel the heat radiating out across the room. It must have been unpleasantly warm sitting in the front row. Smoke began to rise from the bread The Alternator was toasting. He turned to the woman in the front row and removed her toast, took both slices back to the trestle table, slowly and elaborately opened two miniature oblongs of hotel breakfast butter and began to spread. He whistled nonchalantly before returning one slice of buttered toast to the woman. Grinning, he took a bite of his own, indicating she should do the same. Throughout all of this, flames danced around Jordan who remained still and silent and *smiling* rapturously. It was mesmerising. More than that, it was highly unnerving. As the man next to him burned merrily, The Alternator took another bite and addressed the woman with the toast. 'Unsalted butter, unfortunately. All I could nick from the B&B.'

She blinked, holding the toast delicately between thumb and forefinger.

The Alternator took another bite.

The wags in the audience piped up, bouncing heckles off one another.

'Jordie's a bloody kebab!'

'Aye, God man, I can smell burnin''—'

'That's his aftershave.'

'You're doin' great, Jordie. Lightin' up ma life—'

'Aye, well done, mate.'

'Any more o' this and he will be bloody well done.'

Nervous laughter danced over the audience but quickly fell away into a concerned buzz.

The Alternator grinned and nodded. 'Gets a bit disturbing after a while, doesn't it?'

He reached out a hand towards the burning man, spoke a quiet word and the fire leapt upwards, curled into a ball and flowed back as a dense white condensation of heat towards the magician's open palm. He clapped his hands together again and it disappeared.

Still standing in the trug, undamaged and undisturbed, a slightly flushed and bemused-looking Jordan stared about him. Applause erupted with whoops of appreciation as The Alternator shook Jordan's hand and ushered him back to his seat. The magician returned to centre stage, wallowed for a few moments in the standing ovation, took his bow and then disappeared behind a black curtain. He reappeared a minute later to enjoy a few more seconds of applause but an announcement over the PA system asking everyone to leave quickly so that the next act and its audience could take their places put an end to proceedings.

Matt and Kylah stood. But instead of following the crowd out, they stepped forward onto the stage.

'Can you smell it?' Kylah asked.

'Seared meat and sulphur.' Matt nodded.

'Vestigia,' Kylah said. 'That was no illusion. Our friend The Alternator is using the good stuff. That was Shaddara's Fire.'

The girl with magenta hair, dressed in the black and orange of Fringe staff, came in behind them.

'I'm afraid I'm going to have to ask ye to leave.'

Kylah ignored her and pulled back the blackout curtain covering a doorway through which The Alternator had exited.

'Excuse me,' said the girl. 'Ye cannae—'

With an apologetic tilt of his head, Matt followed Kylah through the door into a dingy corridor behind. Steps lead down to a single door with a handwritten sign that read, *Artists*.

Kylah knocked.

A voice answered. 'Just changing. If it's about the fire…'

'Open the door,' ordered Kylah.

Matt winced. He knew that tone. Authoritative, insistent, not a tone one wanted to mess with or ignore. On the other side of the door the sound of shuffling ceased abruptly.

'Who is this?'

'DOF officers. Open the door.'

'DOF? What the hell is DOF?'

'The people who know you've been meddling where you should not have been.'

The noises behind the door returned with renewed vigour.

'Aperio,' Kylah said urgently. Matt fished out the porcelain artefact and Kylah fitted it to the door, turned the knob and pushed, revealing a dim, windowless room containing a small table, a folding chair, a clothes rail upon which three wire hangers swayed and, on the far wall, a full-length mirror. It was through this that The Alternator was quickly disappearing.

'Damn,' yelled Kylah.

'I'll get him,' Matt said and pushed past, only to feel Kylah's strong hand on his arm.

'Wait,' she said.

Matt jerked back just as Kylah's left hand thrust forward in a good imitation of an underarm throw. A buzzing cloud emerged and flew towards the mirror. The Alternator's head and shoulders were still in the room. He grinned and said 'Ciao' before disappearing.

'Why did you stop me?' Matt asked as the room fell silent.

'You would have been dragged through and maybe left half in and half out. Far too dangerous. Never follow a warlock through his Gateway.'

'But the bastard got away!'

Kylah smiled. 'No, he didn't.' She opened her hand and the thin cloud hanging in front of the mirror buzzed back with a high-pitched whining sound.

'What is that?'

'Tracer gnats.' She opened her palm over a small pouch on her belt and the whining increased in volume momentarily before falling silent.

'I think one or two found their target,' said Kylah.

'Do you know what's going on?' Matt asked.

Kylah should her ahead. 'I don't. Not exactly. But this is no ordinary close-up magician. The reports were right.'

Magenta girl appeared in the doorway behind them. 'Security is on its way,' she said in a petulant Scottish accent. 'And how come ye opened that door on the hinge side?'

'No need, we're leaving. And trick of the trade, in that order,' Matt said.

'Where is he?' Magenta-hair did a quick sweep of the room with her eyes.

'Long gone. Didn't even have enough time to give us an autograph.'

Magenta frowned. 'Some people have complained about the act. Said he used fire.'

Matt nodded. 'So that's not normally in his act, then?'

'Of course not. He knows ye can't do that sort of thing. The fire marshal's going to throw a major wobbly.'

Two men appeared behind the girl. They were older and bulkier with yellow security armbands on their black sweatshirts.

'This them?' asked one.

'We're just leaving,' Kylah said, her smile chocolate sauce on vanilla ice cream. 'Just came for an autograph. Looks like we missed him.'

Magenta girl inclined her head and took the opportunity to be clever. 'He's a magician,' she said. 'I suspect he's quite used to disappearing.'

Nobody laughed.

Kylah led the way back down into the courtyard. She pushed through the crowds, finally emerging back on the street.

'Where to now?' Matt asked.

'Back to the office. We need a door.'

The street was busy with Fringe-goers hurrying to, or

from, venues. Excited chatter buzzed around them full of reminiscences of something just enjoyed, or barbed criticism of a wasted hour of drivel. Finally, Matt touched Kylah's arm.

'We passed a dentist's office across the street.'

They crossed, Kylah attempting and failing to suppress the anxiety that lurked at the back of her mind. This was her job. This was what she was trained to do. How many times had she and Matt, or she alone, made visits to purported exponents of so-called magic only to find clever illusionists or deluded charlatans? But this…this was different and genuine and a little worrying since The Alternator clearly had insight enough to run when the DOF had knocked on his door.

She should have felt elated. After all, this was an endorsement. The raison

D'êTRE of an organisation set up to protect humanity from a threat the vast majority of the population were blissfully ignorant of. A world where all the imagined things that went bump in the human night strutted around in broad daylight. Things who'd usually jump, fly or shape-change at the chance of sliding through the cracks and across the border between worlds. And yet Kylah's elation was short lived. The smell of the vestigia was eau de all wrong and repulsed her like she had not been repulsed for a long while. There was something badly out of place. Very badly out of place.

'We could just stand here and wait for them to open on Monday,' said Matt.

Kylah shook her head and focused. They'd crossed and were standing in front of the locked door. She'd done all that on autopilot while her brain searched the filing cabinets of her sub-consciousness for a clue as to how The Alternator had done what he'd just done. 'Sorry,' she said, reaching for the Aperio.

'You okay?' Matt's tone was light, though there was real concern in his eyes.

'I'm fine. A bit surprised, that's all. Never expected to find the real thing here in Edinburgh.'

'Judging by the stink of it, it's a bad one too.'

'You got that as well?'

'I can still smell it. Either that or I stepped on something as I crossed the road.'

Kylah nodded. 'When the bough breaks…'

'You better not be standing beneath it for fear of being covered by several years' worth of guano?'

'Something like that. Come on.' She applied the Aperio and the locked door opened the wrong way into a room that was a tasteful shade of pastel blue.

CHAPTER SEVEN

HIPPOSYNC ENTERPRiSES, OXFORD, ENGLAND, HW

BACK IN HER OFFICE, KYLAH stowed her Aperio and gently pushed at the tailless mouse linked to her computer to wake it.

'I'll do that,' Matt said, taking over the keyboard and immediately typing something into the search engine. 'You run the tracer on the bug.'

While Matt clicked and typed, Kylah opened a cupboard and removed the silver salver etched with letters that were from no alphabet Matt had ever seen and placed it carefully onto her desk. Turning back to the cupboard, she removed two small glass bottles, unstoppered one and carefully poured three violet droplets onto the plate, which began to fill with inky fluid. From the other bottle, she shook two small white crystals into the palm of her hand and tipped them into the dark water. The fluid instantly cleared and gradually a wavy image appeared, clearing again as the disturbed fluid settled to display a shimmering replay of their encounter with The Alternator from the moment the bug landed on the man's lapel. His escape through the mirror in the Pleasance Up and Under venue in Edinburgh was now visible from the tiny insect's point of view.

'It's a hotel room,' Kylah said.

'Which hotel?' Matt asked.

'Not sure yet.'

The bug's attention, and therefore by definition, The Alternator's, zeroed in on the wardrobe. Clothes were frantically removed and stuffed into an overnight bag open on the bed.

'What about you?' Kylah asked, hearing Matt's rapid typing. 'Remind me.'

Matt read from the screen. 'His website lists The Alternator as a budding close-up magician. Twenty-nine years old, single, available for dinners, parties, and weddings. His reviews go from two to three-and-a-half stars and contain comments like, 'I've seen better magic come out of a Christmas cracker' and 'More who didn't than Houdini'.

Without looking up from the silver platter, Kylah said, 'That doesn't sound like someone who can walk through mirrors.'

'Is that every mirror?' Matt asked, looking around to see if anything was a likely candidate. 'Or is it only some mirrors? Didn't I read something about brass being magically protective?'

'Brass mirrors can't be used for porting or spying, you're right. Some with stone surrounds are especially good for two-way communication but the stone has to have a common origin. Speculassult spells for porting are cast beforehand because they take a while to set up. He must have charmed the mirror in the changing room in anticipation. He wanted to be able to implement a quick getaway.'

'And he did.'

In the plate, the gnat's point of view showed the overnight

bag on the bed rapidly filling up as a wash bag and towel joined the clothes.

'There's no doubt this is our man,' Matt commented. 'His profile picture's exactly the same. Born in Derby, flunked university, tried to make some amateur science-fiction films…'

'But nothing about Fae?'

'Nothing that I can—'

'Hold on. We're leaving the room.'

Matt joined Kylah and stared into the salva as the view changed to a corridor, then a lift and finally a reception area, a desk, and the receptionist herself. Unfortunately, there was nothing to give them any clue as to where the hotel was. The receptionist smiled and began typing something.

'He's checking out,' Matt said.

'Where the hell is this?' Kylah hissed in frustration.

In the plate, the receptionist pushed across the printed bill towards The Alternator.

'There!' yelled Matt. 'Letterhead. Crown Thistle, Chester.'

'Come on.' Kylah grabbed her Aperio and thirty seconds later they were exiting the lift into the reception area of the hotel just as The Alternator pushed open the glass exit doors.

'Do we follow?' Matt asked.

'Follow and, when the opportunity arises, apprehend.'

'Very cops and robbers,' said Matt.

Kylah turned to him with a serious expression. 'Matt, this guy is demonstrating abilities way above anything he learned on a magic circle correspondence course. We need to be careful.'

'Right, right,' Matt said but his enthusiasm didn't falter. 'Still it is fun to be out here, just me and you,' he paused for dramatic effect before adding cheerily, 'chasing villains.'

Kylah shook her head. 'This is dangerous. I don't think this chap has any idea what he's capable of.'

'Bit like me then,' Matt said.

'Yes, but at least I'm here to handle your foibles.'

'If only.' Matt gave her a lopsided grin.

Kylah turned away with her eyes towards the ceiling and headed for the door.

They followed The Alternator out into the street. Dusk was fast approaching but the squat figure that was their quarry remained clearly visible as he hurried away, clutching an old leather bag.

'So how do you want to play this?' Matt asked.

'I could call in a Surreptor squad,' Kylah said but it was delivered with little conviction.

'I don't think we have the time to get half a dozen people in position,' Matt said. 'Our friend isn't dawdling. I'd put money on a train or bus station as his destination, though why he doesn't repeat the mirror trick is beyond me.'

'Two reasons,' Kylah answered. 'The first is that he thinks he's got away from us, and the second is that his *Alice Through the Looking Glass* move would have drained him. I saw his face in the bathroom mirror while you were Googling. He looks like he's been ten rounds with Tyson. That sort of thaumaturgy, and I reckon he's used Shaddara's Fire and the Speculassult, which takes enormous power. I don't think he has the energy for anything unusual at the moment.'

'Okay, so let me arrange a little accident.'

Kylah stopped so abruptly that Matt walked right into her and had to stop himself by grabbing her with both hands. She stepped back and looked at him with eyebrows raised.

'What?' Matt asked, shaking his head.

'Those two words. Little accident.'

'We need to do something,' Matt said, his voice a mixture of urgency and protest. 'He'll be on the eight-thirty to Birmingham before we can say Jabberwocky.'

'Agreed, we do need to do something. But can you try and keep it simple for once? Nothing too…elaborate, that's all I'm saying.'

Matt's expression composed itself into feigned hurt. 'I don't know what you mean.'

Kylah looped her arm in Matt's and began hurrying down the street after The Alternator. 'Yes, you do. We both know exactly what I'm talking about. The shapeshifter thief you turned into a human fly, for example.'

Matt shook his head. 'Matter of using what was available. I didn't put that syrup tanker on that road. It was just there. And what better way to stop a fleeing miscreant than turning the pavement into flypaper on the off chance that his shapeshifter head came up with fly as an idea.'

'What about that sniper at the G8?'

'Anyone can trip over a first aid box.'

'Agreed, but not many people end up getting entangled with its contents and bandaged up like a car crash victim.'

'Mummy,' Matt said a little unnecessarily and then added, somewhat sheepishly, 'and he was armed.'

'Not after the mob got to him. If we'd have arrived five minutes later, he would have been neither armed nor legged.'

'Don't tell me you felt sorry for him?'

'What, with two wounded and a security guard dead? He deserved what he got. You're wonderfully inventive, Matt. But sometimes a bit *too* inventive, that's all I'm saying. Yes, he could have tripped and got tangled up, but the chance of those bandages wrapping themselves around his trigger finger, his eyes, and his legs were infinitesimal.'

'But still possible.'

'Yes, but would an ophthalmoscope really have found its way into…the place it found its way into? I mean, come on.'

'He fell awkwardly.'

'He fell and ended up looking like an Egyptian mummy with a medical instrument sticking out of his bottom.'

'No one complained.'

'I think the sniper might have if he'd been able to talk. Questions were asked. And we aren't always going to be able to erase CCTV footage. People have mobile phones, you know. They video everything. It's all so…freakish.'

Matt was silent for a moment. 'That's rich coming from a card-carrying member of the Fae. But okay, I get the message. Nothing too freakish.'

'Exactly,' Kylah said.

'Because chasing a magician who's just burned someone alive with magical fire leaving him unscathed before escaping through a mirror isn't freakish in the slightest, is it?' muttered Matt.

Kylah stayed silent. She had a way of staying silent that said an awful lot. In this instance, it said, *I love you dearly, oh light of my life, but this is work and there is a line across which flippancy becomes tantamount to insubordination and one more word will probably place you just the wrong side of that line.*

Matt had the good sense to listen to that silence and hear every word.

Ahead of them, The Alternator was about to cross the street.

'We're losing him,' Matt said and there was an airy, questioning tone to his statement.

Kylah growled in frustration. 'Okay, okay. I give up. Go on. Do your voodoo, but try and make it slightly less…'

Beside her, in the twilight, Matt grinned. 'Freakish. Yeah, I heard.'

The Alternator crossed the road at a run and headed for a carefully constructed wooden canopy covering the pavement next to a building undergoing renovations. Above, the building itself was doing an impression of a giant scruffy Christmas present having been completely covered in protective plastic sheeting over scaffolding behind which, during normal working hours, construction workers drilled and hammered. Hundreds, if not thousands of pedestrians had walked under the thick, reinforced awning held up by scaffolding poles at the pavement's edge. Health and Safety were rightly proud. But no risk assessment protocol known to man was designed to factor in the presence of Matt Danmor and the 'anything could happen' clause that came with him.

The reason for this was complicated. For a start, Matt was the seventh son of the seventh son of a seventh son descended from a race that occupied the earth for quite a long time before homo sapiens fell out of the trees and started buggering it all up with such spectacular skill. Post Lapsarian was the term Kylah used when she'd explained it to him, but she knew that its Biblical connotations confused him enormously.

The fall of man had all kinds of subtexts but it was one of those terms just nebulous enough and with a nice mythological flavour to do the job of summing up a period in history that was an awfully long time ago. The chapter and verse might as well have been written in Sanskrit for all that it really mattered because you were what you were and that was all down to genes and chromosomes. And in Matt's case, all that DNA had gone into a historical Magimix and come out with a young man with dark hair and a winning smile who, under the right circumstances, could turn luck to his advantage. So long as what took place was a physically plausible series of events, it didn't matter how unlikely they were. He couldn't make winged monkeys appear out of thin air, or walk through mirrors, but he could imagine a sudden gust of wind catching the edge of a sheet of giant tarpaulin covering the building above where The Alternator was walking. He could see, in his mind's eye, that same sheet ripping free of its fixings, wafting upwards like a sail, and then falling towards the open edge of the protective canopy beneath and being blown under it.

The fact that there was very little wind and no gusts of sufficient power to make such a thing happen didn't faze Matt. It made the chance of such a freak occurrence infinitesimal. But infinitesimal did not mean impossible. It meant only highly improbable. And Matt did highly improbable *really* well.

'We need him in one piece,' Kylah said, noting the little smile playing on Matt's lips.

'Obviously,' he replied with a roll of his eyes.

The gust took a great many people, including a whole raft of meteorologists and a few dozen bystanders on the Chester street where it manifested, completely by surprise. It made pedestrians cringe against it, gently buffeted a few others against doorways; made others pause mid stride and turn their backs. As a result, few, if any, heard the snap of ropes breaking or saw the tarpaulin high on the building spiral vertically upwards in an updraft before twisting down in a graceful arc to strike the wooden canopy beneath, unfurl and then slap against the unfortunate Alternator, clinging to him like a wet flannel as he stumbled back, rotating in his confusion. The material wrapped around him, enveloping him, hurling him to the ground next to a sleeping street person who'd made a corner of the narrow space under the canopy his cardboard home and curing said unhoused of a week's worth of constipation in the process.

'Come on,' Matt said, setting off at a run.

The majority of pedestrians, sensing that they were in the middle of some sort of freak weather event, remained huddled in doorways, heads bent against the wind. A few had sought shelter under the same canopy into which the tarpaulin had blown. It was this small and bewildered knot of people that Matt and Kylah now joined as they stared at the moaning, struggling pupa-like figure rolling on the floor, encased in grey plastic.

'It's okay,' Matt said pushing through, 'I'm a doctor.'

Behind him, Kylah muttered, 'You wish.'

'Heard that,' said Matt and knelt next to The Alternator, pulling the clinging material away from the frantic man's face. He managed to unwrap enough to reveal one eye and most of a nose. Suffocation was not on today's agenda, though the tarpaulin was a welcome barrier against the odour pervading the rest of the canopy space. When The Alternator saw who was ministering to him, his struggles and moans grew. A buzz of fresh concern emerged from the onlookers. Kylah took out a small bottle from inside her jacket, upended it and let a couple of drops fall into the gap in the tarpaulin around The Alternator's nose.

His moans subsided quickly.

From the street behind, the noise of a siren approaching at high speed drew the onlooker's attention and a few seconds later an ambulance, complete with flashing blue lights, drew up and parked. Two paramedics in uniform emerged from the vehicle. The larger of the two, six four and built like at least two back-to-back outhouses, went immediately to the rear of the ambulance and opened the doors. The second man, shorter by a good nine inches and slighter with tattoos visible on his arms and neck under a variety of piercings, pushed through the small crowd with determination to join the kneeling Matt.

'What kept you?' Matt muttered.

'Traffic is a sod this time of night,' he said in a voice low enough for only Matt to hear. 'Plus we had a hell of a job nicking the ambulance.' He turned and shouted over his shoulder. 'Alf, hurry up with that stretcher.'

As DOF clear-ups went, it was more or less textbook. Matt's   what-if-the-loose-tarpaulin-managed-to-restrict-speech-and-limb-movement combined with Kylah's little sedative arrangement worked perfectly. He didn't want to let The Alternator's hands create any forma, nor voice incantations. And rather than try and unwrap him there and then, the paramedics, who called themselves Alf and Dwayne because Sergeants Birrik and Keemoch of the Special Elf Service didn't quite fit the bill, hoisted the struggling man straight on to the stretcher. Of course, through Kylah and

Matt's eyes, both the SES sergeants looked like the Sith Fand that they were. Their khaki-coloured skin, long sinewy limbs, and swept-back foreheads were in stark contrast to their projected human forms. Thankfully, no one else in the vicinity had the tenth gate of awareness needed to see them, or their brown SES uniforms as they really were.

'Very convenient wind,' Kylah said, nodding her approval when The Alternator was safely on board the ambulance.

'Well, that's a clear winner in the least likely phrases you're ever likely to hear anyone say on a date.' Matt grinned.

'I'm talking about an almost natural phenomenon that can blow a giant tarpaulin off a building, not something involving evil bacteria in one's gut.'

'I'll thank you to leave one's evil bacteria out of this. They have never done anyone any harm.'

'That's debatable. I still remember a very uncomfortable and cold night after that all-you-can-eat Punjabi buffet you took me to in Brighton.'

'You didn't have to leave the window wide open all night,' Matt argued.

'Yes, I did. It was either that or risk spontaneous combustion the air was so toxic.'

'One was ill,' Matt said.

'Yes, as in chemic-ill weapon.'

Sergeant Keemoch, aka Alf the paramedic, cleared his throat like a thirty-a-day tobacco addict with bronchiectasis. 'If I could suggest continuing this somewhere else, ma'am,' he whispered, nodding towards the gathering crowd of onlookers, some of whom were grinning, some frowning at the nature of the exchange between the good Samaritan who'd acted so promptly to save the unfortunate victim and the attractive woman who'd helped him.

Kylah nodded. Birrik winked at Matt, who shrugged helplessly.

'The General is on take for emergencies.' Kylah said loudly, inviting Matt to respond.

He did so with overt theatricality. 'Yes, the General would be best. He'll need a scan.'

'Right you are, doc,' said Birrik cheerfully. 'We'll see you there.'

The crowd murmured its approval. This was a real-life news story unfolding in front of their eyes. Who'd have thought that nature could be so capricious? And what were the chances of such a strange and extraordinary thing actually happening here and now? This was one story they'd simply *have* to tell the grandchildren.

CHAPTER EIGHT

NEW THAMESWICK, FW

Asher's office at the Bureau of Demonology once served as a storage room for an experimental alchemist. Said alchemist had long departed with a loud bang and quite a lot of green and brown smoke that smelled, curiously, of cinnamon. The clue to his demise consisted of a box marked *MONSTER FIREWORKS* and a charred piece of signed paper with *I accept the terms and conditions* printed on it in Elvish. All that was now left in the room to indicate its previous incarnation was the floor-to-ceiling shelving along the back wall.

Duana Llewyn had the room remodelled, after a fashion, with a comfortable armchair, desk, pongcluetor, a steel 'arms' cupboard with both physical and thaumaturgical locks, and a formidable reference library to replace the frankly dangerous tomes the alchemist had favoured. Asher relished the room's relative emptiness and found it passably comfortable. Best of all, it was not a shared space. Asher argued against the need for the small library, reasoning that if he wanted to know anything at all about demons and the like, he could ask Duana. But she had insisted, arguing that she might not be available at all times. He'd capitulated, conceding that the professor's calendar was rather full during the day with lectures and tutorials. And even fuller after hours, with her evenings allocated to the wide variety of partners she encouraged. When it came to appetites of the carnal variety, Duana was voracious. She'd nibbled at Asher in the past, but their relationship was now on a strictly professional footing. Crouch, on the other hand, was always sniffing around and Asher knew he would do almost anything for a crack at one of the slots in Duana's schedule.

Asher caught himself. Worryingly, he could actually hear Crouch's innuendo-laden voice in his head repeating the phrase with lascivious inappropriateness. He shook his head and turned his attention back to the book he was studying. It was fairly new, just three hundred years old: *Vampires Through the Ages,* by Rhydian Flesch. Though it was not exactly bedtime reading, it gave Asher an inkling into what he'd never bothered to discover about leeches. And in so doing he wondered about that, too. About why he had never bothered to educate himself. But then he knew little or nothing about the origins of pond scum either: it was simply something you encountered now and again and avoided if you could. Because if you dipped your toe in and it came out covered in slime, you learned not to do it again. No need to write a dissertation about it.

But Asher was up to his neck in pond scum now and there was no getting away from the leeches anymore. He put his finger on a paragraph in the book, under a heading entitled *The Origine of Haematophillik Vampyres*, and began to read.

IT IS SAID that in Spag, a childe borne with lack of pigmente in the skin was so beautiful that his parents sought the help of a demon called Shistirrer, known to be of a particularly capricious nature, in order to allow the child a better life than one skulking in shadow. The demon willingly cursed the child for a fee. In order for it to be free to walk under the sun, it had to drink the blood of humans at least once a week. By doing so it would pass the curse on to the bitten. The delighted parents gladly paid the demon, which was very fond of bacon, a herd of Snorter yellow spot. The parents donated their own blood and the child thrived. But his beauty was such that he attracted admirers and soon the contaminant spread to the village residents, all of whom developed the need to ingest the blood of others in order to survive. The clan, also known as the Kindred, were driven out into a mountainous region known as Oneg, where they became an isolated, inbred people, living for many hundreds of years by raiding adjacent countries and terrorising their occupants.

A 'cure' for their illness was found by one Robin 'Swivel-eye' Bowler. Ostensibly a hunter, his unfortunate eye condition meant that he could not hit a princod in an alleyway, let alone a moving target such as a deer. That did not deter Bowler, who lived alone as a trapper. Bowler would frequently run short of quivers on his hunts and would revert to fashioning arrows from the nearest tree. The yew, being poisonous, was always avoided by hunters, except by Bowler who did not know his yew from his elbow. Having fashioned several such arrows and being late and alone in the woods bordering on Oneg, he shot at a rabbit and, missing by many feet, chanced to skewer a vampyre which, at that very moment had emerged from behind a rock and was rapidly approaching in a silent attack on the unsuspecting hunter. Since that time, yew skewers became the preferred method for killing vampyres. They are also known as Bowler shanks. And anyone blessed with unexpected fortune is termed as having Bowler's luck.

ASHER LET his eyes drift up to the back of the room where the shelves, thanks to krudian physics, went up at least fifty feet, though the ceiling ended at seven. Several dust-coated glass jars remained on the topmost shelf, all baring ancient and unreadable labels. The buildings' caretaker, a dwarf named Sach, deemed it prudent not to move the jars, as who knew what sort of thing might be unleashed by any sudden jerk? It might cause an explosion, or risk transporting the person doing the lifting to another planet, the inside of a lamp or any one of countless other unpleasant venues. Yet, though his eyes saw the jars, Asher's mind was elsewhere, thinking about Simla DiFrance and Les Reasonables and their filthy and despicable unconverted brethren, the leeches.

A knock on the door brought him back from his musings.

He called, 'Come in,' and turned in his chair to see Duana Llewyn's shapely figure silhouetted against the lit corridor outside.

'I heard you were here,' she said. 'I've come to invite you to a cafeteria dinner. I am working late, too.'

'I'm not that hungry.'

'Irrelevant,' Duana said. 'Like sex, eating is a physiological requirement. Hunger has little to do with it. This evening, they have borlotti bean stew and pork in cider as specials. I would advise neither if you value your teeth and a night not chained to the water closet. Mrs Sanchez, the sous-cook, specialises in pinchos, which she gets from her mother in Mucha via an illegal portway. My treat.' She walked in and stood at Asher's side, looking down at the open book. 'Research?'

Asher nodded.

'An even better reason to join me then. I wrote an essay on Shistirrer in my final year. What I don't know about that corpulent monster is not worth knowing.'

They adjourned to the cafeteria and ate several delicious plates of veal cheeks, chicken with aioli, and salt cod taco washed down with a nice Rioja, much to the bemusement of other diners chewing their way through overcooked chops. After a brief but enlightening mini lecture on Shistirrer and the punishments he now endured in endless oblivion, Duana refilled Asher's glass and asked with her usual candour, 'So, how goes it with the leech murders?'

Asher sighed. 'It's trademark Sicca Rus. Of that there is no doubt. But it isn't him, either.'

'Is that meant to be enigmatic?'

'Yes and no,' Asher said. He got a scathing glance for his trouble, before elaborating. 'It's his Modus Operandi, no question. But it doesn't make sense, other than as a hate crime. And Rus doesn't do focal hate; he's an equal opportunities hater. So picking out any one ethnic group isn't his style. He'd kill you for the matches in your pocket, but the leeches are so dysfunctional they don't even have lint. They exist; that's all they do. So why, I ask myself, is Rus killing them?'

Duana pondered for a moment before speaking. 'You may be underestimating some deep neurosis or psychopathology. He may do this simply for the fun of it.'

'Rus has three psychopathological conditions named after him already. I am underestimating nothing. But it isn't the way he works. He kills for a reason. That reason may be as little as five scruples, but there is always a reason.'

'So you're trying to work out what Rus' motivation is?'

Asher nodded. 'And I might as well be trying to stem the tides.' He sipped from the wine before asking, 'Remind me of why they are in this state?'

'The leeches?'

Asher nodded again.

'By the middle of the seventeenth century, they'd established themselves in Oneg and were making incursions into neighbouring provinces with frequent and increasingly violent attacks. Believe it or not, they were the beautiful beings, empowered by the Glamour, and had no trouble seducing willing victims. They exude pheromonal charm, strongest in the males. Driven purely and simply by bloodlust, what unites them is an inherited addiction. They can't help themselves, though one or two of them, like Les Reasonables, try. When one particularly nasty raid killed the emperor of Splosh's envoy and family, retribution was swift. The emperor's wizards devised a targeted hex rendering all active vampires hatefully ugly and unpleasant to look at, as well as robbing them of charm and guile, in other words, their Glamour. After the fission hex, they could go nowhere without being stigmatised. Their numbers declined and they were forced to seek asylum in 'friendly' countries. Or at least countries willing to turn a blind eye so long as the leeches stayed in the gutter.'

Asher nodded. 'Why didn't they stay in Oneg?'

'The emperor of Splosh employed an effective and vindictive slash and burn policy, including poisoning the earth. They say it might take two hundred years for the land to recover. Pockets of habitable areas are all that survive. The resulting diaspora led to vampire numbers tumbling. Less than two thousand still walk the earth. There are those who will not be happy until that number becomes zero. But those that do still live seek asylum and, as you would imagine, New Thameswick is a target. They perceive our culture as tolerant, if not exactly welcoming.'

'Sicca Rus seems to have taken it upon himself to dispel that notion single-handedly,' Asher murmured.

Detecting that his mood was like a soiled piece of underwear that desperately needed changing, Duana obliged. 'I spoke with your Miss Miracle yesterday.'

Asher looked up with narrowed eyes. *She's not my Miss Miracle*, he thought. *She's her own Miss Miracle, and woe betide anyone who suggests otherwise.*

'She was here and hoping to catch a glimpse of you.'

Asher shrugged. 'We restrict our socialising to weekends. She's busy with her course and I find enough to do helping Crouch. We both felt it best not to be too…distracted.'

'Too busy for a quick drink, even?' Duana's eyebrows went north.

Asher smiled. 'A drink generally turns into several and then before either of us can say borborygmi, we're practising bedroom gymnastics at my apartment and nursing a debilitating hangover in the morning.'

'Ah. You're still at the 'can't keep my hands to myself' stage?'

'Neither of us has much self-control.' Asher's smile was rueful.

'She is an attractive person,' Duana observed. 'The brightest of the intake, if not of the year, I would say.'

'I'm sure she'd be delighted to know that. But I would be grateful, too, if you keep your paws off her, Professor Predator.'

'She bites for just the one team, I fear.'

'It's bats for just the one team, not bites. Cricketing reference. Though I suppose you don't even know what cricket is?'

'A human game played on a large open field involving willow and leather, usually accompanied by a comedic commentary.'

Asher nodded. 'Got it in one.'

'And does she bat well, Miss Miracle?' Duana Llewyn's face held not one jot of amusement as she delivered this line.

The glass of wine that Asher was about to sip from froze an inch from his lips. He looked into Duana's grey-blue eyes and detected no guile. She was genuinely interested.

'She does indeed. With surprising enthusiasm and a very strong grip on the handle.'

Duana nodded. 'An interesting image I will take with me to my bed. I suggest you do the same. But only on weekends?' She tutted. 'We need to talk about work-life balance, Asher. Your Miss Miracle is too much of a catch to restrict contact to two days a week.'

CHAPTER NINE

'No, Richenda, I am not getting into a round with you and all I want is an elderflower spritzer. Here is the money for it.' Bobby reached into her purse for some coins.

'Oh my gods, don't be so boring.' Richenda rolled her eyes. But Bobby remained adamant.

'Unlike you full time students, I have a job to get to tomorrow morning and I am not turning up to it with a force nine hangover.'

'Okay, we get the message.' Richenda made jazz hands to other Wicca novices seated around the table in the Battery and Broomstick inn. Bobby had tried desperately to sneak off after lectures but Richenda had grabbed her arm and dragged her in for a 'quick drink'. It was late afternoon and Bobby was thirsty, but she was under no illusion as to what a quick drink meant to four trainee witches. Neither the adverb nor the singular form of the noun would apply. In the opposite corner, half a dozen warlocks, including Brigger, were already into their second round and becoming louder with each sip.

It was the kind of pub where the booths and chairs were made of worn and stained wood that smelled of stale beer and smoke, and the sawdust on the floor was there for function rather than effect.

When Richenda returned from the bar a short time later, Bobby was relieved to see a tall glass of fizzing lavender liquid on the large tray of drinks. She was less pleased to see the barmaid following with a separate tray of five shots.

'What are these?' Bobby asked, pointing a finger.

'Brain Steamers. You have *got* to try one.' Richenda handed out the drinks.

'No way,' Bobby protested.

Richenda's eyebrows went ceilingwards again. 'You are not going to be allowed to leave here without tasting one.'

The other novices all nodded.

'Come on,' said Richenda, grabbing a small glass of gently steaming dark liquid. 'I guarantee it'll make you feel better.'

'I don't need to feel better.'

'Super better then.'

Bobby ignored the shot glass, picked up her elderflower spritzer and sipped. She detected no alcohol, but when it came to witches you could never be too careful.

'Come on,' Richenda encouraged the other girls who picked up a shot glass each, 'we're toasting our lovely fellow *mature* student who knows Prof Llewyn like a sister and may even be able get us some hints for the exam.'

They held up their glasses and waited.

Bobby shook her head.

'We will stay like this all afternoon,' said Richenda, 'unless you comply.' She lifted her glass another inch or two. 'To little Miss Mature.'

Bobby sighed. She knew there was only one way out of this. She picked up the shot glass in her other hand and tipped it to her lips, making sure to keep them firmly shut. The other girls threw the drink down with practised ease and while they had their heads raised, Bobby deftly flicked the contents of the glass over her shoulder.

No one noticed.

Though no liquid passed her closed lips, a layer of it remained on the surface and Bobby judged that running her tongue over that would not be too bad and, strictly speaking, qualify for having tasted it. The minute the smidgen hit her taste buds she knew she'd made a very wise move not to drink the whole thing, as a streak of hot, delicious excitement bypassed her stomach and went straight to her brain. She felt like leaping up, punching the air, and roaring. There was music in her ears and everything suddenly slowed down and looked hilarious. She took a quick gulp from the spritzer and waited for the sense of dislocation to disappear. Thankfully, it did.

'Wow,' she said, bending exaggeratedly forward.

The novices screamed with laughter.

'You're funny,' said Richenda, the pupils of her doe eyes now almost as big as her grin. 'Come on, we need a song. Cupula?' she turned to a well-covered girl next to her. 'Give us 'I'd Rather Hold a Warlock's Staff than Fondle a Wizard's Sleeve'.'

Cupula needed no cajoling as she stood and launched into the lewd ditty.

Bobby offered to buy another round. At the bar, she paid for four more Brain Steamers, which she asked the barmaid to deliver to the table. While Richenda, one hand on her hip, was challenging the warlocks to sing an even bawdier song, Bobby, eel-like, slipped away.

Outside, she breathed in the air. It was good to be away from the Brain Steamers' fumes, which continued to drift up from the emptied glasses to hang potently around the table. There was a time and a place for late afternoon drinking, but today was not it. She had an essay to finish and needed a clear head to get that done. Besides, there was the delicious prospect of an early supper with Asher at six and it was to the Haroon Rooms she now headed.

They'd discovered it on one of their lazy walks. A simple doorway leading to a long narrow room and a counter behind which said Haroon met customers with a genuine grin. You ordered from a menu that had sent Bobby's salivary glands into overdrive. She was working her way through it slowly, savouring every dish. Last time it had been the tomatillos and wasabi mascarpone that did it for her, leaving her wide-eyed and almost speechless with pleasure. Best of all, the back room, via a portway, existed on a Mediterranean terrace overlooking the sea and was always just the right side of warm. She couldn't wait.

But wait she did outside the restaurant as the big clock on the Wandmaker's Guild tower across the street chimed six and the big hand moved slowly around to quarter past. Had he forgotten? It was unlike him. In fact, it was he who had suggested they meet up after his work. She let her eyes stray up one side and down the other side of the street, the little fizz of anticipation she always felt buzzing away in the background. At twenty past, he rounded the corner a block away, looking harassed and apologetic.

'Bobby, I am so sorry. I went in search of a vampire expert in the BOD, couldn't find him and got spectacularly lost.' He sounded distraught.

'In a building?'

'Exactly. Only I am beginning to believe that it has at least a dozen more buildings within it.'

'Doesn't matter. You're here now. A hug would be nice since I've been standing here for ages.'

Asher pulled her to his chest and kissed her gently. Bobby decided he tasted even nicer than wasabi mascarpone and twice as spicy.

'See, all better,' said Bobby, but then frowned on seeing Asher's troubled expression.

'What's wrong?'

'I'm afraid we are going to have to call off our supper. Crouch has been summoned to yet another meeting with his colleagues at six-thirty and has asked that I be there. They are discussing the leech murders and I am already late.'

'Oh, okay,' said Bobby. She tried for a brave smile but failed to hide her disappointment.

'Can you forgive me?'

'Not your fault, is it? It's work.' She rubbed his arm, wanting to relieve him of his obvious distress.

'Indeed it is. This leech business is bad. I feel I have to support Crouch as much as possible. But I will make it up to you, I promise.'

'Make it up might not quite cut the mustard, or even the wasabi. I intend to make you pay.'

Asher smiled and Bobby melted just a little as the muscles involved brought his upper lids down and exposed even more of his amazing eyelashes.

'I can always rely on you to cheer me.' Asher grinned. 'What will you do for supper?'

'Beans on toast.'

'Temptress.'

'With Worcester Sauce, I'll have you know.'

They hugged and kissed again and Asher kept saying sorry even as he hailed a cab and got in. Bobby allowed herself one big sigh and turned away, now wanting nothing more than to get back to her flat in Oxford as soon as possible, where she hoped there'd be a little wine left in the fridge. She felt the need for some alcohol-assisted wallowing.

Kylah had set her up with an Oysterperio, which allowed her to travel between the worlds at set points. One of these was the bathroom door in her Oxford flat; the other was the female locker room at Le Fey Academy and it was to there that Bobby now headed without looking back.

Richenda would undoubtedly, right about now, be calling

her a lightweight, but that didn't matter. She'd been called a lot worse.

The evening had stayed bright and breezy, keeping the worst of the street smells from lingering. Bobby watched the driverless horse-drawn carriages clatter along the streets, and the manure collectors dashing back and forth, picking up the waste like ball boys in a dangerous and demented tennis match. Heading downtown, she only had to cross the road once, and did so between the wheel tracks on the giant stepping stones designed to allow pedestrians to avoid the effluent. However, they did not help in avoiding the affluent who, given that this was an ordinary working New Thameswick evening, populated the pavements. And there were all sorts, dressed in an eclectic mixture of clothes that rendered the streets more like a film set where five different movies of wildly differing genres were being shot simultaneously. She would never get used to seeing dark clad witches and globular mountain trolls mingling with bearded dwarves and sly-eyed elves. But then she didn't want to because who, in their right minds, would not give *anything* for this job?

She turned a corner on Hemlock Avenue and stopped. A crowd had gathered to watch a group of protestors on the wide pavement outside a government building opposite. They looked a sorry bunch, covered head to toe in dark rags against the daylight, shambling in a circle, chanting—or rather growling:

'What do we want?'

'More night!'

'When do we want it?'

'Now!'

She read the brandished banners. *Hug a vampire. It's not catching!* wasn't so bad, but *Rights for bloodsuckers!* seemed a little optimistic to say the least.

The rubberneckers choked the pavement on Bobby's side of the street and she had to veer towards the precarious edge

—precarious because a couple of feet below the kerb nestled a good six inches of steaming horse poo—to get around. She'd managed to get two thirds of the way through the crowd when she felt her arm being grabbed and looked down into the face of a wizened old man smoking a pipe and brandishing a crooked walking stick. He looked vaguely leprechaun-like. That was before she saw the shamrock in his hat and the vagueness evaporated.

'Could you not curse the lot of 'em for us, eh?'

'Sorry. Against the law.' Bobby smiled.

The leprechaun frowned and glared at her. 'What's the use of being a feckin witch if you cannot smite your enemy and rid the world of filth?'

'Sorry, I'm training. I can only do laundry charms so far,' Bobby replied with a toothless smile and retrieved her arm before pushing through the rest of the crowd. She hurried on, but glanced back several times at the pathetic little group of chanting leeches as a pang of unexpected guilt took hold. As a group they were easy to hate and were doing a grand job of not helping themselves by slowing down traffic and invoking suspicion under all those rags. But they were members of society and had, by all accounts, a pretty rotten existence. Someone had suggested the authorities create housing reservations but that did not sound like a recipe for cultural integration to Bobby.

Oh well. She'd talk to Asher. It sounded like he'd know more about what was going on now that he was dealing with them directly, if reluctantly.

She made the Le Fey in under fifteen minutes and headed for the locker room. From her bag she took a key card and slid it between the edge of the hinge side of her locker door and the jam. There was a click and the door opened onto her dingy little bathroom in her empty 'shared' Iffley Road flat. Since her flatmate spent much of the week away and Bobby spent most weekends at Asher's, the term 'shared' was a relative one. She stepped through and shut the door behind her.

'Right,' she said to no one but her own reflection in the bathroom mirror. 'Coffee, and then the joys of 'Lycanthropy in the Wool Industry of Skein—A Paradox. Discuss in two thousand words.''

In a way, she was glad of it because it meant she'd be able to distract herself from the crushing sense of disappointment she felt on missing out on supper with Asher. It was only meant to be a quick meal but now that it hadn't happened she grieved for it. No, that wasn't true. She grieved for him. She looked around the dingy flat and knew that it could, it should, be better than this. Their schedules were bloody stupid.

'Come on, you can wallow for England later. Lycanthropy calls,' Bobby said and fleetingly wondered why her eyes were suddenly a little more moist than normal before she bent to her task.

———

THE FOLLOWING MORNING, with the essay finished and proofread, a more sanguine Bobby Miracle caught an ordinary bus into town and walked from the station to Jericho near the canal in Oxford. The further towards the canal she headed, the fewer people she saw. She stopped in front of a heavy wooden door in a grimy red brick wall, under a hanging board announcing: *Hipposync Enterprises: Purveyors of Rare Books and Manuscripts.* There was no keyhole for a key but there was a brass doorknob that turned only for a very select few people, one of whom was Bobby.

Inside, she stuck her head in to the receptionist's office and said, 'Good morning.'

In reply, Miss White-Tandy, the nonagenarian factotum that was the 'face' of Hipposync to any callers, looked up and warbled 'Good morning'.

'Expecting visitors, are we?' Bobby asked.

This sentence came loaded with unspoken meaning, as the silver-haired head looking at her belonged, in truth, to a sleek-skinned and long-limbed being called Tilfeth, who was a highly trained Sith Fand member of the DOF garrison. Seeing her transformed into Miss White-Tandy implied that non-Fae were about. Bobby had of course long abandoned the thought of herself as non-Fae; she was as much part of Hipposync as the mould on the underground bathroom wall.

'Just in case,' said Miss White-Tandy. 'And we already have one.'

'Really?'

'Oh yes. And I always transform when we're on orange alert.'

'Orange alert? Why?'

'Go on down. They're waiting to brief you.'

Bobby had an office between Kylah and Matt, but the voices she heard as she walked down the corridor all came from Kylah's room, and it was on this door that she knocked.

'Ah, Bobby. I'm so glad you're here.'

'What's going on?'

'A genuine case of dark dabbling, we think,' Matt said. He had a hip perched on Kylah's desk and was watching the captain write something on a white board. Behind him stood Sergeants Keemoch and Birrik, the remaining Sith Fand garrison in DOF fatigues. Both nodded to Bobby, who waved back. Her stomach swooped. Something was definitely up.

'Take a seat and I'll run through what's been happening,' Kylah said.

The Edinburgh trip and the Chester recovery did not take long in the telling and it helped to have the key points written up on the board, including The Alternator's real name, Reginald Strayne.

'But this Strayne chap, he isn't really in the hospital, is

he?' Bobby asked when Kylah got to the point where they'd bundled him off in the ambulance.

'No,' Keemoch said. 'He's still charmed and in stasis in the yellow room.'

'That's the one in the basement, right?'

'Yes. The one that's hex proof.'

'We've got an address,' Matt explained. 'So we're heading out now. Keemoch will stay here with you. If we find anything, we'll get it back here so that you can begin analysing it.'

'Great,' said Bobby, her eyes sparkling.

'We don't know what they'll find, yet,' Keemoch said in a cynical tone designed to quash her enthusiasm. But he'd have needed a steamroller. This was what part of being at Hippo-sync was all about and Bobby couldn't wait to get stuck in.

CHAPTER TEN

WARRINGTON, ENGLAND, HW

THE ALTERNATOR'S ADDRESS TURNED OUT to be a drab bedsit in a house in Warrington. Since neither Matt nor Kylah had ever been there before, a local agent was despatched on a recce. The agent, masquerading as a researcher based in Manchester's media city, arrived at the address thirty minutes after Kylah's call. An Aperio got him into the house and the flat, where he quickly confirmed its empty status. He then used The Alternator's bathroom door to link directly with the blue room at Hipposync's Oxford HQ. Shortly after, Matt and Kylah, with Birrik in tow, stepped through from Kylah's office into The Alternator's lair.

'Why is it we always use bathrooms as transit ports?' Kylah asked, turning up her nose at a pair of underpants on the edge of a laundry basket. They looked, disconcertingly, as if they might be trying to climb out.

'So you can answer any call of nature that presents itself at short notice?' offered Matt, taking in the selection of shampoos, deodorants, and shaving equipment stacked, inexplicably, on the floor.

'Does that include wanting to vomit at the sight of other people's…habits?' Kylah swiftly turned away from what she'd just seen in the toilet bowl.

'Probably,' Matt said, flushing the cistern. 'God knows what this chap's been eating. Though I doubt he needs any more fibre judging by the—'

'Can we please leave this room?' Kylah pushed past Matt who followed her into the bedroom. 'Is this what they call a studio flat?' she asked.

'It's what they should call a shoe box,' Matt muttered.

'Put your finger right on it there, Agent Danmor,' Birrik added.

'Really?' Matt said, 'You shouldn't stand so close.'

Birrik snorted.

'Will you two stop it? We're wasting time. Thorough search, please,' Kylah ordered.

'I'll take the DVD collection.' Matt moved purposefully towards a cabinet stuffed with titles and began moving a small pencil-length detector across their spines. 'Very retro.'

'I'll look through the desk,' Birrik volunteered, picking up some letters. We're in the right place. All these are addressed to a Reginald Strayne—'

Kylah shook her head. 'Oh, no. That leaves me with a wardrobe and the drawers. No thank you. Drawers usually contain things people don't want to be found. Sergeant Birrik, you do the drawers; I'll take the desk.'

'Of course, ma'am.' Birrik's reply was crisply sardonic.

Kylah narrowed her eyes, but remained unrepentant. 'We both know you have a nose for vestigia.'

'What about me?' Matt asked, feigning hurt. 'What do I have?'

'A very long walk home unless you pull your finger out.'

Matt turned back to the DVDs, muttering in a thinking-out-loud kind of way to no one in particular, 'Weird expres-

sion that, pull your finger out, don't you think? Quite suggestive in its way. I mean what is the finger in to start with that
you need to pull it out in order to hurry things along? A pie?
Your nostril? A dyke, as per the old fairy tale?'

Birrik snorted.

'Stop,' Kylah said. 'Can you smell that?'

'Wasn't me,' Birrik said, straightening up.

'Vestigia,' Kylah said. 'There's definitely a smell. *That*
smell.' She was closer to the bed than the other two, staring at
the needing-to-be-changed sheets with distaste.

'Are we talking vestigia as in socks, or maybe some very
old cheese?' Matt said with one eyebrow raised.

Kylah shook her head, distracted. 'No, much worse. This
is the stench of the butcher's shop.'

Birrik lifted his chin to sniff the air. 'Spoiled meat? Is that
what you're getting?'

'Something like it.' Concentrating, Kylah tilted up her
face too. The smell was coming from somewhere around the
bed. Warily, she stepped forward and drew back the sheets. It
was empty. But the smell was stronger here. Much stronger.

Matt joined her, brows knitted, sampling the aroma.
'Okay, I get it too. Pretty ripe, whatever it is.' He got onto the
floor and looked under the bed.

'Anything?' Kylah asked.

'Some very interesting literature,' Matt said.

'Anything worth reading?' Birrik asked.

'Not much writing in these publications, I'm afraid. Not
really the sort of thing one *reads* as such. More the sort of
thing you stare at goggle-eyed.'

'Leaving your hands free?' Birrik asked with a sagacious
nod.

'Can you two please be quiet and let me concentrate,'
Kylah ordered. Once again she lifted her nose.

'That snooty look really suits—'

She sent Matt an incendiary glare. It shut him up and she followed her nose to…the bedside table, upon which were a table lamp, a half empty glass of water, and a battered leather bound book entitled, *The Octomeraan Manuscript*.

Kylah leaned towards it and sniffed first the glass and then the book itself. 'It's definitely the book,' she said.

Matt stepped across and reached for the leather-bound tome.

'No.' Kylah slapped his hand away. 'Don't touch it. Could be hexed.' She motioned with one hand without taking her eyes off the book. 'Sergeant Birrik.'

Birrik reached for a pouch on his belt. 'How come I knew that was coming? Doesn't matter if *I* get hexed, I suppose.'

Matt looked worried. 'What if he's hexed?'

'Then he'll have to be hexorcised, won't he?' Kylah proffered an insincere smile.

'Yeah, I know, laugh it up,' Birrik said, donning a pair of elbow-length gauntlets. 'Won't be so funny when I turn into a lamp stand.'

'What if he's turned into a lamp stand?' Matt frowned.

'He won't be. And even if he is, at least lamp stands are useful. And anyway, hexes generally turn people into something disagreeable and ugly.' She turned away and then muttered, 'So it's possible Sergeant Birrik has been hexed already.'

An anxious Matt asked, 'But Kylah, if it's that dangerous—'

'If you picked it up it would be dangerous. Those gauntlets Sergeant Birrik is donning have more protective charms woven into them than he's had hot rogan venk.'

Suitably protected and grinning at Matt's unfounded concern, Birrik picked up the book carefully and opened it. The pages fell open on a battered bookmark. Birrik held it up between thumb and forefinger, his nose wrinkling. 'There is your vestigial source, ma'am.'

'A bookmark?' Matt asked.

'And,' Birrik flicked to the back page, 'the receipt is still in here too.'

'Where did he buy it?' Kylah asked.

'A place called the Inky Well, in York of all places.'

'We all know what can happen in York,' Matt said.

Kylah did not reply, but she knew what Matt was alluding to. They'd been to York quite recently to deal with a nasty case involving attempted murder, inter-dimensional demonic despots and a Bwbach with girlfriend issues. 'Excellent. Let's get this back to HQ and Bobby. Then, we pay a visit to a certain bookshop in York.'

YORK, ENGLAND, HW

The Google Maps street view threw up a gloomy corner property on a narrow street set back from the river. It looked anachronistic and out of place next to an electronics repair shop and a launderette.

'What do we know about this place?' Kylah asked.

'Not much,' Matt sighed. 'No website, no email and the phone goes direct to answering machine.'

'Then we go direct to field ops. Same as before.'

They contacted a local field agent who did a quick recce and set them up with an Aperio link much as they'd done with The Alternator's address. But this time they were more cautious and exited onto Braeburn Street through the door of a launderette and crossed the road to assess their target. The shop window was crammed with hardbacks, spines visible from the street. The only thing not directly book-related sat at the front and centre of the display: a three-legged table on which stood a stone inkwell and a protruding plume of a quill. A thick grey cobweb ran from one edge of the feather to the rim of the inkwell.

Birrik, currently manifesting as Dwayne, pushed open the door to the accompanying 'ting' of an old-fashioned bell.

Given the external appearance, the inside did not disappoint. It was as if they'd wandered onto the set of *Nicholas Nickleby*, the remake. And the Dickensian vibe was augmented by a musty, somewhat unpleasant smell permeating the air. Ceiling-high shelves divided the space into passages and alcoves. Inner rooms led back into a gloomy interior and piles of books made towers in many corners. Handwritten signs roughly divided the stock into *Fiction* and *Reference* with further divisions in each section. Kylah wandered into *Arcana* and studied the books. Many of the titles were not in English, and all were of the last century or before. But unlike the arcane and academic tomes that Hipposync specialised in, these were an eclectic pick and mix.

'What is that smell?' Matt asked with his usual candour.

'Moth balls?' Birrik offered.

'Disinfectant?' Kylah sniffed.

'Yep, I get that too, but I also get something rather nasty that those can't quite mask. Mushroom compost and old meat?'

'Is it the books?' Birrik asked.

'Mouldy books can whiff a bit,' Kylah said.

'Maybe it's the owner,' quipped Matt.

But there was no sign of a shopkeeper.

It was Birrik who eventually said, loudly, 'Here,' to indicate a significant find.

Kylah and Matt joined him at a wooden counter covered in an array of reading-related paraphernalia ranging from clip-on lights for night reading to book-related drinks coasters with coy titles like *Tequila Mockingbird*. But Birrik kept staring at a small pile of bookmarks identical to the moth-eaten example oozing vestigia in The Alternator's flat. The sergeant waved a small wand over them. The wand glowed orange.

'Definitely the real thing,' he said. 'Minimal trace activity.

Nothing like the stink of the last one but there are traces.' He used the wand tip to slide the topmost bookmark off the pile and picked up a propelling pencil to use as a second instrument. 'These markings are the same.' He ran the pencil tip around the ornate scarlet curlicues outlining the perimeter of the oblong card.

'Are they letters?'

'Not in any alphabet I'm familiar with,' Kylah said. 'But there are not many repeats, so they could be letters or sinograms.'

'Who?' Matt asked.

'Sinograms. Like Chinese characters,' Kylah explained.

'The same ochre ink has been used throughout,' Birrik observed. 'But The Inky Well logo is in black. Obviously added later.'

'"The Never Forget Bookmark," read Matt. 'Is that what the other one was called, too?'

'Yup, though it was badly stained.' Birrik turned the bookmark over. The ornate filigree decoration was repeated on the other side, but the top half of the remaining space was taken up by words and symbols: Ѝiәmoʋoḅ repeated in a variety of different fonts all down the length of the card.

'Manufacturer, you think?' Matt asked.

'Could be,' Birrik said. 'There's a URL at the bottom here.' He pointed to the address.

www.Ѝiәmoʋoḅ.org

'We need to talk to the owner.' Kylah reached out and slapped her palm down on the silver bell resting squarely on the counter top.

Nothing happened.

Kylah repeated the summons and Matt, bored with waiting, wandered off whilst Birrik leaned in close to inspect the Never Forget bookmark a little closer. After a few seconds, Matt's voice reached them from somewhere in the labyrinth.

'Here's one for you, Birrik. *The Calmer Sutra*, with a 'C' and an 'L'.'

'Never tried a 'C' and an 'L'. Do they come already lubricated?'

''C' and 'L' as in Calmer, you muppet. *For the less energetic lover*. I think I'm in the racy book section, subsection, humour.'

Birrik smirked. 'We'll come back for you tomorrow, then.'

The smirk stayed until Kylah wiped it off with a threatening look. 'Don't encourage him,' she whispered.

'There are some great titles here,' Matt went on. 'How about *Lady Chatterley's Hoover: How to Have Fun with Cleaning Equipment?*'

'Right, I've had enough of this.' Kylah punched the bell so hard it made her palm ache. But at last, the sound of footfalls descending stairs came to them from somewhere in the building. A door opened behind the counter and out stepped a young, clean-shaven man in his early twenties, dressed in check shirt and jeans.

'Can I help you?' he asked.

'You the owner?' Birrik asked.

The man shook his head. 'That would be my uncle, Connor O'Malley.'

'Can we speak to him?'

The boy shook his head. 'He's asleep. Does that a lot. He's on medication.'

'What's wrong with him?' Kylah asked.

'He's had a couple of strokes and is on loads of pills. I come and help out. I'm here most days.'

'Your name?' Birrik asked.

'Why do you want to know?' The man's eyes narrowed.

Birrik took out a black wallet and opened it. The man peered at it and then looked up. 'What's the DOF?'

'An offshoot of Border Security,' Birrik said. 'Your name?'

'Alistair, Alistair Donovan.'

Kylah said. 'So you serve in the shop?'

'Most days. We're not exactly busy.'

Kylah nodded to Birrik, who took out a photograph of The Alternator and slid it across the counter top. 'Know this chap?'

Alistair nodded. 'He's a regular. Won't see him for months and then he'll turn up two or three times. Why? What's he done?'

'We are not at liberty to tell you that,' Kylah said. 'But we are very interested in your bookmarks. He had one of these in his possession when we arrested him.'

Alistair Donovan blinked and then shrugged. It looked forced and Kylah could see his weight shift from one leg to the other. Mr Donovan was nervous. 'We have them on the counter so's people buying books see them. It works well as a sales strategy. The idea is that they'll never forget where you finish reading. And the funny thing is, they never seem to. Subliminal, I expect. You know, the message is a reminder to put the thing in the right page so it appears like it never forgets.'

'Where do you get them from?' Birrik asked.

Alistair shrugged. 'I don't do the ordering. My uncle does…did that.'

'Then who does your uncle buy from?'

'Lots of people. We have reps calling in all the time, trying to get us to set up window displays and such. But we hardly shift any stock. I think the rep that brought these was called Digsbow. He's been coming in for years. I think he's an independent.'

A light went on in Kylah's head. Digsbow. It made perfect sense. Alistair picked up a bookmark and held it over the counter towards Kylah.

'Want one? There's no charge.'

Kylah looked at Birrik, who shrugged. 'I don't see a problem. Nothing active showing on the scanner.'

Kylah took out a plastic bag and let Alistair drop it in before tucking it away in an inside pocket of her coat.

Matt's delighted and disembodied voice sang out from the belly of the shop. 'Hah, here's a good one. *Fifty Shapes of Clay: A Guide for the Erotic Potter.* Genius!'

Birrik sniggered.

Kylah shook her head and sighed before turning back to Alistair. 'About the man whose picture we showed you. What does he normally do when he comes in here?'

'Scouts around for old books. Magic-related stuff, usually.'

'And each time he buys one, he buys a bookmark, too?' Birrik asked.

'Yes. Always.'

Matt appeared, clutching a book in his hands. 'This'll make a great Christmas present for Mrs Hoblip. *LOLEater: Diary of a Chocaholic Sexter*—geddit?'

Kylah gave him a look with a smile so fixed it would need a jackhammer to prise it off.

'Sorry, am I interrupting?' Matt looked perplexed.

Alistair took the book and typed something into the small laptop on his desk. 'Two fifty.'

'Two hundred and fifty?' Matt eyebrows shot up.

The shopkeeper frowned. 'I wish. No, two pounds fifty.'

Grinning, Matt handed over the money. 'Bargain. Look, I have to ask, what is that smell?'

'We've had some ruptured drains. Sewage, we think. These old streets, you know? Do what I can to mask it until it's repaired, but it sticks in your throat, doesn't it?' Alistair shook his head sadly, inviting his guests to sympathise. 'Would you like your receipt in the bag?'

'Yes please.'

Birrik was already turning his attention to the other items on the counter. Kylah let her eyes drift over the cornucopia of wasted words on the shelves as Matt picked up a rubber monster eraser you could stick on the top of your pencil. The Inky Well was full of distractions. As a result, not one of them saw the shopkeeper slip a Never Forget bookmark between the covers of *LOLEater*, exactly like he'd been asked to do with every sale.

CHAPTER ELEVEN

Subterfuge is a strange beast. Filtered through the imagination of authors and filmmakers, it comes across as glamorous and clever until the floor opens onto the shark tank and suddenly the unpleasant truth is revealed in lurid plumes of scarlet. No doubt there are those secretly recruited few who know how to play the game, take their martinis stirred, not shaken in fabulous penthouses, and look *amazing* silhouetted in a tuxedo. But for the vast majority of the population who drink warm beer in front of the telly, their knowledge of deviousness comes from a tawdry amalgam of gossip and Chinese whispers dripping with schadenfreude. It is the stuff of soap operas and structured reality TV, deliberately designed to blur the lines between verisimilitude and fantasy.

It takes a psychopathic brain or at least six months in politics to become *really* good at it. For most of us, best heed the do-not-try-this-at-home warning stamped in red ink and leave it to the experts because, more often than not, the lies build and the collusion deepens until, like the floor of the shark tank, the tissue finally tears and becomes a fissure wide enough to plummet through.

Alistair Donovan did not drink his martini stirred. In fact, he hated alcohol. But he was knee deep in a genuine conspiracy and already finding that the stuff he was wading through was almost over his wellies.

When the shop bell rang to signal his visitors finally leaving, Alistair hurried out from behind the counter, ran to the door, turned the *Open* sign to *Closed*, pulled down the blind and flicked up the button to secure the lock. He stood with his back against the blinds, letting his racing pulse subside. That little episode had been too close a call. He'd never heard of the DOF but they represented authority and in his experience, dealing with the authorities, whoever they might be, was never a good thing. And for a man in his present circumstances, it presaged disaster on many fronts.

Panic threatened. An overwhelming urge to run upstairs, throw a few essential items into a backpack and get the first stagecoach out of Dodge hammered against the inside of his skull like an insistent child demanding a toy from a locked cupboard. At least that might buy him some time to take stock of what he was embroiled in...

Alistair forced himself to take some deep breaths. Several deep breaths.

No.

That was not how this was meant to go. Not after all the effort he'd put in. There must be another way. A way that would still let him come out of this ahead. The one crumb of comfort from the crushed biscuit of the DOF encounter seemed to be that it wasn't actually Alistair they'd been interested in at all. They were looking for the loser magician bloke and Digsbow. The magician could go screw himself, though Digsbow was a different problem altogether.

When his pulse had slowed to a canter, Alistair crossed the room and flicked off the shop lights. Outside, the afternoon was darkening and with the blind on the front door lowered, the interior of the Inky Well became a place of shadows. But Alistair could navigate the shop floor blindfolded and he walked sure-footedly back to the counter where, instead of exiting via the door behind, he took a sharp left and headed for the travel section. The books here, as everywhere else in the place, were old and contained maps that were decades out of date and travelogues of a bygone era. It was a section that attracted few visitors. None had ever twigged that the book-cases here were of a more modern construction; a lighter wood than the heavily varnished variety fixed around the rest of the shop. The reason for that was that these bookcases were specially made and not all functioned as repositories for the written word alone.

He got to the section he was after, removed a battered copy of *Holidays on Swedish Railways* and pulled the recessed handle hidden behind it. The bookcase swung inwards to reveal another place beyond.

C. S. Lewis would have been so proud.

The room he surveyed had once been a stockroom. A grubby place full of unopened boxes that smelled of old paper, mouse droppings, and candle wax. Alistair entered, flicked on a wall switch and filled the room with light. It was no longer a stockroom. This was Wonderland.

ALISTAIR HAD STOOD on the threshold for nearly twenty minutes, astonished that his uncle had hidden this from him for so many years. With a degree in anthropology, he wasn't eager to join the daily commuter grind and found few oppor-tunities for social scientists at the job centre. Running his uncle's shop while he was ill seemed a reasonable choice, especially with rent-free accommodation, despite the meagre pay. However, when Uncle Connor returned from the hospi-tal, Alistair realised the full extent of his responsibilities.

He was no longer just a bookshop salesperson; he was also a carer. Having been the sole caregiver for his elderly parents, he was familiar with the demands. His father had passed away, and his mother was in permanent care, attended by professionals. But with his uncle, the duties went beyond managing the shop. While Alistair avoided tasks like dressing, undressing, and bathing—left to the visiting aides—he still had to assist his uncle at night and handle the unpleasant job of emptying the commode; a job done on an empty stomach with a peg on one's nose wearing thick rubber gloves.

Alistair's enthusiasm waned, but whether his uncle noticed this would remain unknown. All Alistair knew was that everything changed one night a few weeks after Connor O'Malley's return from hospital all those months ago.

ALISTAIR HAD MADE a student staple of spaghetti Bolognese for supper and cut it up into forkable bites for his uncle. He never ate in the same room; he found it too off-putting, but when he went to collect his uncle's tray, the old man beckoned him near. Alistair hesitated. Several bits of spaghetti had migrated down Connor's stubbly chin and his mouth was rimmed in orange Bolognese sauce. And if that wasn't bad enough as an added antidote to intimacy, Uncle Connor's speech was disjointed and difficult to follow. The stroke had turned it into dysphasic nonsense where every word apart now came out as 'diddy'. But Uncle Connor did not try to speak on this occasion. Instead, he handed Alistair a battered notebook and made the young man read what he'd written in the large squiggly capitals, which was all his left hand could now manage.

That evening, the tremor that accompanied the physical effort of handing over the notebook seemed markedly worse. If Alistair had been asked, he'd have probably said that

Connor O'Malley seemed frankly scared as he handed over the pad.

Alistair had to read the words three times for them to make any sense. Finally, he looked up into his uncle's face and read out loud:

Won't leave me alone. The whisperers. Need their fix. In the DVD player with the mirror in front of the screen. Play their film and they'll leave me alone. Don't talk to them. Don't listen to the promises! JUST PLAY DVD. Travel section. Holidays on Swedish Railways. *S.G. Crabbe.*

Alistair tapped a spare fork on the page. He always brought two in case one got dropped. 'Is the DVD about Swedish Railways?'

Connor shook his head. 'Diddy.'

Alistair rubbed his chin with the ball of his thumb. 'Is the DVD about Holidays in Sweden?'

Another shake. 'Diddy.'

'So Swedish Railways is—'

Connor grabbed the notebook back and waved it with his one good hand.

'Diddy!'

'It's a book?'

Connor, still holding the notebook, mimed removing it from a shelf.

'So take the book down?'

Connor nodded. 'Diddy.' He then mimed opening a door.

Alistair frowned but said nothing as his uncle sat back, exhausted. The effort of this new disclosure seemed to have drained Uncle Connor of all his energy. But once Alistair washed up the supper dishes, curiosity got the better of him. Half expecting to find nothing since he suspected that the strokes might have sent his uncle doolally anyway, Alistair wandered through the Inky Well to the travel section, found *Holidays on Swedish Railways* and spent ten minutes examining it before surmising that his uncle was finally losing it. He was in the process of putting it back when he saw the silver catch hidden on the shelf behind it.

It was curved, a bit like the boot lever inside his uncle's old Renault. He reached in, pulled on the little lever and watched in stunned silence as the bookcase creaked open.

Beyond was the hidden room and fifty years of his uncle's infatuation with all things…strange. Against one wall sat a desk covered with ornate carved patterns. Coiled and serpentine, they wound around the legs and up over the edge of the table like creeping foliage so that they seemed to move as Alistair looked at them. A single naked light bulb hung from the ceiling. But this was obviously not the main source of light because tens of candles in a patterned arrangement of white, red, and black sat on the shelves, their cylindrical shapes grotesquely distorted by melted runnels of wax. Against two walls were more bookshelves, sparsely populated by a few titles with unfathomable names like *Le Grimoire du Pape Morris* and others in Latin and German as well as English. Alistair got the impression that they'd been chosen because of their rarity.

Yet it was what sat between the books that were the strangest of all. Artefacts crouched and leaned in every space. Strange miniature sculptures of animals the like of which Alistair had never seen in any zoo, or upright idols with many arms and extra rows of eyes.

All the better to see you with.

One shelf held a bizarre collection of shrunken heads with strands of wispy hair hanging down so as to frame rictus grins. Two of the walls were without shelves, adorned instead with painted symbols, all black-and-white in shapes that Alistair had never seen before. But some were familiar, like pentagrams, wheels and moons and runes. On the floor, five concentric circles of scorched wood took centre stage.

Alistair shook his head. His uncle, the bookish Connor, a closet student of the arcane. On the desk sat a DVD player linked to a small monitor screen that was placed so that it faced a pewter-framed mirror on the other side of the desk. Flashing LED numbers told him that something—possibly one of the many power cuts brought on by the storms battering Britain that time of year—had turned the system off. Mindful of his uncle's note, Alistair depressed the power switch and watched as the system began to play from where it had frozen.

Somewhere deep in the shop a clock chimed. Alistair returned from his recollections and looked at his watch. Eight o'clock. He adjourned to the kitchen to make some coffee and then returned to the hidden room. Thin wisps of steam drifted up over the rim of the cup into the cold air. It was always much colder than the rest of the shop, even with a fan heater on full blast. He wondered about that again just as he wondered about the stern authority that the female DOF agent had exuded when she'd fixed him with a pair of amazing, gold-flecked eyes.

How much did she know, he wondered? How much of what he'd said would she believe? He'd spoken the truth about Connor being unwell and having strokes. He was still upstairs in his bedroom. But it was what Alistair had left out that might have interested her more.

A lot more.

After the supreme effort of passing on the secret of the hidden room and the weird dvd set-up (and he'd never asked Alistair if he'd even found it), the old man quickly took a couple of turns for the worse. More TIAs, the GP had explained.

And while Connor languished in his bedroom, slowly getting sicker and weaker, Alistair watched the DVD that Connor had set up to play in the mirror several times. Watched it and failed to understand why anyone would want to revisit such a rubbish YA vampire film made from a series of rubbish YA books. Until one day, a TIA had blossomed into a massive stroke, big and bad enough to kill the old man. And when Alistair discovered him dead in his bed, mouth open and eyes staring, he also discovered something else waiting for him in that bedroom.

The whisperers.

After listening to them, Alistair had not rung the GP. Nor the ambulance. Nor, since, a funeral home.

The whisperers had a better idea. One that Alistair, terrified and grief-stricken, had at first resisted. But enough of their power had leaked into the Inky Well to ensnare a hapless youth and twist his mind to their way of thinking.

He sipped at the coffee cradled between his palms and stepped inside his uncle's secret room once more to stand staring around in admiration, his body energised with a new sense of purpose.

He checked the AV equipment. The DVD was playing on schedule.

He was keeping up his end of the bargain.

He thought about the DOF agents again and felt his resolve harden. This was too good a deal to let it all unravel.

NEW THAMESWICK, FW

IN THE VIEWING room at ICHOR, Les Reasonables were fully settled in for an evening's indulgence. On the screen, a group of human thugs had chased a human female into an alley with nefarious plans in mind. She was helpless, cornered, no prospect of escaping their wicked and violent attentions. Out of the shadows stepped a man. Chiselled features, large expressive eyes, skin as pale as milk with hair the colour of bleached straw. The girl was known to him. She made the mistake of enjoying his company and in so doing incurred the wrath of an erstwhile admirer who considered females so much property to own, not relate to. The admirer stood at the head of the male gang who now cackled and cajoled, their suggestions lewd and demonstrative. At last the pale man stepped forward out of the shadows and into the stark sodium streetlight to reveal himself.

The cackling stopped. No one in the audience noticed how the wind that whipped the girl's hair wildly about her face did not displace one strand of the pale man's combed locks. Why should it? He was the master of his universe after all. Either that or continuity was not high on the director's tick list. Les Reasonables knew nothing about cinematography or a director's wiles. They couldn't care less because they were rooting for their hero, the vampire.

On screen, the gang regained their confidence quickly. He was just another bloodsucker, after all. They rushed him and he responded with superhuman agility and strength and moves that had them flailing and broken within minutes.

He turned to the girl. He was hungry, but he did not feed on her. Honour overcame desire.

Les Reasonables gasped as the offer, so overtly presented, was declined. It showed great fortitude. They all want to be that hero, though a good ninety per cent of them knew they would have bitten that neck the moment it was within reach.

Without warning, the action stopped.

A gasp emerged from the crowd as letters appeared on the screen.

WE HAVE HAD VISITORS SNOOPING ABOUT.
VERY INTERESTED IN THE BOOKMARKS.
DIGSBOW NEEDS TO KNOW.

DiFrance stood and walked forward. He leaned in and whispered something into the mirror. More letters appeared.

WILL DO.

The film action recommenced and within minutes, the scene shifted to a forest and a group of dark-haired cannibals plotting a vengeful act. The message was soon forgotten.

But not by everyone.

Unseen in the darkness, one of Les Reasonables slipped quietly away, his silver eyes glittering with purpose.

CHAPTER TWELVE

OXFORD, ENGLAND, HW

Bobby Miracle, wearing a pair of fetching protective gauntlets, thumbed through the confiscated copy of *The Octomeraan Manuscript*, looking for clues. From across the room Sergeant Keemoch watched impassively, his green eyes giving nothing away.

'Anything interesting?' he asked.

'Nah,' Bobby replied. The book seemed to be nothing but superstitious nonsense and folksy prose about hearts beating primal rhythms under the silver moon in a clearing in an ancient wood. Written by someone claiming to be an expert in Wicca, it was all as insubstantial as steam from a kettle.

They were in a small annex of the DOF library with the door sealed shut. All sorts of symbols and letters covered the four walls with a large pentagram inlaid into the floor so that no chalked, painted, or salt scattered lines could be randomly broken. This was Hipposync's safe room. The best place to examine magical artefacts. If anything did explode, escape, erupt, scream, attack or sing, Siren–like, it would be contained within the room until suitable help arrived to clear up the mess.

'It's full of all sorts of twaddle,' Bobby continued. 'All guff, no substance. I mean, 'When the wind doth blow deep from the south, tis time to seal a lover's troth.' I ask you. Sounds like a fairy godmother's line from a bad pantomime.'

'Someone must believe that stuff.'

'Someone probably does. But just because it's written down in a book doesn't mean it's worth anything.'

'So why bother writing it in the first place?'

'Ego? To court controversy? There's always context. Don't forget that this book was written in the early eighteenth century just a few years after they'd executed women in Salem for plaiting their hair in a non-virtuous way or for having a bow in their dress. Though, 'When the wind doth blow deep from the south, tis time to seal a lover's troth' wasn't exactly blasphemy, it was titillating and controversial at the time.'

'Just words, though.'

Bobby nodded. 'But we all know how much trouble words can cause. Some people ascribe all sorts of meaning to things when they're written down. They adopt them as a way of life and castigate anyone else who doesn't think or do as they do. Words are probably the most powerful things we have.'

'They're only shapes and squiggles. I don't see how they can cause so much trouble,' Keemoch said with a soldier's belief in trusting things you could feel and see rather than ideas that you could not.

Bobby shrugged. 'It's not the squiggles and symbols that are the trouble. It's the people who read them. And we all know how good people are at creating mayhem from the simplest of things. Just look at what they've done with the atom.'

Keemoch paused at that.

Bobby turned another page. 'So even though this is all pigswill, someone has had a serious go at it. By that I mean the scribbles and notes and annotations in black ink. Plus, there's an odd set of sentences written inside the back cover in brown ink.'

'What do they say?' Keemoch asked.

'Your guess is as good as mine. I wouldn't know where to start pronouncing some of the words. Who is Agathoth when he's at home?'

Keemoch shook his head and sipped his tea.

'Oh, and where is that bookmark? Might as well have a look at it too.'

Keemoch shook his head. 'Still with the labs. Kylah insisted we send it to the Met for fingerprints and DNA testing. She wanted it all done by the book so their forensics are giving it the once over.'

'I only caught a quick glance at it but I think this writing looks a bit like some of the writing on the back of the bookmark. Either that or a drunk spider's fallen in the ink and gone walkabout on both.' Bobby sighed. 'Ah well. It would have been useful as a comparison, that's all.' She closed *The Octomeraan Manuscript* and peeled off her gauntlets. 'Right. Shall I ask the jolly japer a few questions then? Now that the potion's worn off and he's out of stasis.'

Keemoch looked up at her over the top of his tea mug. 'That wise? Did you run it past Captain Porter?'

Bobby's large eyes became ovals of innocence. 'She asked me to find out what I could. I reckon a few questions wouldn't do any harm.'

Keemoch's expression, unreadable at the best of times given that he was a Sith Fand, sagged with scepticism but he did not object. 'Okay. But I'm coming with you to observe.'

The yellow room stood just off the library, separated from an outer vestibule by a stout layer of hexiglass—so called because it was, of course, impervious to hexes both spoken and leered. The room was similar to the library annex they'd just left in that it had been designed for containment, specifically sentient beings as opposed to inanimate artefacts. The Alternator sat on a stool staring through the glass, looking surprisingly untroubled considering he was in a detention centre against his will and hadn't even been offered a glass of water yet. In fact, he wore the look of a man who'd just been told the world's best-kept secret.

'Mr Strayne?' Bobby said through the glass.

The Alternator returned a compressed little smile. 'Please, call me Reg.'

'Do you know why you're here…Reg?'

Reg dropped his chin. The smile remained. 'No, but I reckon you're about to tell me.'

Bobby sighed. 'I'm not quite sure you appreciate the gravity of your situation.'

Reg's smile slipped as he tried desperately to reassure Bobby that he was indeed aware. 'Oh, I do. I do. Only…well, you know…I always believed. Always. People kept telling me there was no such thing as magic. Not real magic. But,' his grin returned, this time ear to ear, ''well, here we are. I just walked through a mirror and now I'm being interviewed by a witch.'

'I am not a witch.'

Reg gave her a derisive grin that had 'pull-the-other-one' tattooed on its chest. 'And that bloke behind you, he must be an elf.'

Bobby grimaced. Any chance Reginald Strayne ever had of developing a relationship with Keemoch disappeared like a rodent up a drainage conduit. The sergeant liked being called an elf about as much as a homeopath liked clinical trials.

'So, maybe I'm in trouble but I'm excited too,' continued Reg. 'I'm here and this is…real.'

Bobby blinked. This was all she needed. A wide-eyed sycophant who thought he'd just stumbled into Narnia.

'The book. The one we confiscated. Is that where you learnt to perform your 'trick'?'

'Trick, hah. That was no trick. That was a proper spell. I can do spells, you know.' Reg giggled. 'Can you believe that?'

'Yes I can, otherwise I wouldn't be here. Now about this book?'

'Useless pile of crap.' Grinning, Reg leaned forward. 'On the whole.' He tapped the side of his nose and sent his eyebrows skyward.

'Meaning?'

'Oh, come on. Let's stop playing games. You saw what I did on stage.'

'Unfortunately I did not. But I heard it was pretty spectacular.'

'Setting fire to somebody and leaving him unscathed? That's not just spectacular, that's—'

'Extremely unusual.' Keemoch's voice reverberated through the room like the rumble of an approaching train.

Reg blinked. 'Yeah, that too.'

'How did you do it?'

A new expression crept slowly over the magician's face. The wide-eyed enthusiasm faded to be replaced by calculating guile. 'How about we do a swap. I'll tell you how I did it so long as you answer all my questions.'

Bobby glanced over her shoulder at Keemoch. He raised the tea to his lips and shrugged again.

'Okay,' she said. 'Ask away.'

'The two people who brought me here, are they agents for an organisation monitoring the flow and activities of supernatural beings?'

'Supernatural is a word you could apply,' Bobby said carefully, 'though I'm quite partial to extramundane—'

Reginald Strayne leapt off his stool with both arms raised in victorious celebration and a yelled, 'YESSSSS!'

The move took Bobby completely by surprise and despite the toughened, charmed glass partition between them, she reared back in alarm. Reg, however, began riding an imaginary horse, Gangnam style, around the yellow room, whooping, and shouting, 'I knew it! I bloody well knew it. All true, it's all true!'

Bobby stood, nonplussed, until the magician's exuberance took a break. After two very long minutes in which she exchanged bemused looks with Keemoch more than once, Reg finally stopped celebrating, picked up the toppled stool and sat, red-faced and panting, to mop his brow.

'Can we look forward to a repeat performance?'

'Definitely…not,' gasped Reg.

'Right. My turn for a question, I think. Who taught you the spells?'

'No one…taught myself.'

'That may be an answer to my question, but it isn't particularly helpful now, is it?'

Reg gave an exaggerated nod and held up one finger to indicate he needed a moment to compose himself. Judging from the way he was blowing air out through puffed cheeks, it looked more likely that he needed a moment to avoid a cardiac arrest. 'The book,' he muttered. 'Ninety-nine per cent rubbish…except for the stuff at the back.'

'You mean the handwritten scrawls inside the back cover?'

More nods. 'That is the real deal. I tried everything else, but then I got to the back page and tried that first sentence. It's like a key. Say it and the words in the book change and you plug in to the power.'

'What do you mean?'

'It's simple. *Merum venenatus*.'

On cue, the floor beneath Bobby's feet started to tremble. It lasted no more than five seconds but it was enough. 'Wow. Very…impressive.'

'See?' Reg grinned. 'I say those words and then whatever I am thinking about makes a shape in my head and it usually happens.' He frowned. 'Except that this time it didn't.'

'What did you think about?' Bobby asked, smiling.

'That the glass would shatter and I could talk to you face to face.' He grinned back.

Bobby nodded. A bit of her wanted to suppress a shiver, while another bit smiled encouragingly. 'Thought so. You're in a quarantine room. A protected space. Specially built for bad boys.'

'I wasn't trying to be weird or anything. It was just a demonstration.'

Bobby's smile widened. There didn't seem to be anything other than genuine enthusiasm in his words. She believed him. At least a part of her did. The same part that was warming to him, wondering if those bovine eyes of his could get any more soulful. Of course, another part of her was screaming, 'Are you stark raving mad?' but she wasn't listening.

'So, my turn for a question, I think?' Reg leaned forward.

Bobby nodded and, alarmingly, heard herself giggle.

'Other worlds. There must be other worlds, right? Somewhere magic is an everyday occurrence? Please tell me there are because I have believed in that since I first picked up the book.'

'Yes,' said Bobby. 'Yes, there are. Hundreds of them. Some you wouldn't believe. You'd do well in quite a few of them. I know some tribes who go for the fuller figure. And I could probably take you—ow!' She felt something pinch her arm and looked down to see Keemoch's fingers pincering her elbow. She looked up at him in annoyance. 'What are you doing?'

'Outside, now!' Keemoch ordered.

'But I haven't finished the interrog—'

But the sergeant was having none of it as he unceremoniously yanked her out through the vestibule and into the corridor beyond, his grip unrelenting until they were standing with the door to the yellow room firmly shut behind them.

'Why did you drag me out like—' She shook her head as

her thoughts evaporated and she struggled to recollect them. It was like coming to after a very rapid anaesthetic. A momentary blankness followed where she didn't remember quite where she was or why and then it all came flooding back. 'Did I…?' She left the question hanging.

Keemoch grabbed it. 'Yes, you did. You were beginning to flirt with that idiot in there.'

'But I…I mean how could I? He's not exactly…In fact, he's downright…'

'You tell me?'

Bobby thought about it. Had she really considered Reg Strayne as soulful? Judging by the way he was bulging out of his jacket in several places, a better adjective might have been soul food. He wasn't her type. In fact, Reg Strayne was as far from her type as Timbuktu was from Oxford. She paused and considered what her type was. Asher was definitely her type, dark-haired and hard-bodied and…My God, she'd *flirted* with Reginald Strayne but for the life of her, she had no idea why.

Keemoch watched her with a frown. 'Have you worked it out yet?' he asked.

'I haven't worked anything out. All I thought I was doing was asking him some questions and…' Her words tailed off.

'And all of a sudden you were enjoying yourself and wondering if he might be interesting in sawing you in half… without a saw.'

Bobby felt herself flush. 'That's very crude, Sergeant.'

'But I'm right though, aren't I?'

'I wouldn't have put it in quite those terms, but…' Reluctantly, Bobby nodded.

'I knew it. I thought I could smell it.'

'Smell what?' Bobby's brows crowded together in mild panic.

'My Latin isn't exactly brilliant, but those words he said, know what they mean?'

'*Merum venenatus?*'

'It means tainted wine. Crude wine before water is added.'

'So?'

'It doesn't mean wine. Not really. It's a euphemism for something else red and sticky.'

'You mean blood?'

Keemoch nodded. 'Not safe for you to be in there alone with him, Miss Miracle, novice witch though you are. I'm afraid our friend Reg reeks of vampire.'

CHAPTER THIRTEEN

They convened in Kylah's office. Matt brought in a projector and a laptop, and seats were arranged to accommodate the team. They could have easily managed without, but Matt insisted on bringing a little technology to the table. What was unusual was the leather armchair. That was hardly ever needed, but today it most definitely was since its occupant, Mr Ernest Porter, chief of staff at Hipposync, insisted on sitting in nothing else. Kylah never argued with her uncle since he was the venerable head of the garrison, or embassy, or whatever the powers that be back in New Thameswick found it politically expedient to call them these days. But his role was much more than section head, since he also functioned metaphysically as the Doorkeeper and without him there would have been no DOF at all.

With a full head of tufting snow white hair and curiously dark eyebrows, Mr Porter pottered about, mainly reading the ancient texts Hipposync had under their guardianship—titles that were never listed for sale in the catalogue—and advising on matters of inter-dimensional importance. Casual conversations with taxi drivers, community policemen or innocent shopkeepers often left the conversationalists with the impression that Mr Porter might have been an eccentric, retired Don. They were wrong on all counts, yet it was one of the reasons Hipposync was based in Oxford. On the streets, Mr Porter did not look or sound out of place at all. Though in truth he could not have been more out of place than a Starbucks on one of Jupiter's moons—even if they immediately opened another one two hundred yards away.

Bobby Miracle's revelation that Reginald Strayne was contaminated triggered a full outbreak response plan, which began with an evidence review meeting. In the room were Birrik and Keemoch as field agents, Bobby, Kylah, Matt, and Miss White-Tandy, aka Tilfeth.

Kylah called the meeting to order.

'Right, first of all thank you all for coming. You all know why we've convened this meeting but I am also aware that sharing information is vital in such situations and some of us might benefit from being brought up to speed.' She beamed at her uncle.

'Are we having coffee?' Mr Porter asked, beaming himself. 'I do hope we're having coffee.'

'On its way, Uncle Ernest.'

'And will Mrs Hoblip bring some of her excellent shortcake?'

'I'm sure she will.'

'I do like Mrs Hoblip's shortcake, you know.'

Kylah, still rigidly smiling, cleared her throat. 'So, if we could turn our attention to the screen. Matt, could you do the honours?'

Matt stood up and flicked on the projector to show an infogram. Lines began appearing without anyone drawing them.

'As you will see, the road to this point is somewhat winding. Initial reports of Reginald Strayne's unusual prowess reached us via a variety of the usual sources. Our investigations confirmed dark dabbling on his part. A search of his flat led to the discovery of a book, *The Octomeraan Manuscript*, and a likely source of cross-dimensional contamination in the form of a bookmark. Both book and bookmark have been traced to a bookshop known as the Inky Well. From there we learned that Digsbow, a known pedlar with a license to trade in non-wonderworking artisan Faeware, supplied the items. We also know he has meddled in contraband previously. We apprehended Strayne, aka The Alternator, and confined him to the yellow room. However, following an interrogation by Miss Miracle, we now believe that Strayne is in fact also contaminated. The question is, how?'

Kylah caught some movement in her peripheral vision. Mr Porter had turned his attention to the window and the canal outside.

'What about the bookmark?' Keemoch asked.

'Still with the Met labs, I'm afraid,' Kylah explained. 'However, we did manage to find another example at the Inky Well. Our analysis indicates that its manufacture and origin is non-human, though it appears inactive as compared with the example found in Strayne's flat.'

Matt pressed a button and a magnified image of the bookmark's front and back appeared on the screen. Bobby leaned forward. 'That writing in brown. It's the same as on the inside of the back page of *The Octomeraan Manuscript*. I knew I recognised it.'

'We will get that double checked, of course. But I agree, on initial inspection it looks the same.'

Mr Porter chuckled. 'I do believe that an albatross just fished out a sports shoe from the canal.'

Everyone looked.

'It's a large seagull, sir,' Birrik explained. 'And I think that's just an odd-shaped food wrapper it has retrieved.'

'Seen some very funny things on the banks of this canal,' Mr Porter said. 'Saw a vulture once. Great ugly brute with a red neck and eyes so full of evil you felt like bashing it on the head with a shovel just so that it would stop looking at you.'

'Surely not,' Bobby said.

Birrik turned to her. 'Stay here long enough and that'll seem like a very ordinary day, believe me.'

'Had a great propensity for cursing, too, if I remember rightly,' Mr Porter added.

'You do remember rightly, ' Matt agreed. 'Highly skilled in that department was that B', Rimsplitter.'

'Rimsplitter? Yes, that was his name. Odd name for an odd blighter, what?' Mr Porter gave them all a sparkly-eyed look.

'Yes, good, but can I have everyone back in the room, please?' Kylah said.

Everyone turned back to the front. 'I asked our police forensic colleagues to look at the smudges on the bookmark. They report that it is blood containing maemoglobin, confirming that the bookmark is contaminated with vampire blood.'

'Maemoglobin?' Bobby asked.

'It's pathognomonic of vampire infestation,' Kylah explained. 'Causes their blood cells to get bigger, but less effective. Hence the reason they have to top up with infusions. They also get a new carrier protein that transports ingested blood through the lower end of their oesophagus after they have fed, so that it never gets to the stomach acid for denaturing. The morphology is quite fascinating if you're into that sort of thing.'

'And you think it's Strayne's blood on the bookmark?' Matt asked.

'There is more than one blood type,' Kylah said.

There was a knock on the door. It opened and the aforementioned Mrs Hoblip creaked in, wheeling a large trolley laden with two huge silver pots and a couple of plates of golden biscuits covered with sprinkled sugar.

'Excellent,' cried Mr Porter, clapping his hands together once. Kylah did a silent count to ten. Mrs Hoblip, ostensibly Mr Porter's housekeeper, was also a Bwbach who had volunteered her services. And once a Bwbach did that you were stuck with her, or him. Small hardship since Mrs Hoblip's culinary skills were to die for. Thankfully, no one had yet. She surveyed the room with her huge, mournful eyes, arranged a toothsome grin in her pumpkin-shaped head, and backed out, her curly-toed leather slippers sliding silently over the carpet. Keemoch stood and poured the coffee. It took ten minutes before everyone was settled again.

'Okay,' Kylah said in a forced and measured tone, 'now that the refreshments have been distributed, perhaps we can get on.'

'Magnificent shortbread,' said Mr Porter, spraying a plume of crumbs over the carpet in the process.

'So the question is,' Matt continued through a mouthful of biscuit, 'what is the significance of the bookmark?'

'Surely the thing to do is to get the other bookmark analysed,' Bobby suggested.

'As mentioned, we're already on that,' Kylah assured her. 'However, the other important issue is further spread. We need to make sure Strayne hasn't contaminated anyone else.'

'He's a dabbler,' Keemoch observed. 'Is it possible he's used the book to summon something and that's what's given him the curse?'

'Anything is possible at this stage.'

'Any more coffee?' Mr Porter asked.

Kylah sighed. 'Uncle Ernest, I can't help thinking that you aren't taking all of this very seriously. A vampire outbreak—'

'Is a terrible thing,' Mr Porter nodded gravely. 'We should avoid involving our human colleagues as much as possible. They do an excellent job of disguising these things as galloping bleeding monkey virus or some such, but we all know that if such outbreaks aren't cleared up, they have a tendency to come back and bite you.'

Bobby choked on a biscuit.

'However,' Mr Porter said in complete ignorance of his pun, 'it is important to differentiate an outbreak from an isolated case. As Sergeant Keemoch has already pointed out, your magician is a dabbler. It is possible that he has meddled where one should not meddle. I would also be interested to know where Digsbow obtains this… contraband.'

Everyone looked at the screen again.

'Thank you, Uncle. That is an excellent idea,' Kylah agreed. 'We need to trace the bookmark to its source. In the meantime, I need to interview Mr Strayne properly. Miss Miracle, you're with me, as are Birrik and Keemoch. Matt, I'd appreciate it if you continued analysis of the texts.'

'But most important of all,' said Mr Porter after a pause and with some gravity, 'there is only one biscuit left. Anyone mind?'

––––––

REGINALD STRAYNE WAS USING the bathroom when Kylah and Bobby entered the vestibule on the other side of the hexiglass partition. Both Keemoch and Bobby had reported Reginald Strayne's Glamour. Not that she didn't believe them, but Kylah, an experienced interrogator, needed to assess it for herself.

'Kylah, do you mind if I ask you something?' Bobby asked.

'Feel free.'

'Your uncle, what exactly is his role here?'

'In effect he's an ambassador, a kind of senior advisor on all things Fae.'

'He seems…' Bobby searched for the right word.

Kylah obliged. 'Doddery? Oblivious? Maddeningly obtuse? Let me know if you need any more help.'

Bobby flushed scarlet. 'I didn't mean to imply—'

'I know you didn't. And I know how unlikely it seems that he could be of any use at all, other than as a biscuit taster for Harrods. But in amongst the twittering remarks there is always the odd gem. Sometimes a very odd gem. Uncle Ernest has seen it all.'

'Really? How long has he been in the job?'

'You know the apple that Adam plucked for Eve?'

Bobby nodded.

'Uncle Ernest planted the tree.'

Bobby opened her mouth to say something and there it stayed, waiting for words that never arrived.

Inside the yellow room, the bathroom door opened and Reg emerged, holding a book. He looked up and smiled.

'Ah, ladies. Nice to see you. Can I straightaway thank you for providing some very interesting reading matter. I had no idea dwarves wrote poems. Oh, and the breakfast was magnificent. My compliments to the chef. Now, when are you going to let me out of here?'

'Mr Strayne, I am Captain Kylah Porter of the Department of Fimmigration and this is Roberta Miracle, one of our special agents whom you already know.'

'I do. So, when am I getting out of here?'

'Before we can talk about that, there are a few questions that need to be answered.'

'I thought I had answered them. Like I already said, I got the book from the Inky Well. The bookmark came with the book. When I read those funny sentences at the end of the book, things started to change for me.'

'In what way?'

'Isn't it obvious? There's the magic to start with. Before the book, the best that I could manage was to pretend to push a bottle through a table. After the book, I made a bus disappear from the high street and made it reappear in the depot. It didn't just *look* like it moved. It did actually move.'

Kylah took notes. 'Prior to the book, had you made any other attempt at inducing supernatural aid for your work? Had you taken part in a séance, for example? Any kind of ritual or act? Had you visited anyone who promised you arcane power? Anything at all supernatural?'

'Does doing the lottery count?'

'No.'

'Then no, I hadn't done anything different.'

'And apart from the obvious improvement in your magical skills, have you noticed any other changes in yourself?'

Reg frowned. 'Like what?'

'Appetites, drinking habits?'

'Are you a doctor?'

'No. I am simply trying to ascertain why all this is happening to you. Whereas it may seem to you that your boat has come in, our fear is that it is heading very much for the rocks. Anything else?'

'Well, there are the girls.'

'Girls?'

'Yes. You know I've been doing some shows in Edinburgh. First time on the Fringe for me. It's been good. Really good. Especially the girls.'

Kylah put down her pen to listen.

The Alternator brought his stool over and sat a few feet away from the hexiglass. Next to Kylah, Bobby too was giving The Alternator her full attention. Behind them, Keemoch lounged against the door with arms crossed.

'I have to tell you that I haven't been very lucky when it comes to girls.'

A little part of Kylah's brain rolled its eyes up and wanted to say, *No surprises there then, chubster. Lose a few pounds before Uncle Diabetes comes to call, shave off that ridiculous lumberjack beard, and ditch the braces for a start.* But another part of her wanted to listen, was actually sympathetic. There was something in his voice and the way his eyes locked on to hers.

'I haven't had any real girlfriends up to this year,' Reg explained. 'I didn't know how. Didn't know where to meet them. But since I started doing the show I'd go to this pub to meet up with some of the other performers and there'd be girls. And the really weird thing is that they'd start talking to *me*. Said they actually liked red beards. And then they'd suggest we maybe had something to eat and then go back to theirs or mine. Mine was out because I was sharing with three others. The point is that since I started my show, I've gone from zero to ten without passing Go. Don't know whether I'm coming or going.'

'That's not funny,' Kylah muttered.

'Ten?' Bobby asked.

'In how many days?' Kylah added.

'Fifteen.' Reg's face grimaced in apology.

'That's—'

'Quite the bucketful in terms of the milk of human kindness, yes, I agree.' Reg grinned.

'I was going to say, impressive,' Kylah began, but her thoughts were wandering off on their own and were managing to countermand all logic. And it wasn't the sort of landscape Kylah's imagination normally traversed at all. Yet there it was: Reginald Strayne and her, half-naked on a beach with lots of wild horses and crashing waves, and she didn't even mind the sand getting into places sand was better not ever getting into.

'Have you ever considered eleven?' Bobby murmured next to her.

'Right,' Keemoch said loudly. 'That's enough. Let's get out of here before I throw up.'

Through the screen, Reg's face hardened in an instant and the soulful eyes became slits of blackness. 'Do not interfere where you are not wanted, Sith Fand,' he hissed.

Keemoch beamed but there was nothing whatsoever pleasant in that smile. 'And there he is. Nice of you to come out and meet us, bloodsucker. Now piss off.' Keemoch turned to Kylah and Bobby, both of whom wore the same pale, shocked expression. 'Ladies,' he said and as he had done before, took a limp elbow in each of his hands and led them out into the corridor where they leaned against the wall to recover.

From behind the hexiglass, Reg began to hurl abuse. Many of the words were ones that neither Kylah nor Bobby had heard before, but some were very familiar and left them in no doubt as to his previous liaisons with their mothers, their birth status, and their proclivity for foreplay, reproduction, and other forms of sexual gratification.

'Satisfied?' Keemoch asked.

Bobby was breathing hard. 'What just happened? That's the second time my brain's turned into mushy pea—' she stopped talking when she saw Kylah's face.

If it was possible for someone with olive skin to become ash white, then Kylah was proving the theory at that moment. She was trembling, no, *shaking* almost uncontrollably, one hand clutching the wrist of the other as she slouched against the wall. It looked as if she might pass out at any moment. Bobby glanced at Keemoch and saw that the sergeant shared her concern.

'Kylah?' Bobby stepped forward but the look on the DOF captain's face stopped her in her tracks.

'No one goes into that room without my permission, understood?' Kylah snapped her head towards Keemoch. 'Do I make myself clear, Sergeant?'

'Perfectly, ma'am.'

Kylah turned to Bobby. 'Sorry I put you through that. I had to see for myself, but it was silly to expose you again.'

'Expose me?'

Kylah nodded. 'It's strong in him. Stronger than I've ever seen.'

'What is?' Bobby asked.

From behind the door to the yellow room, they heard a terrible banging and the noise of smashing furniture.

'If there's one tiny consolation it's that I don't think he truly knows how to use it. If he did, I…' She shook her head.

'Use what?' Bobby asked.

Kylah didn't answer the question. Instead, she said, 'Come with me,' and hurried out of the room. Bobby followed to the small kitchen where Kylah poured out two glasses of bottled water into which she sprinkled a little yellow powder.

'Garlic,' Kylah explained. 'It's tasteless, but it'll clear your head.'

Both women drained their glasses. Kylah waited for the seasoning to take effect, one eye on Bobby's confused expression as a barometer. The confusion gave way to horrified realisation.

'Did I really just volunteer to be number eleven with…?'

Kylah nodded. 'You did. And as unlikely as that scenario might be in your rational, good taste-endowed, normal mind, it may well have happened under different circumstances. What we experienced in there was the Glamour on speed.'

'The Glamour?'

Kylah nodded. 'All vampires have it to a certain degree. There's a good metaphysical and thaumaturgical reason for it. Something to do with changes in their physiology, the pheromones they exude, the timbre of their voices. It can make people do all sorts of things and believe me, I've seen people do some of the most extraordinary and appalling things for the entertainment of vampires. But I have never felt it that strong before. He has to be quarantined until we find out what is going on here.'

Bobby nodded.

'I will explain all later. But for now, I need to speak to Matt, urgently.'

They found him in the library. The desk in front of him had a couple of reference books open on pages relating to vampires. He had a phone to his ear and held up a hand as they entered, indicating that there was someone on the other end of the line.

'Okay…okay…yes, thanks. I'll wait for your call.' Matt replaced the phone in its cradle. 'Still no joy from the Met as regards DNA, I'm afraid. We'll need a sample from our friend, Reginald, of course.'

'Good luck with that,' Bobby said.

Matt frowned. 'Did it not go well?'

Kylah shook her head. 'He's a vampire. There is no doubt at all about that. He flipped on provocation.'

'Oh dear,' said Matt. 'Did he admit to any summoning?'

Bobby shook her head.

'I'm not that au fait with coffin sleepers.' Matt nodded at the books on the desk. 'Thought I'd brush up on the old lore. I didn't know they could manifest as mist as well as a bat, nor that you can get them with all sorts of things. Iron or silver is good. A crowing cockerel puts the frighteners on them. Then there's running water and the sound of bells, not to mention garlic and poppy seeds and agrimony.'

'What book are you reading?' Kylah asked.

'Jeremiah Boam's *Almanac and Bestiary*.'

Kylah shook her head. 'Waste of time. That was written before blood typing was discovered. The truth is much worse. They are reviled in New Thameswick. They've been persecuted for centuries and with good reason. Everyone knows what they're up against over there. Over here it's a very different story. Our priority is to contain this infestation.'

'Infestation?' Matt made a face. 'Strong word.'

'Not strong enough, believe me. Not once you've seen what it does to a community if it gets a hold.'

'There's an account of that in the book I got from the Inky Well.' Matt reached under the open book and retrieved his purchase. 'Oh, and I found a bookmark inside. Nice of that shopkeeper to—'

Kylah did not allow him to finish the sentence. She smashed the book out of his hands and sent it flying through the air, its pages riffling like an injured bird. It fell with a slap and the bookmark skittered out to lie on the polished oak floor.

'Bobby, get the gauntlets and bag those up, too.'

Bobby left and came back with Birrik, who did the necessary without speaking.

'That was a bit harsh, wasn't it?' Matt asked when the book and bookmark were in sealed bags.

'Not now that we know what this is.' She indicated to Bobby and Matt to sit. 'Our friend Reginald is not himself. He is contaminated. We need to trace all of those girls he's been with. It's a forlorn hope that all they did was exchange pleasantries. However, there is an incubation period of several days if the transmission is by anything other than a direct bite. It's possible to prevent infection with appropriate countermeasures. We can usually get around the truth by playing the STD card and I'll get our colleagues in Scotland on the case. It sounds like all contact in Edinburgh was made at the pub, so we pray that there are CCTV cameras. We'll get nothing from Mr Strayne.'

'Are you sure? You want me to try?' Matt said.

'NO,' Kylah said, louder than she'd meant to. 'No…need. I mean, the least contact the better. There's a charm issue here. It's very deceptive, but Mr Strayne now has the Glamour about him and it is highly seductive.'

'Really,' Matt said with a chuckle. 'Hard to believe. An oil painting he is not.'

'To an unsuspecting victim, he's a van Gogh, believe me,' Kylah said. 'But we mustn't forget that he, too, is a victim, albeit one that has grasped the fanged nettle with apparent alacrity. And dealing with established cases poses a very different set of challenges in terms of treatments and cures. There are certain...elixirs that are supposed to be helpful. They're unlicensed and only available from the odd supplier.'

Matt's eyebrows went up.

'And before you say it, yes, some extremely odd suppliers. So, I thought you might be the best person to deal with that. It'll mean going across to New Thameswick. You can try and track down Digsbow whilst you're there. I suggest you team up with Asher. He's becoming a bit of an expert in vampires from what I've heard lately.'

She looked at Bobby, who smiled wanly. 'He doesn't talk much about his work.'

'Great,' Matt said, grinning. 'Always up for a field trip.'

Kylah frowned. 'Matt, this isn't a jolly. Of all the things you've been involved with for the DOF, this is the least jolly-like. Vampires are the very worst kind of slippery, egomaniacal, narcissistic pieces of filth you'll ever deal with. I want you to promise me to be absolutely on your guard at all times.'

Matt blinked. 'Absolutely. Totally. But I haven't seen Asher for months. We're due a catch up. I'll get on to that right away. What are you going to do?'

'Sort things out this end. Bobby and I need to find out where the Inky Well fits in to all of this. Meanwhile, I'll brief you on what needs to be done regarding the curse.'

When he'd gone, Kylah joined Bobby and spoke to Tilfeth, issuing instructions regarding the tracing of Reginald Strayne's 'victims' with calm assurance.

'Will those girls be okay?' Bobby asked when she'd finished. 'The ones that he…contaminated.'

'I think so. It's a twenty-three day incubation period. Strayne has only been in Scotland for twelve. We still have a ten-day window and we do have things that decontaminate. The sanguinare mundi potion is highly effective, though it often leaves victims with a liking for raw meat. Totally ineffective against the fully infected, unfortunately.'

'Will they really use CCTV?'

'Yes. But they'll also use tracer charms and tracking spells. Vampires leave a very tainted trail.'

'And are Matt and Asher really going to be able to help Strayne?'

Kylah didn't answer right away. It was a good question and she knew that Bobby had a right to know. After all, Asher was her significant other. However, she couldn't think of anyone she'd rather have Matt team up with from the Fae world. And, even with all its dark and arcane dangers, New Thameswick had paradoxically and suddenly became a much safer place for the both of them.

'Perhaps. But what's more important is that they're kept away from the case here.'

'Why?'

Kylah took a breath. 'Vampires were never meant to be here, Bobby. And contamination is not just an infection as with a virus. It's clear that there are strange supernatural aspects involved here, especially once you're bitten. You saw what Strayne did to us without even knowing he was doing it. He has the Glamour. The drive to interact, in all the meanings of the word, with females is very strong in male vampires. Once fully contaminated, female vampires are indiscriminate addicts who will do anything for blood. But the male vampire also develops a pathological and murderous hate for any male it sees as a threat. I have seen that homicidal lust in full flow. I've even lost some good friends to it.'

She thought about elaborating, but decided against it. Memories, half buried under the weight of normality and DOF routine, bobbed to the surface and rolled around in her consciousness like a decaying corpse in a muddy lake. It took a concerted effort to push them back down under the layers of control that kept them in place. It would not do to unburden herself here.

Now was not the time.

It was a decision she would live to regret.

'In New Thameswick,' she explained, 'vampires signed a pact in order to survive. They are stripped of their Glamour there and appear as they really are: ugly and despicable. But they're left alone to avoid extinction. Here, they hide under a veneer of attractiveness but all they are vicious killers. Our friend, Reginald, will soon learn to change the way he looks. And believe me, they can look fabulous as they tear out your throat. It's very selfish of me, I know, but I don't want Matt or Asher anywhere near one of these things here if I can help it.'

Bobby blinked searchlight eyes. 'That's not selfish, it's common sense. And thank you for including Asher.'

'Don't thank me yet. If either of them found out what I was doing they'd explode. Vampires are a testosterone challenge if ever there was one.'

Bobby nodded.

'So this is one little problem us girls are going to have to sort out, agreed?'

She held out a hand. Bobby shook it.

CHAPTER FOURTEEN

NEW THAMESWICK, FW

FOR MATT'S FIRST EVER VISIT to his den at the Bureau of Demonology, Asher pushed the boat out and had coffee brought in. Humans quite liked that, especially when the coffee came directly from a little place in Ipanema. Asher had found Ned the stamp, the youth who brought his post around on a trolley, to be very resourceful when it came to those tricky little extras that he never knew where to find. Extras like paperclips that held together any number of pages, coffee and biscuits and gossip. Ned was of that indeterminate age anywhere between fourteen and seventeen whereby limbs seemed still to be growing and facial hair was still in hibernation. Not quite a waif, the big blue eyes, pale face, and bleached straw hair earned Ned the stamp weekly offers of adoption from the female staff, together with donated home-made sandwiches and cakes in the mistaken belief that Ned needed 'looking after'. So many donations in fact that Ned did a roaring trade in reselling every lunchtime under a pop-up tarpaulin awning in the rear quadrangle. In that sense, Ned was indeed looking after himself very nicely. On weekends, he even had an upturned fruit box in Undergarment Passage market where he also resold pens, paper, cakes, coffee, and biscuits.

Quite the entrepreneur was young Ned, though it was not a word he applied to himself, since spelling was not his strongest suit. His postal round took him to every single floor and department in the BOD without challenge and his knowledge of the hidden corridors and mezzanines was ency- clopaedic. For some reason, he liked Asher and would often spend half an hour of idle chat watching him consult the big books from the library, trying, and inevitably failing, to find out what it was that Asher was working on. His direct approach got him nothing other than impenetrable looks, but to Asher's frustrated consternation, his taciturn approach to Ned's cross examinations merely seemed to feed the boy's interest in him. And worse was the fact that engaging in conversation with Ned required concentration, if not a trans- lator, since the post boy's education had been mainly on the streets of New Thameswick.

'Just so's you know, I can get you anyfink, so long as it ain't nailed dahn, or screams too loud when you togs it.'

'So you're in procurement, is that it?' Asher had asked when Ned had announced this at their first meeting.

'Nah, I'm just waiting for me growth spurt,' Ned replied, straight-faced.

Asher had considered laughing but some inner survivalist section of his brain told him to do so would be to offend. From that absence of a put down had grown an unlikely friendship. Asher did nothing to encourage it, but Ned's imag- ination needed little or no feeding. Having a necreddo in the building was enough for the boy.

Getting coffee from Brazil using an Aperio was not that difficult, but such things were frowned upon as personal frip- pery. Whereas Ned knew every nook and cranny of the BOD and every eccentric experimental alchemist and theoretical thaumaturgist it contained. The details of how Ned procured these things was never volunteered and Asher felt disinclined to ask, though the post boy had hinted at a couple of booths in a locked room of the Lovecraft wing, where Transcon had sponsored a whole department of dark energy research. Rumour had it that the booths were supposed to be not just transcontinental conduits but transdimensional. Unfortunately, no one was entirely sure because both the boffins working on them had disappeared. The booths did, however, function very well as simple, free portways, as Ned had discovered (he did not elaborate on the how).

Matt arrived looking wide-eyed and impressed by his escorted journey through the bowels of the BOD.

'This place is pretty out-there,' he said as Asher beckoned him in. 'I think I saw a pterodactyl circling the whispering gallery.'

'Yes, that will be Temporal Studies on the fifth floor. Perfectly harmless, as they can only occupy fifty square meters of space. It's unfortunate that no one has quite worked out how to tell the contents of their bowels that. Even more unfortunate if you happen to be on the receiving end of a pterodactyl toilet break since, not only is it large, but it also aggregates 150 million years' worth of morphological change as it falls. One broke Spiving's collarbone last week.'

'Nice,' grinned Matt. 'I thought it was meant to be lucky.'

'It was. He sold the rock to a museum for a good wedge. Coffee?'

After Matt had stopped groaning with delight at the beverage, they got down to business and exchanged information.

'That's very interesting,' Asher said when Matt had finished explaining about The Alternator.

'And since we hear you're becoming something of an expert in the Kindred, as well as being hand in glove with the rest of New Thameswick's underworld, it was suggested by the girls I come and see you.'

Asher gave a lopsided grin. 'Not sure I like any of those labels, but, unfortunately, they do tend to stick. First stop would be Digsbow, I guess. I've got Crouch on the case. We're to meet him at Marinade Avenue.'

'Good idea,' Matt got up but hesitated.

'What is it?'

'Don't suppose we've got time for another coffee, have we?'

Asher grinned. Matt was his kind of guy.

———

Marinade Avenue was the type of street where people lurked, even in broad daylight. Not that they were out to cause physical mischief to anyone; this was not that sort of road. They lurked because the many deals that took place there never truly saw the light of day and remained very much on the shady side of things. And if you didn't lurk, you'd miss them completely.

Almost anything could be bought or sold on Marinade Avenue, and yet there were no establishments displaying their wares. This was a street of quite normal houses, wooden framed, leaning in towards one another as if they were preparing for a cosy little chat. And yet knock on one of the doors with the correct tympanic phrasing and when it opened, it might change your world.

Digsbow lived in rooms on the second floor of a rooming house run by Mrs Canticle, a woman of ample girth and absent mirth. She opened the door to Asher, Matt, and Crouch with an expression that was as welcoming as a pterodactyl with the squits. Indeed, her expression was as a good impression of a pterodactyl with the squits as Matt had ever seen.

Crouch stepped forward. 'Mrs Canticle,' he said, bringing a sudden effusiveness to bear. 'And how are you today?'

'What do you want, hawkshaw?'

'Nice day for it, whatever it is.'

Mrs Canticle's one good eye drifted up over Crouch's shoulder and then back down again. 'It's raining.'

'And surely it must be simply a matter of seconds before the sun will grace us with its presence now that you have graced the world with yours.'

'If it's me body you're after, you can look all you want but no touching. This,' she ran thick fingers over a filthy house coat from neck to naval, 'is for my Septimus and no one else. He's due back from sea any day now.' She gave them what probably started out in that part of her brain as a suggestive leer but ended up, once it had negotiated its circuitous route through layers of white matter that had long since forgotten how to flirt, emerging as a frightening grimace. Across the road a cat stopped in mid stride with its tail and fur suddenly vertically rigid.

Matt felt something stir inside him with the label 'queasy' firmly attached.

Crouch continued to grin. 'And what a lucky man Septimus is. How long's he been away now, one or is it two decades?'

'He writes every day. Steamy letters, they are. Full of what he's going to do to me when he gets home.'

Crouch's grin made him look like a death's head. 'It must be such a strain for him. Terrible that his work takes him so far away from you, Mrs C. And living on those tropical islands in the middle of all those heathen hulula girls. I feel for him, I really do. But you and your voluptuousness are safe today. We just need a word with one of your tenants.'

'He isn't in.'

'How does she know? We haven't said who we want to see yet,' Matt whispered to Asher.

'Intuition,' Asher whispered back, 'plus a blanket denial caused by a healthy desire to stay on the right side of several of the shady characters who've used this vermin-ridden hole previously.'

'He will be for us,' Crouch said and pushed past into the corridor.

'Number eight,' Asher said.

'Oy, rozzers, you can't—' Mrs Canticle's protests echoed up the stairs. The sound of several dead bolts thudding home reverberated through the building as tenants, on hearing the warning, battened down the hatches.

'Rozzers?' Matt said.

'Mrs Canticle is very old school,' Asher explained.

They took the stairs quickly, voices dropping to whispers as they travelled up as silently as they could, Mrs Canticle in wheezing pursuit. They tried for stealth but failed spectacularly as every rickety stair had been fitted with a creak charm. Finally they stood outside a battered-looking wooden door with a splintered lock that had been poorly repaired with a nail.

'Digsbow, you in there?' Crouch yelled.

There was no reply.

Crouch repeated the shout, then with still no response, he fished out an odd-looking knife with lots of strangely shaped tools attached.

'You can't do that,' Mrs Canticle protested. 'That's B and E, that is.'

'Can you smell that?' Crouch asked without taking his eyes off the little tool he was using to prise open the nail.

'Smell what?'

'Waccyweed. Unmistakable, it is. I reckon someone's smoking a banned substance.'

Mrs Canticle sniffed. 'I can't smell anything different to what I always smell. Cabbage, used nappies, leftover curry, and mould. Usual healthy smells.'

Asher heard Matt titter next to him. It earned a scathing glance from Mrs Canticle's non-walleye.

'Ah yes, but underneath all of that is an aromatic tone,' Crouch explained. 'If Boots was here, he'd be going bananas.'

'Boots? Who's Boots?' Mrs Canticle demanded.

Crouch stopped to stare at Mrs Canticle. 'You don't know who Boots is? He's our sniffer dog. Trained to detect all sorts, he is. And he's decided that what he likes best is sniffing out waccyweed. And who can blame him? Nice gig if you can get it. Problem is, once he's sniffed it he's useless for the rest of the shift because he's usually on his back drooling and pawing air on account of him having a nose that's ten thousand times more sensitive than ours.'

'I run a sober house,' Mrs Canticle said, hitching up her left bosom, which had sagged a good three inches more than the right.

'Exactly. So, when we smell waccyweed, we know it's a miscreant. That gives me the power to investigate further.'

Mrs Canticle sniffed the air. 'Come to think of it, there is something.'

Asher looked across at a small pile of orange and brown that someone had thrown up to the side of a door a few yards away and had to agree. That was certainly something.

When the door opened, Asher knew instantly that this flat had no occupant. At least, not a living one. There were no aircraft in New Thameswick nor the world it occupied. Yet the noise of a thousand fat and well-feasted flies taking off from the free lunch they were enjoying reminded him of a cruising 747 on a runway, gunning the jets ready for take-off.

Mrs Canticle, straining to get a look into the apartment let out an oath ending in a gagging noise as the stench hit her.

'Ugh, he's left some meat to spoil and buggered off.'

It was Asher who turned to her, blocking her view with the suggestion that she make them all a cup of tea and that Crouch would be happy to pay.

Mrs Canticle waddled down the stairs, whistling.

Inside the apartment, a narrow corridor led to a living room off which was a small kitchen. The smell was coming from the bedroom. Rich and cloying, it seemed to reach into Asher's brain and turn a handle that mangled his stomach. By the look of him, it was having much the same effect on Matt. Asher handed him a small piece of thin wood shaped like an arch. 'Put it over the bridge of your nose,' he instructed. 'It helps.'

Asher slid on his own peg. The sharp, astringent scent of pine forest exploded into his head. It helped a little. But it was no antidote to the horror that greeted his eyes when he followed Crouch into the bedroom. The remains of a man lay scattered over the bed and the floor. Black pools of congealed blood matched the streaks on the walls and ceiling. Some of the more persistent flies were still crawling over the corpse's face. Several feet away, some more were enjoying themselves on an arm and the stragglers were doing what blowflies do on a curly mound of sausage-shaped entrails neatly arranged on the pillow in the shape of a familiar symbol that the more imaginative might interpret as representing Smegrot the Smiter, but which Crouch knew only too well was the calling card of someone else altogether.

'Sicca Rus,' said Crouch. The words emerged like air from a punctured tyre.

'So this isn't Digsbow, then?' Matt asked, trying not to look at anything and failing since everything was on display in all its terrible gory glory. All that was missing there was a Hallelujah.

'It's Digsbow, alright,' Asher pointed to the hand on the bedside cabinet, 'in jigsaw form. He always wears that ring. Won it in a game of call a spade a heart from a diamond merchant. It's his favourite anecdote.'

'Was his favourite anecdote,' Crouch muttered.

'So who or what is Sicca Rus?' Matt asked.

Sighing, Crouch turned away from the horror to look at Matt. 'That's a question I have asked myself too many times. For now, it's enough to know that he's the perpetrator of this little horror show. That,' he pointed to the visceral artwork on the pillow, 'is his attempt at visceral humour. His calling card. Come on, I'll get the squad down here to clean up. I could do with that cup of tea.'

They settled themselves in Mrs Canticle's living room and drank tea from china cups, one of which didn't even have a crack in it. Asher's eyes darted absently between the thick layer of dust on the dresser and the cobwebs in the corners, yet they were welcome distractions from the images of the charnel house upstairs. The three of them sat in silence, letting the strong tea assault their taste buds. It was like drinking sweet essence of iron filings. Finally, it was Matt who gave in and dragged the subject of their visit back out into the open.

'So, did Digsbow have some sort of argument with this Sicca Rus, you reckon?'

'Argument?' Crouch frowned. 'You are making the elementary mistake of assuming that Rus needs motivation for doing something like that.'

'Doesn't he?'

Asher shrugged. 'He might object to you having breathed the same air as him, or being caught in the same rain, or possibly crossing the same street that he once crossed. Rus has a very liberal approach to killing.'

'But it's a bit of a coincidence, isn't it?' Matt looked at Asher and Crouch in turn. 'I mean, I turn up wanting to interview Digsbow and here he is, doing his bit for fly famine in easy-to-distribute pieces.'

Crouch shook his head. 'That might apply were it not for the fact that Rus has been actively practising his considerable skills on a regular basis for several weeks now. Finding a Rus victim is something we've become depressingly used to.'

Crouch shrugged and took a sip of the dark brown liquid in his cup. 'Gods, this tea is terrible. Any more, Mrs C?'

Mrs Canticle fetched a huge pot from where it had been stewing on the stove. The infusion that emerged from the spout looked like creosote and had a flavour that was not entirely dissimilar. Crouch spooned in three teaspoons of sugar and stirred.

'And you can't recall any strange goings-on, Mrs Canticle?' Asher asked with the air of someone casting a spinner into a fast-flowing river and hoping for a bite.

Mrs Canticle cackled. It turned into a bubbling cough and ended with something unpleasantly green deposited in the fire that hissed like a stepped-on snake. 'This is Marinade Avenue you're talking about. We invented strange goings-on. So yes, I seen all sorts of weird people on me stairs. I generally avoid 'em on account of me bad chest and a healthy desire to see me next birthday with all me limbs. I have a duty to my Septimus to keep me looks, I'll have you know.'

The urge to say that Mrs Canticle could keep them preserved in a bottle of vinegar for all the good it would do was trodden on unceremoniously by Asher's good manners and sense. But from the look of distaste on Crouch's face, he'd been thinking much the same thing.

'We thought we had a pattern,' Crouch went on. 'Developed a bit of a thing for leeches, had Rus.'

'Leeches?' Matt asked, and, despite his better judgement, held out his cup for a top up as well.

'Vampires. He's got the stake through the heart technique down to a fine art. Uses yew sticks to turn them into kebabs. But Digsbow is no leech.'

Matt sat forward. 'But our case involves a vampire infestation and a link to Digsbow. Odd that your man Rus seems to object vehemently to both. He must be involved somehow.'

Crouch narrowed his left eye. 'I can see why you get paid the big scruples, Matt. Right, I'm off to fill in forms. I shall leave you sleuths to ponder our next move…unless the two of you fancy some lunch? Do a mean black pudding at the Dress On The Left. It's only a couple of streets away.'

'I'll take that as your idea of a joke, Crouch,' Asher said.

'Take it whatever way you like. I'm starving. Stay honest, lads.' Crouch waved his hand and took his leave.

'Take no notice of him, Matt. Crouch is a hawkshaw under a lot of pressure from his bosses. Rus is a big thorn in his side.'

'So what about Kylah's other instruction?'

'Remind me.'

'The magician, Strayne. He's infected. She said that you'd know where to go to get him sorted out.'

'She said that?'

Matt nodded.

Asher looked down at his shoes and then up at Matt. 'Your Captain Porter has a warped sense of humour, has anyone ever told you that?'

Matt let out a dry titter. 'Don't get me started. But does that mean you don't know anything about vampire cures?'

'Nothing at all. Time we hit the books, I fear.'

CHAPTER FIFTEEN

LONDON, ENGLAND, HW

Kylah and Bobby used the Aperio and emerged inconspicuously from the ladies' toilets in Paddington station. A man in GWR uniform walked past with a hawk on his arm and Kylah did a double take.

'Anti-pigeon patrol,' said Bobby with a shrug.

Kylah tilted her head. 'Crouch would *really* like that.'

They hurried to a taxi rank and hailed a cab. As it trundled along central London's choked roads towards Goodge Street, Bobby turned her thoughtful gaze from the thronging crowds towards a preoccupied Kylah.

'I have to ask, why not use an Aperio to go directly to this address?'

Kylah shook her head. 'The Met hate people appearing out of thin air. It's a security thing. Though they acknowledge our existence and are more than happy to make use of us when needed, it's a love-hate relationship. Still, you'll like Professor Mispickle. She's a sweetie. Can't say the same about Chief Inspector Sewell.'

'What's wrong with him?'

'Let's just say that no matter how hard you might rub, there is no prospect of him ever being a polished one.'

The taxi turned off Tottenham Court Road opposite Goodge street station and pulled up outside an incongruous wedding cake-shaped building incongruously named, The Eisenhower Centre. Kylah went to a side door, punched in some numbers on the combination lock and entered a white painted corridor leading to a lift with polished metal doors.

'What is this place?' Bobby asked.

'It was once a deep underground air raid shelter during World War II. Goes right down below the Tube tunnels. The Met thinks it's the safest place to deal with all things Fae.'

The lift stopped and they exited. A frosted glass door ahead had a stencilled sign that read, *Metropolitan Police Forensic Laboratories—Section F.*

Kylah pushed the door open and they entered a large open plan office space with half a dozen people working at desks. A tall man in a suit and tie stood up from where he was leaning over to look at the computer screen of one of the seated office staff. A look of recognition crossed his face and a vulpine smile accompanied it as he walked towards them.

'Ah, Captain Porter. Always a pleasure.'

How is it, thought Kylah, *that power, even a tiny dose of it, can fool people into believing that they were something special when the truth was the exact opposite?*

Chief Inspector Ralph 'pronounced Rafe, if you wouldn't mind' Sewell held himself in high regard. 'Yes, I am in the police force but I'm afraid exactly what it is I do is classified. Matter of National Security,' was pure Sewell. Kylah was willing to bet he'd even said, 'and if I tell you I'll have to kill you,' with that exact same vulpine smile that would leave lesser mortals with the tiniest suspicion that he actually meant it.

He was a big chap, once a rangy back row forward for the Met rugby team. When it came to women he was a genuinely hopeless case, believing erroneously that most women found him devastatingly attractive. It had taken his two wives twenty-six and nineteen months respectively to discover the reptile under the tan and lead them to run, screaming, for the hills. But this had done little to dilute the man's self-belief. Nor the disdain with which he treated other professionals whose employers were not the Met. Though he had been forced to tacitly acknowledge the existence of supernatural beings in his dealings with the DOF during his time at Section F, Kylah suspected that in his heart of hearts Sewell believed that if it came to a fight, physicality and superior intellect would always win the day. It was a dangerous ignorance that she suspected would literally come back to haunt him one of these long, dark nights.

'Inspector Sewell,' said Kylah in acknowledgement. 'This is Roberta Miracle. She's consulting on the case.'

'It's Chief Inspector now.' Sewell grinned while his eyes did a rapid top to toe and back again assessment of Bobby. 'Are you in mourning?' he asked.

'What do you mean?' Bobby replied.

'The funereal garb.'

'Roberta is a novice at Le Fey Academy,' explained Kylah.

'Oooh.' Sewell adopted a scary voice. 'Please don't turn me into a frog.'

Bobby laughed. It was tinkling and brittle. 'Wouldn't dream of it. I was thinking more Gila monster, actually.'

Kylah coughed. Sewell glowered.

'Very droll. But then the DOF are good at that, aren't they, as your latest little escapade shows.'

Kylah felt something cold break inside her. For a moment, she was lost for words, searching Sewell's self-satisfied smirk for a clue.

'Oh dear, don't tell me you haven't seen it?' He turned to

the nearest desk and punched in a password. He didn't look at them while the search engine found what he'd asked it to. 'Half a million hits so far. You'll be happy to know we're putting out the fire.'

YouTube's page appeared. The heading read, *Amazing Tarpaulin Snake Traps Bystander*.

The cold feeling inside Kylah turned to solid ice. The video was only thirty seconds long, grainy, shaky, and dark. But there was enough light from the sodium lamps to show the astonishing way the tarpaulin disengaged itself from the building, curled upwards and hovered for two frozen seconds at the top of its arc. It was there that the edges of the flapping material seemed to fold and snap into a shape. A flat head, the suggestion of an eye, and a loose rope tongue. Behind Sewell, where he couldn't see her, Kylah squeezed her eyes shut and ground her teeth together.

Inside her head she was screaming. *Matt, you total bloody wazzock!*

Typical. Despite her warnings. Despite her pleading, he'd been unable to resist inserting a little Nagini moment in his performance. He couldn't help himself, she knew that. But it was pure ammunition to gits like Sewell.

'CGI,' said Bobby and Kylah could have kissed her.

'You might think so,' Sewell said, turning back to gaze imperiously at the women. 'However, we have some of the best software experts in the world and they tell me there isn't a pixel out of place. Thankfully, the rest of the population is now so cynical that they assume CGI unless proven otherwise. But we know better, don't we, Captain Porter?'

'We didn't have much time,' Kylah said. 'We did what we had to do.'

'And that meant unleashing some sort of giant plastic snake on the world, did it?'

If only you knew the truth of it. 'We got the job done,' she said, tight-lipped.

Sewell shook his head and turning away again, said, 'Mispickle is in her lab.'

'Wonderful.' Kylah walked past, heading for a door in the corner.

'Was that a bit too strong?' Bobby asked as she followed.

'Gila monster? He deserves every scale.'

Lorenza Mispickle wore a white coat over a woolly jumper, corduroy trousers, and brogues. Her hair was shorn short and flecked with grey. She stood in front of a blackboard with her back to them, chalk dust powdering her shoulders, chalking symbols and wavering lines with quick, sure strokes.

'With you in a minute,' she said in a strong Yorkshire accent without turning around. Kylah and Bobby waited. Finally, the professor finished her scribbling and turned to beam at the women. Her glasses were gull-winged with looped brown string that curled around her neck. The eyes behind the glasses were sharp and intelligent.

'Hungarian recipe for wart cream.' She nodded at the blackboard. 'Promised the PM I'd make him some up. Doesn't want the press to know where it's situated.' She pointed to her buttock, lifted her shoulders, and gave them an exaggerated grimace tinged with wicked delight before stepping forward and grabbing Kylah in an embrace. 'Lovely to see you, Kylah. I expect you've come about the bookmark, am I right?'

'Spot on,' Kylah said. She introduced Bobby and the women shook hands.

'Le Fey?' Lorenza asked.

Bobby nodded.

'Looks like you were born for it.' Lorenza grinned. 'Right. Your mysterious bookmark is over here.' She led the way to a brightly lit bench. The bookmark had been sliced in two and now front and back were displayed side by side.

'Paper is interesting. Not of this world. High flax and clay content puts this squarely at the door of Burper and Sons in the Old Forest region, north of New Thameswick. There's something about the sizing—additives used during manufacture—that I've never seen before. It's probably a rosin that they've used to modify the ink application.'

'Yes, I was going to ask you about the ink. Interesting colour.'

Lorenza put on some high-powered loops and leaned forward over the split paper to adjust a camera on a swinging arm. 'Isn't it just? Probably because it is most definitely not all ink. But we'll get to that. First things first. The decorations around the edge are not simply fancy curlicues. They're a form of character-based language. Logical aggregates; strokes added together to give meaning. The characters here are from old Gng.' The last word of the sentence emerged as a strangulated bleat performed by someone attempting ventriloquism with a heavy cold. She paused for effect and then said, 'The waiting snake shows powerful forbearance.'

'What does that mean?' Bobby asked.

'Context, my dear, is your department.' Lorenza swung the camera over the smudged words on the back of the bookmark. 'However, this is where it gets complicated. You will know that provisional analysis indicated that the smudging over the back surface was blood and typing revealed it to be Mr Strayne's. However, further analysis has thrown up some interesting findings. It wasn't only Mr Strayne's blood. There was a mixture. In all we found three different DNA fingerprints. The one linking factor was the presence of maemoglobin in each.'

Kylah stared at the professor. 'You're saying that more than one vampire has handled this bookmark?'

'Indeed I am. But that is where it gets beyond interesting into WTF because we also have the new, pristine bookmark from the Inky Well. And thank you for providing that because it means we can use it as a control.' She slid the camera along to a different, cleaner image. It, too, had been split in half. 'You can see now that two different colours have been used. The decorative cursive lettering around the edge, disguised to look like simple scribbles, uses green ink. This is a pulped plant extract of *Papaver somniferum.*'

'Opium.' Kylah nodded.

Bobby started. 'It's drugged?'

'Contains a little drug, yes. Of course, the dry ink imparts no effect. But if it was moist and got into the blood stream, it would certainly induce mood enhancement.' She moved the camera to the logo of the Inky Well. 'Black ink is used for the logo and for the words, *The Never Forget Bookmark*. This is classic iron gall made from iron vitriol, oak gall water, and vinegar. An old formula but very effective. It will fade with time but gives a dense black to begin with. But beneath that is what we've assumed to be the manufacturer's website: www.Иiэmoჟoḅ.org. Now, this ink is a brown ochre, as you can see. Except that it isn't ink at all, not really. This is blood mixed with a little gum to make it stick to the paper better. And this blood contains maemoglobin.'

Bobby blinked. 'You're saying that this is *written* in vampire blood?'

'Indeed.'

This time, all Kylah could do was stare.

'And there is one more very interesting thing about these bookmarks.' Professor Mispickle picked up some forceps and lifted the bookmark to demonstrate its edge. 'I use the plural because it is an unusual feature that is common to both. Some kind of technique, and I suspect it is not technological, has been used to hone the edges to make them extremely sharp.'

'Like a weapon?' Bobby asked.

'The material is not thick enough to be used bluntly. No, I suspect the idea is to cause minor injury. A paper cut, perhaps.'

'Why?' Bobby asked.

'So that the bookmark can act as a biological weapon,' Kylah said, her voice low and harsh. 'That's how Strayne got infected. He started to bleed and the blood on the bookmark mingled with his and contaminated him with just enough opiate mixed in to make him not notice the pain, or even enjoy it a little.'

'Precisely my conclusion,' Lorenza said, nodding with satisfaction.

'Wow,' Bobby said. 'That's pretty…diabolical.'

'The question is why,' Kylah mused.

'Mischief?' Lorenza suggested. 'Always a possibility where Fae are involved.'

'Agreed.' Kylah nodded. 'Though instinct tells me otherwise. But right at this moment we need to confiscate these bookmarks. Matt is already in New Thameswick searching for Digsbow.'

'The delightful Matt is well, I trust?' Lorenza beamed.

'Very well and sends his regards,' Kylah said. 'Let's hope he finds some answers. In the meantime, I need to get back to the Inky Well. We need to trace everyone who's been given or sold one of these lethal things.' Kylah started towards the door but hesitated because Bobby wasn't moving.

'What's wrong?' Kylah asked.

'The website address. www.Ѝiɘmoɔoḅ.org. We've tried the URL, I presume?'

Lorenza nodded. 'It doesn't exist,' she said. 'At least not in this world.'

'There is no internet in New Thameswick or in any part of Fae world,' Kylah explained. 'I suspect they've used that arrangement to pander to human convention. To make it look authentic and smart.'

'So who, or what is Ѝiɘmoɔoḅ.org?' Bobby asked.

'When we know that, we'll know who's behind these bookmarks.'

Sewell was waiting for them as they passed back through the Section F office.

'Productive meeting, my little fairy friends?'

'Did you just say fairy friends?' Kylah asked.

'I did. Because that is what you are, isn't it?' Sewell's smile was so supercilious it wore a vest emblazoned with a capital S.

Kylah answered with an even tone that seemed at odds with the sparks that flared in her irises. 'First of all, the term is Fae. Fairy, the way you use it with an 'i' refers to a romantic Victorian idea of a pixie with little wings. Last time I looked, I don't think anything was growing out of the back of my shoulder blades.'

'How do you know I meant it with an 'i'?'

'Because it's slightly derogatory and it makes you feel better to denigrate that which you don't understand.'

Sewell lifted his face to the ceiling with a sardonic laugh. 'I'm not scared of ghosties and ghoulies and things that go bump in the night. In my experience, they go less bump once you've clobbered them with a nightstick.'

'Ah, the clobber it and they shall squeal approach.'

'Works for me.' Sewell grinned.

Bobby joined the fray. 'Do you mind me asking…If you're so sceptical, how is it that you were given this job in the first place?'

Sewell kept the smile on his lips, but his eyes became all Nordic glacier. 'There are jobs you apply for and there are those you are given.'

A light went on inside Kylah's understanding cupboard as the door clicked open to let in a little packet of insight. Somewhere along the line, Inspector Sewell had blotted his copybook. Perhaps he'd called a WPC something inappropriate, or made a move on someone vulnerable who quickly realised that rank had two very different meanings and neither of them was nice. Said blotting may not have been enough to merit frank disciplinary action, but enough to get him sent a hundred feet down under the streets of London, where he could take his lumps out of everyone's sight while realising that the job, top secret though it may be, was a punishment.

'And it's my job to make sure that those ghosties and ghoulies never disturb your dreams, Inspector.' Kylah smiled, deliberately avoiding the 'Chief'.

Sewell shrugged. 'Very nice of you, Captain. But you know what? I'd like to see some real hard evidence just once. Hysterical reports and beyond the veil hints are ten a penny.'

'What about the O'Hoy case? Have you forgotten that?'

'The Scotland Yard brass might have taken your word for it, but where was the proof that he'd nicked something from 'over there'?' Sewell used fingers in the air around the last two words of his sentence.

'Weren't you briefed by Green, your predecessor?'

Sewell's eyelids descended to half-mast. 'He obviously needed a holiday.'

'Dave Green is a nice guy.'

'I'm sure he is. But he also reads graphic novels and plays bloody computer games. What I need is something I can get my teeth into.'

'Okay, I'll bear that in mind, but don't say I didn't warn you. Now, if you'll excuse us…'

'Of course. There's a world waiting to be saved, I'm sure.'

Kylah said nothing as she rode up in the lift and kept her gaze away from Bobby's troubled face, her thoughts a silver pinball bouncing around a mental table dotted with obstacles and holes.

It was a mistake to let idiots like Sewell get to her. The man had no idea. Of course, his was not a unique world view, polarised though it might well be. Many people preferred to live their lives convinced that there could be nothing outside of getting up in the morning, going to work, sausage and beans every Wednesday, and a couple of glasses of Sauvignon or a pint of artisan beer on a Saturday night. That was life and the little extras made it bearable. All very well to let the metaphysical into your house in the form of ghost stories at Christmas and enjoy scary movies about dark forests and vile crones who somehow still managed to look desirable even after four hours in monster makeup, but that was all fantasy. It was controlled and a story and in stories everything usually worked out. The trouble came when the barriers really broke down and good, hard-working people were confronted with the truly inexplicable. Human brains weren't wired to cope with such things. Even the ones that truly knew.

Kylah's brain most definitely was and it replayed the tarpaulin video and she grimaced. Matt was a prime example. He had been involved in a nasty incursion by a whole race of cannibalistic idiots called the Ghoulshee, who'd stolen count-less people before he'd stepped in, found his place in the world—worlds—and sorted the whole thing out through a mixture of luck and good-hearted judgement. Yet even he still struggled to comprehend exactly what his place on the whole smorgasbord was. He possessed a wonderful, astonishing power, but remained woefully unprepared for the many dangers that lurked around every Fae corner. He trusted in luck—and why not since it was the currency he dealt in—but she couldn't help but worry that he remained an ingénue when it came to comprehending what the Fae could throw at him. Usually wrapped in something foul-smelling and nasty.

A freeze frame flashed into her head displaying the giant tarpaulin snake's head and she squeezed her eyes shut. Some-times she thought that life was all just one big joke for him and it made her worry, really worry, about him.

It was all such a contrast with Bobby, whose grandmother was a genuine Fae hero. Bobby, who had embraced the culture and involved herself with training and catch-up since joining their ranks just a few months before. The reports they were getting back from Le Fey were little short of astounding She was clearly talented and was a shoo-in for the style since she was Goth through and through. She would make an excellent witch. A very good thing to have on your side when the ghoulies and ghosties came to call, in Kylah's experience.

Neither Bobby nor Matt was your run-of-the-mill human. In fact, there were enough genetic herbs in the cake mix to make them both honorary Fae. The same could not be said for Sewell and his ilk. And it was Kylah's job to protect that ilk. Those ignorant, cynical, helpless humans. Her job to ensure that those Fae who were functioning in the human world—and there were many of them—did so appropriately and with all the checks and balances in place such as camouflage charms, curbed appetites, and definitely no contraband. The vast majority of the population had no idea that the driver of the number 73 to Newington Green was, in fact, a banshee who liked mechanical things and wanted to give his kids a better education. Okay, he might have joined a choir as a soprano as a sop to his wailing needs, but that was all the Fae that showed because that was the deal.

However, as per good old Reginald Strayne, the bad stuff was out there too, and required cooperation from authorities on both sides of the divide in order to deal with it. Having an out-and-out sceptic as the Met's Chief Inspector was a challenge Kylah knew she could well do without.

'What a slimeball,' Bobby said after several more seconds' silence.

'Could not have put it better myself,' Kylah said with a sigh straight from the heart.

'I'd love to wipe that smirk off his face—'

Kylah stopped suddenly. Bobby swivelled around to stare at her boss who was grinning at her.

'What?' Bobby asked.

'You've just given me a great idea.'

'Comes naturally,' said Bobby with a shrug, 'even if I haven't a clue what idea you're talking about.'

'I think it would be appropriate to invite Sewell to accompany us on the next part of our investigation. Get him out into the field.'

'Preferably one dotted with invisible cowpats?'

The lift stopped and they exited. Kylah's grin widened. 'Bobby Miracle, I'm sure you and I must be related. We obviously share the same sordid thought patterns.'

CHAPTER SIXTEEN

NEW THAMESWICK, FW

MATT AND ASHER SPENT A fruitless morning searching through the books in Asher's limited library at the Bureau of Demonology.

'We could always ask Duana?' Matt suggested, shutting yet another dusty tome with finality.

Asher made a face. 'We could, but she'd want to know why. And even if you didn't tell her, she'd work it out by looking into your eyes. That woman is frighteningly bright. The truth is that there is no cure for vampirism. Not officially.'

'Then what is Kylah on about?'

Asher shrugged. 'It's rumoured that some people have weaned themselves off.'

'Like those leeches I've heard about?'

'Most certainly not like those leeches. They're still vampires but sustained on non-human blood. Grume, they call it. And if you saw what that does to them physically, you'd understand why.' Asher shook his head. 'And these are not fanatics like Les Reasonables, who have decided to stay vampires but who suppress their addiction in an attempt at proving to the world that the Kindred can be assimilated into normal culture without the threat of imminent drainage. What we're talking about are those rare individuals who've fallen under the curse but who have decided that they want to be rid of it. Mortality with the certainty of death versus immortality and a life of eternal craving. Though you and I can't comprehend why, some might see that as an ethical dilemma.'

'But if cure was possible, why doesn't everyone do it? I mean, leeches have a horrible life.'

'Ah, but you're forgetting the mindset. Even the ugliest, smelliest leech thinks he's better than you or I. They survive in the gutter because of a conviction that there will be a revelation. After all they are the chosen ones and when the apocalypse manifests, it is they who will emerge superior and lord it over the rest of us. They see us as nothing more than cattle. Cattle who've managed to carve wooden stakes and harvest garlic, but cattle nonetheless. That conviction runs through them like quicksilver.'

'Do you mean revelation or revolution?'

'Revolution is off the agenda. They're too arrogant and lazy to organise themselves into an army. I mean revelation. Some act or individual that will change the world for them. And you can't convince them otherwise, no matter what you do to them. Their plan is to create a Nosferate, a socio-theological state in which vampires hold sway and we, the people, feed their cravings.'

Matt winced. 'It all sounds depressingly familiar.'

'There are, of course, religious parallels in your world. Like you, we consider ourselves progressive and have encouraged preternatural freedom. All creeds are welcome. The trouble is, all creeds are not equal, or at least don't consider themselves to be.'

Matt shrugged. 'It's a difficult tightrope to walk, I know.

Libertarianism versus sectarianism and bigotry. We've had lots and lots of practise and are no better at it now than when the lions ate Christians for lunch.'

Asher nodded sagely. 'Here it's a matter of twisted political correctness. Anyone who has converted to vampirism, whether a volunteer or a victim, is subject to strict codes of practise and their addiction supported. No one can stop you being a vampire if you want to be one. It's enshrined in the laws of non-human rights. If someone suddenly came up with a 'cure', it would be tantamount to admitting that it's an illness or a disease in the first place. So it's all gone underground. Oh, there are rumours, but that's all they are.'

'Worth following up?' Matt asked. 'Should I talk to a vampire? Ask them what they know?'

'Be like trying to ask a scorpion to cooperate.'

'Isn't there someone here?' Matt waved vaguely at the four walls making up Asher's office and the building beyond.

'I don't know the place well enough.'

The noise of someone whistling cheerfully on another floor brought a sudden smile to Asher's face. 'But maybe I know a chap who does. Fancy another coffee?'

They found Ned outside the typing pool trying to find room on his post trolley for a bag of Eccles cakes. This was a struggle because the trolley was already overloaded with a couple of Victoria sponges, some profiteroles, three bags of chocolate chip Vogtel lambosts and a tray of cupcakes with pink icing.

'Looks like a good haul,' Asher observed.

'They fink I need feedin' up. S'nice, though. I do eat a few, but the rest go to waste unless I flog 'em. Fancy a profiterole? That's gratis, that is. Taste of the merchandise, if you like. I can let you 'ave that Victoria sponge for two scruples fifty.'

'Not just now, thanks. But we do need your help. Who is the expert on vampire reconversion?'

Asher had been prepared for this to be a difficult question for Ned to parry. After all, such esoteric intellectual pursuits were usually the domain of New Ron University, New Thameswick's Internationally renowned seat of learning. Unfortunately, since their Department of Krudian Physics' last experiment with temporal displacement fields had gone ever so slightly wrong, the whole university was now on a ten-week delay. It was possible to write them a letter, but it was unlikely to be opened for two-and-a-half months and a similar delay could be expected for any return correspondence. Matt had wryly commented that the exact same problem had dogged the DVLA in Swansea for the last decade and they didn't even have the excuse of being staffed by wizards, trolls, dwarves, and the undead. Though watching the staff arrive on a winter's morning after the Christmas party, one might be forgiven for thinking otherwise. Ned, however, was up for the challenge.

'You'll be needin' to speak to Shonkin in Demon Relations. He's up on the tenth floor.'

'There isn't a tenth floor,' Asher said.

'Ah, feoretically, no. But there is a button marked ten on the sahth tower lift. It takes five minutes after leavin' the eighth floor but it gets there in the end.'

Asher sighed. 'And is Shonkin approachable?'

'Oh yeah.' Ned waved a dismissive hand. 'As demigods go.'

Matt laughed. But seeing Ned fail to reciprocate, it fizzled out into a troubled frown.

'He knows all abaht the Frozen Ostrich,' Ned went on.

'Frozen Ostrich?' Asher asked in a way that suggested he would regret it fairly soon.

'What?'

'You said Frozen Ostrich.'

'Yeah,' said Ned. 'That's what they call it on the street. It's a bit like cold turkey but five times as 'orrible and with a kick that can knock your 'ead off.'

They followed Ned to the south tower. It took a while since Ned knew everyone in the building and was happy to exchange a word or shake hands with everyone he met.

'Charismatic chap,' observed Matt.

'You could say that. But watch closely when he shakes hands. Something is usually exchanged. Generally notes. If I was a betting man, which I am, I'd say our Ned is more commerce than charisma.'

Finally, they reached the lift. Surrounded by ornate iron-work that doubled as the balusters of a stair that wound upwards, it consisted of a dark wooden box large enough for no more than six people. The box sat humming gently. Ned pulled back the concertina cage doors and ushered them in. Illuminated buttons inlaid into one wall showed 0-8. At the top, separate from all the other buttons, was the number 10.

'There's no need for you to come with us,' Asher said.

'He's due some post.' Ned nodded at his trolley. 'Plus 'e's partial to the odd pastry. If I were you, I'd take some cakes. Break the ice, know what I mean?'

Asher looked at the pale, innocent eyes staring back at him. They appeared guileless in much the same way as shark-infested waters could appear calm. You didn't know what was going on beneath until it was too late and you were flopping away minus one limb and trailing a red slipstream.

Ned put a key into a slot, turned it and pressed the 10 button. The lift rose smoothly, rattling slightly as it negotiated the floors and slowing as it approached the eighth.

'Brace yourselves,' said Ned, clutching the handrail.

With a lurch, the lift rose though a dark space and then seemed to plummet for several seconds before rising again and coming to a stop. Ned pulled back the doors and wheeled his trolley out into a well-lit corridor with half a dozen doors. Lilting evocative music from a mandolin played somewhere.

'What is that?'

Matt piped up. 'Lindisfarne's 'Lady Eleanor'.'

Asher gave him a sideways look.

'My mum was almost hippy once,' Matt shrugged. 'I've heard this song a million times.'

Ned led them to the third door on the right. A sign read *Demonic Suppression*. Ned knocked and they heard a male voice. At least it could have been a voice. Either that or a recording of a car skidding to a halt on a gravel road. 'Come in.'

Ned opened the door and pushed in his trolley.

Asher wasn't sure what he'd been expecting, but a stick thin man dressed in leather jeans with his shirt open to a hairy navel and face that badly needed ironing was not it. The room was little more than an office divided into a bank of wooden index card filing cabinets on one side and space where Shonkin sat in a battered and overstuffed armchair, wearing a pair of large earphones. A wire ran from the earphones to a boxful of dials next to a record deck. A huge collection of vinyl records sat stacked upright against one wall and a neat coffee machine and an old-fashioned telephone were the only other items on the desk.

Shonkin took off the earphones and stood up. 'Ned, my man. You got cake?'

Ned nodded. Shonkin's craggy face split into a toothsome grin as he waited expectantly. Without the earphones, Shonkin's ears stuck out like trophy handles either side of two ragged brown eyes rimmed with black eyeliner. A knitted rainbow headband held a woolly mass of greying hair up off his face. Asher shook a sandpaper hand while Ned made the introductions. As pre-arranged in the lift, he then broke out the Victoria sponge and Shonkin made them coffee.

The cake was excellent, the coffee passable, though not as good as the Ipanema Arabica Asher had given Matt last time. Largely, for the first few minutes, Shonkin's conversation consisted of grunts of approval through a very full mouth as he devoured three portions of cake. But it was Matt who fired off the opening salvo by commenting on an album cover lying on the desk: a colourful geometric design with Picasso-like cubist elements and a central motif of a pair of eyes and an open mouth.

'Is that Medusa?' Matt asked.

Shonkin stopped chewing and stared at Matt with keen interest. 'You know Trapeze?' His accent was somewhere south of London with a lazy drawl that ran his words together in the slightest of slurs.

'I know that album cover. It was on the wall of one of my mum's friend's lounge wall. She was into hard funk rock. I must have heard *Black Cloud* about a hundred times.'

Grinning, Shonkin leaned forward and flicked a switch. A cowbell beat and strong rock chords filled the room. Ned made eyes at Asher, who started tapping his hand. After a good thirty seconds of guitar solo, Shonkin turned the volume down.

'So, are you a kind of DJ for the BOD?' Matt asked.

Shonkin's eyes hardened and for a short but highly uncomfortable second, Asher thought that a storm was coming. But then he leaned back and laughed out loud, displaying a dismayingly large volume of half masticated Victoria sponge in the process. 'Hah. You could say that. Yeah, you most definitely could. What do you fancy, a bit of Deep Purple next? Or maybe a little Zep?' Shonkin shot them both expectant glances.

Matt returned a toothless smile and wiggled his head noncommittally; a clear indication to Asher that he was way out of his depth. Shonkin meanwhile slid out another vinyl disc and set it on the turntable. He got up, walked to one of the large varnished filing cabinets and slid out a drawer stuffed with hundreds of cards. He riffled through, pulled one out and slotted it into a small box next to the amplifier before setting the needle on the groove. 'Kashmir's driving, urgent strings kicked in.

'So, what is it I can do for you gentlemen?' Shonkin said, settling back into the armchair and turning down the volume.

'We're looking into vampire reversal,' began Matt. 'Ned here thought you were the man to see.'

Shonkin's expression was unreadable.

Asher shifted in his chair. 'Perhaps if you could you tell us what it is you actually do here, it might help.'

Shonkin turned to Asher. 'You're the necreddo, aren't you?'

Asher nodded.

'See Ned, I do read the memos.'

'Nice one,' Ned said, nodding at the in-joke.

'Well, Asher, what I do here is monitor the Bureau's auditory suppression policy on demonic transgression.'

Asher's frown was a mirror image of Matt's. But it was to Matt that Shonkin addressed the next part of his explanation.

'How many times, Matt, have you read, or heard, people claiming that popular music in the twentieth and twenty-first century is the work of the devil?'

Matt responded. 'Are you talking about those nutters with megaphones that stand on a box in the high street telling us to repent and claiming Elvis was the Antichrist?'

Shonkin nodded. 'That's it. You got it in one. Those 'nutters' you speak of represent the extreme end of a spectrum. You'd be surprised at how many punters think that all modern music is, in fact, the work of demons. Rhythmic drumming is known to alter brainwave activity and frequency, resulting in altered states. Entrainment of neuro-cortical chemistry was a known phenomenon as far back as your seventeenth century, though they didn't call it that, since they still thought that ground-up desiccated toad was an effective cure for the bubonic plague. Fact is, there are grounds for concern in that many demons use sound both to terrify and control. More coffee?' Shonkin replenished the cups.

'And it doesn't take much to modulate that sound and incorporate it in instrumentation, arrangement or, even, the human voice,' he continued. 'Lots of examples over the centuries. There was Cooper the Beguiler, for one. A few words from him and you'd be handing over all your wealth and removing your undergarments before you could say, 'Not now thanks, I've just eaten.' And then there was Sofia the Sly, whose voice could charm snakes. Ah, what a woman she was. Her voice could coax the robins from the branches or the gold fillings from your teeth, it could.' Shonkin lost himself in a fond recollection for a moment and then, as if seeing Matt for the first time, came back to himself. 'Of course, demons have no qualms about crossing over to the human world whenever they can. There have been some significant infringements over the years with you lot. Now let me think of the best example…'

'Tom Jones? He can usually get undergarments off after one verse of 'Sex Bomb',' Matt said.

'Nah, Tom is one of us,' Shonkin said, shutting his eyes in concentration. 'Like I said, it's not always music. There's the orators. Who was that berk who caused a bit of rumpus…' Shonkin hesitated for a moment longer and then his eyes snapped open in triumph. 'Got it. Hitler!'

Luckily for Matt, he was able to grab a large envelope from Ned's trolley to use as a shield with which to absorb most of the coffee and Victoria sponge that sprayed explosively from his mouth. Everyone watched and waited in helpless fascination as he gasped for air and his bulging eyes gradually started to recede.

'Something go down the wrong way?' Ned asked.

'Yes,' Matt said in a rasping voice. 'Hearing 'bit of a rumpus' and 'Hitler' in the same sentence.'

Asher took up the strands of conversation that Matt's

convulsion had left frayed and swaying in the breeze. 'So you're telling us that Hitler's voice was influenced by a demon?'

'Cloacastic the Revener. Took us a long time to get him back in his box, I can tell you. The bunker helped. Crap signal thirty feet underground. But that was why, some ten or so years after the rumpus, we decided to bring in rock music.'

Matt, still wiping crumbs from his face, looked up. '*You* brought in rock music?'

'Of course,' Shonkin said, sounding mildly affronted. 'We chose rock and roll as the simplest vehicle. Scattergun approach. Seemed to be the most effective in suppressing the majority of demonic frequencies. Hard rock followed, but then the demons fought back with happy house and polka music. Of course, over here, we've gone the folk route and my colleague on the other side of the corridor keeps tabs on that. I have to say that human technology has helped a lot. He used to have to go out to all the taverns of the land listening to 'My Woggle is a Dangler' a dozen times a week. He was close to burnout last year. At least now he can mix it up with a little rap if he wants to.'

Asher leaned forward keenly. 'So, if I understand this properly, you play selected music and…'

'Listen for the howling protests on the cans.' Shonkin picked up the earphones and wiggled them. Asher followed the wire to the wooden box with two dials. He noticed now that where there should have been numbers were strange symbols and what might have been runes.

'So you dial in the demon's number?'

'Not exactly, but it's a speed incantation. They're summoned to respond and I play them their favourite track to make absolutely sure it's causing them agony and pain. Only has to be heard once in a year and a day to suppress their ability to use the same cadence and frequency.'

'So radio stations…' Matt said.

'Do the job for us. But as tastes change, it's important we keep alive the old stuff. And, of course, there's research into the new. What do you think of tribal dubstep?'

'Umm,' Asher floundered.

'Definitely demonic. Take some liquorish tea before listening and you'll be fine.'

'I had no idea,' Matt said, and then turning to Ned added, 'but I don't see how any of this helps us.'

'Ah, but there's demons and there's demons, ain't there, Shonk?' Ned said.

Shonkin nodded sagely. 'Young Ned here has an old head on those young shoulders. He is right, of course. You're interested in vampires, right? Well, like all sentient beings, they too, are plagued by demons. You wouldn't think anyone would bother, would you? But the truth is, they are.'

'Shonk's done research into vampire demons, ain't you, Shonk?'

'My master's thesis was on the Demonology of the Kindred, that's true.'

'And that helps us how exactly?' Asher asked.

'Most demons have the simple aim of making everyone's existence as miserable as possible. That's their bread and butter and include in that the sandwich filling of eternal damnation. But when it comes to your vampire, he, or she—and some of the nastiest ones are female—is already eternal. So, their demons threaten mortality. The exact opposite of what most people fear. One of their demons, called Suty the Seditious, has a wailing curse that can turn a vampire back into a mortal being. Obviously, in the interest of fair play and equal opportunity, we have found a passable inhibiting frequency in Linkin Park's 'Blackout'. Know it?'

Matt nodded. 'Vaguely.'

'However, the correct modulation and frequency of the original Suty wail that keeps vampires honest occurs in a song called 'Caper 'Cross the Campions'. But only if sung in the style of one Tiny Tim.' He nodded at Matt. 'Every time a vampire hears that track it's like pouring acid on its soul. A dozen bars and the curse is ripped from him and he's mortal. He, of course, sees this as a terrifying punishment. And, come to think of it, so do I whenever I listen, but that's not the point. The song is banned everywhere that vampires exist. However, rumour has it that a Tiny Tim impersonator has been found in Tobler.'

'At the Frozen Ostrich clinic,' Ned said, looking pleased with himself.

Shonkin nodded. 'All highly illegal and difficult to prove. But if you're looking for answers, there may be some in Tobler and 'Caper 'Cross the Campions'. Now, how about some Wishbone Ash to finish off?' He got up and selected another vinyl from the shelves. ''Blowin' in the Wind' sends Poxter the Togre apeshit and it's about time he got a bit of gorilla guano.' He set the track up and then turned to his audience with another gap-toothed grin. 'Now, more cake anyone?'

CHAPTER SEVENTEEN

NEW THAMESWICK, FW

Simla DiFrance faced his audience in the basement at ICHOR with a heavy heart. A sea of powdered white faces stared back at him expectantly, waiting for him to speak. Though he had done this many times before, stood in front of the covered mirror to address the brave souls who fought their cravings daily, it had never been with such despondency. Gone was the excitement he'd felt on setting out on the venture. An excitement he could vividly recall the day he'd first put forward his plans with anticipation coursing through his veins like white water.

Emancipation, he'd called it. A new existence in a place where they could live safely in society. A stigma-free existence where the Glamour was so strong they could dispense with the embarrassing powdered faces and the ridiculous clothing and demonstrate how the control and discipline they followed would keep everyone safe. The visions had shown him the way. Shown them all what was possible. And his followers believed because they could see it for themselves.

But now someone or something was threatening to ruin it all.

DiFrance cleared his throat and began. 'You will all be aware of the spate of dreadful killings that are terrorising our brethren, those who eschew rehabilitation. The constabulary's visit here and their questions were unpleasant, but I have it on good authority that they are no further forward in finding the perpetrator. You will also be aware of the intelligence we received about unwelcome activity from our friends in the human world and that our colleague Digsbow needed to be warned. In a new and sinister twist, I regret to tell you that the warnings came too late. Cocket Digsbow has also fallen victim.'

A hiss skittered over the audience. DiFrance held up his hands.

'Details are as yet few and unformed. Suffice to say that Digsbow's mutilated body was found yesterday in his apartment, on the street outside, and, inexplicably, up the chimney.'

Les Reasonables fell silent.

DiFrance's tone remained grave. 'I know how shocking this must be for you all since some of you, if not all of you, knew Cocket personally. But it is vital we understand the ramifications this has for our purpose. Cocket was our sole distributor. Our link with the human world. His demise means that this vital and invaluable link has been severed. It means that we will be unable to forward any more totems to our distribution source. We must hope that what we have achieved thus far will carry us through and we *will* succeed in our goal. Remember, it will take only one human to open the door that will lead to our emancipation.'

'Will the visions continue?' A lone voice spoke up from the crowd.

DiFrance's chest constricted. The desperation and hope in that voice was almost palpable.

'There is no reason for them not to. Patience, my friends, is all that is required. Though we had a loyal ally in Cocket Digsbow, I will strive to find another, equally staunch supporter of the cause to carry us on to glory.'

The truth was Digsbow would do anything for a couple of hundred scruples and cared about as much for Les Reasonables' cause as anything living in a pond might. But the purely mercenary nature of their arrangement would not have fitted DiFrance's narrative well and he therefore avoided mention of it.

'Once I have more detail, I will, of course, inform you all. We will reconvene here this evening as usual.' DiFrance attempted a reassuring smile but the muscles of his face felt stiff as he forced his mouth into the correct shape. The result threw up a grimace of such horrifying proportions had Edvard Munch seen it he might have titled his masterpiece *LOL*.

Slowly, Les Reasonables rose in ones and twos and began to file out. DiFrance watched them go, standing alone as he always did, making himself available for any of the believers who wanted to talk. He stood, patiently, while the room emptied until only one white face remained near the back of the room. DiFrance peered and tried to make out the identity of the seated figure. Though he prided himself on his ability to do so, it was quite often very difficult to differentiate one powdered visage from the other, especially at a distance.

The figure remained in his seat until the last of the others left. The door swung shut yet the figure remained, staring at DiFrance until the leader felt compelled to speak.

'Cutlam, is that you?'

'There is another way,' Cutlam said, calmly and with conviction.

'Ah, Cutlam, ever the impatient one.'

'The bookshop. We could use the boy.'

DiFrance flinched and stuttered, 'How do you know about the boy…and the bookshop?'

'Digsbow and I were close. He confided in me.'

DiFrance took a few steps forward, dropping his voice low. 'He had no right to do so. It is best not to talk of such things. Our arrangements are delicate and secret. It is vital they stay so.'

Cutlam ignored the warning. 'Sitting here like sheep waiting for the wolf to call and hoping for the best is not a plan. We have to do something. We both know this is our only chance to cross over.'

Despite his determination to show fortitude, DiFrance's shoulders slumped. Cutlam's words cut through him like a stiletto since they vocalised the thoughts and feelings that preoccupied DiFrance for most of his waking hours of late. 'I realise the situation we now find ourselves in is frustrating. As the newest member of our order, I have found your enthusiasm invigorating and remarkable. But haste is the careful man's enemy.'

Cutlam dropped his chin and looked up at DiFrance with hooded eyes. 'Are we men, then?'

'No. But we can live like gods amongst them if we are patient.'

Cutlam shook his head. 'You've used that word more than once today. Patience! We both know you've used the darkness to animate the boy's uncle.'

DiFrance flinched and leaned in towards Cutlam so his urgent, desperate whisper would not be overheard. 'Digsbow had no right to discuss such things.'

'Use it again to help the boy understand what is required of him. It would be simple to—'

'It is not simple.' DiFrance hissed out the words, glancing left and right to make sure no one else could hear. 'What you suggest would involve possession and…' He shook his head vehemently. 'That I will not sanction.'

Cutlam glared defiantly. 'Then if not the boy, use his uncle. I know he is a revenant.'

'It is true we have delayed his passing for the moment, but that is not the same as willing the dead to—'

'Willing the dead is our only hope. You know it to be true.'

DiFrance shook his head. He was not used to discussing such things with the novices. With anyone. Yet Cutlam spoke with such assurance that DiFrance found himself marshalling his arguments instead of dismissing the discussion out of hand. 'Such acts require great power and the darkness would need paying. The price is too high.'

'But you could do it, couldn't you?'

Though Cutlam's eyes were hooded, a strange silver light glinted within their depths. Once again, in defiance of his instincts, which were to deny all knowledge of such dark acts, Cutlam's cutting, perspicacious questions forced DiFrance to consider the answers. He should deny all knowledge, yet such a denial would be a lie. He was skilled in many arts, it was true. Probably more skilled than any other of his kind. His tortuous course through a torrid life had taken him in many directions to arrive at this point. Several of his sojourns afforded him the luxury of study, more often than not at first hand; studies that did not feature on any curriculum in any university but were of a nature known to only a very few. Though his heart balked at the prospect, he felt compelled to answer Cutlam's question truthfully.

'Yes, I could. But it is not a thing to contemplate lightly. It requires a—'

'Sacrifice?' The word slipped easily from Cutlam's lips. So much so that DiFrance flinched again.

'Exactly. And so it is impossible. I will not be a party to another killing.'

Cutlam stood abruptly. He was not as tall as DiFrance, but his frame seemed suddenly to fill the vast room.

'We both know it's our only chance. Tell me what you need.'

DiFrance laughed. A dry, hollow sound. 'Nothing. I need nothing because it is never going to happen.'

A moment's silence followed in which the two stared at one another. It was Cutlam who broke the silence. 'What if I told you I could provide whatever is needed?'

'You cannot. For it to work the sacrifice has to be one of us. One of our own.'

'That can be arranged.'

DiFrance's eyebrows shot up to his thin red fringe. 'I will not be party to a murder.'

Cutlam smiled and on seeing it, DiFrance's innards flipped over like a tossed pancake.

'Who said anything about murder? I can get you a volunteer,' said Cutlam.

'Preposterous. Who in their right minds would…'

Cutlam pointed at his own chest. 'Me. I'll do it.'

DiFrance stared in horror. 'No, you can't. How could you even consider such a thing?'

'How long do you need to prepare?'

DiFrance suddenly couldn't think. He couldn't speak. Cutlam's proposition was monstrous, and yet the seed had been planted and was germinating like some putrid fungus in the black peat of the darkest portion of his brain and he was helpless to stop it. Still he could find no words to use.

'How long?' Cutlam repeated the question and its tone was such that DiFrance finally found his voice.

The reply slid out like an adder from under a rock. 'Half a day.'

'Will you need the mirror?'

'Yes, but—'

'I'll tell the others there will be a delay in tonight's visions. I'll meet you here alone. Send a servant with your list and I will fill it.' Cutlam turned and swept from the room, leaving

DiFrance quivering with shock. This went against everything he believed in and yet…and yet…his racing heart knew it to be the only way. Since he'd set his audacious plan in motion, he'd allowed himself to hope. But the light of expectation had faltered many times and, with Digsbow's demise, had sputtered and all but died. But now it flared again with renewed energy.

Could Cutlam be right?

He had already stepped over the threshold and used the darkness to good effect. The revenant spell had not been difficult to cast and Digsbow's instructions to the boy had been concise and accurate and he had complied. And complicity meant the boy was embroiled in the arrangements. Yet possession of a revenant asked much of the necromancer. It required a delicate touch as well as the violence of the sacrifice. DiFrance had studied such things on a purely academic level; it had to be that way since many of the texts were banned and anyone found in their possession was subject to severe penalty under New Thameswick's stringent necromancy laws. But what the law was ignorant of, it could do little about.

Though it ought not be, it could be done. And he, Simla DiFrance, could do it. With a new spring in his step, DiFrance left the viewing room and hurried up to his quarters. There he kept a black mirror that gave no reflection. But when his hand slid through the glass it would find a locked box. He hurried along. What he needed nestled inside that box.

CHAPTER EIGHTEEN

TOBLER, FW

As MOUNTAINOUS REGIONS FULL OF lakes and peaks go, Tobler was about as corrugated as they came. It had fjords and glaciers and, even at this time of year, was mostly covered in snow. If it had been a human country, it would probably have been overrun by artists with contracts for painting chocolate box covers and dippy nuns trying to find themselves through the medium of song.

But this Tobler was in Fae country and had once been a gnome enclave where tribal sectarianism held sway and where men feared to tread for fear of treading on a gnome, which usually resulted in the wrath of a thousand of the little buggers being visited upon the treader. In the bad old, pre-banking, pre-tobogganing, and pre-hoarding days, a dozen gnomes could swarm up an unsuspecting trouser leg—given that they were no more than nine inches tall—in five seconds flat, armed with very sharp implements. Seeing hardened warriors freeze and go deathly pale as they realised their most precious possessions were at the point, literally, of being scythed, stabbed, needled or otherwise rendered inoperative in a variety of painful ways, had led to the saying, 'Gnome is where the hurt is'.

However, as civilisation—or what passed as civilisation in a world where a mountain troll could, with one burp, set off an avalanche that could engulf three villages—advanced, the Tobler gnomes' other skill of magically secreting things in places no one could ever find them became a much sought-after commodity. Gnomes were quick and nosy and belligerent. Owning, and more importantly, keeping property safe had resulted in a branch of shamanism in which almost every gnome took part. You created a space in another dimension in which to keep your—or anyone else who cared to pay the rental's—stuff, and it stayed safe so long as you remembered the password. Since gnomes believed this space was in fact their own little corner of heaven—one they could access prior to death, a bit like picking out your own burial plot—and since they believed that heaven was a kind of endless snow-free mountain high in the sky, they called their independent magical storage system the meCloud.

The Frozen Ostrich, or, to give it its proper title, Vor Zen Ost Reich, was situated in the village of Klap, high in the eastern mountains. It took a good three days by cart from the capital city, and for many months of the year Klap got cut off by deep snow. Luckily for Asher and Matt, Shonkin had visited several times and, with the help of an Aperio, took the three of them off to a small hotel on the side of a snowy slope. The Kiefernzapf Spa was all dark wood and rickety stairs, but Shonkin managed to find them a room with a roaring fire at a reasonable cost. Outside, on the mountain, people were sliding down slopes on sleds and throwing snowballs at each other.

Matt went to the window to admire the view.

'Can't see anyone skiing or snowboarding,' he said after a few minutes of peering up and down.

'Whating?' asked Shonkin.

'Skiing. You know, on skis.'

Shonkin stared back with a blank expression.

'Two skis—like planks of wood— strapped to your feet so you can slide down in a controlled manner. Or, in the case of snowboarding, one piece of wood, a bit like an ironing board.'

'They do that where you come from, do they?' Shonkin asked.

Matt nodded. 'Yes, and pay a lot of money to go to somewhere like Tobler where it's cold and icy.'

'And it's easy to do, this…skiing?' Shonkin asked, his curiosity piqued.

'No. Takes a bit of practise. And a lot of falling over. All part of the fun.'

'And wearing these planks contributes to the falling over?'

'Well, yes.'

Shonkin frowned. 'Snow and ice are pretty slippery at the best of times. At least with a toboggan you're sitting down. Why would anyone want to make it more difficult to stand or walk on than it already is?'

'It's a sport,' explained Matt in exasperation. 'There are competitions to find out who can ski the fastest around obstacles. They even have ramps that send people skiing up into the air.'

'So they can fall further?' Shonkin asked casually.

'They tend to land. It's very graceful.'

'Sounds bloody dangerous to me,' Shonkin said. 'Anyway, I'll leave you two to it. Good mulled wine in the bar and the specialty cheese fondue is great, so long as you don't want any sleep.'

'Heartburn?' Asher asked.

'It's not called that, though that's not a bad attempt. The villagers who make it call it the flytrap, on account of it being able to attract flies—even when left adjacent to an open sewer. Has double the fly-trapping quality once it's passed through the human digestive tract and emerges as gas. So,' Shonkin gave them both a lopsided smile, 'I'll leave you to it. Don't be strangers. Sometimes I get really mellow, put on some Tangerine Dream and eat some mescaline cupcakes with a little LSD topping. If you're ever around, it's a trip.'

Matt and Asher watched him exit through the bathroom door.

'What a great guy,' Matt said.

'Who or what are Tangerine Dream?' Asher asked.

'The daddies of electronica,' Matt explained. 'German ambient, Krautrock, call it what you will. Still going as far as I know. Hey, did you think Shonkin looked a bit like…you know, that guy from the Stones?'

'What stones do you speak of, Matt?'

'Don't come the confused Fae. You know who I mean. The eyeliner, the headband, and the quasi-anorexia are a dead giveaway. I know Bobby's a fan.'

'She is indeed. And I agree, there is a passing resemblance. However, isn't it possible that said artist might have, in fact, modelled himself on Shonkin rather than the other way around?'

Matt's guffaw died when the look on Asher's face didn't change. 'Are you serious?'

'Shonkin has been around a long time. Maybe he turned up to some of the early gigs. Before the band members had settled into their iconic roles. Maybe someone fancied his look?'

'It would explain—'

'A lot. Yes, I know.' Asher nodded. 'Now, what about the Frozen Ostrich?'

Matt shrugged. 'We stick to the plan. We just have to get in there. See if there's any truth to the rumours.'

'And if there is?'

Matt tapped his pocket. 'We go the tech route.'

'Will your technology work here?'

'Yes. It's sealed in a krudian bubble field. I made sure of that.'

'Okay. But getting in promises not to be at all easy. Shonkin said their application process is rigorous.' Asher stared pointedly at Matt.

'If you have any better ideas, I'm willing to listen,' Matt replied.

Asher shrugged. They'd been through this a hundred times and still Matt's idea was by far the best one. 'Okay,' Asher nodded. 'I'll go down to the bar for a bit of reconnaissance while you change.'

The lounge at the Kiefernzapf Spa had made an effort in order to attract the après-tob crowd. The pale wood and burnished steel furniture was a great improvement on the dark and gloomy stained pine featured everywhere else. But the presence of at least four cuckoo clocks on the walls meant no escape from Tobler's tourist mantra.

Asher ordered a small beer from a pigtailed blonde barmaid dressed in a frilly white blouse, red skirt with frilly hem, and black bodice with ruched trim. At some point, the designer of the garb might have visualised a traditional Tobler costume, but then had gone away and decided to revamp it using a third of the necessary material. It might have looked great on a ten year old, since it was clearly cut to fit someone of that age. Unfortunately, the barmaid had seen ten, quadrupled it and added a few more for good luck. Asher was left wondering if a crowbar made up part of Heidi's wardrobe accessories, since she'd obviously used something with leverage to cram all that flesh into those wire reinforced cups. She poured Asher's beer into a glass, or rather poured two inches of beer that frothed up to fill the rest of the glass, and delivered it with a smile and a deliberate leaning forward of her upper body to reveal two good reasons for Asher to want to jump on the nearest toboggan.

He thanked her and took his beer to the far end of the

lounge where a booth, much like a confessional, had been set up. Shonkin, in passing, had mentioned these gnome booths and they intrigued Asher. He paused to read the printed sign.

Family Heirlooms?
Art?
Gold?
Precious items?
Confidences?
Allow us to creatively secrete it for you in our labyrinthine meCloud vaults.
Guaranteed authority-proof storage.

Asher pulled back the curtain and peered in. On a chest-high ledge sat a very small...person with a white beard and spectacles, dressed in a pointy hat and leather waistcoat. He looked up as the curtains opened.

'Vot can I do for you, young man?'

'Can I ask you some questions?'

'Kvestions? About vot?''

'About what it is you actually do?'

The gnome shrugged. 'Vee are happy to help people when zey have money, or ozer valuables, to keep safe.'

'And does it matter where those valuables come from?'

The gnome sat forward, steepled his fingers and peered at Asher over his glasses. 'Possession is nine tenths of zee law. Here zee other tenth is ignored unless it turns up with a sword vile zee transaction is being undertaken, in vich case vee usually return zee items.'

'And this applies to individuals and countries, I take it?'

'Vee like to stay neutral. Money does not bleed. Secrecy is our vatchvord.'

'And what about the rest? What about confidences? What does that actually mean?'

The gnome peered at Asher thoughtfully before sitting back. 'Please close zee curtains.'

Asher complied.

'Now, Mr…?'

'Lodge.'

'Now, Mr Lodge, it occurs to me zat you are not simply a tourist here.'

'I am not. What I need to know is if the rumours are true. Can you keep anything in those vaults? Secrets, even?'

The gnome nodded. He pointed towards a wire helmet hanging on the wall. 'Vith zee geegnome extractor, vee can remove anyzing for safe-keeping. Thoughts, secrets, ideas.'

Asher smiled. 'Really? And how much might that set one back?'

'Thirty scruples per month. Of course, vee allow a twenty-four hour cooling-off period in case someone changes zeir mind.'

Asher grinned. 'What a great idea. Could you give me a minute?' He ducked out of the booth, took a healthy swallow of beer, which dealt with almost all of it bar the froth, and then took the stairs back to the room two at a time. As he entered, something large and white with a face as pale as bleached bone crossed in front of him.

Asher started and picked up a convenient chair to brandish.

'Trick or treat,' said Matt and gave a twirl.

'Wow,' Asher said, putting the chair down. 'Love the colour scheme.'

'White is in, so I've heard.'

'It is that. In your hair, the carpet, and the walls.'

'I had a bit of a problem opening the tin of talc. Wouldn't unscrew but then sort of exploded when I tapped it against the edge of the table. Anyway, question is would I pass as one of Les Reasonables?'

Asher looked at Matt appraisingly and managed, with

some effort, to conclude that anyone who cared to dress exclusively in oyster-coloured trousers and a light grey tunic and powder their face the colour of a frosted doughnut would probably pass, but instead said, 'Brilliant.'

'Right.' Matt sighed. 'Should we go through the story one more time. We are lovers—'

'Brothers,' corrected Asher.

'Shouldn't we move with the times?' Matt protested.

'This is Tobler, not San Franchenko.'

'It's San Francisco,' Matt corrected.

'Foggy place with a red bridge. Whatever.' Asher walked around the frosted Matt appraisingly. 'I am convinced blood ties will hold more sway.'

'Okay, okay.' Matt nodded and sent a begrudging eyes-to-the-ceiling look back at Asher. 'We're brothers from New Thameswick—'

'From East Charmony. It borders Oneg and would lend a great deal more credence to our story.'

'What's it like, East Charmony?'

'Lederhosen, compulsory sausage for breakfast, an inability to say the word 'squirrel' and no sense of humour. But don't ever tell them because they do not find it funny.'

'Okay, East Charmony it is. I was seduced by an Oneg girl, got bitten and now despite having tried rehab, I am desperate to convert back to being human, right?'

'Correct. And your name?'

'Dieter Kruger.'

'And I am Andreas Kruger.'

'Right,' Matt said. 'Let's go.'

Asher didn't move.

'What?' asked Matt.

'I've heard they interrogate people pretty thoroughly in this place. There are always do-gooders trying to poke their noses in. They have a thing about people getting in under false pretences. Journalists especially.'

Matt's expression was unreadable under the talc, but his tone implied irritation. 'Well, we'll just have to tough it out, won't we?'

'Have you done much undercover work?'

'Only with Kylah.' Matt's grin looked grotesque in his floury face.

'You know what I mean.'

'No. But I've watched the boxset of *The Wire* if that's any good.'

'Just as I thought. But the good news is that we are in Tobler,' Asher said. 'And Tobler is renowned for its gnomes. And these gnomes are experts in hiding things.'

'Yeah?' Matt said in a tone clearly suggesting that he was struggling to follow Asher's train of thought.

'There's a gnome booth in the bar. Why don't I let him explain?'

'You want me to go into the bar dressed like a terminally anaemic Cambodian dictator?'

'Pretend you're on a bull do.'

'It's stag do, and anyway, who in their right minds would dress up as a quasi-rehabilitated vampire on their stag do?' Matt paused to think about what he'd just said and then nodded. 'Yeah, okay. Stag do it is.'

In the bar, Matt drew a few glances, but it is astonishing how a determination to enjoy oneself after a hard day's tobogganing refuses to allow annoying distractions like Morris dancers, students playing beer pong or even a rehab vampire to distract one for too long. Asher went straight to the booth and made the introductions. The Gnome listened, pointed toward the geegnome, agreed on a price and, after not much persuasion, Matt saw the sense of it.

———

TEN MINUTES LATER, Dieter and Andreas Kruger left the Kiefernzapf Spa and made their way along the snowy pavements towards Klap's commercial sector and a pink four-storey building sandwiched between two larger half-timbered houses. On the wall of the pink house the panels between the first and second and second and third storeys were elaborately decorated with images of birds and trees beneath window boxes full of Christmas cacti. The sign over the door had a silver pointed spear as its motif under the words, *Vor Zen Ost Reich*, and underneath in a text that kept changing to suit whomsoever was looking at it, said, *Enter Only the Pure of Heart*.

Matt looked at Asher. There were tears in his eyes as he spoke. 'At last Andreas, here vee are.'

Asher nodded. 'Yes, Dieter. At last.' He took Matt's arm and led him across the street to the studded front door of The Frozen Ostrich. A sonorous C-sharp tone rang out inside the building when Asher yanked on the brass bell pull. He was glad of the distraction since he didn't want to look at Matt, who gazed in awe at the carved panels like a troubled, sick patient might gaze at the entrance to a famous hospital, or the caves at Lourdes. In his eyes burned hope for salvation. Asher found that look troubling. He'd known Matt for as long as Matt had been a part of the DOF and was more used to a look driven by a cynical humour and an almost manic determination not to take anything too seriously. But that was long gone to be replaced by a highly uncomfortable mixture of loss and terror.

The door to the Frozen Ostrich opened to reveal a serious-looking dark-haired woman dressed in a white floor-length tunic under a blue apron. She wore an old-fashioned coif over her hair and an even older-fashioned expression behind dark-rimmed glasses on a face that seemed to have forgotten what a smile was.

'Yes?'

'Ah, yes, hello,' said Asher. 'I won…von…vonder if—' His

stumbling explanation ended when Matt fell to his knees in supplication.

'Please, please help me. I am a soul in torment. Zee red river flows vizin me. I lust after zat which gives life, and yet to satiate my cravings I must rob ozers of zeir lifeblood. Please… you must help me. We haff travelled from East Charmony to get here.'

The nurse, because that was what Asher had decided she must be, looked up from the distraught Matt at Asher. 'Do you haff an appointment?'

'No, we haff travelled far in the hope that we might—'

'Entry is by appointment only.'

'But—'

'Please,' wailed Matt. 'Do not tax my brozer, for he is simple of mind.'

Asher glared at Matt.

'Zis is not a valk-in clinic,' explained the nurse.

'Zen I must valk the streets for I feel zee hunger come upon me.' Matt made a sucking noise with his teeth that told everyone in the vicinity, namely Asher and the nurse, that what he lusted after was warm and red and packaged in pink.

The nurse's eyes narrowed and, Asher noted, softened from diamond to tempered steel. 'Many people try and gain entry under false pretences. If you are here under false pretences, zee consequences for you vill be severe.'

'You can see my brother is desperate. He wish…vishes to be rid of the red fever before he causes more suffering,' Asher said.

The nurse paused, looked down at her clogs and then back up at Asher. 'Very vell. You may come in. I vill take you to zee reception area vere vee vill interview you.'

She led them along a soothingly lit corridor to a tasteful seating area.

'Vait here,' she instructed and closed the door, leaving Asher and Matt alone in the stark corridor.

'You're doing great,' Asher whispered. 'I think she's taking the bait.'

Matt turned to him. 'Vot is zis bait of vich you speak, Andreas?'

Asher frowned. 'So you have absolutely no recollection of the gnome?'

'Ah yes, zee gnome. Remember vat our little old grey-haired mozer told us about Tobler? It is a place full of userers and vomen of loose virtue. If vee see a gnome vee must run zee ozer way for fear of zem stealing our memories. I do not believe all our poor mozer tells us, but still, it vould be better to stay true to our task, yes?'

'And Shonkin?' Asher said airily.

'Why should I not remember our village butcher's dog? Andreas, are you vell? Has the journey taken its toll upon your mind?'

'My mind is ticking along fine, thanks for asking.'

Matt sent a nervous glance towards the closed door. 'Vot do you zink she is doing, Andreas?'

'Not listening to this conversation, I hope.'

'They say zat Vor Zen Ost Reich vill eizer cure or send a vampire completely mad.' Matt turned to Asher and grabbed his coat lapels in both hands. 'If I go mad, svear zat you will look after our mutti and our little brozer, Helmut, and our dear little sister, Kamilla. I know zat your vish is to join zee navy and vear a hat viz a pointy spike, but if I am not zere…'

'I'll look after them, don't you worry,' Asher said and received a full-on Matt bear hug in response. 'Just after I've planted those magic beans I've swapped for our cow,' he muttered into Matt's white tunic.

Matt pulled back. 'You have magic beans?'

'Joke,' Asher said.

Matt frowned. 'Joke?'

'Ah yes, what was I thinking.' Asher nodded. 'We are from

East Charmony after all. Fun and frippery are dirty words there, aren't they?'

Matt blushed. 'You know I do not hold vith svearing, Dieter. Promise me you vill vash your mouth out vith carbolic.'

Asher nodded again, half turned to face the back door and wiped his hand through his hair as he said, to no one in particular, 'I have a feeling this is going to be a very, very long day.'

CHAPTER NINETEEN

NEW THAMESWICK, FW

SIMLA DIFRANCE WALKED THROUGH the ICHOR building without seeing a soul. Admittedly, he was making a journey he normally made an hour later in the day, yet the place felt eerily deserted. In this time after their evening meal, most of Les Reasonables took the opportunity to meditate. And today, after the dire message he'd given them, there was indeed much to contemplate. He realised, too, that his own sense of excitement and anticipation at what he was about to do had heightened his awareness to such an extent that he felt he might hear the scratching of a mouse behind the skirting, if any mouse dared stray into a building where the presence of a warm-blooded animal resulted in the occupants tearing down the wall in a feeding frenzy to get at it. There was such a thing as temptation and so vermin control was a top priority at ICHOR.

The doors to the old ballroom were locked and though he had a key, Simla knocked gently.

'Who is it?' whispered a voice from the other side.

'It is I, Simla DiFrance.'

The lock clicked and the door swung open to reveal Cutlam on the other side. Simla slipped through and heard Cutlam lock the door behind him. The sheets had been removed from the large mirror. On the floor in front of it as DiFrance had instructed, Cutlam had laid out a circle of salt with thirty candles forming a ring of light beyond.

'Are you ready?' Cutlam asked.

'Are you?' DiFrance replied. He had decided during his preparations that afternoon to allow Cutlam an opportunity to retract his offer at any time. He would allow it without recrimination. What had passed between the two of them would remain between the two of them and no one else need ever know. And yet, DiFrance found himself once again astonished by the total absence of any sign of nervousness on the part of the rehab novice.

'Oh, I am,' said Cutlam. 'I'm always ready. And I know how much we're all going to benefit from what we do here tonight.'

DiFrance nodded, disconcerted yet again by the smile that crept over Cutlam's lips. Here was true believer in the cause and no mistake.

'My preparations should not take very long,' DiFrance said and laid out the contents of the bag slung around his shoulder: blackened bones, black candles, something very dry and flaky that had once hopped, several vials containing a variety of dark liquids, and a ripe plum.

'Is the plum of a special kind?' Cutlam asked.

DiFrance looked up in confusion. 'The plum? No, it needs only to be ripe. Unfortunately, I missed half of this evening's meal and I will undoubtedly be hungry. Now, give me room to arrange things.' DiFrance moved towards the prepared circle and began setting out the black candles in the shape of a pentagram.

'Difficult to do this necromancy lark then, is it?' Cutlam asked from a safe distance.

'The spells and incantations are there for all to read in any grimoire you'd care to purchase.' DiFrance said. 'However, as with all aspects of thaumaturgy, there is much to be learned in the preparation and delivery.'

'Bit like cooking then, is it?'

'I suppose—'

'I mean, you and I could get exactly the same ingredients from Condiments the grocer and you might end up with a soufflé and me with scroggled egg.'

'Yes, I—'

'S'all about flair and knowing just how long to whisk the whites, how hot the pan needs to be, and how long to grill it for.'

DiFrance paused in his labours. 'You seem to know quite a bit about food, Cutlam?'

'Yeah. Thought about being a chef once. But I was no good at all that prep. What I was good at was foraging and hunting. More garrotte than carrot, if you know what I mean.'

'Indeed,' DiFrance said.

'So with this stuff you're doing, saying the words is only a part of it, right?'

DiFrance lit the candles. 'Yes, it is the tone and enunciation that holds all the power. A reasonable analogy might be opera singing, I suppose. The great castrati, Jean de Collette, used to say that he would see the notes as shapes in his head. Presumably he had neither the need nor drive to imagine any other shapes. But that's exactly what one does here. The words take a shape and it is that shape that is sent out into the world and takes on power.'

'Words,' Cutlam said.

'Words,' DiFrance agreed.

'And once they're out there, I suppose it's hard to take them back?'

DiFrance nodded. 'That is why such things are so dangerous. Dark energy tends, like water, to flow towards a larger body. Damming it and controlling it is the key. Not controlling it leads to disaster.'

Cutlam's eyes glittered so brightly they made DiFrance stop what he was doing. 'You seem very interested.'

Cutlam nodded. 'Death's on his way here. I have the right to know how he's flying in.'

'Certainly,' DiFrance said in an earnest voice. 'Certainly. I'll be happy to explain.'

Of course, 'happy to explain' was usually just a throwaway remark. Something you said after conveying complicated and unpleasant news, such as the need to remove someone's gall bladder through a hole the size of a ha'penny using long bits of metal not unlike unbent coat hangers. A dangling invitation offered in the expectation that it was highly unlikely to be taken up. Most people, when faced with such an offer, simply swallowed in the hope that they might retain their lunch and decline with a shake of their heads. They didn't *need* to know, not really. So long as the bloke explaining *did*. That was the basic contract between expert and punter.

But then there was always one clever dick who harboured dreams of being a surgeon, or a thaumaturgist, who'd want to know all the gory details such as the gauge of sutures used, or the precise wording of the incantation voiced. Cutlam, it seemed, was definitely a gauge of sutures sort of bloke. DiFrance found himself explaining things in the finest detail to a rapt listener who, though he obviously did not understand all of it, gave the impression that he almost, *almost* did. And the effect this had on DiFrance, in defiance of all his misgivings about what they were about to do, was to turn on the academic tap. DiFrance had been given little or no opportunity to talk about the arcane things he'd learned to anyone, so now that he had an avid listener, the floodgates opened.

'This conjuration is my own modification of those used by

the practitioners of old. I have modelled it on more, how should I put it, *modern* wonderworking techniques. Though it is of course essential that the performance of such an invocation should only be undertaken by one whose imagination and will has been honed by and attuned to the supernatural world. It remains the case that such invocations require much energy. However, in my modification I do not use the head of a cat who has been fed nothing but human flesh for a week.'

'Glad to hear it,' Cutlam said. 'I quite like cats. They're… mysterious.'

'However, I do use a cap embroidered with the signs of Moon, Jupiter, and Pluto. We will burn camphor and storax. We have, in the bottles, blood from a variety of sources, namely goat, bull, and bat. I do not use the ashes of the dead as the salts. Here we have refined the spell to use nothing more than nail clippings.'

'My old dad used to keep all his in a stone jar,' Cutlam reminisced. '"Never know when they might come in handy," he'd say. By the look of it he was right all along.'

DiFrance cleared his throat. 'The alchemy is also distilled from my own studies. The cypress and alder wood fire is now nothing more than two lit sticks coated in amber. This is necessary, for the invocation will open the gate and allow us to communicate with Aerich, a demon whose strong point is not personal hygiene.'

'Looks like you've done your homework.'

DiFrance nodded. 'We will break the circle once Aerich is here. The boy's uncle, O'Malley, will be compelled to listen and do as I say. Then it will be time for human blood to be spilled. Then, and only then, must we weald the knife and this you must do yourself. I have sharpened the weapon so that one, perhaps two strokes will suffice.'

'So, how do we start?' asked Cutlam, his eyes shining once again with that intense light.

'Candles. A circle within the circle drawn in blood with a

dagger used for death. We leave a gap in that inner circle. It is through this gap that I will communicate.'

Cutlam nodded. 'So we're good to go?'

'Except for thirty minutes of chanting the invocation.'

'Thirty minutes?' Cutlam protested.

'Please, it used to be five hours.' DiFrance finished his preparations, fell to his knees and began to chant in a language known to only a very few and whose inflections and correct pronunciations was known to even fewer. After a minute he opened his eyes and spoke to Cutlam.

'Now, give me that blackened bone. It's O'Malley's thumb. Shot off during some war or other.'

Cutlam picked up the piece of blackened bone and examined it carefully before handing it across the circle. DiFrance took it and closed his eyes to begin the invocation again.

'*Jasch keot, pelindras torgu ad sjost et funudoth. Jasch keot, pelindras torgu ad sjost et funudoth. Jasch keot, pelindras torgu ad sjost et funudoth Jasch keot, pelindras torgu ad sjost et funudoth...*'

As the words flowed, so the light in the room began to diminish. DiFrance remained conscious of Cutlam sitting, his face intense and alert, but gradually, to match the dimming light, his awareness of the surroundings faded. In its place grew another awareness. One that cleared just as reality diminished. After fifteen minutes the ballroom disappeared to be replaced by a vast, treeless plain. Stunted grass and corkscrew bushes were all that was visible except for a doorway in the far distance that grew slowly as it moved towards him. He'd been to this point many times before during dress rehearsals for the real thing. But always he'd stopped before the door opened. Once he had seen a violet light appear through the tiniest crack and had beaten a hasty retreat by ceasing the invocation. But today there would be no retreat. Buoyed, DiFrance concentrated on his chanting and saw the door accelerate, fed by his conviction and desire to finally see this through.

A wind began to blow, fierce and dry as if from some vast desert with the hint of something foul, almost tidal, on its breath. DiFrance felt his lips begin to smart and crack, but still he persisted for he knew that these were merely challenges, tests for the uncommitted. He persisted, the seconds turning to minutes as the words flowed one after the other.

'*Jasch keot, pelindras torgu ad sjost et funudoth. Jasch keot, pelindras torgu ad sjost et funudoth…*'

The door came to a halt within reach of his outstretched hand. He touched the surface and it felt smooth and yielding, more like flesh than wood. This then was the final act. It was up to him to open the door and interact with what was beyond. Steeling himself, the chant now an automatic mantra he had no need to control, DiFrance gripped the doorknob and turned the handle. The door flew open and DiFrance squinted against a violet light that suddenly flared white. The screams of a thousand tortured souls beat at his ears and the smell of fetid decay and corruption made him gag. A figure appeared in the centre of the light. It moved forward, shadows dancing forth like a dark aurora. The noise of the wind redoubled, so forceful it threatened to blow DiFrance over. He reached for the doorframe with one hand to brace himself, the other shielding his eyes from the battering, hot wind, which swirled and gusted about him. And all the while the dark figure grew and grew until, at last, it stepped through onto the plain.

The wind died instantly and, blinking furiously, DiFrance opened his eyes to confront the demon Aerich, his mouth paper dry, his brain reeling.

Though he'd read extensively of demons and seen his fair share, nothing could have prepared him for what stood in front of him on that vast metaphysical plain. Aerich stood six feet tall, its features strong and moulded unmistakably into that of a male with untidy, frizzy hair of shoulder length. But it was how Aerich was dressed that momentarily befuddled

DiFrance. First of all, there was the large bow attached to a white hairband and worn to one side of the crown of Aerich's head. The bow almost matched the pale blue colour of the puffed, short-sleeved calf-length dress it wore. A white pinafore with frilled edging, white stockings, and ballet pumps topped off the look.

'Aerich, guardian of the doorway, I command you to—'

'Yeah, yeah,' said Aerich. 'Forget the schtick. Who is it you want to communicate with? I haven't got all day. I'm late for my ceramics class as it is.'

DiFrance frowned. 'Ceramics class?'

'Yes. Ceramics class. It's what's trending. Demons have hobbies too, you know. It can get bloody boring waiting eons for the next call. So, we've started a little group. Pottery in a frock. Suits some of us, pisses off a whole lot of others.'

DiFrance could only nod. If there were any words suitable for the occasion, they were in a dark wood somewhere at dusk without a compass.

Aerich watched him, its eyes slitting in calculation. 'It's the dress, isn't it?'

'Well, I…' DiFrance's inadequate reply sputtered and died.

'I knew I should have worn that dogtooth suit. But last week that tart Soffit turned up in an evening dress, so I thought, sod you, Soffit, I'll go all Alice today. But this bloody bow…the colour is all wrong. The dress is cornflower and the bow is moonstone. I knew it as soon as I saw it, but what's a girl to do?'

'What…indeed.' DiFrance was so nonplussed he was almost a minus. 'And you do this because?' He let the sentence dangle.

'For a bit of attention, obviously. But this is mild compared with some. You should see Conrach the Violator. He comes in a vulture feather fascinator and spike heels. Bloody show-off.'

'I see.'

'No, you don't. But do I give a tinker's? No, I do not. But I'm here and I don't want to be, so who is it you want again?'

'O'Malley.'

'Ah yes, you did dial in with his thumb bone. Sorry, I was distracted. Right, here goes.' Aerich stood back and let DiFrance cross the threshold. He stepped into the bedroom above the Inky Well. The smell of decay was worse here. Connor O'Malley lay motionless on the bed, little more now than a bag of bones.

DiFrance recommenced the incantation. '*Jasch keot, pelindras torgu ad sjost et funudoth. Jasch keot, pelindras torgu ad sjost et funudoth…*'

O'Malley's inert body twitched and, with a distressing squelch, one eyelid opened to reveal the pallid globe behind, the cornea as dull as a cod's. Slowly, DiFrance moved across the floor, conscious of the fact that his feet did not tread on solid ground. From his robe he removed a piece of parchment upon which were written instructions. DiFrance scrunched the parchment into a small ball and inched forward, O'Malley's baleful eye watching his approach. When he was near enough, the old man's mouth opened to reveal a few grey teeth and a white and yellow-coated tongue. DiFrance leaned in and placed the parchment ball into the corpse's open mouth. The teeth closed and the body jerked once, twice, and then shook violently.

'Follow these instructions to the letter,' said DiFrance.

O'Malley's body convulsed and then lay still. The scene was already fading as DiFrance took one backward step to find himself standing on the wrong side of the doorway with Aerich standing guard. 'Get what you needed?'

'I have fulfilled the task.'

'Good, good. So, payment in full and you get to cross back over.'

'I need to speak to my assistant.'

Aerich shrugged and smoothed down its apron with hands tipped by four-inch-long painted fingernails.

DiFrance leaned forward, both hands on the doorframe. The vast plain ended there. Beyond lay the ballroom and the circle of candlelight. Cutlam was waiting on the edge of the circle. 'Now,' said DiFrance. 'You must do it now.'

Cutlam had the knife in his hands and both of his wrists bared. In one swift movement, he shot out his right hand and grabbed the hair on the head above DiFrance's obligingly craning neck, thrust his forearm between the vimp's teeth and yanked his head forward. DiFrance's canines penetrated skin and sliced through muscle and veins until Cutlam yanked the head backwards and pulled his arm free.

DiFrance spluttered. There was red blood all around his mouth. 'What are you doing?' he protested. It was the last thing he ever said. The knife moved smoothly in several long, practiced, scything slices. There were a few rasps, and a lot of pluming red stuff, and then DiFrance's head toppled lifeless to the floor.

On the other side of the doorway, Aerich watched and shrugged. 'Okay, I admit I wasn't expecting that. Still, payment is complete.' The demon leaned forward and stuck its painted face through the door. It appeared two feet above Cutlam.

'Nice one,' Aerich said, taking in the white face. 'But I think you've overdone it a bit with your foundation. The task will commence immediately. Good doing business with you.' It pulled back and disappeared.

In the ballroom, Cutlam stood in front of the mirror and waited.

CHAPTER TWENTY

TOBLER, FW

Matt and Asher—sorry—Dieter and Andreas did not have long to wait. The nurse returned within a few short minutes and this time she was not alone.

'Your names?' the nurse asked.

Asher answered. 'I am Andreas Kruger and this…zis is my brother…brozer, Dieter.'

She nodded. 'My name is Sister Eva Mia Sofia Laura Varengewissenschaftschaferswessenschafewarenwohlgepflege-undsorgfaltigkeitbeschutzen. Patients usually call me Sister Ems. My two colleagues behind me are orderlies.'

The two alpine trolls behind her grunted. Both of them had slight stoops from having to negotiate ceilings not designed for their kind.

Sister Ems sat, her hands folded primly on her lap. 'Now, in your own vords, please tell me of your journey.'

Matt obliged as Dieter. He told her of how a hunting trip in the forest bordering Oneg led him to stray from the party and to meet up with a girl who'd told him she was foraging for mushrooms. They struck up a friendship. She was very beautiful. Whenever he could, Dieter would find his way to the little glade where they'd first met and they would talk. She told him of her lonely life and of how her father, the woodsman, forbade her from seeing other people. Dieter became desperate to help the girl, but she would not let him touch her during daylight because the woods had eyes and ears. Finally, after days of persuasion, she agreed to meet him in an after-dark tryst. It was his undoing. And Matt's descriptions of what took place after midnight in the moonlit glade involved quite a lot of undoing. Asher listened to the embellishments with growing disquiet, but one look at Sister Ems's face told him that Matt had judged things perfectly. More than once, the po-faced nurse had to run a finger around the inside of her collar. Particularly when Dieter described the poignant moment he got bitten. A moment involving some moaning from Matt and a lot of head movement on the part of the vampire in an area well south of the jugular.

Of course, it helped enormously that Matt actually believed all this had happened.

'Zat is one of the vorst cases I haff come across,' Sister Ems said when Matt finished.

The old Matt would have muttered something coarse at the innuendo, but he didn't. Dieter wouldn't know what it meant.

'Seduction of zee innocents is so despicable.' Sister Ems shook her head.

'And since zen I haff had to feed at least once a veek.' Matt wrung his hands. 'Livestock mainly, but zen zere was zis one poor boy who I almost…'

'Please,' Sister Ems got up and knelt in front of Matt, taking his hands in hers, 'do not torment yourself any furzer. You haff done zee right zing. You haff come before zee fever has taken complete control. But vee must subject you to a trial of concept. Zee treatment is long and difficult. Vee haff to know if you are vone of zee lucky vones.'

'Vat if he is one…vone of the…zee unlucky vones?' asked Asher.

'Zough vee haff excellent results here at zee clinic, not everyvone is susceptible. A sad but very true fact. In your brozer's case, vee vould subject him to a short exposure to see if he responds. It prevents us from giving false hope.'

'And we…vee can do that now?'

'Of course,' she said. 'It only involves a few short minutes. If zee response is positive, vee can enrol Dieter into zee program. If it is not, vee can put you in touch with our sister organisation, VAT.'

'Dare I ask?' said Asher.

'Vampirisch Asylum Toblergnomen.'

'And zat does vot, exactly?'

'Locks away dangerous recidivistic monsters in an isolated castle. Now, all vee need Dieter to do is follow us and remove all of his cloze.' Sister Ems smiled. 'He needs to shed his past.'

Matt immediately began taking off his robe.

'Not here,' said Sister Ems.

Asher did not like the light that flickered in her eyes nor the shadow of a smile that twitched across her lips.

'Am I allowed to come, too?' Asher asked.

'Of course,' said Eva. 'It is important. If everyzing goes to plan, it vill be your opportunity to say goodbye to your brozer for the next two veeks. Vee do not allow any contact until zee program is complete.' She turned to Asher. 'If I could ask you to fill out zee forms vile Dieter gets ready.' Sister Eva handed over a clipboard.

Asher took it and embraced his 'brother', Dieter. An awkward moment followed while Asher slid off a small jade amulet in the rough shape of a fish with golden fins from around his neck. 'I know you said he needs to shed his past, but can he vear zis? It is our family symbol. We have many vaterfalls in East Charmony. The fish haff to leap tall in order to travel up rivers to spawn. To us zey represent perseverance and success. I want him to vear mine since Dieter's vas taken by zee monster who did zis to him.'

Sister Ems hesitated, but then nodded and Asher slipped the amulet over Asher's head. A cascade of white powder fell at Asher's feet.

'Now, by zee time you complete zee details, vee vill be ready for zee trial. Come, Dieter, no harm vill become you here. You are amongst friends.'

A quill in an inkbottle sat on a small desk next to the window. Asher sat and scribbled the fictitious details provided for them by the BOD. When he'd finished, he rang a small bell. One of the orderlies returned and, expressionless, took the clipboard. 'Follow me,' he grunted.

Asher followed through several doors and along half a dozen corridors down into the bowels of the building. And as they descended, so the doors got thicker and the locks more elaborate until at last they came to a gate of heavy iron bars. Asher walked through into a gallery area separated by thick glass from a room below. A room whose walls were padded with sheep's wool. To one side sat a cot and sink and bucket. Matt sat on the edge of the cot wearing nothing but a white towel and the amulet Asher had given him.

Sister Ems appeared at Asher's elbow. 'Ah, Mr Kruger. Glad you could join us. Vee are ready to commence zee proof of concept. Vee vill simply observe from zis vantage point.'

'Vot are you looking for?' Asher asked.

'Zee appropriate reaction.'

'Wit…sorry, vitch is?'

'Vee vill know ven vee see it.' She nodded back at the orderly, who quickly disappeared from view. A few seconds later, one wall of the padded cell Matt occupied slid away to reveal more bars, this time more widely spaced to allow a clearer view between them. Beyond was a small and dimly lit stage. Asher watched in fascination as onto the stage stumbled a man clutching a ukulele. The man lurched slightly and Asher wondered if he might be slightly drunk. Tall and gangly, the man wore a brown and mustard checked suit and a Tyrolean hat complete with feather. He had teeth that looked like they could chew through the mast of a ship in ten seconds flat.

'Observe,' said Sister Ems.

On the stage, the man strummed a few chords and then, in a high falsetto voice and a rapid vibrato, began to sing 'Caper 'Cross the Campions'. Though a well-known ditty amongst the citizens of the continent, never had Asher heard it sung like this. Grotesque and fascinating in equal measure, Asher found himself staring at the figure on the stage, who seemed lost in the performance. But after only a few moments, he felt his arm grabbed by Sister Ems, who pointed animatedly at Matt in the cell.

'Observe,' she whispered.

Matt had risen off the bed to stand at the bars of the wall so as to watch the performance. But now he was retreating, taking faltering steps backwards, his hands over his ears, stumbling in his haste to get as far away from the noise as possible. The towel fell unceremoniously from his waist to reveal his pale, naked form. Thankfully, his knees found the edge of the cot and he sat clumsily, still clutching his ears, his head shaking back and forth as a moan of horror escaped his lips. He jerked his head up towards Asher and the nurse with a look of such venomous hate and terror, Asher had to take a step back himself.

'Pleeeeaaaase,' moaned Matt. 'Pleeeease no.' He fell onto the cot and curled up into the foetal position with his back towards the stage.

Sister Ems stared at the terrible scene for a few seconds more before nodding once again to the orderly. Instantly, the light dimmed and the singing ceased.

Sister Ems turned to Asher. 'Zere. It is done. You can see

yourself zat your brozer is vulnerable and defenceless in zee face of zee treatment. I have a feeling he vill do vell.'

Asher nodded. 'So vat happens now?'

'Now you leave and allow us to do our vork, Mr Kruger. Please feel free to visit in seven days to check on our progress. You must also sign a vow of secrecy. Vee haff to protect ourselves, as you can see.'

'And the singer?'

'Oh, he lives a life of normality in a resource protection program far away from here. Zere, he sells used carts in order to project a semblance of normality. He is very vell paid for the vork he does here.'

'But how did you find him?'

Sister Ems gave a Tobler shrug. '*Tobler's Got Talent.*'

'I'm sure it has, but—'

'No, zee popular zeatre show, *Tobler's Got Talent*. He vas at an audition and killed five of the Kindred who vere hiding in zee audience and planning an unprovoked feeding party. Luckily vone of our people vas zere to see it. Vee vere able to offer him some excellent terms for his talents. Far more than *Tobler's Got Talent* could offer. Zat year it vas von by a goat who could eat a whole copy of zee *Tobler Gazette* vile bleating zee chorus of 'Wie Mach La Vuolpa'—a traditional Tobler song.'

'Vill Ma…Dieter be alright?' Asher stared down at the trembling Matt.

'Yes. He must rest now. Complete rest in full darkness for his psyche to recover. Zat part of him taken by zee red fever knows zee end is near. A great battle vill be fought. He is in good hands, Mr Kruger. You did vell to bring him to us.'

The orderlies escorted Asher from the building after he signed his vow of secrecy using a gobbet of his own spit mixed with iron gall ink.

CHAPTER TWENTY-ONE

ASHER WENT DIRECTLY TO THE Kiefernzapf Spa, ordered room service coffee, which tasted of burned wood and which Bobby Miracle would have classed as tar water, and waited.

Inevitably, as they almost always did these days, his thoughts strayed to the girl he had fallen for and their missed supper. He hadn't seen Bobby in days. She'd declined staying over in the week because of her workload at Le Fey and Hipposync. Worse, this weekend she was off to a cousin's wedding. She had asked if he'd like to accompany her in a half-hearted, 'I'm not even going to ask you because I know you'd hate it' kind of a way. She was right, but Asher began to think he'd rather be bored at a wedding with Bobby than be bored at home alone without her. There was a good chance she'd find some of the best man's jokes funny and she'd laugh her socks off when he told her about Matt and Sister Ems. He thought about her laugh now and it made him pause, because it was one of the things he loved her for.

Though Bobby was quick to smile, she saved her laugh for the real thing. And that meant the real thing had to press the right buttons, because when her laugh arrived it did so as an expulsion of air before diving down into a slow vibrato with breathy mewling squeals behind the hand she'd use to cover her mouth for fear it let out something worse. And there'd usually be tears of joy that she'd dab at ineffectually with, for some inexplicable reason, the ball of her thumb in a hopeless attempt at stopping her mascara from running. She'd often try and speak through the laugh, which only made things ten times worse. Bobby's laugh was a thing of wonder.

So much so that the first time Borodin, Asher's cat—or at least the cat who deigned to spend some time with Asher at his apartment—heard it, he bolted for the door and had, so far, not returned.

Gods he missed her. Bobby, not the cat. She had been distraught by the effect her presence had on the feline, but Asher reassured her, 'He will return when he is ready. Borodin is a free spirit. He once went away for two years.'

Asher gave the Frozen Ostrich half an hour before walking into the hotel room bathroom with his Aperio. He attached it to the bathroom door and let his mind fill with the memory of Matt's padded cell. When he had the image clear in his mind he turned the Aperio and opened the door from the hinged side. A barnyard smell filled his nostrils and he realised it must be from the sheepskins. It was almost pitch black beyond and the light from the bathroom filled only the centre of the room.

'Matt,' whispered Asher urgently.

No reply.

'Matt. Are you there?'

A shape flew at Asher with flailing arms. It hit the necreddo squarely in the chest and sent him tumbling backwards into the bathroom, where he ended up on his backside against the toilet. He was on his feet in an instant only to find a pale and sweating Matt staring at him.

'Andreas?' Matt asked. 'Vat folly is zis? Vy haff you come for me? And who is Matt?'

Quickly, Asher yanked Matt through, slammed the door shut and removed the Aperio. 'Matt is…there,' Asher pointed to the shower mat before beaming at the real Matt. 'There's been a change of plan.'

'But I heard zee vailing man. I knew zee demon inside me could hear too and he vas in agony. I felt exhausted. Sister Ems came with unguents to massage into my body and—'

'Spare me the details. I could see she had her eye on you.'

'She said she needed to inspect my bites—'

'As I said, keep that to yourself.'

Matt looked around at his new surroundings in horror. 'But Andreas, how am I to be cured if I leave zis place?'

'Temporary diversion. You will be cured I can promise you that. But first there's someone we need to see. Of course, I realise there's nothing more you want than to be subjected to the noise of someone sounding like he's got his foot caught in a mangle and be molested by a sexually repressed zealot. I mean, who wouldn't?'

'It is zee only vay I can rid myself of—'

Asher nodded but remained insistent. 'First things first. Now get dressed. We're on the clock here.'

Matt, his eyes wild and fearful, turned, threw open the bathroom door ready to bolt back to his wool padded cell but found only the hotel room. He whirled around. 'Vat sorcery is zis?'

'Sorcery you'll thank me for later.'

'But—'

'Trust me, Ma…Dieter.'

'I vant to, Andreas, but I am haffing great difficulty.' Matt started backing away.

Asher thought desperately. 'You know those magic beans I told you about?'

Matt nodded.

'Our dear old mutti gave me one and it has conjured this safe room for us to do one task before the cure. She insisted.'

'Zis is all Mutti's doing?' Matt's eyes were runny ovals of emotion.

'Of course it is.' Asher felt no guilt at the lie. After all, at this precise moment, Matt was actually living a lie so one more should make bugger all difference.

Matt nodded and slowly began to dress, insisting on applying more white powder to all the exposed parts of his skin. Asher didn't argue.

Early evening in the bar at the Kiefernzapf Spa saw it teeming with people who'd had enough of sliding down a hill for the day and were quickly trying to make up for any dehydration. Asher took Matt straight to the gnome booth.

'Hi, we're back,' he said to the surprised-looking gnome.

'So soon?'

'Yes. Not quite working out for us, I'm afraid.'

The gnome nodded. This was business as usual for him. 'You are vithin the twenty-four-hour cooling-off period. I assume you vant me to return the memory we haff removed and stored?'

'If you wouldn't mind,' Asher said.

'Of course, zere is zee nominal twenty-scruple administration charge,' said the gnome and smiled.

Asher felt suddenly glad he hadn't eaten. 'Of course. I read the clause. Very, very small print under the heading, Daylight Robbery.'

The gnome looked mildly offended. 'Our services are—'

'Worth every penny.' Asher handed over a purse. 'It's all there.'

The gnome opened the purse and poured the contents out onto a scale. He smiled, showing a row of very pointy teeth.

'And we are in a bit of a hurry,' added Asher.

'Of course.' The gnome turned to Matt. 'Now, sir, if you vould put on zee geegnome apparatus.'

Matt looked troubled. 'Vat magickary is zis, Andreas?'

'Nothing to worry about. Just a few things we need to get you to remember.'

'But I remember everyzing.'

'Not quite everything. Here, let me help you put it on.' Asher fitted the headgear onto Matt's head.

'Ready?' said the gnome. 'Now, just close your eyes.'

Matt did and the gnome uttered a few words in a tweeting voice that sounded like two budgerigars fighting. A strange purple light filled the booth and Matt's eyes snapped open. He looked at the gnome and then at Asher and blinked several times.

'Matt?' said Asher, not liking the way his friend frowned. 'You in there?'

'Yeah, I am,' replied Matt in a shaky voice.

'You remember what happened?'

'Yeah. Especially the bit when Sister Ems inspected my bites. Which she did for quite a long time and quite vigorously.'

'Ouch,' said Asher but he grinned as he spoke.

They thanked the gnome and Asher bought them both a frothy Tobler beer from the bar. Matt drank his in three swallows before clutching at his chest convulsively.

'What?' Asher asked.

'The amulet,' Matt said, horrified.

'It's here,' Asher opened his hand. 'I took it off you before you dressed.'

'I'm probably going to have to shower again to get all this powder off.'

'Good idea. You do look like someone who's fallen into a flour mill.'

'Yes, sorry about that. But ten minutes ago I thought I was a blood-sucking monster allergic to daylight.'

Asher grinned. 'We may have something for that. Let's hope we recorded enough.'

Matt nodded. 'Even if we got a bit of it, I know how we can tweak it. Or rather, I know a man who can. But first I need a shower.'

They were attracting stares from curious onlookers as the bar filled up.

'How about you shower at mine,' Asher said. 'I think we'd better get away from here before word gets out to the Frozen Ostrich there's an escaped wannnabe-able-to-die-again vampire in the bar.'

As they headed for the stairs leading up to their room, Asher's fears about them attracting attention surfaced in the form of the two alpine trolls brandishing unpleasant-looking clubs barging through reception. Matt and Asher hared it to their room, grabbed their belongings and were opening the door to the bathroom with the Aperio just as the door to the room smashed open with a shouted, 'HALT!'

Both men jumped forward as Asher slammed the door behind him, but not quickly enough to prevent a club the size of bowling pin sailing through the narrow gap and missing Matt's head by a whisker. It clattered against Asher's apartment wall and rolled over the floor into the centre of the room.

'Persistent gits, weren't they?' Matt said, reaching for the club. His fingers were inches away when he was sent sprawling by a shove from Asher's booted foot.

'Oy,' Matt said, sounding suitably muffled and irate with his face in the carpet.

Asher, meanwhile, grabbed a tea towel and threw it over the club. 'Sorry, Matt. Probably a contact poison. Don't know if you noticed, but our visitors were wearing gauntlets.'

Matt sat up and blinked. The powder spared his blushes.

'You get changed while I deal with this.' Asher nudged the covered club with his toe.

Fifteen minutes later, a scrubbed Matt and a refreshed

Asher were sitting in a coffee shop eating waffles with the 'amulet' on the table in front of them. Matt broke it open to reveal the small, very human tech recording device within.

'How will we know?'

'I could take it back to Hipposync and connect it up to my PC, but it'll take me forever to do what needs to be done. On the other hand, did you ever meet my mate, Paladin?'

'I don't think so.' Asher frowned.

'AC/DC, Xbox, second life?'

'I did not know you could speak East Charmon.'

'Stop playing the berk.'

Asher shrugged. 'I know of these things, of course. But only as interpreted through the eyes of Bobby Miracle.'

'Paladin, real name Malcolm, is an expert in all things technological and a lover of all the aforementioned. He consults for us and is our go-to guy for this sort of thing. If anyone can sort out our sample, it's Malcolm.'

Matt had never been to Malcolm's place, but as a Hipposync consultant he was a part of the communication network. Back in the human world, all Matt had to do was pick up the phone or text. But from New Thameswick, he had to approach things a little differently. In general, artefacts and charmed items that worked perfectly well in a Fae environment lost all but minimal power when they were transported to the human world. Dream catchers that did exactly what they said on the tin in New Thameswick ended up as so much wood and feather tat on New Age stalls in Newbury market in the human world. That was why the Inky Well's bookmarks had stirred up so much interest. How they had been imbued with power and by whom remained a mystery because it took some juice and old thaumaturgy know-how to do that. The same powerful krudian thaumaturgy someone at the BOD had used to make Matt's fish amulet functional. But the reverse applied too. Certain communication devices designed to allow links between Fae and human worlds did exist. Especially for DOF operatives. One of these was a small and opalescent conch Matt now took from his pocket, applied his lips to and blew softly. After a few seconds a voice emerged.

'Hello?'

'Malcolm? It's Matt. Need some help with a tech issue. Any chance I could pop over?'

'Sending you the visual link now.'

Matt held the conch away from his face and waited while a thin wisp of what looked like steam emerged to form a cloud. Within it, an image of a small room stuffed with monitors and wires appeared. Matt stared at it, stored the eidetic signal, and then took Asher's Aperio and attached it to the bathroom door. A minute later they were in Malcolm's bedroom.

Matt made the introductions and Asher shook the hand of a stocky man with red hair and a confident grin.

'Cut your hair and lost the beard, I see?' Matt said.

'And going to the gym,' Malcolm said almost regretfully.

Matt nodded. 'Malcolm's better half is a warrior clan leader on Moldarrenovia.'

'Really?' Asher said.

Malcolm shrugged. 'She's got me learning to ride a horse bareback. Three times a week, an hour at a time whilst firing arrows from a bow.'

'Sounds interesting,' Asher said.

'Sounds like a sore coccyx to me,' Matt opined.

'So what can I do for you gentlemen?' Malcolm asked.

Matt showed him the recording device and Malcolm slid it into a USB port and winced as the recorded rendition of 'Caper 'Cross the Campions' emerged.

'Well, at least it is there,' Asher observed.

'Did whoever made this noise have his or her foot caught in a mangle by any chance?' asked Malcolm.

'Unfortunately, no. And it's a him.'

'Could you loop that twenty seconds worth together into a three-minute blast?' Matt asked.

'No problem.'

Malcolm applied himself to the software at his disposal while Asher watched in fascination. The pongcluetors he used utilised elephant mites as memory and sprite scribes could rapidly sketch images onto the screen as visual artists.

'So,' Malcolm said without looking up, 'how did you get hold of this little bit of demonic caterwauling?'

Asher let Matt tell the story. And as he listened, something vague and unsettling began to gather in his brain. Too unfocussed to have any real meaning other than a tantalising awareness that he had missed something important along the way, it worried at him while Matt told the story. It was still doing so when Malcolm sat back and handed over the USB stick.

'There you go, three minutes' worth of 'Caper 'Cross the Campions'.'

'Malcolm, you're a genius,' Matt said.

Asher used the Aperio, but instead of taking Matt back to his apartment, they entered through the door of the Five Bells, which, being the closest pub to Asher's apartment, served as his local.

'What are we doing here?' Matt asked, following Asher to the bar.

'I could do with something to wash down that glass of foam we had in Tobler,' Asher said. 'And since it's lunchtime, this is where we'll find Crouch. Fancy a pint of Bombdropper?'

Matt shrugged and waved at Crouch sitting in a corner.

They took their pints and joined the constabulary man. Asher took a healthy swallow of beer. 'Ah. Nothing like a pint of lukewarm ale.'

Matt sipped and grimaced. 'I'm more a chilled wheat beer fan myself.'

'It'll grow on you,' said Crouch, 'and if you spill any on your lawn it'll stop things from growing full stop.' His eyes strayed to Matt's hairline. 'Oh, and you've either walked under a leaky flour hopper or you've got galloping dandruff.'

'It's neither,' Asher said and proceeded to fill Crouch in on what they'd been doing.

'Tobler, of all places,' Crouch said with distaste. 'And all this bloke does is sing 'Caper 'Cross the Campions'?'

'There's some long-winded explanation about identical modulations and banshee wails which Shonkin from the BOD would be happy to provide you with, if you were able to find him.'

'Nah, I'll take your word for it,' Crouch said.

Matt took another sip, grimaced as the initial bitterness took hold and then smiled as the sweeter flavours found the appropriate taste buds and settled in. 'Cheers,' he said, holding up the glass. 'Here's to a successful operation.'

They clinked glasses.

'So after this we go back to Hipposync and find the girls, right?' Matt said. 'I don't want to be anywhere near when they try out 'Caper 'Cross the Campions' on The Alternator. I'm going to be plugged in to something tuneful and relaxing like Slipknot.'

'Are they one of those quartets that play poncy stuff by wossname, Mazerati?'

'No, not classical, more growling nu metal. But compared to 'Caper 'Cross the Campions' their stuff is chamber music.'

Asher said nothing; too busy studying the thin froth on his beer. He studied it for so long, in fact, Crouch felt obliged to comment.

'See anything in there? Westminster dog track winner?'

'I see nothing but ale,' Asher said, looking up. 'And that is what bothers me. Until you take a sip, all beers look more or less the same. It is only the taste that differentiates them.'

'Stone the ravens, he's gone all philosophical on us,' Crouch said with a lopsided grin.

Matt nodded warily. 'How come I get the feeling that this is leading us somewhere I'm not sure I want to go?'

'We've just penetrated one of the most secretive places in Tobler,' Asher said.

'Yes…' Matt nodded using an upswing on the word to make sure Asher knew he was listening.

'And it was not difficult. Not really.'

'No, not when I'd parked all memory of my real self with a gnome valet service so that I actually believed I was Dieter Kruger.'

'Of course.' Asher nodded. 'But what also helped was you hiding behind the robes and the powdered face.'

'I didn't see it that way—'

'No, of course not. But it's what everyone else saw.'

'What is it you're trying to say, Asher?' Crouch put down his beer as Asher sat up and looked at them both with a slightly manic glint.

It was all crystallising inside his head now. The nagging, gnawing intangible awareness had suddenly solidified into a horrifying realisation. Asher centred his gaze on Matt. 'You said it yourself. You dressed up and asked me if you would pass muster as one of them.'

'So?'

'So when everyone looked at you they saw one of Les Reasonables and nothing else.'

'I'm hanging on your every word, but I have to say the hand holds are quite slippery.' Matt frowned.

'It's an iconic dress. A statement of intent. Crouch and I visited ICHOR and got the tour. They showed us what they were doing. Making cards and stationery and papery dross. But we didn't really pay much attention because you can't really see anything beyond those painted faces and the traumatised eyes.'

'The bookmarks,' said Matt abruptly.

Asher nodded. 'The bookmarks. It's so obvious, it's criminal. I think we need to talk to our friend Simla DiFrance once again, don't you?'

'ICHOR is only four streets away,' Crouch said, on his feet and heading for the door in a heartbeat. He didn't even bother to finish his beer.

CHAPTER TWENTY-TWO

YORK, HW

Alistair Donovan was making himself beans on toast when he heard the chime of the Inky Well's bell. He paused, butter-laden knife in mid spread, and frowned. This was an old house with old-fashioned call systems. The small sitting room next to the even smaller kitchen on ground level had been meant for staff use. A wire via a pulley linked to a bell had, at one time, informed the staff of anyone requiring their services. The three bells were arranged on the wall above a small fireplace in the smallest room. One for the shop door, one for deliveries at the rear, and one linked up to the bedroom upstairs. The bell that rang the most was the one linked to the shop door.

Alistair frowned. He was sure he'd locked that door. He put the knife down on the plate and went into the sitting room to look at the faded wooden panel and its trio of bells, as if staring at them in annoyance might prevent them from ringing again.

It was well after six o'clock and the shop closed at five. Every one of his regular customers knew that. Probably some tourists chancing their luck. Alistair sighed. He had no time for this now. He'd send them on their way and if they really wanted something they'd have to come back tomorrow. He turned to enter the shop when the bell rang again. The noise drew his eyes and he froze, a strange and uncomfortable thrill working its way up from somewhere down in the depths of his innards.

Not possible.

The bell vibrating at the end of its coiled brass ring did not link to the shop door. This wire ran horizontally along the passage and then vertically up, to the first floor and to a push button to the right of his uncle's bed.

His dead uncle's bed.

Suddenly, Alistair's appetite for beans on toast took a nosedive off a high cliff. He turned to the small radio playing inane pop and switched it off. In the silence that followed, the north wind moaned and whistled in its effort at getting into the house, negotiating the chimney and forcing itself into all the gaps and drafts the old place had to offer. Alistair stood, rigidly listening as he tried to understand what all of this might mean. It didn't take long for him to conclude he'd really rather not find out. He did not want to go upstairs. Despite the ring of mothballs around the door and the bowls of disinfectant on the floor and stairs, his uncle's reek had ripened of late. He knew he'd have to face it at some point: after all, the plan was to get at least thirty cheques signed as soon as the new cheque book arrived and then…then he'd have to find a way of explaining away his uncle's rotting body. There were some old wells just north of the ring road. He reckoned that once this was all over he could transport the corpse, chuck it down one of them and then go away for a few months. He'd already arranged—at the whisperers' suggestion—for Connor to write a suicide note. When he'd come back from his travels, Alistair would report the note and his uncle's absence, and by the time they found him, rot would have done its thing. And why not? He'd seen it done a zillion times on TV. It couldn't be *that* hard, could it?

Well…truth was, he'd had enough of messing about with those effing whisperers on the other side of…whatever they were on the other side of. Uncle Connor had been fascinated because he was into all that stuff. But Alistair was getting a bit antsy. Digsbow had promised that he'd be rewarded—gold had been mentioned—but the greasy salesman hadn't been around for days, if not weeks, and dealing with his dead uncle freaked Alistair out. Having the police or the DOF thingummies' call had put the willies up him even more. So, he'd decided to forget the gold and move the schedule forward. He'd 'borrow' some money from the old man's bank account. Once the cheque cleared, he'd get rid of the body, shut up shop and take that gap year, or gap three months, with whatever he could get. He'd always wanted to see Vietnam and Cambodia. This would be his chance for freedom at last. And that part of Alistair's conscience that knew how awful and corrupt his plan was remained locked away in a mental filing cabinet marked *Hexed*. Next to the very dusty one marked *What-the-hell-are-you-playing-at-even-talking-to-the-whisperers-you-idiot*.

Digsbow had a lot to answer for.

The bell rang again. Alistair shuddered.

He didn't want to go up those stairs but he knew he must. It was the only way to stop the bell ringing. But then his uncle hadn't moved much in the last several weeks. In fact, he only moved when Alistair put the pen in his hand. So who, or what, was pressing the button?

Alistair went back into the kitchen, took the bubbling beans off the stove, and grabbed the largest and sharpest knife he could find.

The bell rang again.

Cursing silently, Alistair went to the stairs and stood at the bottom. Even though the lights were all on, it seemed dimmer somehow around his uncle's bedroom door.

'Uncle Connor? Is that you?'

The only answer came as a gusting moan from the wind.

'Shit.' The oath slipped unbidden from Alistair's mouth.

Slowly, he walked up the stairs. The lights did not flicker, the door to his uncle's room did not rattle mysteriously, nor did the doorknob turn of its own accord. Yet Alistair, despite everything he'd done and accepted as other-worldly, shivered and trembled and blew out the breath in his lungs that seemed to be coming much quicker than it had minutes before.

He stood outside his uncle's door and knocked gently. 'Uncle Connor? Did you ring the bell?'

Something shuffled on the other side.

'Shit,' Alistair whispered again and did a little anxious dance. Had his uncle fallen off the bed? The way things were going the last time he'd been in there, it looked like most of Uncle Connor's bits were on the verge of falling off the bed individually. He took a deep breath and told himself to get a grip.

He also told himself that being scared was understandable.

Alistair remembered how he'd almost bolted the first time moribund Uncle Connor's hand had twitched when he'd put the pen between its fingers and the chequebook in front of it. The movement had been mechanical and repetitive, like some automaton at a grisly fair. So why was this new turn of events having such an effect on him?

He knew why.

The button for the bell was on the wall next to the bed, which meant Uncle Connor must have moved several feet to get to it unless his arm had grown by that much or…

Alistair swallowed loudly and muttered for the third time, 'Shit.'

The wind moaned.

Squeezing his eyes shut, he put his hand on the doorknob and twisted.

The door opened, or rather flew open with Alistair's hand still attached to the handle. He fell in, heard the door slam shut, and found himself on his knees in the dark, with the stench of rotting corpse all around him. For a moment he didn't move, couldn't move as terror gripped him and paralysed every muscle. He could hear his own wheezy rapid breathing, but when he held it, another noise emerged in the darkness. A slow, shuffling, creaking noise.

The room was stygian, the stink awful, his imagination on turbo drive. But though he did not want to see, he knew he had to. He felt his way across the floor, found the foot of the bed and reached out for the wall beyond. He felt for a shoulder-height switch next to the doorframe, found it and slowly dragged himself up until he stood with his back to the wall, a wavering forefinger on the plastic toggle.

He shut his eyes and pressed.

Behind his lids he saw light fill the room. Several seconds crawled by before he allowed his trembling lids to slowly drift apart. What was revealed to him would haunt his nightmares for years to come.

Uncle Connor was on his feet next to his bed, except that one foot had snapped at the ankle and so the corpse listed to the left. One finger was pressed up against the call button. Much of the digit had become a dark mashed pulp. In his other hand, Uncle Connor held a Never Forget bookmark, like the ones Digsbow brought. Luckily, the old man's head hung bowed.

But then Alistair's luck ran out.

With a sickening click, the head snapped up and two dried-out grey corneas stared at Alistair. In that moment Connor O'Malley, dead for seven weeks, started to breathe. The noise was like a low expansion of ancient bellows. It sounded painful, but worse was the bubbling noise that followed, like gas forced through a channel of water. Five times the breathing repeated itself until at last O'Malley spoke in a dry, straining voice.

'You...have…a task.'

Alistair didn't speak. It was all he could do to nod and pray his jeans were dark enough not to show the warm stain blooming in his crotch.

O'Malley's left hand cranked upwards. It held out the bookmark.

'Mirror…read…mirror…read…mirror…read…mirror… read.'

'Okay,' said Alistair, his voice high and terrified. 'You want me to look in the mirror and read?'

'Yessss,' croaked Connor.

'Read what?'

'Mirror…read…this.' The pale, yellowing hand inched up further, thrusting the bookmark towards the boy's face.

'Read the bookmark?'

'Yessss.'

'But there isn't—'

Something growled deep inside O'Malley and Alistair shut up.

'Mirror…read…this.'

The growl didn't sound like Uncle Connor. Not even this husk of Uncle Connor. Instead it sounded like something else, something much worse. Alistair made himself concentrate. They wanted him to do something and so he would do it. Mirror, read, this. Mirror, read, this. His brain threw the information around and around.

'You want me to read what it says on the bookmark into a mirror?'

'Noooo.'

'Then?'

'Read words…words…in mirror.'

'Okay. Hold the bookmark up to a mirror and read what it says?'

'Yesss.'

Alistair nodded wildly. 'Okay, okay. I can do that. I will do that.'

'Nowww.'

'Okay, now.'

Alistair reached out to take the bookmark. It slid out between the papery flesh of the animated corpse's fingers. Below his uncle's right leg, dark viscous fluid was pooling around the limb end. The smell churned Alistair's gut and he turned his face away. That was why he did not see the dead fingers snap closed around his own wrist and yank him forwards such that his face ended up inches from Uncle Connor's grey, decrepit flesh.

'Do…it…now,' hissed his uncle from behind a mouthful of grey and yellow teeth.

Alistair dare not inhale. If he did he'd throw up, he knew it. Instead, he nodded quickly and many times, his face turning gradually aubergine as he tried, in desperation, to hold his own air and not suck in any zombie breath. But it was no good. The breathing, if that was what his uncle was actually doing, died away. But the fingers remained clamped and firm. He reached down for the bookmark, but couldn't free his other hand.

He tried to prise the digits away, eyes bulging against the trapped CO_2 in his lungs. Finally, he could not hold it any longer. In desperation, he thrust his clamped hand upwards and heard a crack. Air exploded from his lungs as he yanked open the door and fell on his knees in the corridor, gulping in air. It was only after three deep lungfuls that his eyes focused on the bookmark in his fingers and on his uncle's snapped-off hand. A hand that now remained adorned like a bone and ragged flesh bracelet around his wrist. Moaning, he tried again to prise away the fingers. But they remained like forged steel. And something inside Alistair Donovan told him they would remain there until he fulfilled his promise.

He got to his feet, staggered, leaned against the wall as the stink pervaded his nostrils again. But this time he knew it had nothing to do with the room he'd just left. It came from the hand.

Gagging, Alistair ran for the bathroom and its big mirror.

In his haste, he slammed into the sink and felt a burst of pain in his hip. Whimpering, he looked in the mirror. His face was a mess. Streaked with tears and something else, a spray of dark fluid that could only have come from his uncle's mouth. He pawed at it automatically only to feel his uncle's hand brush its cold flesh against his chin as it stuck out from his own wrist.

He let out a gargled, 'Aaargh,' and almost gave up and jumped into the abyss of beckoning madness. But the pain from the jarred bone at the front of his hip helped drag his mind back.

'Come on, Alistair. Come on,' he whispered from lips trembling violently from adrenaline and fear.

Slowly, trying to blank out the sinews and skin dangling from the accessory hand, he brought the bookmark up to the mirror and started at it. All he saw was the Inky Well logo and the words *Never Forget bookmark* in reverse. He read it out in a halting stutter…

'The nu…never fu..fu…forget bookmark.'

Nothing happened.

He read it again.

'The never forget bookmark.'

And again.

'The never forget bookmark, the never forget bookmark, the never forget bookmark.'

It was then that he felt the pressure on his wrist. Almost gentle at first, it grew in strength. He started at it and saw, with horror, the fingers on his uncle's hand slowly tightening and twisting. He resisted, whimpering some more, but the unyielding pressure forced his own hand to crush the section of bookmark he held. Pain seared the soft pulp of his palm as the sharp edge of the paper bit home and a trickle of his own blood flowed and smeared the surface, mingled with the inky marks. But the pressure from Connor's disembodied hand was insistent. Alistair let his own wrist follow the applied torque and watched as the now blood-smudged bookmark rotated in the mirror until the rear was reflected. The rear with the strange shapes around the edge and weirdly repetitive letters that were not quite letters and did not quite spell out a word. And then there was the manufacturer's website:

www.Ǹiɘmoɔoḃ.org

He stared afresh at the writing he'd looked at so many times, realising they were familiar and yet different, seen as they were in the mirror. And as he stared, Alistair suddenly understood that though the words were not separated, the letters that were not quite letters suddenly did spell out something legible.

ḋocomeiǸ

Do. Come. In.

'Do come in?' Alistair whispered.

The house shuddered around him. As if something seismic had shifted beneath its foundations.

'Do come in? Is that all it is?' Relief brought with it a high-pitched laugh that ended abruptly as a new sound met his ears.

Something moved downstairs. Not the wind this time. Furniture scraping on a hard floor. As if someone was moving about in unfamiliar surroundings. The pressure in his palm eased as his uncle's fingers relinquished their grip and the hand clattered to the floor.

Alistair stared at his own hand and the cuts left by the bookmark. Two thin trickles of blood dripped onto the carpet. He did not like the sight of blood.

Correction, he *used* to not like the sight of blood because suddenly, the sight of it triggered a spurt of saliva flooding into his mouth. With it came an overwhelming urge to lick that blood. Lifting his palm to his lips, Alistair let his tongue run up the flesh. Salt and copper exploded into his mouth and fired off a pleasure torpedo that struck home in that part of his brain that shared the same primordial wiring with alligators and cheetahs and anything else that tore its prey apart to feast on the red stuff. But it was watered down wine. This was *his* blood and though it promised much, it did not deliver. There was something missing, some element that would satiate and fulfil like nothing else ever had before and would never again.

He heard a thumping downstairs from the shop. The sound of someone trying to get in, or out, of a confined space.

Perhaps it was warm blooded?

The thought galvanised him.

Alistair kicked his uncle's hand away and walked out of the bathroom aware only that something had changed both in the world and inside his own head. The door to his uncle's bedroom remained open. A crumpled form lay on the floor, twitching intermittently. It held no interest for Alistair because that decaying husk of a corpse contained no fresh blood. And yet he was grateful for his uncle doing what he, or rather the decrepit collection of flesh and bone that remained, had done for him. In a part of his head that was still the Alistair Donovan who'd helped out in the shop… a faint alarm sounded at the thought that both he and Connor O'Malley had been played by a puppet-master. The whisperers had talked to his uncle like they had talked to him.

They promised riches and more.

Perhaps poor Uncle Connor should have got it in writing. Insight was a wonderful thing, but of less value when it came after the event. What might something that could make the dead write cheques and hiss out instructions through functionless lungs consider riches? But it was nothing but a fleeting agitation, that thought. Like a troublesome fly that strayed near an ear and then buzzed away in an instant.

He glanced down at the blood on his hand and on the carpet. Another surge of ecstatic desire fizzed through him. Something was happening inside his head and body. Something empowering and fantastic.

He heard wood scraping against more wood from somewhere in the shop.

The hunger inside him blossomed and swamped all other thoughts as he turned and ran down the stairs.

CHAPTER TWENTY-THREE

NEW THAMESWICK, FW

Asher, Matt a carriage and pulled up outside the ICHOR building on Scrap Street to find Crouch waiting, and a small crowd gathered. In New Thameswick, that meant 'entertainment', in the broadest sense of the word, was in the offing. Said 'entertainment' might mean a juggler throwing up burning torches, or a pop-up pea and cup merchant complete with audience stooges and heavies ready to fleece the innocent. It could mean someone on a soapbox preaching the forthcoming apocalypse, or an ex-pirate busker called Small Jack Pewter with a banjo singing songs from his limited repertoire such as, 'Boiled Beef and Parrots' or, 'They Call the Wind Mariaaaargh'. Today, however, something much more sinister was on the variety bill.

'Right you lot,' Crouch said, addressing the small group of onlookers clustered around a very distressed young lady Asher immediately identified as one of ICHOR's Tealand receptionists. 'What's going on 'ere?'

The receptionist, her white painted face streaked with tears and her hair uncoiling in dishevelled strands from the black bun it should have been, sniffed miserably. 'It is awful. Something terrible has happened.'

'What exactly?' Crouch asked.

The girl stood, or rather wobbled, since one of her wooden sandals had lost a heel. 'Les Reasonables have become very…Unreasonables.'

'In what way?' Asher pushed through the crowd, which seemed intent on listening to the exchange and was closing in.

'In a very unpleasant way. It was horrible. They started sniffing at us. Like you might do to some cooked meat. One of them licked my face.'

The crowd ooohed.

'What's your name, Miss?' asked Crouch.

'Sherry Blossom.'

The crowd aaahed.

'Okay, Sherry, were you alone in there?'

Sherry shook a petite head and batted eyelashes as long as a crow's wing. She reached for and removed a bun-piercing chopstick, allowing more lustrous black hair to spill out onto a pale shoulder.

The crowd gasped. Someone moaned.

'Pale Leaf and Mountain Mist are still in there. I think they have barricaded themselves under the desk.'

'Where's DiFrance?' Crouch asked.

'No one can find him. The ballroom is locked and there is no key.'

'When did all this start?' Asher asked.

'Immediately after the dinner bell rang. They were all restless. They did not receive their envisioning session this evening.' Sherry shook her head again. Her hair followed on a half-second delay. Someone in the crowd said, 'Phwah.'

'What time is dinner?'

'Seven. Usually it is a subdued affair, but today, there was much running around and much sniffing of the air.'

Asher and Matt exchanged glances.

Crouch tilted his head. 'What do you think they were smelling?'

'We could not smell anything different,' Sherry said with a sniff. 'Just the usual charred vegetables and beetroot soup.'

'So there's something in there only they can smell and it's making them a bit agitated,' Crouch mused.

'More than a bit agitated,' Sherry corrected him.

'I'd put my money on spilled blood,' Matt said.

Everyone looked at him.

'Vampires are haematophillic. I remember reading somewhere how their olfactory systems are highly attuned. Up to ten thousand times more sensitive than us to anything… bloody.'

'Light bedtime reading, was that?' Asher asked.

'Kylah's recommendation. Says I need to bone up.'

Crouch turned to the crowd. 'Right you lot, bugger off. Nothing to see here.'

'There's Sherry,' said a voice.

'And maybe Pale Leaf and Mountain Mist if we're lucky,' added someone else.

'And there'll be the feel of this stick if you don't get lost.' Crouch raised the fox-headed vampire slayer in his hand.

Grumbling, the crowd, mainly youngish men Asher now noticed, began to drift away. Crouch whistled up a police carriage and spoke to the horse.

'Ah, Portnoy. Hang on for ten minutes. If we're not out by then take this young lady and anyone else we manage to extricate to the station house, will you?' He turned to the shivering girl. 'When you get there, ask for Sergeant Vood and give her this note.' He scribbled on a scrap of paper. 'Condalisa's a good girl. She'll look after you until we sort this.'

Matt helped the girl into the carriage, a feat hampered by the tightly restrictive dress she wore. When she was safely seated, the men stood together on the pavement.

'Plan?' asked Asher.

'Stay here,' Crouch said and ran across the road to a greengrocer's. He came back a minute later with a small sack. 'Help yourselves,' he said, upending the sack onto the floor to reveal three strings of wild garlic.

'Will this be enough?' Matt asked.

'It'll have to be,' Crouch said. 'Of course, there's always this.' He held up the nightstick with the silver fox's head.

'Are you going to stun them with a dance number from the musical?' Matt asked.

'It's a skull-cracker,' Asher explained. 'Though seeing Crouch tap dancing might be enough to quell any riot.'

'Yeah, go on, laugh it up,' Crouch said. 'We'll see who's laughing when there's a pair of fangs inches from your jugular. We ready?'

Matt and Asher draped a string of garlic around each of their necks. Crouch simply stuffed a few complete garlic heads into his pockets. Finally, he turned to the door and knocked.

No one answered.

Crouch knocked twice more to no avail.

Asher applied the Aperio. It did not work. 'Probably charmed,' he said with a sigh.

'Looks like an old door,' Matt said, stepping up and studying it carefully. 'Bit of rust on the hinges. Sometimes they can decay right through, in which case a sharp tap on that side may case the whole door to fall in.'

Crouch laughed. 'What are you like? This door has stood for centuries. It'd be a miracle if that—'

Matt slapped at the hinged side of the door. It gave with a snap. Using his index finger, he pushed gently and the whole door toppled inward.

'Ye Gods,' Crouch said.

'Bit of luck.' Matt shrugged.

'Luck?' Crouch spluttered.

Asher took him by the elbow. 'I'll explain it all later,' he said and pointed at the corridor in front of them, where three

Les Reasonables were trying to tear up the heavy oak desk. The crashing door distracted them and they turned en masse to regard the three men with expressions best described as maniacally hostile.

'Oy, you lot,' Crouch yelled. 'Get away from that desk!' His dusky skin was now dancing with iridescence; a sure sign that the hawkshaw was getting miffed.

There is a moment in any altercation between offenders and the law when both parties have to weigh up the options and decide. Sometimes such decisions rest with individuals. That is why armies have a chain of command and why orders such as 'Take cover' or 'Smash 'em, lads' are quite important. Hence the reason recruits have to shine their boots with saliva and spend winter weekends on mountains in the back of beyond with no food, armed with nothing but a penknife and a bit of string. It encourages discipline, camaraderie, and the ability to listen even when the bullets are flying, else there is never going to be any lunch. Leaders, in these kinds of situations, emerge like dragonflies from nymphs.

With rabbles, it's very different. When a mob is driven by anger, a sense of injustice and the need for revenge or gratification, sense, and sensibility goes out of the window—usually tied to a brick. The only weighing-up that takes place is a vague awareness of which gap between the water cannon and the riot squad to make for once you've delivered your missile, or flammable cocktail, or, if you're very, *very* angry, a clattering blow with a cardboard banner on the end of a long stick. Sod the consequences (STC) is what applies in general. But if a rabble is stoked on enough STC, even that thin veneer of a survivalist instinct rubs off to leave naked violence beneath.

For the knot of Les Reasonables attempting to disassemble the desk and enjoying every decibel of the distraught screams of terror they were inducing in the two secreted receptionists, their STC was airborne and smelled of copper.

Crouch's words were nothing more than a warm breeze fanning the flames of wanton destruction that roared within. All three snarled and leaped off the desk as one.

'Let 'em come,' Crouch said though gritted teeth, lights doing the cha-cha over his skin. 'Grab a clove of garlic in each fist, wait until you can see the red of their eyes, and let 'em have it.'

In their haste to get at fresh meat, the three vampires almost fell over one another, but then they were sprinting down the corridor, eyes wild, fangs bared.

Crouch retreated outside, waited for the first one to emerge onto the pavement and swung his nightstick. The fox's head struck home with a cracking noise and turned the vampire into Orpheus fodder in an instant.

Matt watched the second one come straight for him and stuck out his fist. The garlic slowed the bloodsucker down but didn't stop him. What did was a DOF-trained kick to the knee followed by a neck punch and then, with his opponent on the floor, Matt grabbed a throat with his garlic-laden hand. Instantly, the vampire froze and became very still.

'Ah, Van Heflin's grip. Very smart,' Crouch said, dancing past.

Asher, meanwhile, parried a couple of blows—more pawing grabs, really—from his little beauty and waited as Crouch circled. Without warning, Asher fell to his knees in supplication. 'Oh no, please don't. I don't want to become one of you.'

'Too late, human,' snarled the vampire.

He was right. Well, half right. It was too late, but not for Asher, since the blow from Crouch to the vampire's cranium ended proceedings from its point of view rapidly and igno-miniously.

Asher and Crouch approached the desk and spoke to a very frightened Pale Leaf and Mountain Mist, who were crouched under the table and barricaded in by several chairs.

It took some persuading but eventually Asher managed to convince them it was safe to come out and they ran into the waiting arms of Sherry Blossom safe in Portnoy's charge outside.

Crouch tied a head of garlic around the neck of the not-so-reformed vampire Matt had incapacitated. 'That should keep him catatonic for a while,' he explained. 'Now what?'

'The ballroom?' Asher suggested.

They walked along the hallway, hearing strange whoops and calls echo through the building.

'Bit different from the last time we were here,' Crouch said with an air of wary irony.

Asher didn't answer because he was staring at the end of the corridor. The sub-basement door stood open and light streamed in behind them from the smashed-down front door, yet the steps leading down seemed bathed in a kind of soupy darkness. Neither fog nor shadow, it was as if the light were being pushed away and not allowed entry.

'What is that smell?' Matt asked. 'It reminds me of a dead whale that washed up on a beach in Cornwall once. Stayed there all summer getting slowly riper and providing sushi for the seagulls.'

'Vestigia,' Asher said. 'And a foul one to boot. But there is another smell. There is old blood beyond this door.'

Crouch tried the door. It rattled but remained locked.

The three men looked at each other. 'I don't think we have much choice,' Crouch said finally.

Asher nodded and took out his Aperio, fitted it to the locked door and pushed. Once the door was opened, the dimness hovering around the entrance seeped back into the room and clung to the ceiling like thin smoke.

'Wow,' breathed Matt as he and the others took in the scene.

Crouch put his hand over his nose and mouth in an

attempt at masking out the worst of the stink. 'This is even worse than I expected.'

Asher said nothing. He was the one trained in demonic activities and he didn't need to be told that what had gone on here measured off the scale. His eyes darted around the room but the miasma seemed to mask the detail. Asher knew this was deliberate, a fogging left behind by whatever had been here in order to cover its trail. But he was up for the challenge. Reaching into his waistcoat, he removed a small glass marble, which he cupped in both hands. He felt its smoothness between his palms, shut his eyes, and imagined the shape and form of light that it needed to take. He opened his palm and light exploded into the room from the epicentre of the marble. It drifted up to the centre of the ballroom ceiling, causing the darkness to crawl towards the huge mirror at the end of the room where it funnelled at speed through a huge crack.

'That will be where the demon entered from,' Asher said.

'Who is this poor bugger?' Matt walked forward and stared with distaste at the decapitated head lying on its side and staring back at the mirror.

Crouch kneeled, careful to stay outside the circle of salt. 'Name of DiFrance,' he said.

'It's his blood that's sent his disciples wild,' Asher commented.

Another strange yell echoed down from the corridors above.

'We ought to re-lock the door,' Crouch said.

Asher did the needful. When he turned back towards the room, Crouch was walking towards the mirror. 'I wouldn't get too close if I were you,' Asher warned.

Crouch stopped and turned back. 'What do you know?'

Asher shook his head. 'Not much, but there has obviously been demonic activity here. The vestigia tells us that.'

'Did a demon cut off this chap's head?' Matt asked.

'Maybe. But usually physical injuries from demons are much more imaginative. Turning people inside out or separating them into thirteen pieces are much more their style. This is too clean cut.'

'So what's your theory?'

'The circle of salt and the symbols all point to some sort of summoning ritual. DiFrance is inside the circle. From that we can guess he did the summoning. But the rest of it I can't put my finger on. Someone else must have been in here. Someone capable of doing *that*.' He nodded towards the body. 'But where is that someone?'

'Maybe he made his escape and locked the door behind him?' Matt suggested.

'Probably,' Crouch agreed.

But Asher was less convinced. 'I think we're missing something here. DiFrance obviously succeeded in summoning the demon, but why?'

'Doesn't look like we'll find any answers here, anyway,' Matt said. 'The dead don't talk.'

'Not to us…' Crouch sent him a look before turning to Asher.

'Worth a try, I suppose,' Asher said.

'But you said yourself, leeches are wild when they pass.'

'But DiFrance was a vimp, remember? Maybe…'

'Well, rather you than me,' Crouch shrugged.

'Or rather never you, always me,' Asher clarified Crouch's statement and got a reluctant nod and a grin for his trouble.

Matt wandered around to the other side of the circle where he knelt to study something that caught his eye. 'There's something here. Looks like a coin of some sort.'

Asher and Crouch joined him. Crouch took out some gloves and put them on.

'Glad to see you came prepared,' Asher said.

'When I'm on a case with you, I'm always prepared,'

Crouch said drily before picking up the object and holding it up for them all to see.

'Is it a coin?' Matt asked.

Crouch studied it for a moment and then said, 'Winker.'

'There's no need to be like that,' Matt said.

'He means it's a warming link. A charmed artefact. They're worn as amulets or rings, sometimes just kept in pockets. You might give one to your friend or significant other, or closest relative. It transmits warmth to its twin when you hold it, no matter where the other is. Often used as a token of affection, or to signal to someone, or something, in a prearranged fashion. Once set up the link can't be broken.'

'Looks like it rolled out of DiFrance's robes when he fell.'

'His foot is out of the salt circle here,' Matt observed.

Crouch looked from Asher to Matt. 'The winker is flesh-triggered, right?'

Asher nodded.

'Even dead flesh?' Matt asked.

'There is one way to find out.' Asher placed the winker on the corpse's exposed ankle. The artefact immediately began to glow a deep heliotrope.

'So the flesh does not need to be ali…' Crouch's words died on his lips. Something was happening to the mirror. All three men looked up to see the ballroom's reflection disappear. In its place they saw a woodland full of evergreen pines under a grey sky.

'What the venk is this?' Crouch whispered.

In the mirror a huge wolf padded forwards. It spied a man through the trees. The man stood tall and thin, dark hair cut clean, his clothes tight fitting, his face chiselled and smooth. The wolf turned and ran, leapt from ten yards away and transformed in mid-air into a man who landed on two elegant feet to stand and shake the first man's hand.

'Are we looking through a window at another world?' whispered Crouch.

'I am not sure,' Asher answered.

'It is another world,' Matt said. 'The one imagined by Hollywood producers. This is *Rhage*. First in a trilogy of films about the vampire clan wars.'

'Is this a history of Oneg?' Crouch asked.

Matt laughed. 'It's a history of someone's overwrought imagination. They're films of novels that were bestsellers about ten years ago. You know the sort of thing.'

'No, I don't know this sort of thing, Matt. Are you saying this is not really happening?'

'No, it did happen. This is a recording, but it isn't true to life. These are actors.'

'But what is its purpose? That shapeshifter—'

'Doesn't look like any shapeshifter I know.' Crouch winced.

'That shapeshifter gets a silver bullet through his left eye thirty minutes in.'

'And so this is play acting?'

'Yep.'

'I did not know shapeshifters acted,' Crouch said, unable to take his eyes off the screen.

'He didn't really change from a wolf into a man just then.'

'But he did. I saw it. Perhaps your eyes were hooded from the truth.'

'Oh, I saw it too. But it's just CGI.'

'Seegeeeye?' Crouch asked. 'Is he a sorcerer?'

'Look, it's a film. A story. Made up. An emotional potboiler—though you'd never guess it from the wooden performances. He's the ultimate bad boy attraction. And for the blokes there are hot vampire girls who want to bite you as soon as look at you. What's not to like about that?'

'But what is this…'film' doing in the mirror?' Crouch looked very confused now.

'I think it's time I talked to DiFrance, don't you?' Asher said.

CHAPTER TWENTY-FOUR

YORK, HW

ALISTAIR REACHED THE BOTTOM OF THE stairs conscious only of the fact that something that could move furniture generally had arms and legs and, by definition, blood pumping through them. Nothing more he needed to know. He hurried through the darkness of the Inky Well, listening, stopping occasionally to smell the air and taste that coppery deliciousness. It was like an invisible string guiding him and he could have followed with his eyes shut. Rich and heady, like slow-cooked casserole on a winter's evening, it drew him forward between the stacked shelves and narrow aisles with a promise of satisfaction. But as the aroma of blood grew stronger, he sensed something else there too. A faint taint in the delicious tang that grew the deeper into the shop he went. This was a different smell. Musky, almost, like the sprayed mark of an animal on a tree or a path. The trail led on into the bowels of the shop and the spoor was coming from the same place as the blood. Perhaps this was always how it was, he reasoned, or at least transiently thought because reason had no part to play at all in the wild, ravenous, instinctive lust pulsing inside his head. Yet something set his teeth on edge. The blood he'd be happy to sniff all day, but this other scent made all the little hairs on the back of his neck stand to attention.

More scraping and a rattle. Alistair reached the DIY section, paused and listened.

Another rattle, like a locked door being tested. By now Alistair had reached the middle of the shop, approaching *Travel*. The only door anywhere near here doubled as a book-case and guarded his uncle's secret room.

The room he thought only he knew about.

Slowly, Alistair reached for *Holidays on Swedish Railways*, removed it, and depressed the recessed handle. The door swung open to reveal a man in a grey tunic. For a moment, Alistair at first thought he'd been terribly injured since the figure was covered in bright red blood smearing his face and staining his clothes. But then he caught the man's eye and it was not the look of suffering he read there. Rather the expression smacked of cold calculation. But Alistair's senses instantly registered the fact that this man was the source of both the blood that attracted him so *and* the sour scent tainting the blood. And now that scent was so overwhelming Alistair forgot all about the blood pumping within the flesh.

'Who are you?' asked the man.

'No, hang on, this is my shop. Who are you?' Alistair asked, surprising himself in the process.

'Cutlam. The name is Cutlam.'

'Who attacked you?'

'There was an accident but never mind that. Is this the place? Are you human?'

'*Was*.' Alistair drew himself up. It felt like he was attached by string to the ceiling. 'Not so sure anymore.'

'The visions, then. Do you supply the visions?'

Alistair frowned. 'Visions?'

And, as if it had heard, from behind Cutlam there came a weird orange glow. It came from a coin-shaped amulet on a cheap desk set against one wall. From a cardboard box, something small shuffled out and started jumping up and down in a warm-up routine. Cutlam turned to look. Alistair already knew what was going on.

'What is this?' Cutlam asked.

'That's a winker,' Alistair said, pointing at the glowing coin-sized amulet. 'It's signalling.'

Both men watched as a small terracotta man, no more than nine inches tall and carrying a rubber-tipped pencil, strode mechanically along in front of a bank of equipment, stopped and jabbed the pencil at a button. The machine clicked, whirred, and then hummed into life. The automaton checked the lights and then, satisfied all was well, trudged back into its box.

'Why do you have a golem?'

Alistair looked at the stranger impassively. 'Automation à la the other side. The winker signals the golem that they are ready and voilà, the golem turns the machine on so they can watch the DVD wherever 'they' are.' The quotation marks came out as implied. 'But then you'd know all that because that's where you're from, isn't it? Over there.'

The man who called himself Cutlam didn't answer. 'I need to change and get out of these bloody robes. The smell…it's not good to be bloody.'

'No,' agreed Alistair, swallowing loudly, 'it isn't.' He still had a knife in his hand. 'I'll show you the bathroom, but no funny stuff, okay?'

Cutlam nodded. Alistair found some old clothes and waited outside the bathroom door. He heard water running and, a few minutes later, the door opened to reveal Cutlam mercifully without the blood. The musky smell persisted but it was less intrusive. Dressed in jeans and one of Alistair's old shirts, Cutlam looked as if he might be around thirty. Alistair was an-out-and-out heterosexual yet he couldn't help but notice there was something very attractive about this man, now that he'd brushed up. Perhaps it was the silvery eyes and the dark hair cut neatly in a modern style.

Cutlam caught him looking. 'What? Is there more blood?'

'A little,' said Alistair quickly, pointing to his own forehead to indicate where traces remained on Cutlam's face.

'I couldn't see any,' Cutlam explained, using his sleeve to remove the stains from his face.

'Do you have bad eyesight?' Alistair asked.

'No. It's your mirror.'

Frowning, but with the knife still clutched firmly in his hand, Alistair stepped into the bathroom behind Cutlam, who'd turned back to look into the mirror. Even from the offset angle Cutlam's reflection was blurred and unfocussed.

'Does it need a wipe?'

'I have tried wiping.'

Alistair took another step to stand behind Cutlam to see for himself and…frowned. His face appeared smudged and unclear, just a vague oval framed by a mop of chestnut…

Alistair's hair, the last time he'd looked, had been a mousy brown cut close to his head.

He jerked back and stepped out of the bathroom.

A new expression crossed Cutlam's face. 'What did you see?' he demanded.

'I didn't. I couldn't…it's blurred.'

'But you saw something. You saw a blurred…something.'

Alistair shook his head. He had seen something. Something different. And he felt different. There was no doubt about that.

Cutlam's eyes glinted. 'Tell me what you see when you look at me?'

'What?'

'Tell me what you see?'

'Tallish, slim, dark hair, thick on top, silver eyes, dark eyelashes, full lips.'

Cutlam nodded. 'And I see someone well built with chestnut hair, long in the back, hazel eyes, and a freckled face that is not unpleasant to look at.'

'Don't talk shit,' Alistair said.

Cutlam shrugged. 'It is what I see. And what you see is as unfamiliar a description of what I normally see in the mirror as mine so obviously is of you.'

'What does it mean?'

'It means we have no reflection when we look at ourselves. Yet we project a very different image when others see us.' Cutlam paused. 'The Glamour.'

'What Glamour?'

Cutlam grinned. It made an already handsome face devastating. He looked down at the knife in Alistair's hand and the smile widened. 'What is your name, boy?'

'Alistair.'

'Put away the knife, Alistair. I would have killed you already if I needed to. But I can smell you, Alistair. You are not a man. You are like me and we can be of help to one another.'

'Like you?'

Cutlam smiled and this time he opened his mouth wide. When he did, two large fangs, not normally visible, extended downwards on either side of his incisors.

'Try it,' he said to Alistair. 'It doesn't hurt. You only need to open your mouth a little wider than normal.'

'I can't do that.' Alistair shook his head.

'Try it.' Though Cutlam's voice was calm, this sounded more an order than a request.

Alistair complied. Cutlam was right. It didn't hurt. It felt just like popping a blocked ear canal with a swallow. He gingerly ran a fingertip around his new teeth. They were very sharp.

'But what does this all mean?' he said after extending his fangs for the third time.

'It means the world outside, your world, is our playground. Are you ready to play, Alistair? Are you hungry enough?'

Before he could answer, the shop doorbell rang.

CHAPTER TWENTY-FIVE

YORK, ENGLAND, FW

In all honesty, Kylah could have just as easily not taken Sewell with her and Bobby to the Inky Well, but it was about time he had his eyes opened and his cynicism skinned and roasted once and for all. Something was rotten in York, so why not let him discover it with them? It would be one way of finding out if his sphincter control was as good as he professed it was.

As ideas went, it turned out to not be one of Kylah's best.

Rules still applied when the Department of Fimmigration was doing something official in the human world. And the police had little sympathy for breeches of protocol. So, though Kylah and Bobby could have simply opened any door and walked right into the Inky Well using an Aperio, human rules demanded they knock and ask to be let in on the basis that Alistair Donovan needed to answer a few more questions with regard to their enquiries into unlicensed thaumaturgical activity.

They could, of course, have simply obtained a warrant. A few judges remained sympathetic and Sewell would have had no problem had he so wished. Many judges over sixty, as most of them were, still remembered some of the more celebrated cases where Fae played some nefarious or capricious role. What only a few select judiciary knew was that the MP expenses scandal of the early 2000s was, in part, Fae-related. The reason one MP claimed for the building and maintaining of a waterfowl bungalow in the middle of his pond was that he'd been seduced by a very attractive shapeshifter who managed to get an animorph spell sorted so that said MP became transformed into a duck on weekends. Quite apart from an enjoyment of swimming, it meant a corkscrew appendage and being able to copulate in public with no comebacks. Ticked all sorts of boxes for the honourable member—in both senses of the word—who otherwise would undoubtedly have ended up on the sex offender register.

Not exactly an excuse for the misspending of public money, but it demonstrated the fact that sometimes a politician's behaviour required a multi-disciplinary approach in order it be understood. Some of them were greedy, self-serving, egomaniacs who could be trusted about as far as one could spit into a force nine gale. Others were greedy, self-serving, egomaniacs who were also away—or at least having it away— with the fairies. Oddly enough, Fae found politicians alluring in the same way a mild-mannered accountant saw a trinket on a fairground stall a must-have item. Though undoubtedly tat, when it comes to using an air rifle to hit those targets, the gloves were most definitely off.

Fathering alien children, accusing women who don't clean behind the fridge of being sluts, waterfowl bungalows—they were the stuff of political pantomime. What Fae could resist a cry of, 'Look out behind you!' when their Widow Twanky or Buttons thought nothing of waving a flag and wearing a crash helmet and a suit whilst dangling on a zip wire.

You couldn't even make it up.

But Kylah knew Sewell. She could see in his eyes that he

wanted, more than anything, to prove her concern over this case was so much reactionary hot air. A load of old BS perpetrated by some bored amateur magician nerd who'd found something written in an old book and thought it fun to prank the public and the Met. He remained unshakeably convinced Alistair Donovan was in cahoots with Reg Strayne, who'd used smoke and mirrors to bamboozle a couple of gullible, D.O-give-me-a-sodding-break-F officers. In Sewell's mind, what this called for was simply a touch of the strong arm to put the frighteners on and he was very good at that. Five minutes alone in a room with this spotty herbert, Donovan, and it'd all be sorted out with minimal bruising. Then he could get back to proper policing with villains who knew that if Chief Inspector Sewell was on their case, they could expect at least a kick in the kidneys for giving him the trouble of calling on them.

They used the launderette on Braeburn Street as their exit, much to Sewell's disgust, and hurried along, leaning in to a sharp northerly breeze that whipped their coat-tails around their legs. The weather did not invite conversation and so, heads down, the trio hurried to the Inky Well. This was Kylah's case and she was the lead officer. Even so, it came as no surprise to see Sewell knock on the door of the closed shop firmly with three quick raps. Silence. Sewell repeated the knock and tried the handle. The door remained firmly locked.

'I'll take a look around the back. You ladies stay here out of the wind.'

Bobby watched him go with a shake of his head. 'Does he think that us 'ladies', being so frail and weak, might get blown away in the breeze?'

Kylah gave her a sour smile. 'Thing is, this is a shop, agreed? And shops, by definition, invite ingress.'

'Not when it says 'Closed'.' Bobby pointed to the sign hanging in front of the drawn blinds in the glass pane that made up the upper half of the door.

'But what if it said 'Open'?'

'Then I'd say we would be free to enter.'

Kylah slipped the Aperio on the door, opened it, reached in front of the blind and turned the sign around. 'There, now it says 'Open'. So, we're being invited in, aren't we?' She pressed a button on her lapel radio. 'Sewell, the door was open all the time. You must have been using the handle the wrong way. We'll be inside waiting, out of the wind.'

Sewell's expletives came back over the radio but Kylah ignored them. She pushed the door fully open and stepped inside with Bobby just behind her. The shop bell tinkled and a foetid, sickly stench hit them right away.

'Oh my God!' Bobby exclaimed. 'Has something died in here?'

'Possibly. But it's just as likely this is bad vestigia. Something appalling has happened or is happening here.'

'Should we wait for Sewell?'

Kylah nodded. 'Oh yes, we wait for him. Wouldn't want him to miss anything now, would we?'

They did not have long to wait. The Met's Section F officer wore a face like a toddler who'd lost his sweets as he hurried around from the rear.

'It seems you forgot to try the handle, Sewell,' Kylah said.

'It was locked. And the sign said 'Closed'. This is trickery.'

Kylah gave him a sympathetic pout. 'It's dark, we're all tired and some of us obviously emotional. We're only human, after all.'

'Are we?' said Sewell.

Kylah shrugged and Bobby had to turn away to hide her smile.

'Right, let's get on with this.' Sewell made a move to walk in, but Kylah stepped in front of him. 'Better let me go first,' she said. 'We don't know what's waiting inside.'

'Nothing a good nightstick can't sort out.' Sewell pulled

out a small cylindrical object and flicked it forwards. It extended telescopically and locked with a click.

'My, that's a big one,' Kylah said.

'Verbiage,' muttered Bobby.

'Big and hard.' Sewell smiled. 'Not let's get on with this, ladies, shall we?'

Kylah stood back and let Sewell through. She caught Bobby frowning behind him. 'Feel protected?' Kylah whispered.

Bobby shook her head. 'He's an idiot.'

'Shines right through like an insistent stain, doesn't it?'

CHAPTER TWENTY-SIX

NEW THAMESWICK, FW

ASHER WALKED AWAY FROM THE mirror and sat cross-legged outside the salt circle, making sure he was within reach of DiFrance's foot. The whoops and heavy footfalls of the blood-lust-energised vampires in the ICHOR building above seemed to be getting louder. They were a distraction. But Asher had been here before. He took some calming breaths, reached out towards DiFrance's cold flesh and shut his eyes. The express elevator feeling took him immediately, though sitting down did help the gut-swooping descent. His mind fell through the wispy clouds separating the living from the dead until, abruptly, it stopped. He was relieved to find he was not in the complete darkness—stygian or otherwise—preferred by the dead leeches he'd tried communicating with previously. Instead, Asher found himself in a small, old-fashioned lecture theatre, sitting a couple of rows back in one of the tiered and numbered seats rising vertiginously from the central desk and blackboard.

Asher was always surprised by the venues he ended up in at such times. They were, after all, nothing but imaginary constructs, a manifestation of the very essence of the recently deceased whose central core was laid bare. Sometimes he would find himself in a harem, or the biggest shopping centre in the world. Sometimes on a boat fishing for Marlin, other times in a pub with no closing time. Once, memorably, in the heart of a volcano surrounded by golden rings and fish bones, though that particular dream merchant was a suspect in a cross-dimensional transgression investigation. The fact of the matter was that at the end, the dead came to face the dream, or nightmare, that drove their lives. They could not hide anymore behind lies or the layers of defence and pretence the living wore like cloaks to conceal what lay beneath.

A door to the left of the blackboard opened and DiFrance walked in. He looked dazed, staring about him like a man in a dream. Confusion was also quite common at this point, especially in those who died sudden and violent deaths with no time for preparation. They ended up spending more time worrying about who was going to feed the cat than pondering any religious or supernatural considerations.

Existentialism came a poor second to Tigger.

'Hello?' DiFrance said, looking up at Asher.

'Mr DiFrance. I am sorry for your loss.'

'My loss…yes…I suppose…could I ask you to make sure Sherry Blossom feeds Blofeld?'

'Blofeld is your cat, I assume?'

DiFrance nodded.

'Of course,' Asher said.

DiFrance seemed to relax visibly. He walked to the desk and turned to the blackboard, both hands sweeping the chalky surface before turning back to face Asher.

'This is a temporary venue, I take it?'

Asher shrugged.

'I have studied transitional manifestations, of course. It is particularly ironic to find myself exploring my own.'

'It lasts until final arrangements are agreed,' Asher

explained. This was always a delicate discussion. Some people panicked at this point, wanting to know what exactly 'final arrangements' meant. And Asher never had an answer for them. Unless they'd made arrangements themselves, paid in to a scheme or, like the wizards at the university, set up a metaphysical college where deceased faculty members could still interact with the student body, you just faded. Witches, of course, 'retired' to a tropical island with bare-chested young men seeing to their every need. But for the majority of people, there was simply a fading away. Eventually, in a few years, Asher might come back to visit DiFrance and find nothing but a faint spectre running his hands over the blackboard, unsure and unaware of why and who and what.

'I always wanted to teach,' DiFrance said. 'When I learned I was a vimp I dedicated my life to finding a way to help my brothers.'

'Very noble,' Asher said. He wasn't buying. The dead could afford to believe their own invented narrative. The living could not. 'So why does a teacher summon a demon?'

DiFrance frowned. It was as if he knew the answer was there somewhere but he needed to clamber over some obstacles of logic before he arrived at it. 'I spent a lifetime studying vampire history and lore. Their heritage, my heritage. Some call us a freak of nature, others a necessary evil. There are sects in countries adjoining Oneg that consider us vital to maintaining a healthy population. They see us as hunters designed to cull. Where we flourished, only the agile, the cunning, the strong, the best of the herd could survive.'

'Your lot would kill and keep killing until there was no one left, we both know that.'

'From what I see of New Thameswick, it would do no harm to impose a little Kindred law.'

'You mean like stonings and crucifixions for decrying vampirism? Compulsory bloodletting? Abolition of alcohol and music? All in the name of blood?'

'That is a possibility,' DiFrance conceded. 'The bloodlust is a wondrous thing to behold. And yet I have never known the ecstasy, will now never know what bliss the taste of human blood brings. The more I learned, the more I yearned. And all the while I watched my kindred, the leeches, decline in stature and turn into something less than the grume they were meant to feed upon. I realised I must find a better way.'

'What better way?'

'Digsbow, of all people, a simple pedlar of trinkets, held the answer. Or rather, his trading licence did. He could sell to humans. He could sell the toys and omens we made.'

'But it's a fact that powerful artefacts here lose all power once they cross the trans-dimensional border. It's krudian law. They are little more than fancy decorations over there.'

'And yet they exist. Devoid of all physical and thaumaturgical power, they still exist.'

Asher frowned, trying to gauge where all this was leading. 'Let me guess, the bookmarks. Were they your idea?'

DiFrance nodded. 'Simple, harmless, inanimate objects of thick paper. I called them Never Forget to suggest a little arcane power. They like that sort of thing, or so Digsbow told us. A simple piece of thick paper loaded with more power than a cauldron full of Kritax. Their construction was a work of art, a design that took me years to perfect. The edges are as sharp as paper allows. Vampire blood colours the words and decorations. All it takes is one small paper cut, so easily obtained by an uncaring handler.'

'But why?'

'Have you not studied the bookmark, Mr Lodge? Really studied it?'

'No.'

'Oh, you should. You really should. But be sure to wear thick gloves when you do.' DiFrance, as dead as a doorknob, actually seemed to be enjoying himself. Asher decided he needed a reminder of his situation.

'You have a limited amount of time in which to wallow in success, DiFrance. How does your bloody bookmark tie in with summoning a demon?' Asher demanded.

DiFrance flinched. 'I no longer want to discuss this with you. I have other things to complete before…before…'

That was the thing about the dead. Usually, in the early stages, you could not shut them up because they needed to talk about their situation, unless of course they had something to hide. Some had a secret they really wanted to take with them to the grave. And then there were those souls who began to realise what this all meant for them. And that could quickly lead to fear and hopelessness. But DiFrance's reluctance was something else. Guilt perhaps?

Asher stood up. Necreddos were not simply collectors of gossip or the outpourings of the wronged. There were rules here and if DiFrance wanted to play by them, so be it.

'We could do this the hard way.'

DiFrance's lips stayed shut.

'You're a bright chap,' Asher said. 'You know how this works. Do I need to load the gun?'

DiFrance looked defiant.

Asher sighed. 'By requirement of the nexus so arranged, I, Asher Lodge request that the encapsulated entity once known as Simla DiFrance—'

'There is no need for that. I will answer your questions.' DiFrance's shoulders slumped.

Asher waited.

'The demon was an afterthought. With Digsbow gone, the chance of a human becoming transformed and mirror-reading the invitation—'

'What invitation?'

'It is written on the bookmark. An invitation to enter. The only true way for a vampire to gain ingress. I thought…I *believed* that if I were invited, I might at last fulfil my destiny. The part of me that was a vampire might truly be allowed to blossom and become whole.' DiFrance's eyes glittered with zealous belief. 'I had to try,' he whispered. 'Surely you see that?'

'What I see is murder most foul.' Asher shook his head. People were always meddling in things they did not know enough about, heedless of the fall out.

'It was my destiny.'

Asher stifled a groan. Destiny. Someone should rewrite the dictionary and add death and disaster as synonyms. 'You were clearly the summoner. Why did the demon attack you?'

'Who said it was the demon?'

Asher leaned in to the rail. 'If it wasn't the demon then—'

'Cutlam,' said DiFrance and the pain in his expression was plain to see. 'He was one of ours. He volunteered himself for the sacrifice the demon required. Perhaps I should have suspected a different motive.'

'Where is he?'

DiFrance hesitated once more. He was losing it as the dread realisation of his situation overtook his intellect. 'I…I did not make the transition. It is he who has been invited across.'

'Invited to where?'

'The human world. The promised world…Cutlam was not what we believed him to be.' DiFrance frowned. 'He made me bite him.'

Asher went cold. 'What?'

'Cutlam planned everything…I had no choice or control. He made me bite him.'

Asher stared at the spectre of DiFrance. 'Let me under-stand this. Cutlam made you bite him and then he—'

'Cut off my head.' DiFrance moaned on hearing the words. 'Cutlam did this…Cutlam.'

This was new. New and extremely troubling. Asher's mind raced. 'Tell me about the Inky Well?'

'I tire of our discourse.'

'Someone warned you about Digsbow, didn't they? How?'

'Messages. The mirror in the ballroom, it is old. I found it under the city in a vault that should have remained locked and undisturbed. But I took it and used it. Connor O'Malley and then his nephew, Alistair Donovan, showed us miracles. The Glamour is so much stronger over there. We have seen what we could become. Beautiful, strong, revered—' DiFrance paused, his face crumpling. 'No more,' he whispered.

'Who else knew Digsbow was under suspicion?' Asher tried to take all of this in but DiFrance was turning back to the blackboard, confused again.

'Who else knew?' Asher pressed the vimp for answers. 'Did Cutlam know?'

DiFrance nodded. But his response was vague and troubled.

Asher's mind galloped, computing all of this new information and coming up with a calculation that was horrifying in its implications. DiFrance, meanwhile, began to look around him like a man seeing his surroundings for the first time and Asher knew the imagery would begin to blur as his transient grip on this post mortem construct began to loosen. It sometimes caused great agitation and tension in the ghosts. He needed to get DiFrance to concentrate on the task in hand before the cords anchoring his mind to this manufactured existence frayed.

'If Cutlam *made* you bite him, it means he was not a reconditioned vampire like the other Reasonables,' Asher said.

'How long will you stay?' The question sounded incongruous, but Asher knew where it came from.

'A little while only.'

'Please stay.' DiFrance's voice was full of pleading.

Asher tuned him out. Cutlam knew about Digsbow and that he was going to be questioned. Cutlam pretended to be an on-the-wagon vampire when he was nothing of the sort. Cutlam then made DiFrance bite him to become contaminated before murdering him as payment for the demon who somehow then allowed the murderer to cross over to the Inky Well.

Why? Unless…

DiFrance walked across and held up his hands pleadingly. 'Please stay. There is so much to do. I—'

'I can't,' Asher said. 'I'm sorry. But there are people who still have some living to do and they deserve a chance.'

DiFrance's face distorted with misery, but Asher was already closing his mind to the ghost and sliding up through the layers until, at last, he snapped open his eyes to find himself back in ICHOR's ballroom.

'Cutlam,' he said out loud, getting to his feet. 'One of the novices. That's who killed DiFrance.'

Crouch and Matt, both inspecting the mirror, swung around on hearing Asher speak.

'Oh, and I wouldn't get too close to that thing. There's definitely a bit more to it that just a reflector.' Asher brushed chalk dust from his trousers.

'Who the hells is Cutlam?' Crouch asked.

'Good question. Great question. Who knows what lurks behind the mask of a white painted face?'

Something loud hit the floor above their heads. It sounded like a body.

'So Cutlam, the murderer, is one of Les Reasonables?' Matt asked with a confused frown.

'Yeah. Except he wasn't a vampire then, though he is now.'

'You been on the gin, Asher?' Crouch asked.

'The thing that really irks,' Asher explained, ignoring Crouch's stab at humour, 'is that DiFrance tried to contaminate humans using the bookmarks. Trying to recruit in the hope one of them might invite him or the others across.'

Matt nodded. 'Of course. That's the only way—'

'A vampire can enter a building, yeah, we know all that,' Crouch said.

'I'd forgotten,' Asher said grimly.

'So is that what's happened to Cutlam? Has he been invited across?'

'Forget Cutlam. Cutlam doesn't exist,' Asher said. 'It's just a name he used while pretending to be a born-again vampire here.'

Crouch and Matt were vying for deepest frown of the day.

Asher shook his head and clarified his thoughts. 'Can't you see it? Matt just fooled a clinic in Tobler into believing he was a vampire from ICHOR by dressing up as one. No one else in their right minds would want to *pretend* to be one of Les Reasonables unless they had an extremely good reason. And who do we know who might have a diabolical reason to hide under that same perfect in-your-face disguise? Hide until the opportunity arose for him to escape into another world?'

Crouch blinked as he touched down on planet Asher with a bump. 'Sicca Rus,' he breathed.

'Exactly.' Asher was on his feet, pacing. Matt and Crouch watched with wary expressions. Both of them looked like they wanted to ask questions, but were wise enough not to hinder Asher's concentration. He would not have answered them even if they had spoken. He was too busy cursing himself for being a blind and bigoted bloody fool. 'Rus targeted leeches. Tortured and killed them. Giovaise was on the brink of trying to be rehabilitated. He probably told Rus this and a great deal more. It gave Rus an idea. Somewhere to hide, disguised and in full sight of the world. Once there, DiFrance's mad plan gave him a tantalising glimpse into another world. A new world to wreak bloody havoc in, where the Constabulary can't get to him. Must have been like twenty birthdays all rolled into one. All he'd have to do was become a vampire. And then some poor misguided idiot in Matt's world would invite him in. So, to put it succinctly, or as Crouch might say, to put the bloody cherry on the rhesus positive cupcake, Sicca Rus is somewhere else in the universe and is also, by choice, a rapacious vampire.'

CHAPTER TWENTY-SEVEN

YORK, ENGLAND, HW

Kylah and Bobby followed Sewell into the dark and musty interior of the Inky Well. The instant they crossed the threshold, the smell not so much hit them as assaulted their olfactory nerves with grievous intent. Sewell, his coat up over his nose in an attempt at repelling the stench, switched on a torch and its bright beam bobbed drunkenly over the stacked shelves. 'Looking for a light switch,' he said.

There was a click followed by nothing.

'No good,' Bobby whispered. 'Electricity's off in here.'

'Your powers of deduction are truly astounding, Miss Miracle,' Sewell muttered.

'Ignore him,' Kylah said, adding tersely, 'Sewell, switch off that bloody torch.'

'Great idea. Plunge us all into darkness, why ever not? But then that's de rigeur for ghosties and ghoulies, isn't it?'

'It might also allow us to zone in on the light I caught a glimmer of before you switched the damned torch on.'

There was a moment's contemplative silence while Sewell

considered a riposte. But nothing was said and the light flicked off.

'There,' Kylah whispered.

A faint glow oozed into an aisle to their left. Sewell flicked the torch back on and shone it into Kylah's face. 'Well spotted. I'll go first. And we ought to charge someone for not flushing in here.' He shone the torch into his face and gave them a horror-movie grimace. The beam then slid away and moved off towards the source of the glow to Sewell's accompanying shout of, 'This is the police! Show yourself!'

At the rear, Bobby whispered, 'We'll give stealth and guile a miss then, shall we? So far, I've come up with crass, overbearing, and prat as Sewell-related adjectives.'

Kylah whispered back over her shoulder, 'Not a bad start. Rest assured, there will be more.'

'That smell is sickening.' Bobby forced herself to swallow.

'The odour of bad things.' Kylah quickened her step.

The light, when they eventually found it, leaked out from a room glimpsed through a partially open door masquerading as a bookcase. Sewell stood in the doorway. 'Candles, TV, DVD player, computer stuff. There's blood too. Smudges all over the table. Otherwise it's empty.' He walked in. 'I'd put money on there having been a ruckus here.'

Kylah joined him and as soon as she stepped over the threshold, she felt it. A change, not simply in temperature, but in the reflex desire to turn and run for the hills it induced. It was Bobby, however, who summed up the all-pervading horror of the place. 'Are you sure there's nothing dead in here?'

Kylah shook her head. 'Worse. I think that something that died long ago may have stuck its foot through the door.'

'Alternatively,' Sewell spoke without looking around at the two women, 'we have a simple case of blocked drains.'

'It isn't the drains,' Kylah said carefully, though the look she sent Sewell threatened to take the varnish off the door.

'Thaumaturgy, or any congress with the unnatural, requires energy, or sucks it away. The net effect is cold as in an exchange of atmosphere or a chemical reaction. Generally speaking, the dirtier the act, the lower the temperature and the worse the smell. Love charms smell of lavender. Strengthening charms give off a hint of cedar wood or burnt metal. This stench suggests something altogether different. It suggests that a very bad act indeed took place. It also suggests the consequences of that act are still here.'

'Or the drains need unblocking,' Sewell said, sounding unimpressed. 'All we know for *certain* is that that this room looks like a junk shop and smells like a khazi on the last day of the Glastonbury Festival. Oh, and there's a bit of blood. Maybe this lad Alistair cut his finger.'

'Let's hope it wasn't on a bookmark,' Bobby said.

Kylah moved about the room, taking in the books and the weird artefacts. The TV was on, a DVD still in the player. 'I wonder what someone was watching?' She picked up a remote with a gloved hand and pressed play. The TV screen flickered into life. Even though she was not a regular cinemagoer, she recognised the actors and the film they were in instantly. Difficult not to since the distributors made certain that everyone on the planet saw trailers, or read adverts on the sides of buses about the relationship between the misunderstood heroine with a face like a smacked arse and the uber-perfect hero who saves her from herself and his bloodthirsty Kindred without turning her into a bloodsucker. Just why an immortal super being would want to:

A) Establish a relationship with a moody teenager, or

B) Avoid all sexual contact other than the odd stroke of a neck or a snog,

remained a mystery to anyone with a toehold in the real world. But this, Kylah suspected, formed a part of its attraction where a mythical, immortal creature sees the appeal in the purity of a non-sexual teenage girl. Of course, if you're the girl, it's a lottery win. The looks, the beef, the power—it's all there without the yuck of dirtying the sheets. If you're a boy/man, you're watching the film thinking, *Yeah okay, but what would I really do if I had all that power?* Only one in a thousand came up with 'hold hands and listen to poetry' as an answer.

'What a surprise,' Sewell said. 'He's into a vampire films. The worst kind of made-up cobblers. I think it's time we talked to the boy's uncle, don't you?'

Sewell did not wait for approval or discussion. He turned to leave and came face to face with two figures standing in the doorway behind him.

'Fee, foo, flim, flig,' said Alistair—the new Alistair, 'I smell the blood of a filthy *pig.*'

'Very droll,' said Sewell who, to his credit, did not flinch. He was bigger than both of these men, his steel baton at the ready. 'I hope you have very good reason for being here.'

'We do,' said the second man. 'It's to watch you bleed.' He opened his mouth and it kept opening a good six inches wider than was normal. When it stopped, two large and very pointy fangs extended downwards in front of his existing row of pearly whites.

'Nice party trick,' said Sewell, though Kylah thought she heard a faint waver in his timbre for the first time. She also fervently wished he'd shut up and recognise, for once, that this was strange and dangerous ground. But he was having none of it.

'Now, stand back from the doorway,' Sewell ordered and stepped forward, baton held in front of him. He did not make it any further. The second, be-fanged man simply flicked his wrist and Sewell fell forwards, arms outstretched. He did not reach the floor but in a flailing dive over which he clearly had no control, catapulted out of the room and pivoted upwards in a move that pinioned him against the ceiling of the shop while his baton clattered to the floor. Invisible bonds pinned arms and legs and his face, for once, bore a look of bemused terror.

Below him, the thing that was not really Alistair looked up. 'Stay there, little fly, until the spider is ready to slime you up and suck you dry. And be quiet.'

Sewell opened his mouth, but no words came out. Even as Kylah watched, she saw the policeman's lips begin to zip up from the corners of his mouth, sealing off the gap.

The second vampire turned his attention to the two women. Kylah froze. Next to her, Bobby gasped.

Kylah knew what was going on here. But knowing did little to prevent the hormonal response spurting its message like a pinch of cayenne pepper into the neurochemical soup of her brain.

The vampire was beautiful. No, he was beyond beautiful, he was an androgynous angel; slim and sleek with a mane of hair and features that sucked at her gaze with magnetic attraction. She saw and all she could think of was letting him sink those teeth into her. Feel them penetrate her flesh hopefully at the same time as his flesh was penetrating—

Her thoughts, lost on a charabanc of ecstasy, hit a speed bump as something hard struck her back with force. Kylah turned in irritation to see Bobby pushing past with a look of wanton desire flushing her cheeks and sparking in her eyes. But they weren't looking at the vampire that had so magnificently pinned Sewell to the ceiling. Bobby had the 400°C hots for Alistair.

Kylah risked a glance. He, too, was sex on legs, but maybe one notch down from the delicious specimen she'd bagged. Bobby pushed a second time and Kylah stumbled, head jerking back to hit a bookshelf. Not hard, but hard enough to agitate the content of her skull.

Hard enough to bring a stab of pain.

Hard enough to see a few stars that shone a thin but stark light onto what was happening.

She pushed off the wall, grabbed Bobby roughly by the arms and slapped her hard enough to jar her fillings.

'Oh, you—'

'Don't look at him,' Kylah ordered. 'Do not look directly at either of them.'

'What are you—'

'Don't look!' yelled Kylah.

'Okay, okay,' Bobby said, massaging her cheek.

'This is the Glamour. Never felt it so strong, but it is definitely the Glamour.'

'What are you talking about?'

The vampire's head tilted back and the perfect eyebrows crept together minimally in annoyance. He flicked his hand at the ceiling. Sewell's wrist snapped and the big policeman let out a groan of pain.

'Look at me, little lady,' said Sicca Rus.

Kylah threw him a darting glance. The sneer he wore did nothing to detract from his languid beauty. Her stomach swooped as a wave of uncontrollable ecstasy surged. Kylah's head was full of dancing in loud bars; long, languorous days on sun-soaked beaches; and the promise of some bedroom rodeo in the late afternoon. She could see herself lying on a towel in the hot sand next to this exotic creature who would, she knew, sport dark serpentine tattoos coiling over the corded muscles of his limbs. But in his sneer there was also cruelty. An imperiousness that warned her not to hesitate because he knew of her weaknesses. Kylah Porter, who could stop traffic with a flick of her hair, caught her breath as harboured doubts she never voiced sailed out on the tide of her consciousness and bobbed there on full display.

The way the bones of her knees felt a little too prominent. Her eyes a little too large. The way her mouth somehow became crooked when she laughed. The tiny chip in one tooth from fighting a sea hag when she was seventeen.

Matt would have doubled up with laughter if she ever told

him these things. He'd probably suggest she walked about ringing a bell to warn people of her coming. Then he would put both his hands on her buttocks and yank her to him, pelvis to pelvis.

He'd done exactly that after half a bottle of wine just a couple of weeks before and she had not minded, though the same could not be said of the other people in the restaurant.

Matt.

But this…*this*…was the Glamour and the vampire behind it could sense her doubts and fears. All so superficial and vain and laughable. Yet he knew how to magnify them with dysmorphic expertise. She fought against it, but in her head she sensed that this creature in front of her was doing her a huge favour. She would never have such an opportunity again. The wonderful ones were in town and the prize she just happened to be in front of had an appetite for a plain Jane like her. Did she really want to pass up this one, delicious opportunity? This chance to taste the forbidden fruit?

Another sickening snap from the ceiling. The moan that followed was harrowing. Unnecessary cruelty, the vampire creed, like a cat's unspeakable need to torture a helpless rodent. It cut through her fog of longing.

'Trespass,' said Kylah making a huge effort to keep her eyes fixed on the vampire's feet. 'Under the powers vested in me I arrest you for illegal ingress.'

Sicca Rus laughed. 'I'm here, right in front of you, girl. Look at me. Alistair invited me in and there's nothing you can do about it. Come here and let me offer you the curse.' Even the voice held power and seduction. This one was in a West Texas drawl.

Kylah felt a tug behind her navel pulling her towards the vampire. It drew her forward with faltering steps until something powdery rushing past her face distracted her. It fell to the floor with a brittle drum roll. She looked down to a white line appearing across the threshold of the room as Bobby's voice broke in.

'This room I call my dwelling.

This room where I abide.

No spirit dead or living,

May cross where I divide.'

A sudden buzzing in Kylah's ears and the pulling sensation in her navel stopped. She threw Bobby a look.

'Guardian charm. It will not last,' Bobby said.

Kylah breathed out a warning. 'Sight and sound. The Glamour does both.'

'Is there nothing we can do?'

'Not while he has Sewell.'

'Witchery?' said Rus, looking down at the line of salt. 'You may be safe in there, but your friend is out here with us. And perhaps he might look more agreeable to everyone as he vomits his own liver out through his mouth. Ever seen that, witch?'

'No,' said Kylah, keeping her eyes averted. 'An exchange. Me for Sewell.'

'Both of us for him,' Bobby added too quickly for Kylah to object, though she did try.

'No—'

'Too late. The bargain is struck,' laughed Rus and spat on his hand.

Sewell began to slide over the ceiling, folding around the top of the door frame with accompanying agonised screams of pain as his broken wrists dragged across the surface.

Once over the threshold of salt, Sewell's legs and then his body fell downwards until only his head stayed attached. It was the last to cross and break the spell. He fell heavily, his arms useless to break the fall. Bobby threw some powder into his big pale face and he fell instantly into a sleep.

Rus stood back to await the woman's exit, Alistair behind him.

'Oh so noble,' said Rus, looking at Sewell's crumpled form.

'Can I go in there and kill him?' Alistair asked, drool running down his chin.

'Later, boy,' Rus said as Kylah and Bobby, heads down, started for the door.

'No, now,' said Alistair and lunged at the open doorway. A noise, like something hitting a steel drum followed as Alistair's body met with the salt line of the guardian charm. He fell, clutching his shoulder.

'The charm remains until the witch removes it,' Rus drawled, tutting. 'Perhaps you could do somethin' 'bout persuading her?'

'Run, Bobby. Run!' Kylah yelled and pushed Bobby out through the door.

Alistair, still clutching his arm, swore and lunged at her legs as they sprinted past. He missed. But the movement galvanised him and he got to his feet and stumbled after her.

Kylah, however, did not move.

Rus kept his gaze on her. 'And so we are alone, you and I. I sense your presence here is no accident. What am I to call you?'

'Captain Kylah Porter, Department of Fimmigration. And you are under arrest.'

'So you say. So, arrest me, Captain Porter. Do what you have to do, girl.'

He held his hands out and for one moment, Kylah thought she might actually try and put on some restraints. But as she reached for the leather-coated iron-wire ties in her back pocket, his hands twitched. Like a good agent, she kept her eyes on those hands and followed them up to where they ended their rapid motion—in front of his face. It was then that she realised her mistake.

It was also when she heard the shop bell ring.

CHAPTER TWENTY-EIGHT

NEW THAMESWICK, FW

Constabulary reinforcements arrived at ICHOR and the reassuring figure of Tock, all eighty-five inches of him, stood guard at the door of the ballroom.

The body had been covered with a blanket and Asher was examining, at a safe distance, the mirror. 'I suggest we bag up the winker and take it back to Hipposync. These VDs—'

'DVDs,' Matt cut in to correct him. 'VD is normally an acronym applied to hanky-panky acquired infections.'

'Hanky Panky?' Crouch asked. 'What's the prime minister of Klap got to do with it?'

Matt opened his mouth to speak but then remembered where he was and decided against it.

'DVDs then,' said Asher. 'They are human technology. Clearly there is cross jurisdiction here. The winker is our link to wherever Rus might be and I suggest Hipposync is the best place to begin a trace.'

'Agreed,' said Crouch. 'I'll get this mess cleared up and see what we can dig up on DiFrance from the remaining Les Reasonables. Though I suspect they're unlikely to be in the slightest bit reasonable now they've had a sniff of the red stuff.'

Asher and Matt left Crouch issuing instructions and garlic to his men. Before Matt left, Crouch grabbed his arm. 'Take this. You never know.' He held out his fox-headed cane.

'Thanks, but I don't think—'

'Might not be a bad idea, Matt.' Asher looked pointedly at the beheaded corpse.

Matt shrugged and accepted the weapon awkwardly, before slipping it through his belt.

He and Asher adjourned, via the blue room, to Hippo-sync. There they met with Sergeants Keemoch and Birrik, who listened with nothing short of incredulity to the story they had to tell.

'We, uh, need to find this winker's partner as soon as possible, Keemoch,' Matt said.

The two Sith Fand took the bagged-up artefact and were about to leave when Asher asked, a little too causally, 'Is Bobby about?'

Keemoch's expression was the nearest thing to a leer a Sith Fand could manage. 'Sorry, Asher. Both she and Captain Porter are with the Met.'

'We could have saved them the trouble now we have DiFrance's confession,' Matt said.

'You two boys will just have to play cards until they're back,' Birrik said, grinning. 'Or there's always the cold shower.'

'I have contacts at the BOD, don't forget.' Asher gave both SES soldiers a steely look. 'Prof Llewyn is always looking for well-trained volunteers for clearing geist mines.'

Keemoch held up his hands in surrender. 'Banter,' he said, all innocence. 'Just banter.'

When they'd left, Matt said, 'I'll text Kylah. See what they're up to.' He sighed heavily. 'We never got to finish that drink at the Five Bells, did we? Why don't we go to the Trout while we wait for the trace? I'll see if the girls can join us there.'

Matt left word with Keemoch to contact them once they had results and he and Asher made for the Trout—a country pub nestling on the River Thames just north of the city—via a convenient bike shed door Matt was very familiar with. He ordered a wheat beer and Asher plumped for a pint of best.

'Nice pub,' Asher said.

'Yes. Brings back lots of memories,' Matt nodded.

'Isn't this where you…'

'Almost got killed by a terrorist Thames tsunami? Yes, it is. And I'm glad you remembered all my boring stories.'

'That one comes straight from the archives,' Asher said. 'Recommended reading at the academy.'

They drank in silence for a while, savouring the calm atmosphere after the horrors they'd encountered at ICHOR, but neither of them able to shake off the anxiety of knowing that a killer was out there, somewhere.

'Cheer up,' Matt said after a while, noting Asher's glum expression. 'We did good, as they say.'

'We did. I am sorry if I seem…preoccupied.'

'We'll catch him, you know. Sicca Rus.'

Asher nodded. 'I truly hope so.'

'But that isn't why you're worried, is it?'

'I was hoping to see Bobby. It's been a while.'

'Nothing wrong, is there?'

'No. But this case has preoccupied me. Duana says I need to redress the deficit in my work-life balance.'

'She's a deep one, that Duana.' Matt took a healthy slug of beer.

'She is a wise woman. And it is true, I feel I am not making as much of an effort as I should.'

'You're both busy people…'

'That is not an excuse.'

'Well, sometimes a little bit of distance doesn't hurt, you know.' Matt studied his drink.

Asher looked surprised. 'Are you and Kylah…?'

'We're good. Very good. It's just that lately I've sensed she's a little tetchy when we work together. Says I don't take things seriously enough.'

'Perhaps you, too, need to look at that balance. Working and living together can occasionally be a…'

'Challenge?' Matt interjected.

'Conflict was the word I was going to use,' Asher conceded with a smile just as Matt's phone signalled several incoming messages in short succession.

'Three at once and all from Kylah. Bloody krudian shift plays havoc with this thing. The last one was sent half an hour ago. *Bobby and I have decided to drag Sewell the sceptic along with us to shut him up. See what he makes of Alistair Donovan.*' Matt frowned. 'They've gone back to the Inky Well.'

Once again Matt's phone chirped.

'This one's from Keemoch. He says the partner winker has been traced to Braeburn Street in Yo...' He paused mid word, his face draining of colour.

'What is it?' Asher asked.

Matt looked up. 'The Inky Well is on Braeburn Street.'

For the second time that day, both men bolted for the door, their drinks unfinished. Matt used the Aperio on the bike shed and forty seconds after receiving the text, he and Asher stepped through into the Inky Well's dark interior, triggering the bell above the door. Asher threw a *placatus* hex, which shut it up instantly, but not before it had given warning of their entrance.

'They need to open a window in here,' Matt whispered, wrinkling his nose.

'If I had to put a name to it, I might plump for Eau de Sicca Rus,' Asher hissed in reply. He tried the light switch to no avail.

'This doesn't look or smell very good to me,' Matt said, switching on his phone to light the way.

They moved through the maze of books, Matt trying to remember the twists and turns. They'd gone only ten steps when the house shook with the noise of slamming doors somewhere on the floors above them.

'Sounds like someone's a bit pissed off,' Matt said.

'Then perhaps we should hurry,' Asher replied grimly.

They rounded a few more corners until Asher pointed out the flickering glow of candlelight down one aisle. They crept forward past the open door to a room where a big man lay sprawled unconscious on the floor, his hands pointing in unnatural and disconcerting angles. Matt moved to enter but Asher held him back.

'It's guarded,' he said, pointing to the line of salt. 'There is no way in.'

Another volley of violent banging and slamming reached them from upstairs.

'I don't think that's the removals men. Maybe we should find out what's causing that ruckus,' Matt suggested.

'We will. But first I suggest we follow our noses.'

They did. Literally. The bad smell led them towards the rear of the shop, the serried ranks of books on the crammed shelves the only things marking their stealthy progress. They took a couple of turns and with each the smell worsened until they met an alcove and stopped dead, the only noise Matt's sharp and involuntary intake of breath.

Two figures were silhouetted against the window. One, male, sat nonchalantly on the sill, one leg bouncing on the other knee, beating time to some rhythm only he could hear. Before him stood a woman. She too was calm, her face serene in the guttering candlelight. At least, as calm as someone with a huge knife held to her throat could be. But then, Kylah Porter was not someone prone to theatrics, Asher knew that. And yet this was an odd, unnatural calm he read in her face.

And the way her eyes locked unseeingly on first him, and then Matt, sent warning ripples along the hairs of both his arms.

'Kylah?' It was Matt who croaked out her name to break the tense bubble of silence enveloping them as they stood in that alcove. It emerged from his lips unbidden, his voice a warble of concern.

Her response was nothing more than a vague frown. She looked at Matt but without recognition, or worse, recognition but little or no perturbation. A look pretty women sometimes use to repel unwanted attention.

'It's the Glamour,' said Asher, looking again at the mocking expression the man wore and seeing it for what it was. His appearance was nothing but a shiny shell over the darkness beneath, though the shell itself was admirable. Yet, when Asher looked away and then back again quickly, he saw, for a moment, the flickering truth: a man in a bloody tunic, wiry and intense, holding a knife and grinning like he was about to deliver the punchline of the best joke in all the world,

'Glamour?' said Matt as if he hadn't heard the word before.

'Vampires use it all the time. Or rather, used to use it, according to Duana. It's banned in New Thameswick. Part of the deal they did to be allowed to live amongst us was to relinquish that power. It controls the way they appear to us. When it does work it's at its best between the sexes.'

'But—'

'He doesn't really look like that. But it's what Kylah sees, and she doesn't smell what we smell either. The Glamour works at all levels. They say there's a musk, though to me it smells like sour milk.'

'Pheromones?' Matt asked.

'I am not familiar with that term but I do know Kylah can't help herself. If you look away and then back again, you'll see what he really is. Just a scruffy, psychopathic criminal.'

Sicca Rus spoke for the first time, or rather sneered in his affected smooth West Texan drawl. 'I smell copper.' 'Smell' came out with a sibilant 'S'.

'Sicca Rus,' Asher said, 'You are under arrest.'

'Second time someone's said that to me. Funny thing is, I'm the one with the knife.' He used the flat end of the wicked-looking blade to turn Kylah's face towards him. When she did, her lips parted and she inhaled sharply. 'Captain Porter here had the chance, but we decided it was a non-starter, didn't we, hon?' He blew a waft of stinking breath at her and she closed her eyes in delight.

Next to him, Asher sensed Matt go rigid.

'Matt, that isn't Kylah. Understand that. She's charmed by the Glamour and I sense it is very strong.'

The noise of a locked door being smashed open thundered through the ceiling above, causing Asher to glance up reflexively.

'That'll be Alistair. He's on a witch-hunt.' Rus sniggered.

'Bobby,' whispered Asher.

'That her name, the little witch?' The face Rus projected to the world split into a wide grin showing a row of perfect teeth that would have made any toothpaste manufacturer drool.

'What have you done with her?' Asher croaked.

'Better ask Alistair.'

Asher turned to Matt. 'I'm going after Bobby. Remember, what you see isn't real. He's a criminal, a murderer and Kylah doesn't know what she's doing. I'll be back.'

It was an open invitation for Matt to reply with 'Hasta la vista, baby,' but his brain, though automatically considering the reply since it was programmed to do so, knew this was neither the time, nor the place, for such frippery. Close call though.

Asher turned and headed for the corridor. That would be the best place, he reasoned, to find the stairs.

————

ALISTAIR, the *new* Alistair, with scant regard for the property he was bound to inherit from his uncle, systematically tore the first floor apart. Nothing mattered now that he was infused with the hexed priviron that caused such mayhem in the human haematological systems. With a predilection for bone marrow, once the infective agent reacted with the stem cells to modify haemoglobin into maemoglobin, the transcription was ridiculously rapid. Not content with mauling the red stuff, it also headed for the brain where it threw out the driver by flooding the cerebrospinal fluid with clever cocktails of its own making. Cocktails that altered perception and augmented bits of the brain normally kept hidden for fear of causing damage, both to the owner, and to any innocent bystander. One of those augmented corners of white matter controlled aura projection—the Glamour by any other name. Like lighting up a roman candle.

The priviron was not amenable to any form of conventional Fae or human treatment. Shistirrer had made sure of that when he'd cursed the child in Oneg centuries before, though certain frequencies of sound were known to be highly destructive to its fragile matrix.

But that was knowledge gleaned in Tobler. This was the Inky Well. And here, in Alistair's young and juicy brain, the priviron was already creating synaptic links between his pleasure centre and a hereto-untried lust for the taste of blood— and probably flesh, too—that drove him on relentlessly. And he sensed fresh fayre nearby, could smell its coppery aroma like he might a fondly remembered roast dinner.

A different, fainter aroma, more complex and sharp, drifted up from below. That belonged to the other woman.

Alistair felt little desire for that. It was a taste for an altogether different palate. If Rus coveted that taste, good for him. Alistair required fresher meat. Meat that had leapt over him out of the guarded room and careered blindly into the shop and up the stairs.

Initially he'd blundered through whichever door was nearest, locked or unlocked. But his damaged shoulder ached and he wondered if he'd broken something since his arm on that side felt heavy and weak. It slowed him down, but it had not stopped him because the pain was as nothing compared with the all-pervading urge to tear down the walls in order to get to the girl and rip her flesh open to expose the crimson nectar inside.

He'd demolished the top floor and the attic. There were four doors left on the first floor and he'd smashed opened two. He threw open the third now: his uncle's bathroom.

Empty.

That left only his uncle's room. The room of the dead. He did not want to go in there. Did not want to smell the stench of the liquids seeping from the corpse or see the wasted limbs and the bloated torso. For a moment, he hesitated. Surely the girl would not have gone anywhere near either…would she? But she was nowhere else to be found. And perhaps she was smart enough to have chosen this room for all of those terribly *wrong* reasons.

Cunning bitch.

Enough of the real Alistair remained to understand that his uncle—his dead uncle— had been unreasonably denied his rest at the whisperers' behest and their last meeting had not been pleasant. Perhaps he should just walk away?

He opened his mouth wide and felt his new fangs extend. He thought of the woman's pure, unsullied neck and had to swallow twice to clear the saliva.

Sod that. He needed blood. Even so, this time, Alistair knocked.

'Uncle Connor? Are you…awake?'

No reply.

His voice dropped. 'I know you're in there, bitch.'

Without waiting, Alistair threw open the door. Uncle Connor lay where he'd last fallen when the demon finished using him. The bitch stood on the far side of the bed with pieces of rolled up tissue stuffed into her nostrils against the stench, a brass candleholder in her hand.

Visions of her gore filled Alistair's head. He tilted it back, let out an animalistic gurgle, and lunged towards her.

———

A TINY PART OF KYLAH, alone on an island in the chemical swamp of her brain, understood perfectly what was going on. She'd been taken by complete surprise by the power of the vampire's aura. And yet his very presence in the Inky Well meant that the way had been paved under her very nose. And worse, on *her* watch.

What was certain was that she'd underestimated the danger. Perhaps she'd spent too long amongst humans. Of course, they had glamour, with a small 'g', too. And, though less dangerous, was no less important. Whole industries were built around the damned thing. Magazines, fashion, TV, films all designed to cajole and deceive the morbidly obese into believing that wearing a dress modelled by a six-foot-tall clothes horse on a catwalk could materially transform their lives. Having a handbag bearing the emblem of a small tree made you powerful. Wearing underwear as worn by a footballer specialising in bending balls around human walls might, if you lost a few stone and practiced every day for a quarter of a century, allow you to do exactly the same.

The human race was in good hands.

Laughable? Perhaps. But the people doing all the laughing were the CEOs wheeling their barrows full of gold all the way to the banks. There was nothing at all wrong with turning a profit but what they'd done in the process was make the population believe they needed glamour as much as food and shelter. They'd made it a necessity. And now here were the vampires. Users who could pluck all that need and desire from the air and turn it into something tangible and totally uncontrollable.

Kylah knew Sicca Rus held a knife to her throat. She also knew that the man she wanted to spend the rest of her life with was standing in front of her, looking scared and a little hurt and very, very confused. But more than all of that, she knew that Rus was the most exotic of creatures. That he smelled and looked and felt wonderful—

No he wasn't…

The Glamour, his Glamour, possessed her and held her. She looked at him and saw something her subconscious projected. It said a lot that in this manifestation Sicca Rus looked a lot like Matt, but with added features copied and pasted from a lifetime of Kylah's existence. And in Kylah's case, that meant an awfully, awfully long time.

It isn't real.

Of course it wasn't *real*, but Glamour had nothing to do with reality. It was aspirational and fed on desire and imagination and there were no limits.

Rus spoke, or rather, drawled to Matt. 'If I was a betting man, which I am, judging from the look on your face I reckon I'd get pretty good odds on you having feeling for this filly.' Rus ran the blunt edge of the knife against the side of Kylah's neck. She arched it obligingly because that is what he wanted her to do. 'Thing is, she likes me. Thinks I'm special. Don't you, hon?'

'Leave her alone,' Matt said, emotion thickening his voice.

A small tear appeared in the corner of Kylah's eye.

Sicca Rus grinned. 'Right now, I mean, as of this moment she would do anything for me. I'd give y'all a demonstration but it'd be too distracting. And anyways, I've only got ten minutes, though that's usually more than enough for me.'

Matt looked at his watch. Kylah didn't need to see it to know it would be midnight in ten minutes.

'Yeah, that's right. Midnight in ten. You look like a nice enough fella. Educated an' all. My old mom wanted me to stay in school but my daddy, he needed money for shine so he sent me out to work when I was ten. Only work then was as a soil-treader. Know what a treader is, college boy?'

Matt didn't respond.

'Nah, you wouldn't know. A treader works at the town midden. He waits for the night soil boys to come in with their loads and then treads the filthy contents, looking for coins and the like that someone might have swallowed. You'd be surprised at what us boys might find. Though the smell was something terrible.'

Matt gagged.

Sicca Rus laughed.

'Kylah,' Matt said. 'Kylah, can you hear me?'

Rus shook his head. 'She won't answer. Look, watch this. Give my thigh a little squeeze, baby. Show me some love, uh-huh.'

Kylah's brain flooded with delicious messages at the very centre of which was an idea that her hand might stroke this creature's thigh.

It did.

'See,' Rus beamed. 'It's real easy.'

Matt's eyes snapped up to engage Rus. 'What happens at midnight?'

'I'm gone. I'm scootin' the coop.' Rus tapped the window behind with the handle of the knife. It stayed within six inches of Kylah's neck the whole time. 'The world will then be my crawfish, as my old daddy used to say, when he was capable of speaking. There'll be lots of new places to visit. Lots of little girls like Kylah to engage in conversation and to play with. So you and me and your girlfriend here are goin' to sit tight for ten. And if we're all nice and quiet I might, I just might give her back to you. What do you say to that, eh?'

'You murdered DiFrance,' Matt said.

'I won't deny it.'

'And Digsbow.'

'Yep, that was me.'

'And half a dozen leeches.'

'You got me there. But you know what? It's my creed. Just keep dying, baby.'

'Then I can't let you leave,' Matt said and held up Crouch's cane.

Rus grinned. 'Now what do you think you're going to do with that little bitty thang?'

CHAPTER TWENTY-NINE

YORK, ENGLAND, HW

Creeping up the stairs, Asher heard another door thrown open followed by Bobby's anguished yell. He abandoned creeping and sprang up the rest of the way, reaching the landing just as Alistair made his lunge. Asher plunged forward, taking in the weird tableaux as if in slow motion: the splayed corpse, Alistair tangling with its dead limbs and Bobby with her eyes shut, brandishing a brass candlestick with sweeping strokes against a foe she dare not look at.

Confused, Asher lost concentration and stumbled, hand outstretched to save his fall. In his desperation to regain balance, he grabbed and clamped on to something cold and hard which, for one desperate moment, he thought was Alistair's leg.

Too cold for that.

It was Connor O'Malley's leg.

It helped necreddos enormously if they could see the deceased person they were trying to communicate with. Physical touch, as with DiFrance, was a direct line to the person of interest with no waiting for a dialling tone. But still, establishing contact usually required a bit of effort.

This time the connection was instant and violent and it took Asher just a fraction of a second to realise that something was badly off kilter. Asher was used to dealing with victims. Unlike the cool DiFrance, recently murdered spirits were usually only too glad to unburden themselves with as much graphic detail as they could muster. There was always heavy emphasis on citing the miscreants who had done the deed. The long dead, on the other hand, unless they were possessed of arcane power such as a warlock or a witch, usually needed help remembering. Occasionally, when confronting the long departed, Asher would take something with him as an aide memoir. Something to help him focus.

But Connor O'Malley was in a different league. He was angry, had been recently used and abused most terribly and, to cap it all, was Irish. The first thing he did was punch Asher in the face. But having no corporeal existence, the fist sailed harmlessly through, though not before it made Asher duck.

'Come on, you bastard,' the ghost Connor growled. 'Try it again. Just try it again, you gobshite.'

Asher should have asked what Connor was so upset about. It would have been the polite thing to do. But Bobby was still waving her candlestick and Alistair was drooling like a rabid dog. There simply was no time for niceties. Of course, the physical contact made it easy. The hard part was separating the octogenarian wheat from the chaff. Asher took the liberty of stepping inside Connor's head, psychically speaking. Not something he usually did, but needs must. Within seconds he knew why Connor was so pissed off.

The punch thrown by O'Malley's angry soul had been aimed at the denizen who'd had the temerity to disturb him, and worse, make his dead and decaying body do things no self-respecting corpse should ever do. It was humiliating and uncalled for. He'd been taken for a ride and was certain the whisperers had duped Alistair, too.

All of this burst into Asher's consciousness and managed to make him even angrier than he already was. Reanimation was no joke. It wasn't right. It was degrading. 'So,' he said, stepping out of Connor's mind and addressing the ghost directly, 'how about a little payback?'

On the bed, Connor's petrified lips cracked into a tiny but terrifying smile.

A slavering Alistair finally managed to extricate himself from Connor's rigor-rigid legs and knelt on the bed, waiting for his chance to grab the candlestick and whip it away from Bobby.

'Stay away!' Bobby yelled. 'I'm warning you.'

Attagirl, thought Asher.

Alistair growled and the sound was nothing like the noise humans make. He reached up and waited until the candlestick reached the apex of Bobby's swing before swatting it away and sending it clattering to the corner of the room.

Bobby's eyes snapped open. She gasped. Alistair giggled and opened his mouth, bending slightly to ready his leap.

That was when Connor's dead legs scissored Alistair's waist, causing the latter's leap to become nothing more than a powerless bounce as the bedsprings groaned their resistance.

'Get off me,' screamed Alistair, pawing at the yellow limbs long enough to allow Asher to tear off the garlic scarf he'd been wearing and wrap it unceremoniously around the vampire's neck.

The effect was instant. Like seeing someone terrified of snakes suddenly have a tree python drop down on them from a great height. The dilemma was obvious and written all over the horrified face. He could throw it off, but that would mean touching the garlic with his hands. Whether it was pure fear or the effect of the garlic itself, the net result was a frozen panic. Alistair knelt on the bed, quite still, as

Connor's limbs fell away, his last act as a zombie gratifyingly complete.

'Is he safe?' Bobby asked in a quavering voice.

'A garland of garlic should hold him.'

Bobby nodded. Rapid little movements that mingled with her trembling. Her eyes never left the vampire. 'He looks different.'

'Garlic has that effect. It cuts through all the Glamour. Move past him. It's quite safe.'

With her back to the wall, she inched past the faintly quivering form of Alistair, whose eyes were wide and staring at the garland around his neck.

'I was actually about to let him…' she whispered.

'I know,' Asher said. 'But perhaps I will do for the moment.'

He reached out to her and she took his hand. He pulled her out of the room and closed the door before folding her into his arms. She gave a small shudder and Asher respected her for that. The embrace lasted two seconds before Bobby pushed back, her face full of sudden panic. 'Where's Kylah?'

———

THE WOMAN in question remained lost to the Glamour. It was like being in a coma, or coming round from surgery loaded up on quality pain relief drugs. She could hear all the conversation around her, knew the man opposite was someone she cared about, yet felt completely comfortable and at ease standing next to this other man holding a knife held to her face. It was dangerous, he was dangerous, and it felt all so *right* despite it obviously being so *wrong*. Enough of the real Kylah Porter, squashed into the corner of a very overstuffed central nervous system struggling to cope with all the Glamour-induced hormonal fireworks, twigged that she ought somehow to do something. Otherwise, this was all going to end very badly. She could feel the violent energy in Rus. Knew that he was not going to walk away with business unfinished. Unless she could somehow distract him…

'Put down your pretty stick,' said Sicca Rus. 'Throw it behind you.'

'No,' Matt said and took a step forward.

'Don't be stupid.' Rus pressed the tip of the blade into the soft flesh beneath Kylah's eye. Her fingers crept up to where it pressed and Rus drew it away. But when Kylah pulled her finger away, a red bead of blood welled and trickled down her cheek. Matt threw the silver-headed stick behind him and heard it clatter into the darkness.

'See, we can still be friends,' Rus grinned.

From somewhere in the darkness, a clock began to strike midnight.

'Well, well,' Rus said. 'Doesn't time fly. I'll be on my way now.' He sniffed the air. 'Fee foo flim flood, I smell the perfume of female blood. Oh, man.' He shut his eyes in ecstasy and opened his mouth. Saliva oozed down his chin and onto the floor as if someone had turned on a tap. 'Sometimes you do somethin' knowin' it's a big mistake, but you do it anyway. I think it's time I explored what bein' a vampire is all about.' He ran his finger along the trail of blood on Kylah's face and pressed it to his lips. His eyes flared wide and he opened his mouth violently, the fangs sprang out and he plunged them into Kylah's neck.

The pain brought her back. She had a fleeting realisation it should not have been painful, but it was and she reacted by throwing her arms up to swat the thing away before falling to her knees and seeing Matt's frozen expression of abject horror.

The window smashed behind her. Sicca Rus, sensing freedom, turned to make his escape. She threw Matt a glance and from somewhere dragged up the words in a low growl.

'Now would be a good time to sort this bastard out as only you can.'

Matt's eyes widened a fraction and then he looked at Rus, at the bloodstained lips, the gloved hands smashing out the panes. Something was happening to the vampire's body. It was collapsing, morphing into something hunched out of which wings were sprouting.

The shock and horror lasted only a second or two before Matt's eyes narrowed in that way they did when the answer to a thorny problem came to him. Research was a wonderful thing.

Kylah registered that look and knew she'd love him forever.

The window, which now revealed a chilly York night, began to fill with the sound of bells and a rooster crowing. A wind howled and from nowhere, a rusted corrugated sheet blew up from the street to block most of the window. With the wind came rain and the sudden downpour made a curtain of running water from the overflowing guttering beyond the rusty iron sheet.

'What superstitious bullshit is this?' snarled Rus.

'The sort that has you trapped, I'd say,' Matt said.

Rus turned away from the window, his face now elongated and angular, his hands and fingers a good twelve inches longer than moments before.

Matt hurled his garlic garland at the thing. It struck and Rus screamed. He snarled and flew, literally, past the two of them into the gloom of the building with a leathery rustling of wings.

Matt rushed to Kylah's side and she motioned feebly. 'We can't let him get away…'

There was a loud crack, a noise like something quite heavy colliding with a wall followed by the repetitive clatter of a large number of books falling off shelves, and then silence.

Kylah had her hand over her neck. She could feel warm

blood oozing between her fingers and Matt's arms around her shoulders.

'Shit,' Matt said. 'That bloody little bloodsucking shit.'

'Iron, running water, the sound of bells and a rooster?' said Kylah, trying to muster a smile.

'I thought I'd make absolutely sure,' Matt said.

'I'm contaminated, Matt,' Kylah said. 'You ought to move away. Bites work almost instantly.'

'Maybe we can stop it,' he said, his voice choked.

'What do you mean?'

Matt fumbled with his phone. 'I want you to listen to something.'

Kylah could only nod weakly. A growing tide of nausea fought with a burning desire for some rare steak. Matt's fingers tapped at his phone and all she could think about was finding a restaurant with a chef who would make it blue. Or maybe she should cut out the middle man altogether and chomp on the nearest cow, or horse, or cat or dog. Anything warm-blooded would do.

She turned her face towards Matt's arm. She could feel its heat, hear the warm blood pulsing through it softly and regularly.

Matt's tinny phone speakers burst into life. Some sort of ukulele intro followed by a high, shrill voice singing 'Caper 'Cross the Campions'.

Kylah forgot about the blue steak and immediately threw up instead.

Asher and Bobby arrived, drawn by the heaving sounds. Asher held Crouch's vampire slayer. There were bits of hair and blood on the fox's nose.

'Did you see Rus?' Matt asked, wincing at the noise from the phone but making no attempt at all to turn it off.

Asher held up the slayer. 'What does the fox say?'

'Nice one.'

'He is going to have the mother of all headaches tomorrow,' Bobby said. She didn't sound the slightest bit sympathetic. She frowned at the phone as the looped track began again. 'What on earth is that noise?'

'Music to soothe the savage breast,' Asher said.

'Can someone please get me a bucket?' Kylah moaned.

They tied Alistair and Sicca Rus—thankfully regressed to semi-human vampire form—back to back in the hidden room with garlic necklaces. Kylah lay in a foetal position on a scruffy sofa on some clean towels. Matt bluetoothed the phone through some speakers and sat with Kylah holding the bucket. At first she got rid of the chicken and roasted pepper wrap she'd had for late lunch, then came black bile, but now some thirty minutes after she'd begun it was only dark smoke that emerged with each retch, hit the bottom of the bucket and curled up and away into the air. Matt kept his face averted. That smoke looked purposeful, as if it was searching for something to inhale it. But once it entered a candle's heated airspace, the smoke dissipated and broke up.

Kylah's gastric spasms finally ended fifteen minutes later. She sat up, her colour back. On the floor, Rus and Alistair were whimpering.

'What I'd really, really like now is a glass of cool Slavabad water,' Kylah said.

'I'll pop out and see if anywhere's open,' Matt said.

'Or, we could go to the source. To the mountain that has the spring in it.'

'Are you sure you're up to it?' Bobby asked.

Kylah nodded. 'The contaminant barely had time to take effect. This 'cure' is brutal but effective. I've responded really quickly.'

'I'm game,' said Matt.

'We should all go,' Asher said. 'Now Birrik and Keemoch are here.'

The two Sith Fand stood just inside the doorway. Both wore large headphones, nodding in time to whatever protective sounds they were listening to. Both considered 'Caper 'Cross the Campions' a health and safety risk. Matt could not resist asking them what their jam was.

Birrik said. 'Zeppelin compilation. My own mix. Quintessential stuff. 'The Lemon Song'.' He tilted his head and lifted one earphone away from his head, twisting it in offer to Matt.

'I'm good, thanks. 'Ramble On' does it for me, but if you're into the Zep, we need to introduce you to our friend, Shonkin. And Sergeant Keemoch, what, may I ask, is your poison?'

Keemoch said, 'Andrew Lloyd Webber Gold collection.'

Matt gave him a raised eyebrow nod. 'You're into musicals?'

Keemoch sent him a disdainful stare. 'It's a cold sore treatment.'

Matt could find no answer to that and so, with the other three, he left the inky well.

CHAPTER THIRTY

MOUNT SLAVABAD, FW

The cabin was small and well-kept with a path swept clear of the previous evening's snowfall. The temperature was far below freezing, but the fur coats—ethically sourced from predator kills—were highly effective. The spring ran only a dozen yards from the back door, but in the depths of winter you could lose a nose if you spent too long getting from cabin to water. Kylah insisted they all dress properly before she led them to the burbling stream running clear through the rocks and into a hole in the snow.

She'd provided them all with cups—plastic obviously (metal had a habit of annoyingly freezing to finger skin at this temperature). She could, of course, have simply taken a flask and filled it with the spring water and taken it back to them in the cabin, but seeing was believing. And a running spring in the middle of this frozen wilderness was definitely worth seeing. There was no magic here. Well, none bar nature's. This water ran because it boiled at its source deep in the craggy volcanic mountain hidden beneath the snow. The geothermal explanation sounded banal, but a boiling pot of lava somewhere below provided the furnace to superheat the water and give it enough pressure to force it through the ice sheets, losing temperature as it flowed until, a few yards from the cabin, it ran clear and cool and pure.

They each filled their cups and took them back to the warm cabin. There was no supernatural ritual here; the water was simply rejuvenating. Spas all over the world promulgated exactly the same spiritual connection with nature. And Kylah's family had been coming here for eons. And so, in the cabin the four of them shed their heavy coats and sat around the fire with their cold cups of eons old water.

As good a place as any for a debrief.

Bobby sipped and her dark eyes widened. 'Wow. This is amazing. It's like drinking fresh air. How does it do that?'

'It's the oldest water there is,' Kylah explained. 'This place has been frozen and stayed frozen from the beginning. Even when the poles melted and the magnetosphere flipped the very first time, this place stayed as it was. You're drinking water that was truly life giving.'

'But I don't even need to swallow,' Bobby said. 'It's like drinking a smooth fizz bomb.'

'More like a smart bomb. It will replace much of the water in your body with the freshest there is.' Kylah sipped and felt the water enter her stomach and rush through her veins, driving out the final remnants of the poison with which Rus had infected her.

Within a day she would be completely cured of the curse. Though it would leave her with a need to eat her steak much pinker than she was used to. But the water of Mount Slavabad was not the real reason she'd brought them here. Sighing, she put down her cup and looked up, her lips smiling, but anxiety dragging down the corners of her eyes.

'I need to apologise to all of you.'

They all looked at her, each of them wearing different expressions: Asher with his eyes slitted warily, Bobby confused, Matt smiling but still with that slightly concerned frown he'd had since Rus had bitten her.

'I underestimated the enemy,' she said.

'Many before you have, Kylah,' Asher said and added darkly, 'and many have died as a consequence.'

'But I put you all in danger. You especially, Bobby. I am so sorry.'

Bobby flushed. 'Kylah, there's no need—'

'But there is. Oh, you excelled in the field as I fully expected you to, but it was an unnecessary risk.'

Bobby started to protest again but Kylah stayed her with a raised hand.

'Asher and Matt, sending you to Tobler was—'

'A stroke of genius?' Matt said.

Kylah shook her head. 'It was far from that. In fact, it was meant to be anything but that. My motives were, shall we say, questionable.'

Asher frowned, but said nothing. Kylah had not finished what she needed to say.

'I sent you both because I expected you to find nothing. There were wild geese at the end of that garden path, or so I'd presumed. Fortunately for me, I underestimated you both, too. However, it does not excuse my motives.'

'But if you thought it was a hopeless cause, why send us?' Matt asked.

Here it is, thought Kylah, *the nasty creepy-crawly under the rotten bit of bark at last*. 'I sent you both because I wanted you out of the way. Once we'd seen the bookmark, I knew this was vampire-related and I wanted you two at a distance because...because I knew that vampires, off the leash, kill male threats first and don't even bother to ask questions later. I've never told anyone this, but I was involved in the mop-up operation in Oneg. After the treaty was signed, pockets of resistance remained. Rogue factions deep in the forest. We'd had reports of kidnappings and we went in as a clean-up squad. Combat-trained elite SES, all of us. We found the villagers, but it was an ambush. That was the first time I'd seen the Glamour in all its glory. It was mesmerising. Now we have combat filter charms, but back then we had nothing. There were just three of them but they made us believe they were hundreds. They made us believe we were worthless. I saw one of our boys get up and walk straight into the fangs of a waiting leech with a great big smile on his face. I don't know what he thought he was seeing but it wasn't the vampires. They tore him to pieces in front of our eyes. Or rather they tore bits of him to pieces because they wanted us to hear his screams for as long as possible. It happened to three more before one of the other females and I finally had the sense to use silver-tipped arrows. We'd been trained for it, but somehow the memory of that training just dissolved into nothing. Even then it came back to me only because I wanted to put one of our own boys out of his misery.' She shook her head. She could feel her nails digging into the soft tissue of her palm.

Asher remained slitty-eyed, but Matt sat back, shaking his head. 'Wow. That's—'

'Unprofessional and self-serving, I know. I let my feelings get in the way of clear thinking. I thought I could deal with one more vampire, but I hadn't bargained on it having the extra value of being Sicca Rus. We almost lost Bobby…' She stopped there, hearing the quaver in her own voice.

'But you were trying to protect your colleagues. You did what you had to,' Bobby countered.

'I let emotion get in the way of sound judgement. That's what I did.'

'But we need emotion, Kylah. Without it we are no better than Rus and his kind.' It was the first thing Asher had said and Kylah could have kissed him for it. But she was determined to see this confession through. She looked at Matt and he returned her gaze with renewed and quizzical interest.

'Hang on, at the end with Rus in the alcove by the window, he said he was making a mistake when he bit you. But he couldn't help himself could he? Because he could taste your blood.'

'Matt, he's a vampire.'

Matt shook his head. 'But a calculating one. It wasn't his knife that drew your blood; it was you. You did it with your own fingernail. You knew what it would do to him. You knew he'd bite you. Send him into a bloodlust frenzy. All so that he wouldn't bite me?'

Kylah didn't answer. She should have known he'd see through her subterfuge. 'I made a call. And I made that call on an emotional level that could have backfired badly. The truth is it's all far too dangerous for everyone. It can't go on like this. I can't…'

Bobby's eyes were now like dinner plates, the words blurting out of her mouth before she could stop and think. 'Oh my God, no. Not you and Matt—'

'I don't know what I'm doing anymore, that's the point.' Kylah's hands were trembling so badly she had to put down her cup.

Matt's comical, accusatory expression had left the building. He looked pale and shocked. 'I can see how you might feel that,' he said. 'I can see how working with me is—'

'Dangerous,' Kylah finished his sentence for him, eking out each syllable of the word. 'You treat everything so lightly. You made the tarpaulin into a snake's head.'

Matt started to say something but some survival instinct kicked in and shut off the words.

'A bloody snake's head. And someone did video it. *So* funny. But one day that joke is going to eat you, or turn you into ash, or bite you on the neck and I'm scared stiff I won't be able to protect you and do my job…' She shook her head.

Bobby stifled a sob.

But Kylah persisted. The most difficult thing she had ever

done in her long life so far—twice as hard as offering her neck to Sicca Rus—was to *not* drop her cup completely and run to Matt at that moment. But her heart felt suddenly as if it was made of glass and she could hear it crack as it slowly started to break.

'So what do you want me to do?' Matt's voice sounded equally as brittle. 'Go back home? Back to being me? Back to good old med school Matt with an empty Fae head because here I'm just the weird bloke who turns windows into iron walls that can stop psychopathic vampires, right?'

'Iron, water, cock-crow and bells. A four-pronged attack. Genius,' Asher muttered. Bobby shot him a quelling glance.

'Because if staying here means us not being us, I think I'd rather go back to ignorance and normality,' Matt said, defeated.

Kylah looked at him, her insides in a tumble dryer on turbo mode.

'I'd rather you robbed me of my memory than leave me knowing I'd been robbed of you,' Matt whispered.

Kylah sat frozen to the chair, feeling her world crash about her ears. 'Matt, I—'

'Before another word is said, may I make a suggestion?'

Everyone turned to look at Asher, Bobby a hands-down winner when it came to astonished surprise at hearing him interject at this of *all* points. 'Since we are exposing our dirty laundry, as I think the expression goes, I think I, too, need to apologise. In particular, to Bobby. Why it has taken a professor of demonology whose promiscuity is the stuff of legend to point all of this out to me I have no idea, but the truth is one cannot let one's job rule one's life. I should know, because I have trodden that path for many years and it leads to nothing but bitterness and too many evenings eating, or drinking, alone. And even when Borodin deigned to sit watching, I was still alone. Use all the high ideals you like, but they will not keep you warm on a cold winter's night. And I have spent too many winter nights in a cold bed, alone.' He turned to Bobby. 'I think I need to do something about it.'

Bobby blinked.

Kylah shook her head. 'I know what you're trying to say, Asher, but that doesn't change the facts of my relationship with Matt getting in the way of—'

'Are you also a clairvoyant now, Captain Porter?' Asher said sharply.

Kylah blinked. Normally her eyes would have flashed a warning, but she was in no state to argue.

Asher continued. 'Matt has accompanied me on a dangerous field mission. I understand he has been employed on a consultative basis by the DOF, but he excelled in Tobler. Putting himself in harm's way without a qualm. Therefore, may I suggest we eschew his consultative role and second him to the BOD to let him work with me. I would be happy to mentor him in all things Fae and he, I am sure, will be able to mentor me in all things human. This way he can learn what needs to be learned about our work and you will not feel the need to constantly protect him from the dangers he might encounter in the field, or from himself. That is, if you trust me?'

Kylah's heart, aching and hardened the point of shattering a moment before, suddenly melted.

Asher. Brilliant, damaged, deep Asher.

It *was* another way. One she'd not been able to see through her fog of misery. 'With my life,' she managed to say after a couple of swallows. But she looked at Matt when she said it.

Matt's expression, however, remained flinty.

'How about it, Matt?' Asher turned to him. 'Could you stand my company for a year and a day? It would be a year and a day by the way, standard Fae contract. Or would you prefer to think about it?'

'I've thought,' Matt said. 'What do you say, Kylah?'

'I think it's a plan,' she said, astonished any words came out at all.

Matt nodded and held out his hand to Asher. 'Should I spit on it?'

Asher shook his head. 'Terribly unhygienic habit.'

They both smiled and embraced.

'But what about your boss?' Matt asked.

'Professor Llewyn will consider you an asset and a fresh dollop of clay she will be delighted to mould with her fair hands. Make sure you have no free evenings.' Asher turned to Bobby. 'Now, Roberta Miracle. I suggest we leave these troubled people in peace. Drain your cup because I would like to take you to supper. The Haroon Rooms await.'

Bobby sent Kylah a tight-lipped smile of encouragement and hope together with a double thumbs-up, and followed Asher to the door.

Kylah watched as she and Asher used the Aperio. As they exited she heard the tail end of Bobby's question, '… exactly did you mean when you said you needed to *do something* about it?'

And then she was alone with Matt. Alone and trembling because she could not take back anything that had been said and could not read his expression. Here she was with the man she spent the last two years worrying about and sharing her life with, feeling like a complete stranger all of a sudden. What was he going to say?

'You turned yourself into a bloody vampire for me.'

'A girl's got to do what a girl's got to do.'

'You are such an idiot—'

'You have every right—'

'—but not half as much as I am.' He smiled then. A smile at least 100 degrees warmer than the roaring fire blooming roses on Kylah's cheeks. 'I'm sorry I made you feel like that. I know I can seem a fool a lot of the time. It's just the way I see the world. I can change. Or at least I can try.'

'Don't you dare,' said Kylah.

Matt snorted. 'What are we like?' He remained where he was, several paces away. 'Look, I'll go if you need some space. I realise this is a sanctuary for you.'

'Do you want to go?'

'No.'

'Good.' Kylah walked across and pulled Matt to her so they were pelvis to pelvis. It was clear she had no intention of either pelvis leaving the building.

'In fact, if you're in agreement, I suggest we stay here and be complete idiots together. It's safer for the rest of the world that way.'

————

IF ANYONE EVER ASKS, fur pelts, real fur pelts—ethically sourced, of course—make the very best floor covering for naked cavorting in front of a real fire with the Slavabadrian winds howling outside the windows. Matt even suggested posting a review on TripAdvisor.

Kylah told him he was an idiot.

CHAPTER THIRTY-ONE

ALISTAIR DONOVAN WOKE UP WITH a headache to find that his old uncle Connor had passed away. Apparently, quite some time ago. Maybe even on the first day of the three-week hiking trip Alistair had been away on, which explained the fairly advanced state of decay of the corpse when he found it.

The Inky Well and all its contents became his via his uncle's will. Using eBay and a variety of other online platforms, Alistair culled the inventory significantly. It never failed to amaze him what people would buy. Why anyone wanted a copy of a 1976 edition of *A Touring Guide of the Mendips* was beyond him. But he sold it, and a whole lot of others nonetheless.

With the money from the sales and the small amount of cash in his inheritance, Alistair funded his delayed postgrad gap year trip to New Zealand. One month after his return from that trip a visitor called at the shop. The girl, young, all in black with aubergine lipstick and DMs on her feet, introduced herself as representing Hipposync Enterprises, dealers in rare books. There had, apparently, been prolonged correspondence between Hipposync and Uncle Connor while he was alive. Correspondence regarding the sale of some books which, as a result of Uncle Connor's untimely demise, remained incomplete. Alistair listened while she outlined her interest in purchasing some of these esoteric texts.

At first, Alistair had no idea where to look, but it was suggested they might be 'in storage' since they were too valuable to have on display. Fortuitously and curiously, after the girl, who announced herself as a Ms Roberta Miracle, drew out a tissue from her bag accompanied by a cloud of powdery talcum that billowed into the room, Alistair suddenly remembered the old storeroom. There he found *Grimoire du Pape Morris* and several others with titles in German and French. If he had concerns about wanting to part with them for sentimental reasons, they disappeared when he saw the size of the cheque–signed in proper ink because this was Hipposync–Ms Miracle offered him. Alistair, the whisperer-free Alistair, may have had a soft spot for his uncle, but he wasn't stupid.

With the money, Alistair converted the top two floors of the rambling accommodation at the Inky Well into flats. The shop itself he modernised and it now sells coffee and new books as well as the old stuff. The only things not for sale are bookmarks.

For some reason, Alistair found he'd developed an irrational dislike of the things.

Matt suggested they use CCTV footage from a camera on the corner of Braeburn Street to trace all callers at the Inky Well. Once identified, each one had a surreptitious visit from a very discreet imp team, whose job it was to find and quarantine the bookmarks. They, of course, were known as the Impounders. Only once was the team discovered and then only by a small boy of about eight who, to this day, remains convinced he'd met a real house-elf.

———

AERICH THE DEMON WENT UNPUNISHED. Duana reasoned that it was pointless; it would be like trying to scold an earthquake. However, the incantation DiFrance used for the summoning was hexed such that anyone trying to use it with deliberate intent turned into a myotonic goat for two hours. Which was considered a more than adequate period of time for whoever it was to ponder the wisdom of what they were doing and 'bleat a hasty retreat'.

When Matt explained the pun to Duana, she laughed for almost three minutes solid and then asked him what he was doing for an hour next Tuesday. Asher made sure Matt and he were busy.

The authorities, acknowledging the need for bridge building in terms of vampire relations, closed down ICHOR and established a drop-in centre in New Thameswick. They appointed a fully-fledged leech as its head. A wise old head who went by the name of Lapotaire.

———

BACK IN THE HUMAN WORLD, Chief Inspector Sewell was hospitalised and both arms put in plaster from wrist to elbow. As awkward situations to find oneself in go, being unable to use either hand, even for a short time, must be in anyone's top three. It takes not much imagination to come up with several…*difficult* scenarios. Sewell was, unsurprisingly, not in a relationship. He did not have a girlfriend, boyfriend, relative who could stand him, or slave, and was far too arrogant and proud to ask for any kind of nursing help from the NHS.

Kylah let him stew for three days before she and Bobby paid him a visit. He was in a real state. Unwashed and dishevelled in a sweat-stained T-shirt and jogging bottoms, his flat littered with takeaway food wrappers. A five-day stubble did nothing to improve his appearance.

'There was no need to make an effort for us,' Kylah said when they walked into his apartment without knocking.

'Most people ring. If you had, I'd have said I was out.' Sewell wore a scowl. He was watching TV. Reruns of something from the seventies that been politically sectionable the first time around, and looked much worse now.

'So, how are you, Sewell?' Kylah asked. She liked to think the plaster technician knew full well that Sewell was a misogynistic, card-carrying arse and that was why he'd given him bright pink casts. The soft lint padding had unravelled at the end nearest his elbow. It already looked dark and stained. 'No, don't answer that, I think I can make a fair guess.'

The scowl deepened. 'You try living with both wrists broken in these poxy casts. I can't do anything. I can't wash. I can't wipe.'

'There's a third 'w' in that triptych,' Bobby said.

'Verbiage,' warned Kylah.

'Very droll,' Sewell steamed.

'Remember much about the incident?' Kylah threw an empty pizza box off the settee and sat down.

'Not much,' Sewell said. 'I remember the Inky Well and that hidden room.' His eyes drifted back to the TV. Or at least away from Kylah's. 'Bilateral wrist fractures like this are rare and usually involve falling from height onto both hands. I must have fallen and knocked myself out. Post concussion amnesia, I reckon.'

'Really?' Kylah said.

'Yep. Probably in pursuit of someone. Used my hands to break the fall, snapped both wrists and then passed out.'

'Correct on all counts,' said Kylah.

Sewell shot her a look full of relieved surprise. When he saw her smiling, it turned into a frown of suspicion.

'Except for the falling, pursuing, and passing out bits,' Bobby said. 'What do you really remember, Chief Inspector?'

He did not look at either of the women when he

answered. 'Not much. What bits I do remember were stuff my imagination made up under the influence of the drugs they gave me before they set my wrists. End of.'

'I see,' Bobby said. 'So you don't remember being dragged out of the hidden room by the vampire who snapped your wrist with a wave of his little finger, pinioned you to the ceiling, and snapped your other wrist when we wouldn't give in to him. And you don't remember us making a deal with the monster to use us as hostages instead of you and get you safe under a guardian charm.'

Once again Sewell's eyes stayed away and he muttered a surly, 'No.'

'We could help,' Kylah said.

'Don't need any.'

Kylah looked around, slowly and deliberately. 'No, I can see that.' She stood up. 'Okay then, hope you get better soon. Bobby and I will see ourselves out.'

They got the lounge door before Sewell said gruffly. 'Wait…I…God, you have no idea how hard this is for me. I can't do any bloody thing. You're the only visitors I've had and—'

'We *can* help.' Bobby said.

'How?'

Kylah explained, 'We can arrange for someone to be here with you while you recover. They'd be able to do whatever you ask.'

'How much?'

'No charge. However, I have to file reports as you know and so do you. It will seem very strange to the powers that be if our reports differ hugely. What we'd need is that you wrote the truth, not some whitewashed version supporting your pathetic insistence that the extramundane is pure Scotch mist.'

'Or haar say, even,' quipped Bobby.

Sewell's face added defeat to his already haunted look.

Various bits of muscle seemed to be working at odds with a whole bunch of others as an internal battle took place. Finally, he sat back and said, 'I remember a feeling of being dragged out of that hidden room. I lost my baton and then there was this pain in my wrist. Thing is I was looking at it when it happened. Out of the blue. And then I heard him laughing and I knew he'd done it. He wanted me to feel his power. And then he lifted me. Me! Lifted me like I was made of paper and stuck me on the ceiling like a bloody Christmas decoration. I couldn't move. As helpless as a bloody fly. And then he broke my other wrist and I must have passed out. When I came to, I was in the hidden room again and there were other people there and ambulances and…ever since, I haven't been able to sleep. I see him in my dreams. Ugly, wizened little psychopathic bastard.'

'The Glamour didn't work on you then.'

'Oh, I saw what he was trying to be, but I could see what he really was too.' Sewell hesitated, looking down at his useless, pink-clad hands. 'But if I admit that it's the truth, what's to stop him coming here? Finding me again. Doing worse things…' Sewell swallowed hard and straightened his leg out to stop the trembling.

'He can't because we won't let him. He's in custody in New Thameswick. He was a vampire, Sewell. That's what vampires are like.' Kylah's tone was soft and sympathetic. Well, almost.

Sewell nodded.

'You need to write it like that.'

'And if I do?'

'Wait just a moment.' Bobby went into the corridor beyond and a minute later came back with two youngish women of Malaysian appearance. 'May I introduce you to Emilene and Janine? They are Mendelian Bwbachs and they like a challenge. They have nursing skills and actually do like playing house.'

Sewell's mouth dropped open. Kylah wished she had a camera. Luckily, Bobby did.

'You mean…?' Sewell croaked.

'They will look after you. Cleaning, cooking, washing… wiping. So long as you fulfil your end of the bargain, I am sure all of this can be made easier.'

'You mean a happy ending?' Sewell said. It might have sounded lascivious, but the tone was more tinged with pathetic hope than lewdness.

'Please,' Bobby said with a frown.

'I am sure they will accommodate your every need,' Kylah added carefully. 'Believe it or not, this is what they live for. Bwbachs are very odd creatures.'

'They don't look that odd to me,' Sewell said.

'Appearances can be deceptive,' Bobby said.

'Well?' Kylah asked.

'I'll do it. You might need to wait for the report until I can type,' Sewell said. The glint in his eye told Kylah that by the time his hands healed, his mind might have changed too.

'No. Emilene and Janine can type. I need the report on my desk by tomorrow morning or the assistants leave the way they came in.'

Sewell shook his head but he was already sold. 'Okay.'

'Get well soon,' Kylah said and she and Bobby exited via Aperio to the blue room at Hipposync.

'I feel sorry for those girls,' Bobby said as they walked briskly to Kylah's office.

'Don't be. They really do enjoy all that. And they aren't girls. Between them they have a combined age of a hundred and seventy-three. And Bwbach emancipation is like saying 'dog perfume'. It's a nice idea but it'll never sell. Look at Mrs Hoblip. Gratitude and enjoyment is what they thrive on and there is nothing we can do about it. There are exceptions. Mrs Hoblip's son George may well buck the trend, but he is young and I bet he'll join the special elf service in the end. They make brilliant soldiers.'

'I thought Sewell was going to burst when he saw the girls, though.'

'Yes. I can't wait to see his face in twenty days' time when the transfiguration potion wears off and he sees them as they really are. I expect there'll be no happy ending that day.'

'What a wonderful thought.' Bobby smiled.

––––––

THAT JUST LEFT THE ALTERNATOR—our friend, Reginald Strayne. The ambitious magician whose meteoric rise to fame triggered the whole sorry episode. His response to treatment was the most surprising. Side effects proved minimal with a permanent cure after only half a dozen exposures. That, combined with an amnesia charm, saw him free of the priviron and back to normal in no time. The worrying bit was hearing him humming along to 'Caper 'Cross the Campions' during the treatments and, indeed, for a long time afterwards.

All his Fringe contacts were traced and subliminal exposure to 'Caper 'Cross the Campions' instituted with complete success using Shonkin's expertise. This consisted of hacking every victim's phone ringtone. They could change it back, but only after 'Caper' had played at least a dozen times.

Reg's enthusiasm for legerdemain continued. Though he never repeated the success of his Edinburgh Fringe performances, overnight his close-up magic technique improved no end. He went on to have huge success at weddings and corporate events, lost a few pounds—thanks to an urge to mainly eat protein—and even found love.

She, a willing participant in one of his wedding party shows by volunteering the prop for The Alternator's put-the-ring-in-a-wine-bottle trick, fell hook, line, and sinker. She thought he had hidden depths, a notion in part explained by the fact that her Twitter handle was @HGWRTSLATERS.

They would go on to co-author a successful children's educational series of books entitled *Hex Your Way Through Maths, English, History,* etc.

They would also name their first child Draco.

———

THREE WEEKS after the case concluded, Bobby handed her coursework in to Duana Llewyn at the end of the morning lecture. Richenda conveniently dropped her notes on the floor within eavesdropping distance, but Bobby didn't care.

'I would have given you extra time to complete this, you know?' Duana said. 'After all you've been through.'

'I enjoyed it. Plus, it took my mind off fangs.'

Duana leaned in, grinning. 'Congratulations, by the way. Sicca Rus captured and a vampire infestation contained. One for the CV, I think.'

They shook hands and Duana walked elegantly away. Richenda was still on pins when she and Bobby convened in the Battery and Broomstick for a sandwich five minutes later.

'Right, what was that all about?' she demanded. 'She's congratulating you even before reading your coursework. I smell a rodent. You're not sleeping with her, are you?'

'What? No, of course not. Look, I can't tell you why she was congratulating me: it's classified. Besides, you wouldn't believe me if I did.'

Richenda had gone quite pink as the idea of Bobby and Duana Llewyn took hold in her overblown imagination. 'My Gods. No wonder she smiles and waves at you. Sleeping with the enemy, that is. Oh my Gods, wait until I tell the others.'

'Richenda…' Bobby shook her head.

But Richenda was already searching for the other novices

over the top of the heads of the other pub goers. She was on the point of calling across the bar when her eyes locked on a man who had just entered and who seemed to be waving at her. Her hand was almost vertical in a return wave when she realised that Bobby was waving, too.

The man, with long dark hair, an angular face and dressed in a velvet coat, smiled broadly and walked over. Richenda's eyes grew larger with every step until he stood right in front of her. She had time to note the full mouth and long eyelashes before Bobby said, 'Richenda, this is Asher Lodge.'

'Nice to meet you,' Asher said, holding out his hand. 'Mind if I steal Bobby? We have some business to attend to.'

Bobby squeezed out from the booth and, to her friend's dumbfounded surprise, kissed Asher on the cheek as he squeezed her waist with his hand. Richenda, spluttering, mumbled an apology and ran to the loo.

'What's wrong with her?' Asher asked.

'You've just performed an imaginationectomy without anaesthetic, I'm afraid,' Bobby said. 'Well, this is a nice surprise. I wasn't expecting to see you until tonight?'

It was still unusual to hear herself say that. She'd moved in with Asher earlier that week. It made sense, in that her apprenticeship at Le Fey would increase to two-and-a-half days a week from the following term and Hipposync were willing to pay her for attending, too. Mr Porter considered it an 'excellent addition to the team' to have a witch on board.

What was he like?

'I've just come from the Rus trial,' Asher explained in excitement. 'Matt and Kylah are at the Five Bells and they sent me to get you.'

They were waiting when she and Asher arrived, all smiles, and, Bobby knew, much more relaxed than they had been for ages.

'Well,' she said when she finally sat down at their quiet corner table. 'Isn't anyone going to tell me?'

'He didn't get the death sentence,' Kylah said, straight faced.

'What?' Bobby's voice shot up an octave.

Kylah grinned. 'He didn't because the judge said death was too good for the evil sod.'

'For 'such harrowing crimes' was what he actually said,' Matt chimed in.

'So they gave him two hundred years.' Kylah shrugged, the grin still fixed on her pretty lips.

'Wow,' was all Bobby managed.

'And he responded very poorly to Frozen Ostrich treatment while on remand, though the clever bods who know this stuff said that 'Caper 'Cross the Campions' did mildly suppress his psychopathy,' said Matt.

'So the judge recommended at least thirty minutes of enforced listening every day,' Kylah added, gleefully. 'That was the only point at which the bugger showed any emotion.'

'And that was only a whimper.' Matt nodded.

'If he's very good, they might let him die when he's 150,' Asher said, returning with Bobby's drink.

'So…' Kylah held up her glass. 'I think we ought to toast another Hipposync success.'

Asher said, 'But I am not Hipposync.'

Matt shook his head. 'Since you are now officially cohabiting with our marketing director, we've decided to make you an honorary member.'

'If that is the price I pay for Bobby adding some much-needed class to my apartment, then I am more than happy to accept.'

They clinked glasses.

Bobby blushed. Asher knew how to press all of her buttons.

Kylah saw it and asked, 'Penny for them?'

'Later,' she muttered over the top of her glass. Although how she was going to explain a smile brought on by imagining Asher pressing all of her buttons she had not yet quite worked out.

ACKNOWLEDGMENTS

As with all writing endeavours, the existence of this novel depends upon me, the author, and a small army of 'others' who turn an idea into a reality. The Hipposync Archives are a work in progress. Special mention goes to Ela the dog who drags me away from the writing cave and the computer for walks, rain or shine. Actually, she's a bit of a princess so the rain is a no-no. Good dog!

But my biggest thanks goes to you, lovely reader, for being there and actually reading this. It's great to have you along and I do appreciate you spending your time in joining and the team at Hipposync and in New Thameswick where anything is possible.

CAN YOU HELP?

With that in mind, and if you enjoyed it, I do have a favour to ask. Could you spare a moment to **leave a review or a rating**? A few words will do, but it's really the only way to help others like you discover the books. Probably the best way to help authors you like. Just visit the book's page on Amazon and leave a few words, or a rating, if you have the time. Thank you!

FREE BOOK FOR YOU

Visit my website and join up to the Hipposync Archives Readers Club and get a FREE novella, *Every Little Evil*, by visiting:

https://dcfarmer.com/

When a prominent politician vanishes amidst chilling symbols etched in blood, the police are baffled. Enter Captain Kylah Porter, an enigmatic guardian against otherworldly threats. With her penchant for the paranormal and battling against cynical skeptics, she dives into a realm where reality blurs. Her toxic colleague from the Met is convinced it's just another tawdry urban crime. But Kylah suspects someone's paying a terrible price for dipping a toe, or something even less savoury, in the murky depths of the dark arts.
She knows her career and the missing man's life are on the line. Now time is running out for the both of them…

Pour yourself a cuppa and prepare for a spellbinding mystery.

By signing up, you will be amongst the first to hear about new releases via the few but fun emails I'll send you. This includes a no spam promise from me and you can unsubscribe at any time.

AUTHOR'S NOTE

Once upon a time, in the swirling mists of the last century, my journey into the fantastical began. A devotee of the greats like Tolkien, I found myself drawn deeper into Terry Pratchett's Discworld and Tom Holt's tilt at the modern—the holy trinity of the Ts, if you will.

Two decades ago, I embarked on a series of stories of wonder and the fantastic. Satirising our turbulent modern world with snarky humour by displacing the hapless participants of these tales into situations and places where things are very different. And, come on, who wouldn't want a quick trip to New Thameswick, or have access to an aperio? And all under the umbrella of The Archives.

Can't Buy Me Blood is my attempt at a vampire novel with a difference. A reaction to all the glamour surrounding the lore. Having worked in the medical world, I know from first hand experience that blood is messy, precious, and a bugger to get out of T shirts and sheets. Plus, it gave me a chance to bring Matt and Kylah back to centre stage and to explore a little more of Thameswick with all its foibles.

All the best, and see you all soon, DCF.

READY FOR MORE

Troll Lotta Love

Wanted: Rare plant. Reward: Apocalypse. Inquire within.

When Kenwyn Wimbush's botanical expedition turns into a run for his life, and Captain Kylah Porter's sinkhole problem starts speaking in tongues, you know it's going to be one of those days.

Toss in a mysterious banished cult escapee, a trainee witch named Miracle (no pressure), and a drug that makes users think they can fly (spoiler: they can't), and you've got a recipe for multidimensional disaster.

Who knew saving the world(s) would be this awkward?

'brilliant series. Loved all of the books. Will wait impatiently for the next one, characters are brilliant & I do hope there will be more buffing the vampire slayer to come! AMZ review.

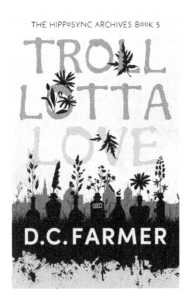

Printed in Great Britain
by Amazon